WHITECHAPEL, 1888

The Symbiont Time Travel
Adventures Series

Book Three

T.L.B. Wood

Cover and Book design by eBook Prep
www.ebookprep.com

epublishing Works!
978-1-61417-838-5
February, 2016

DEDICATION

For Amos, Sam, Sophie and Lily

"The wicked flee when no man pursueth, but the righteous are bold as a lion."
Proverbs 28:1

CHAPTER 1

Sunlight filtered through the thin canopy of early spring leaves with an enviable ease. It was mid March, and the oaks and poplars had yet to fully awaken from their winter dormancy. A solitary warm beam of light became entangled in the auburn fur of Kipp's back as he wandered across my back yard, exploring the natural world as was his habit. He turned, once, to catch my gaze and wagged his plumed tail; his coat burned in the light like a newly struck copper penny. Kipp's thoughts mingled easily with mine, much as a tendril of smoke weaves through a dense thicket in the woods. Telepaths have no need for spoken language, but we still use it, from time to time.

"I love you, Petra," he wordlessly conveyed over the short distance.

I raised my cup of coffee in silent salute and agreement. "Ditto," I shot back at him.

We resided together in my small, cluttered house on a narrow, tree lined street where the sidewalks were broken and uneven from the intrusion of stubborn roots that erupted from underground. My neighbors, humans all, knew me as Petra Goodgame and thought of me as a mildly eccentric member of their species. However, in my four hundred plus years on earth, I had been called by many names; most recently I had been addressed as Petra

Totheroh and Petra Mendez Howard. Although my identity changed frequently in my profession as a gatherer of historical facts, I maintained the given name of Petra as a silent salute to my nomadically inclined mother.

My appearance was deceptive to those around me. While I looked to be a reasonably attractive young woman with dark hair, hazel eyes, and a sprinkling of freckles across a too large nose, I was, in reality, a symbiont. My kind are telepathic time travelers, and I was a historian with a passion for solving past mysteries. Kipp, to the people on the quiet street—many of whom who were retired or worked at the university in Chapel Hill—was a friendly dog. They only appreciated the fact that he didn't bark all night long and keep them from their slumber. In truth, Kipp possessed a complex and multifaceted mind—with intelligence greater than my own—that was concealed within his large, furry, and conspicuously canine body.

Not all symbionts are equally gifted, and, for certain, not all travel in time. Those who travel require a bond, such as the one that Kipp and I shared. Avoiding false modesty, I will state that I was considered by my peers to be relatively talented. But Kipp was in a singular class and strayed from the bell curve in so many ways as to make him exceptional. While my species suffered the effects of some degree of genetic degradation over thousands of years of existence, Kipp, who came fresh from prehistoric times to our current century, was the, uh, real deal, to state it simply. He put the rest of us to shame with his unvarnished and unsocialized approach to the world.

"I dreamt of Perdy last night," I commented out loud, my voice breaking the silence.

"Yes, I know," Kipp replied.

When I first realized Kipp dared to monitor my dreams, I was slightly unnerved since such violations of the ethical code were prohibited by my species. It was even more surprising when I discovered he could manipulate my dreams in such a way that a different, more positive outcome would result. The rest of our kind had developed certain social rules that ensured survival, and polite boundaries are a must between telepaths. But I had allowed Kipp to remain natural and untouched; he might observe the requisite distance with other symbionts, but he could travel anywhere in my brain that he desired—even to the dark recesses where I hid my shame as well as my fears.

Kipp walked over to a bunch of daffodils and dipped his head down into the golden warmth of color. "I like these," he commented. "They seem happy, somehow."

I smiled; Kipp's perspectives were always refreshing. "Always have been a favorite of mine, too," I remarked.

"*And then my heart with pleasure fills, and dances with the daffodils,*" Kipp reflected, parroting the thoughts in my mind. "What is the origin of that phrase?"

"A fragment from a poem by William Wordsworth," I replied.

There was no doubt I was feeling moody and pensive; this often happened following a time shift. Kipp and I had recently returned from what was meant to be a vacation trip to Tombstone, Arizona during the time of Wyatt Earp and Doc Holliday. We, unexpectedly, encountered a lost symbiont who had fallen into the world of criminality. It was sad and disappointing for me to find a fellow member of my species who used his gifts in a self-serving manner. The fact he was a nephew of a close friend of mine complicated things, in that Kipp and I would have to bury this knowledge; there was no need to bring pain to our friend.

"It's time for you to get over it," Kipp commented. He returned to my side and plopped his furry behind down in the damp grass. Kipp's slanted amber eyes were ringed with dark fur, and somehow the natural eyeliner enhanced their expressiveness. "John Gold made his choice and is just a sad memory now."

The bond between symbiont companions was unique and closer than any other relationship that I could envision. Without that connection, time travel was impossible. John Gold, due to his descent into evil, was abandoned by his ethically grounded symbiont and consequently lost the ability to return to contemporary times.

"I just hate it for Fitzhugh. Gold was his nephew, and I feel I'm living a lie by not telling him the truth." I tossed out the remainder of my cold coffee and stood. "But the truth would bring pain for no good reason, and there is no satisfying resolution."

"Let's go in and watch a movie," Kipp suggested, happy to change the dismal subject. "Today is western Saturday on AMC and *The Sons of Katie Elder* is on." His eyes glowed with anticipation of any John Wayne movie.

Kipp, despite his brilliance and too- numerous- to- count capabilities, didn't have opposable thumbs and thus could not operate a remote. I turned on the television and went to the kitchen to fix popcorn.

Kipp, not knowing he was supposed to chafe under the restraint of arbitrarily set limits, had broken through the wall of ignorance in our symbiont community. Lupines were raised to believe they lacked the ability to read and comprehend spoken language. My Kipp, thinking the world was boundless, learned both and discovered he could watch or read a one dimensional medium and enjoy it. I often found him with a newspaper or book on the floor as he read the printed word and communicated the content to me through his thoughts.

I finished pouring the popcorn—the mere fragrance made me salivate—into a large bowl when the telephone rang. My first inclination was to ignore the blaring sound, and I paused, frowning, as I deliberated. Finally, my curiosity overcame my need for solitude, and I picked up the cordless phone. Popcorn in one hand, phone in the other, I walked into the living room and placed the bowl on the floor in front of Kipp.

"Hello, Petra," a familiar voice boomed.

"Hi, Philo," I responded. "What's up?"

Despite my abilities as a telepath—and a good one at that—symbionts had their boundaries on how far thoughts could be transmitted. Even Kipp had limits, and I fell somewhere far below him.

"I hate to call with bad news," Philo began.

I felt my shoulders bunch with tension, and Kipp rose from his position on the floor as he picked up my worry.

"Fitzhugh has had a heart attack," he continued. After clearing his throat in what I viewed to be a poorly disguised delaying tactic, he said, "He's alive, and it was minor, but he was taken to Duke and will be monitored there for a couple of days." After a brief pause, Philo laughed. "Do you think the doctors will figure out Fitzhugh is more than thirteen hundred years old?"

Kipp's amber eyes met mine as he ducked his head beneath my hand so that I could caress the dome of his skull. He was fond of Fitzhugh, as was I. In the past, the old historian had harbored a distinct dislike for me due to my reputation as a reckless traveler with more than a few loose rules of engagement. But in recent times, he had developed a grudging respect for me as I assisted him in cataloging the massive amount of material that formed the history of our species. Being stuck in the basement of Technicorps was not my idea of fun, but I just worked there and had little say over such things.

"I need you to come over to Technicorps and fetch Lily," Philo said, making the request sound more like an order.

I almost groaned. The young cat was rescued by Kipp as we walked past a lonely field, and the creature attached herself to Kipp as if he were her mother. We'd finally pawned her off on a fawning Fitzhugh, who doted on her incessantly. Lily had a destructive, playful nature and the last time I was with her, she ran up my leg as if it were a tree, clinging there securely with all twenty claws. I obviously didn't reply with enough alacrity to suit Kipp, and he roughly head butted my hip.

"Okay, sure," I finally responded. After finishing the call, I retreated to the large closet in my small, dark bedroom. There were plenty of windows to allow light, but I preferred the shuttered, dim closeness of the room; somehow, it made me feel safe. Kipp followed and intruded into my thoughts. Plowing relentlessly through the minds of humans was acceptable, since it was part and parcel of our business. Becoming accustomed to Kipp's thoughts constantly present with mine had taken some adjustment on my part, but my history with him was unique; it was my fervent hope that his natural inclinations would not be stifled by the contemporary mores of our community. So, Kipp meandered methodically through my brain in his endlessly curious manner. To keep him entertained, I tried to box off a stray thought and enjoyed his pursuit of it like a hound after a fox.

"Ha!" I exclaimed, as I pulled out the small back pack I had once used to transport Lily when she was younger. While I was in my closet, I took a moment to hang up the jacket I'd tossed carelessly on the floor. I was not a total slob, but no one accused me of being neat.

After I pulled on some jeans and a hoodie, I made my way to the front of my small home. Pretty much every wall was covered with paintings and drawings; the tables were cluttered with odd bits of junk, but all were things I considered to have a history. It only made sense to me that a time traveling historian would enjoy being surrounded by little reminders of the past. Maybe I am, at heart, sentimental. A stray piece of pottery would cause me to muse over the many hands through which it had passed and wonder what became of all those past souls. Kipp dashed to the door ahead of me and, for a moment, reminded me of his superficial resemblance to a dog; his plumed tail waved slightly over his arched back.

"You are just too handsome for words," I commented as we departed, and I locked the door behind me. The walk ahead was pleasant, and the two mile hike would do me good.

Kipp strutted a little in a playful manner. In his guise as a canine, he wore a collar, which he despised, and I had a leash in hand if anyone raised an eyebrow in our direction. Kipp, even when trying to blend in, stood out due to his large size and reddish color. I once referred to him as a

Chinese Crested Mastiff and got away with such nonsense being uncontested.

"When are you going to get a girlfriend?" I asked, nudging him slightly with my forefinger on the back of his big head.

"I'm still just a growing boy," he replied with a laugh. "Why are you so eager to pawn me off and get me out of your life?" he asked, rolling his eyes up in his head as he looked back at me.

Of course, the opposite was true and telepaths can't lie to one another. Even if I were to try and hide my feelings from Kipp, he could dig like a coal miner and pull them loose from my resisting brain. One part of me wanted to be loving and generous and encourage Kipp to find a mate and have a family. But the other side was terrified that he would do just that and leave me. It was an accepted part of symbiont life that a humanoid could bond with a compatible lupine for purposes of time travel. But many of our kind didn't want to face the rigors of such a life and chose, instead, a compatible mate for companionship and a family. My friend, Philo, was one such symbiont who had been married for many years and had adult children. Kipp suddenly stopped walking, and I almost plowed into the back of him.

"It's a beautiful day," he commented, looking up at the sky.

Indeed, the early spring day was flawless, with pleasant temperatures, low humidity and a sky whose blue canopy seemed unmarred and endless. There was little stirring until, off in the distance, I could hear the yapping of a small dog which caused a cascade of other dog voices to join his crusade.

No one, including him, knew Kipp's real age, but he was roughly half my age, and I had passed the four hundred mark. For my species, I was considered to be relatively youthful—a young adult. Kipp folded his haunches and hit the sidewalk; I knew he would not go any further until he expressed himself to me.

"Petra, we've had this discussion before," he began with an irritatingly patient tone. "I'm happy being your partner and have no wish to do anything else now or in the foreseeable future." He twisted his head up and winked at me. "When I change my mind, you'll be the first to know." Kipp's expressive lupine face became serious. "You don't need to feel guilty over the ambivalence you feel towards me. I realize you want the best for me and for me to be self-actualized. It's also okay to worry about what life would be like for you if I left."

Kipp was much more mature than was I, and I was not so foolish as to not comprehend that fact.

"I just want you to not let me influence you," I began.

"Petra, shut up," Kipp broke into my dialog. With that, he reached out his head and caught my hand between his impressive jaws. Before I could pull away, he gave me a nip that took my breath away. "If you start this again," he commented, "I'll give you a bite that will make you cry for real."

I shook off my mood and focused instead on the trees and flowers. The early bulb plants were waning and giving way to magnificent azaleas of all colors and sizes.

"You can run, but you can't hide," Kipp said, laughing at my attempt to redirect my thoughts.

We passed the expansive, overgrown field where Kipp discovered the irrepressible Lily. A slight mist still hovered, even this late in the morning, over the dew damp grass; before long, the sun's relentless rays would burn away the moisture. It didn't take long to make our way to Technicorps, a huge multistoried building that served as a base for our local community. The business was parked in the midst of the Research Triangle and was an actual, functioning entity that was listed on the New York Stock Exchange. There were multiple aspects to the business, and all was overseen by a governing body of humanoid and lupine symbionts. As was true of us as a species, we worked side by side with humans at Technicorps, and they had absolutely no clue that we were of a different species.

The dog lovers among the humans were just happy that they landed in a work environment where they could bring their canine companions to work!

In general, our purpose was to surreptitiously work to benefit humanity. Past experiences with misusing our talents had led to a lack of humility and the temptation to change history in such a way as to enrich ourselves. But we finally overcame that desire and learned to control the darker half of our nature by working within tightly control regulations. Most important was the dictum to not interfere with the progression of history. No species could handle that type of power except by deliberation and reason.

Although I generally had positive thoughts about my own kind, I had experienced those of us who were destructive and consumed with the hot fire of selfish motives. In Tombstone, I experienced firsthand what history told of our species: without boundaries and rules, the temptation to manipulate history to benefit oneself could be overwhelming. In retrospect, perhaps John Gold was not totally corrupt, or at least he, at one point, had a more blameless soul. Exposure to his example of our species left me not wanting to travel again for a while until I could heal my disappointment.

It was not unusual for a time shift to leave the symbiont pair with unresolved trauma, both physical and mental. During my first fact finding trip with Kipp, he suffered a severe physical injury that was life threatening. The fact he'd been trying to defend me at the time did nothing to alleviate my guilt. Our second time shift—the one to Tombstone—left me feeling depressed and empty. It was no wonder that fewer and fewer of us were willing to make trips back in time. These risky journeys were inherently aging to the body as well as the soul.

Technicorps loomed ahead, a modern, sterile appearing building that held no hint of the complexity of the beings inside, many of whom had lived multiple centuries. I thought that Doric columns might be more appropriate on the façade considering the age of many of its inhabitants.

Fitzhugh was almost 1400 years old, a record to be envied.

We began to walk a little faster, prodded forward by the myriad of symbiont minds working in concert. I could tweak out the thoughts of Philo and Juno who were undoubtedly the closest friends we had in our community of humanoids and lupines. The unforeseen illness of Fitzhugh proved to me that no one's future is certain, and the very essence of life is to manage the unexpected.

CHAPTER 2

We made our way to the lowest level where Fitzhugh reigned over the library like Hades ruled the underworld. I had never been a favorite of Fitzhugh, and his rigid interpretation of our business as symbionts was grating to me. The arrival of Kipp had compelled us to work on research in concert, forcing Fitzhugh to reluctantly conclude that I might possess a positive quality or two.

I think our relationship was sealed, and in a good way, when we gave him Lily. That was a happy day for me, for the little cat was a complete aggravation to all but the normally stern Fitzhugh. Having had him hit my knuckles with a ruler when I leaned my arms across a valuable manuscript, it was irritating to watch him allow Lily to sit smack in the middle of an ancient parchment so that she could give herself a tongue bath. He acted like a permissive father with an overindulged child.

As I entered the library, the various odors associated with old books, stacks of musty documents and the unexpected fragrance of bergamot lingered like a transparent fog in the thick air. Fitzhugh always had a cup of Earl Grey in hand and a pot in waiting. Looking up, I appreciated that this was the one area of Technicorps where the industrial gray and putty colors were not in use. Fitzhugh commanded that rich, deep tones, such as were popular in Victorian times, be used on the few visible walls. He even had a desk in his office that was at least a couple of hundred years old and imported from England. He appreciated the rigors of traveling and had done it himself once upon a time.

A youthful symbiont rushed forward to greet us. "Hello, Petra, Kipp!" he called out, his dark eyes rounded with anxiety.

"Hi, Peter," I responded. It didn't require my telepathic mind to discern the origin of his stress. Peter, an apprentice, was much too young and inexperienced to be left at the wheel of the library facility. Although some made jokes about the amount of time and diligence paid to the keeping of the records, Fitzhugh almost single handedly was in charge of the history of our species. It was our story, and Fitzhugh's job was to cut through to the truth and maintain an accurate record. True, we symbionts had some episodes of which we were ashamed when our more primitive natures took command. The only way to avoid such things from happening again was to catalog and incorporate an awareness of failures and faults; just as with humanity, the only way to avoid repeating bad history is to have an understanding of true history. It seemed such an endeavor was becoming more and more difficult in a politically correct environment—for humans as well as us.

Before Peter could speak, I felt the familiar mental tingling that announced the arrival of my friend, Philo Marshall. He was one of the Twelve and sat on the board that governed the activities of our local community. No one could time shift without permission in our modern society. I turned to Philo and welcomed him warmly, as always. He was the one who could be bracingly honest to the point of pain; all of us, human and symbiont, need at least one individual who can offer that sort of vicious prod toward introspection.

"I'm sorry about Fitzhugh," I began. My vision darted down to catch the sight of Juno who walked at Philo's side. She was another favorite and perhaps the oldest lupine I'd ever known. Her age and wisdom—as well as balanced temperament—placed her on the governing board with Philo.

Kipp, having lost his mother at a young age, enjoyed the gentle and loving presence of the elderly lupine, and darted forward to touch noses with her in greeting. With the manners and solicitude of a courtier, Kipp escorted Juno forward and hovered until she could maneuver her arthritic hips into a comfortable position on the floor near an area where several chairs were clustered. Kipp circled, in the manner of dogs, and lay next to her, placing his muzzle across her flank. Taking the cue from our friends, Philo and I sat in the comfortable chairs that were meant to entice one to relax and read.

"Why is this the only place in the entire building where you can find a good chair and some attractive color on the walls?" I asked, gazing at Philo.

He shrugged his shoulders and stared back, his dark eyes expressive and sad in the soft lighting. Philo was attached to Fitzhugh, too.

"Well, when you become head of the Twelve, you can just wave your hand or sign a command or something and take care of it," I commented.

He frowned in response. "You know I have no interest in that position," he replied.

Peter approached and inquired if we would like some tea. In the absence of Fitzhugh, the patterns of the old symbiont seemed to be almost ingrained into the walls of the library. We thanked him and replied in the affirmative. Peter disappeared through the stacks to the small kitchen in the back.

"You know they will force you to do it," I kept on, feeling the need to be pushy with my friend. "The last two they recruited were power hungry creeps who couldn't be trusted." My eyes flicked down briefly to Kipp, who returned my gaze with his amber eyes. "Look at all the mischief they wanted to bring to Kipp," I commented. "Max wanted to create little Kipp clones, and I'm not sure what all Andrea had in mind." I made a face and grimaced.

"I hope to never feel their thoughts again…made me feel like I needed to take a good bath."

"Well, that discussion is best left for another time," Philo replied. There was irritated finality in his voice. "But," he added, "I have met with the Twelve, and we need something from you."

I could have used my telepathy to pull it from him, but our rules would have made that a vulgar intrusion. So, I waited patiently. Kipp, I knew, wanted to go ahead and plunder Philo's thoughts as he did mine on a regular basis, but he showed an unusual level of personal restraint. The standards of how to behave had changed from the time he was a young pup to now, and Kipp had proven to be remarkable resilient throughout the massive upheavals in his life.

"I told you I'd take Lily until Fitzhugh is back in the saddle," I replied, feeling like a grand martyr at my noble gesture.

"And that is appreciated," Philo answered.

"No one else wants her because she's an uncontrollable little monster," I commented.

As if on cue, Lily made her grand entrance and raced down one of the narrow pathways between shelved binders. Peter, who was balancing a tray with a teapot and cups, almost became entangled with the flying ball of striped fur and muttered an oath that was not the mark of a gentleman, as Fitzhugh might have remarked. Lily was attached to Kipp and felt emboldened to make a high, arcing leap through the air to land on Kipp's broad back.

"Ouch!" he exclaimed, leaping to his feet. The cat had managed to latch on with her twenty mini scimitars and leaned forward to bite him on the back of the neck for good measure. Kipp darted to me and exclaimed, "Get her off!"

Laughing, I leaned forward to pluck her from his back. The young cat began to wave her four legs in the air, looking for another victim. I finally managed to capture her and wedged her on my thighs with the hope she would become calm.

Philo cleared his throat. "We, uh, I mean the Twelve need you to take over the reins here at the library until Fitzhugh is able to return." At my look of horrified alarm, he added, "And we do expect him to return. He's in remarkable health, and of course his mind is clear and focused."

I desperately wanted to whine but an inner voice told me that there was really no way for me to turn down this request. After all, my business was traveling, and there was no pending assignment for me in respect of the recovery time needed after my last journey. Kipp was busy helping Juno mentor a new generation of lupines. I was supposed to be working and received a paycheck from Technicorps; the Twelve probably didn't want to pay me for sitting at home doing little to nothing.

I shrugged my shoulders. "Okay," I replied simply as I enjoyed the look of amazement on Philo's face.

"No argument?" he asked.

"None."

In the mysterious manner of a cat, Lily settled down and began to purr; her claws kneaded my thighs as if she were rolling out the morning biscuits at Hardees. I took my chances with her unpredictable moods and gently scratched her little noggin, enjoying the way she screwed up her pretty face in pleasure.

Peter arrived with the tea and actually poured for us, having learned some grace and skill at the task from Fitzhugh. I had experienced several opportunities to perform this simple chore over my lifetime, and I always managed to scrape out a poor job. The expression on Peter's face was comical as he realized that he wouldn't have to take on the responsibility of the library on his own. After Peter drifted off to the rear office, Philo tilted his head at me.

"I realize that it has been a strain for you and Kipp to keep your knowledge of Fitzhugh's nephew from becoming obvious to him," he commented. After blowing on the rim of the teacup, he took a cautious sip. "It's good," he commented, sounding surprised at Peter's skill level.

"Well, Kipp has helped some with the concealment," I commented.

Fitzhugh's gentle and proper heart would be broken had he known about his errant nephew. I tucked the knowledge away, and Kipp used his projective telepathy to further block any suspicious remnants of the memories of John Gold from Fitzhugh, who was understandably curious about my journey. Only Philo and Juno knew what we had encountered on our trip through time.

"Do you have time to drive out to Duke Forest?" I asked.

"No, but let's go anyway," Philo replied, setting the teacup on the table.

Kipp jumped up, his plumed tail waiving over his back like a fringed auburn fan. There was nothing he enjoyed more than an unrestrained romp in the wilderness. Our sojourns forth in a vehicle typically involved a brief visit at a drive thru where junk food abounded; Kipp had a solid reputation as a notorious French fry hog.

Juno glanced up and mentally smiled. "I think I'll stay here," she commented.

Her muzzle was completely gray, and she walked with a slow and careful gait due to the limits arthritis had placed upon her flexibility. The lenses of her eyes were becoming dense with some degree of cataracts; in fact, she was scheduled for surgery within the next couple of months. Juno was living proof that Kipp was not a complete phenomenon. With his coaching, she was learning the English language. Instead of just telepathically deciphering thoughts, she could actually listen to spoken language with a fair level of comprehension. Also, Kipp was slowly introducing her to written words, and she was using a basic primer to add to her vocabulary.

Scrounging on the floor, I located my backpack, which served as a cat carrier. Lily was not unaccustomed to this transport and associated it with good things, such as a run in the woods. After the cat was tucked inside, I stood and leaned forward to give Juno a gentle kiss on the top of her broad head. She looked up and winked at me.

"You all be good," she commented.

She opted to remain where she lay, since she had found a pleasantly lit nook and her legs were folded into a position of ease and comfort. The rest of us took our leave, and it was only a few minutes later before Kipp and I were crammed into Philo's small car. He drove with the aggressiveness of a stock car racer, and it required restraint to sit in the passenger seat and not offer a running commentary on his skills. As we swerved around one corner on two wheels that squealed in protest, Lily stuck her face from the small opening in the back pack and meowed pitifully. Kipp, who was thrown across the back seat, finally regained his legs and poked his nose into the back of Philo's neck.

"Hey, take it easy," he commented.

We rolled along the piedmont of North Carolina, which was the midway point between the ocean shore and the mountains. I'd lived there for many years but realized at some time I would be transferred out. It was an obvious fact that my human neighbors might wonder why I literally seemed ageless as they all progressed towards senior center memberships, comfortable walking shoes, and white hair. For symbionts, there was a complicated grid that managed our lives. I guess, on some level, I could understand the occasional rebel who would chafe under such control. I had much of that in me but chose to pick my battles. Our long life spans carried with them the curse of choices poorly made that lasted countless years.

The youthful green of spring caught my eye, as I silently enjoyed the passing scenery. Philo rolled the windows down, and my hair waved in a chaotic tangle like a flag whipped by the breeze. Kipp, dog-like, stuck his big head out the small window and allowed the wind to flatten his upright ears against his head. I was rather glad we made the drive in virtual silence.

Philo found a vacant parking spot at the congested entrance. The forest was relatively busy with visitors due to the lovely weather and all the shut-ins who had struggled against being confined indoors for the past winter, which had been unusually harsh. Those who studied plant life could enjoy the rebellious outbreaks of early wild flowers randomly spread on the floor of the forest. I wasn't as well versed in plants as I could have been but enjoyed the proffered beauty for its rawness and just because.

Philo had a pair of running shoes in his trunk, and after he changed shoes, we began to walk. He was uncharacteristically quiet, and we found our roles oddly reversed. In the past, he would have been trying to draw me out; as we brushed past a cluster of dark ferns, I found myself wondering what he had hidden in his mind since we usually had no secrets from one another.

I released Lily from the carrier and off she darted like a wildcat. There was no concern for her safety, because Kipp could keep up with her and likewise benefit from the exercise. I couldn't determine the content of Lily's mind, but Kipp could, to a degree. His thoughts of enjoying the primal experience of running unimpeded across the forest floor mingled with hers, and the two disappeared from sight in less than a few seconds.

"Don't go too far," I called after Kipp in my thoughts.

Beneath our feet, the spongy, moist ground gave way so that we could walk in relative silence, in contrast to the thick layer of leaves in the fall that betrayed one's passage with a crunchy salutation. I loved spring, but my favorite time of year was autumn. Not only was the color palate appealing to me, the smell of the leaves as they said goodbye to the world resonated with history—a musty, earthy smell that felt old but somehow vital.

Philo glanced up and smiled, but the emotion didn't make it to his dark eyes which seemed distant and remote.

"Yes?" I said, tilting my head in what I meant to be an inviting manner.

He broke the eye contact and looked off into the distance. "I'm not quite ready to talk about it, but I will soon, I promise."

Reaching out, he clasped my hand in his. There was no

flirtation between us; we were as close as brother and sister. He had been a good friend to my husband, and I was to his wife, Claire. How could symbionts be anything but close, I wondered? We either had to love one another or find something to despise. It was our true nature to be without guile and any hidden secrets. I only knew I trusted Philo implicitly, and he'd stood by my side when others doubted me because of my high spirited nature. Suddenly, a striped piece of fur with legs raced back towards us, followed by an energetic Kipp.

"She's wearing me out!" he mock complained, laughing as he streaked past us.

"I'll never understand Fitzhugh's love of that animal," I said, shaking my head. "She managed to ruin at least two manuscripts from my count, and there's no telling how many others, since I'm convinced he covers up for her evil deeds."

Philo laughed as we stopped to sit on a downed oak that made a convenient sofa in the wild.

"One can never tell what is really within the heart of another," he commented. "Even us, with our supposed talents." He glanced at me; again, that half smile that betrayed no mirth crossed his face. "Any of us can have dimensions at which others can only guess."

I sighed and stretched my head back. Philo was speaking in riddles and obviously was not ready to share what was causing him worry. Instead, I gazed at the clusters of new leaves hanging in dense patches overhead; a few rays of the bright sun worked past the barricade of green to focus little spotlights on the forest floor. Somewhere close by, a blue jay was cawing, his voice harsh against the otherwise quiet background.

"Philo, you're being much too vague with me. It's obvious something is bothering you, and you keep hinting at it but won't tell me." I glanced at him. "Should I have Kipp do one of his amazing stealth runs into your brain?"

Philo's eyebrows pulled together into a foreboding unibrow.

"No, definitely not. I'll tell you what's on my mind but in my own time, thank you very much." He was clearly peeved at my suggestion.

I decided to change the topic and artfully introduced an honest concern of my own: what on earth was I to do with the library while Fitzhugh was out of action.

"You know he's a perfectionist, and no one can please him," I whined. "He will be furious at everything I do and blame me."

Philo reached out and pushed my shoulder playfully. "Well, you might be interested to know that Fitzhugh asked for you to help. I actually had someone else in mind," he added, raising his eyebrows so high that they almost disappeared into his hair line.

So, I thought with a sense of satisfaction as well as surprise—Fitzhugh wanted my input and leadership in his beloved, sacred library. Life was a continual mystery, and there was no doubt about that truth.

CHAPTER 3

———◆———

With a deep sigh, I stretched back in my chair and paused to rub the bridge of my too large nose with a thumb and forefinger. A dusty, worn pile of manuscripts was laid out in a purposeful pattern on the large work table. I had spent four hours just figuring out what was the best sequence to follow, since none of the papers were numbered. They dated back some four hundred years—about the span of my lifetime—and deciphering the spidery, quaint ink etchings scratched with the point of a quill pen was going to be agonizingly slow. Why on earth anyone would want to do this sort of work, perpetually, was beyond my level of comprehension. Only Fitzhugh, I thought with disgust, I definitely needed to find a new job in between time shifts.

Lily seized the opportunity to do a high octane romp through the library and landed on top of the desk, scattering my carefully assembled montage of fragile parchments. I sat, horrified, staring at her; she looked back at me, too, wearing that silly expression cats assume when they appear startled. Her eyes were opened wide, and her ears were twisted half back in a way that did not bode good things. With a flourish of feline attitude, she hopped off the table, and the last thing I heard was the sound of her paws beating a rapid retreat between one of the stacks.

"Oh, no!" Peter exclaimed as he set down a small tray

that contained a freshly brewed pot of tea and a delicate teacup. He glanced at the stony expression that was fixed on my face, uncertain what to do. Finally he said, "I'll be glad to help."

"No, Peter, but thanks," I replied, waving him off.

He couldn't read French and would be of no assistance to me with translations. In actuality, the young man, who was quite the computer buff, had become very helpful in scanning actual documents into the system and cataloging them; that way, some element of the originals would be preserved after the actual ancient parchments fell into total decay.

"Please put Lily in the back until I can finish reorganizing this group of papers," I requested.

Peter, a good enough sort, was not settled with his own future. He wanted to ultimately be a traveling symbiont such as I, since the position held with it a great deal of mystery and romantic whimsy. On more than one occasion, I'd told him it was hard work that caused disruptions in family life, but he was still drawn to it, since it seemed to be the highest calling to which we could aspire. His mother, however, was adamantly opposed, and until he passed the fifty year mark, there was no way she would relinquish her control over him.

As Peter went in search of Lily, I knelt on the floor to begin carefully collecting the scattered papers. So busy was I, that I failed to hear the opening of the library door and was startled when a big head thrust its way next to mine; the head was followed by a rough tongue that planted a sloppy, lupine kiss on the side of my face.

"Hey, Petra," Kipp commented. He dipped his head downwards and sniffed. "I see Lily has been up to her usual," he added.

"Lily is about to find a new home," I huffed, not meaning it but wanting to sound tough and heartless.

"Aw, she's just a baby," Kipp said, laughing.

With that, he trotted to the back to help Peter corral the cat, which had managed to climb up to the top of a high shelf and was swatting at Peter as he tried to grab her. Kipp managed, with his pied piper effect, to get her to drop her stance, hop down, and go curl up in Fitzhugh's office chair.

I finally managed to get all the papers stacked carefully back on the table and took a moment to pour my tea. Kipp rejoined me and watched my activities with a critical eye.

"You never do that well," he observed.

"And, I might ask, what is your particular talent with pouring tea?" I asked.

"I have a good reason why I can't," he replied.

Kipp poked his head up to the edge of the desk and began to examine one of the yellowed manuscripts.

"What language is this?" he asked.

"French," I answered.

"After I completely master English, I plan on learning other languages," he remarked casually.

I raised an eyebrow and tilted my teacup at him in silent approval. Such a task would easily fall within his capabilities. As I sipped the tea, which was surprisingly refreshing, I sat back and let Kipp tell me about his day with the young lupines he and Juno were mentoring. His presence had opened up an entirely new aspect of our nature as a species, and our lupine brothers and sisters would never again be confined to what had seemed to be a secondary and lesser role. Other than the ability to physically speak a human language, the lupines had every skill that we humanoids possessed. Oh, well, they couldn't pour tea, but then I barely could myself. After circling a couple of times, Kipp managed to settle down on the floor. He was being deliberately circumspect, but it was not in his nature to keep the lid on anything for long, so I knew I only had to wait for him to choose his avenue of self disclosure.

Peter walked by and announced he was going on a break. I cared not and was definitely not the aggressive task master that Fitzhugh could be. As the door closed softly at his exit, I glanced down at Kipp, who was busy licking his paws. The cocoon-like atmosphere of the library was surprisingly soothing and reminded me of the snugness of my own home. After stretching my neck from side to side, I began reading the parchments, translating the archaic French dialect into contemporary wording. As I worked, I typed the translations into my computer. Eventually, this ancient symbiont tale would become part of a database that could be shared worldwide with our peers in other countries.

"You've been having disturbing dreams again," Kipp said. He was hesitant to remark because he knew I didn't want him manipulating my dreams to have different outcomes. From my point of view, dreams were a necessary expression of the subconscious, and I didn't want the impact of mine to be diluted by my well-meaning partner.

I stopped my work and stared at him hard. "Kipp, please don't focus on things that are not problems."

"But I hate to see you upset…even when you are asleep." His eyes met mine across the short, but dimly lit, distance; Kipp's pupils were so dilated in the low lighting, that the golden amber irises of his eyes were lost in liquid pools of black.

I knew he meant well but needed for him to worry less. The loss of his mother when he was so young had left him far too anxious that something might happen to his new significant other….in other words, me.

"Kipp, I'm not afraid of my dreams. They're important to me just as yours are to you. Our brains work out issues while we sleep." I reached down and scratched the crown of his big skull. "I don't mind you listening in, but you need to let go of your worry about me." With a smile, I added, "I'm not going anywhere." After a brief pause, I deliberately changed the subject. "Tell me how things are going with your students."

That query opened the flood gates, and Kipp entertained me with tales of the classroom while I drained the pot of tea Peter had prepared.

"There is one young female," Kipp began, "who shows an unusual aptitude for written language."

"Is there something you need to tell me?" I asked, not able to keep from grinning at him.

"Oh, Petra, really!" he exclaimed. "She is just a baby compared to me, and I am, after all, her teacher." His face didn't reflect the disgust he felt, but his thoughts did as he raced to the moral high ground.

I sat back in my chair and stretched out my legs. Talking with Kipp was preferable to slaving at the computer screen until my vision blurred with fatigue. The amount of work was endless, and for a moment I wondered who would take this over when Fitzhugh could no longer keep up the pace. Peter had been forced into this job but had no interest in it. For a moment, I felt alarm bubble up as I wondered if the Twelve, behind closed doors, were pigeonholing me for this task.

"No, I don't think they'll ask you to do it," Kipp replied to my thoughts. Yes, being telepathic was a time saver with only the rare moment required for clarity.

"Why not?" I asked, somewhat miffed that perhaps I was not considered due to some flaw in my character or abilities.

"You'd be miserable, and they would prefer to find someone who enjoys this degree of tedium. It takes dedication, which you lack." Kipp resumed licking his paws.

"Gee, thanks, Kipp," I answered. Staring down at the table, I glanced at several binders full of translations that I had completed.

"Oh, I didn't mean it that harshly," he explained. "I meant it takes someone who likes doing this sort of work. You do it very well but are unhappy."

Our back and forth was interrupted when the door to the library pushed open, and a beautiful young lupine entered. Ducking her head politely, since she was intruding without an invitation, she walked slowly forward until Kipp's head rose.

"Hello, Elani," he said. After a brief introduction between the youngster and me, he inquired as to what she needed.

"I was hoping to get some time with you to help me with my reading," she responded.

If Kipp had been humanoid, he would have blushed. Since I was monitoring his thoughts, I knew he was a little embarrassed that she had sought him thus. She was indeed lovely, with a gray coat that was tipped in silver and blonde colors that caught light even the dimness of the room. Kipp officiously told her that he would meet her after lunch in the classroom. She ducked her pretty head, again, and departed as quietly as she had arrived.

"Don't start," Kipp said, showing his teeth as he stared at me.

"Oh, pull your lips back over your gums and don't give me the stink eye," I replied. "She is really pretty, Kipp. Has she brought teacher an apple or any other gift?"

Kipp gave me another look that became mildly alarming in its intensity.

"Just remember, when you fall asleep at night, I'm right there in your thoughts. Your dreams can be good….or they can be very, very bad." He blinked his eyes slowly.

"Aw, I'm just kidding with you, Kipp. Actually I'm very proud of your ability," I remarked, reaching out to tousle the auburn fur on his head.

I was about to say more but the door to the library opened again—it was Philo. I was momentarily surprised he had caught me off guard since I normally would have detected his presence before he actually drew that close. On his best days, Philo was a little disheveled and paid scant attention to his attire or hair, which usually stood out as if he had just run agitated fingers through the mass. But today, he had dark circles beneath his eyes and lines of worry crisscrossed his face.

"Kipp," he said, nodding his head at my companion. He hesitated, and Kipp recognized the cause without having to pry into the depths of Philo's private thoughts.

"I'll go so that the two of you can talk," Kipp said, making to stand.

Philo settled him back with a gesture of his hand.

"That's not necessary, Kipp." Philo, noting the worry on my face, flashed a reassuring smile at me. He became silent and began to pace the small space around the work table. The bright bulb that shone upon the manuscripts suddenly seemed hot and unwelcomed, so I reached up to turn it off. We were left in the snug intimacy of the library where the dark colored walls seemed to close in around us.

"I, uh, that is we—Claire and I—are having a problem and would like to come talk with you two about it."

Philo stopped his pacing. I was glad because he had a tiny squeak in the sole of his right shoe that reminded me of a mouse in distress. It was with effort I resisted the urge to reach out, grab his coattail, and yank him into a chair. He darted a look at me; some level of my thought must have been obvious, and he dropped into one of the more comfortable upholstered chairs that flanked a small round table Fitzhugh used for serving tea.

"Peter isn't here and has left on one of his curiously long breaks," I commented, raising an eyebrow at Philo. "You know I don't have the heart or soul of a manager and am letting him get away with not working and getting paid pretty well for doing little to nothing on a daily basis."

Philo raised his shoulders but did not smile despite my attempts at humor.

"My point being, I can make you some tea but it will probably be a poor second. Peter, as it were, makes a fabulous pot of Earl Grey." I left my rigid work chair that was diabolically designed to keep me—or anyone else—from falling asleep. I plopped down in the other vacant upholstered chair and pulled my legs up under me; the soft fabric and overstuffed cushions had issued an invitation to me from early that morning.

Philo seemed to have lost the desire to talk, so Kipp, who had the talents—but not the timing—of a motivational speaker, decided to break into the lull.

"I heard you were nominated to be the leader of the Twelve," Kipp remarked.

Philo's head snapped up. At least Kipp had his attention.

"That has not been announced, Kipp, and I don't appreciate your digging around in my head to get the latest gossip." Philo's dark eyes blazed for a second before resuming their former dull, tired appearance.

I wanted to intercede for both of my friends but decided that they needed to work out this conflict on their own. Nervously, I folded my hands in my lap and stared at my kneecaps.

"Point taken, Philo. But I didn't go digging for the information, as you describe it. One of your peers told me—in confidence, of course." Kipp remained unperturbed by the tension that was circling in the air.

"I'll speak to Juno," Philo replied.

"Well, you can speak with her, but it wasn't Juno, and I'm not telling you who it was."

One thing I had learned about my Kipp was that he had unflappable self confidence. He was literally the new kid on our particular block but one would never recognize it by his attitude. Kipp knew who he was, and his experiences in unbridled telepathy formed a profoundly tough outer shell.

Philo stood and ran his hand down his leg to try and subdue the unsightly creases in his trousers. "I could continue this battle with you, but, to be honest, I'm too tired to outwit you and too distracted to outtalk you." He looked up and smiled, but the expression did not reach his dark eyes. "We'll call it a draw."

I'd finally grown irritated and impatient with both of them and was not too shy to make myself known.

"Now that you two have concluded your male chest bumping display, I'd like to know what's bothering you, Philo." I stood, too, and reached out to touch his arm. "It's obvious something is wrong."

A noise rang out from the back of the library; Lily had become restless in her confinement in the lounge and was attempting an escape. Kipp artfully took his leave and trotted through the stacks to the rear of the room. She was his charge, after all.

"It can wait until we come by if that's okay," Philo said.

His voice was soft, and I thought I detected a mild tremor in the tone.

"Sure, just name the day," I answered. "I'll fix vegetable soup, and we can have some dinner together…just like the old days," I added, smiling up at him.

The smile came at a price since it provoked a memory of my spouse who had died, along with my baby, in an accident. Once upon a time, Philo and Claire were our best friends, and they were godparents to baby George. I pushed my sadness deep, lest it be evident in any manner to my friend; he certainly didn't need to share the burden of my grief.

Philo took his leave, and I was rejoined by Kipp who had managed to open the door to the lounge, freeing the wild and willful Lily.

"I didn't mean to be rude," Kipp began, before I waved him off.

"It isn't important, Kipp. There are bigger issues at play," I remarked. "But it will have to wait until tomorrow evening."

At my comment that I would be fixing vegetable soup, Kipp grimaced.

"Don't worry. I'll find something for you and Lily to eat, too," I said, reassuring him.

CHAPTER 4

"Kipp, if you can manage it, please try and keep Lily from completely wrecking the table setting." The tone of my voice betrayed the subtle degree of stress I felt. No entertainer was I, and my house rarely passed muster. It didn't take much effort to spy a dust bunny rolling across the worn hardwood floors like an errant tumbleweed caught in the hot breeze of the desert.

Darkness had fallen; I kept the lights low—not to camouflage my messy house but rather to create a pleasant ambiance. I'd always enjoyed the flickering, unpredictable light of candles and set out several in strategic locations. In my four hundred plus years on earth, the majority of my years had been spent with no electric lights, and dependency upon candles and oil lanterns was nothing unusual for me. Perhaps, the act of surrounding myself with familiar old friends, in the form of a wax taper or towering pillar, provided comfort on some subconscious level.

From the kitchen, a fragrant aroma drifted into the small adjoining living room. I peeked out the large front window before chiding myself for the useless gesture; telepaths had no such need for visual cues. With consideration for the carnivores with which I lived, I had set out a bowl of chopped chicken mixed with rice. There was no use for separate food containers since Kipp was accustomed to sharing his bounty with the greedy and ever hungry Lily. As I mixed batter for cornbread, I glanced over to watch. Kipp, in his pose of Sphinx, was crouched, his large jaws hovering over the bowl. Lily, with no fear of her adopted mother, wedged herself between his front paws, and her small, triangular shaped face was almost pushed down into the food in her haste to consume as much as possible in a short span of time.

"Watch her, Kipp. She'll eat too fast and then throw it up; I don't have time to chase her from room to room to clean up." When would our nanny hood of Lily end, I wondered?

I pulled the heated iron skillet from the oven and poured the cornbread batter, noting with satisfaction the popping sound as the batter hit the hot grease. No, I was not a particularly good cook, but my mother had taught me how to make a truly wonderful cornbread. Opening the oven door, I shoved the skillet inside and set the timer.

"I might try some of that," Kipp offered.

"Fine with me, but don't turn up your nose if you don't like it," I replied lightly.

His head went up just a moment before mine; Philo and Claire had arrived and were in the process of pulling their car close to the curb. My short driveway only allowed one car, and my battered little vehicle was currently in residence. Kipp's skills were better honed than were mine and certainly less dulled by constant lessons on how not to use telepathy with one another.

After pausing to wipe my hands on a towel, I walked to the front door and opened it just as Philo poised to knock. He wore the same preoccupied expression from my last meeting with him; his dark eyes were hooded. But the appearance of Claire was startling. I'd not seen her in a few weeks, and she looked as if she had lost significant weight. Tall and lean to begin with, she really had little excess to spare. Tonight, in the dimness of my candle lit living room, she appeared gaunt and exceptionally fragile. She was almost Philo's height, and I noticed that where her arm tapered down to slender finger tips, the blue stain of prominent veins marred the ivory perfection of her skin.

Kipp had met Claire briefly on a couple of prior occasions. Nevertheless, I cautioned him to avoid any mental intrusion upon her. Philo had a mild tolerance for Kipp's exuberant and boisterous behaviors, but Claire would be grossly insulted and perceive any uninvited telepathic advances to be a violation.

Claire murmured a soft greeting to me and leaned down to gently kiss my cheek; her lips felt cool and dry against my skin. The subtle scent of a soft, feminine fragrance drifted across the small gap between us. She was roughly a hundred years my senior, but with our kind, that was almost insignificant.

"Hello, Kipp," she said in greeting.

Kipp's ears flattened in a submissive manner, and he wagged his tail in response to her low voice.

"I hope you like vegetable soup and cornbread," I said, my spoken words echoing almost too loudly in the otherwise quiet room. "You recall, Claire, I'm not much of a cook," I said, laughing.

"Oh, that's not true," Claire responded. She smiled, but just as quickly the animation left her face and almost immediately she appeared strained and consumed with worry.

Kipp had the ability to dig into either of my friends' hidden thoughts, communicate them to me and block any awareness that he was doing so. It was something we had been forced to do in the past, but it felt very dishonest, and I would never intrude upon a friend in such a manner. Kipp's ears were still flattened to his big head, and I knew he was barely restraining his curiosity.

Both Philo and Claire held an aversion to formality and trailed after me as I returned to the kitchen. My small dinette set—a battered relic from a second hand shop—was neatly set with some of my mother's old china that was chipped but still maintained an air of dignity. Lily, in her guise of structural engineer, was in the process of determining how much lift she would need in order to leap from the floor to the top of the table. Kipp handily interrupted her spring and managed to get her to settle down between his paws. Actually, he sort of held her between his paws and began to clean her face with his rough tongue. It only took a few seconds for her to look as if she was wearing a reverse ducktail.

I had prepared the ubiquitous sweet tea of the south, and in a jiffy, the cornbread was on the table and soup was ladled into bowls. The discussion during the simple meal was kept equally simple. Philo discussed a few projects that were on the drawing board at Technicorps, none of which involved me or Kipp. Claire, an accomplished musician, taught piano and violin to some of the children of the symbionts who worked with us. She had pioneered a unique technique of using her telepathy and an empathetic connection with her pupils that enhanced their learning.

"I wish I had the ability to play the violin," Kipp announced unexpectedly.

"Why is that?" Claire asked, glancing down at my companion.

His eyes lost their usual crisp focus for a moment as he considered how best to answer.

"When I hear a violin, it's as if it is speaking to my heart. I feel things that sometimes I keep bottled up for fear of being overwhelmed with emotion." Kipp looked up at Claire.

Her expression softened as she nodded her head in understanding. "That is exactly the way I feel about it, too, Kipp."

"My money is on Kipp," Philo remarked. "I don't think there is anything he can't do," he added.

"Well, he seems to not be able to help with dishes or laundry," I commented, fixing my eyes on Kipp. "But on the other hand, he is the only creature I know who can subdue Lily."

We continued with some idle chit chat until it became obvious that my guests were ready to move on and launch into whatever issue had brought them to my home. I almost had to push Claire from the kitchen, since she offered to help me clean up the mess. Assuring her I would take care of it later, I herded everyone, including Kipp and Lily, to the living room, and we chose seats; I dropped into my favorite wing chair. Our movements in the room caused the light from the candles to dance, throwing oddly shaped shadows on the walls. There was dessert, but it could wait until later, I thought.

Philo leaned forward and put his elbows on his knees, as he stared down at the floor as if he was in the midst of an exciting new discovery of some type. His hair, as usual, stood on end, and when he looked up, he caught my glance.

"Well, it's apparent we have something bothering us," he began. His voice quavered with a mild tremor, as he stopped to clear his throat. He glanced at Claire, and I saw her fists clench in response to his expression.

"We need to ask you for a favor," she said. "A big, horrible favor," she added. "Kipp, too."

"Uh, sure, Claire. What do you need?" I replied, daring a quick glance at Kipp who remained silent.

"You know our son, Silas," Philo began. His face reddened slightly, and he paused to clear his throat again. It didn't require the skills of a telepath to gauge the emotional tension present. "He hasn't lived with us for a long time and has been working out of a community on the west coast. For as long as I can recall, Silas wanted to time shift to Victorian England to do research on the state of journalism during the time of one of the most notorious crime events ever—the Jack the Ripper serial killings.

"Since he teaches journalism at several colleges, Silas believes that living through critical points in history to actually view the evolution of the art of journalism will help him in his teaching." Philo paused for a moment. "He has made several such targeted time shifts….he and his symbiont, Vashti."

"So, he is no novice," I remarked. "What do you need from Kipp and me?"

"This time, Silas did not return," Philo said, reaching out

to clasp Claire's finely boned hand in his. "We need you to go after him."

He glanced at Claire; his lips compressed as the tears began to flow, unchecked, down her high, angular cheekbones. I saw his hand tighten over hers in what was meant to be a gesture of comfort.

Kipp stood with care, trying to not disturb Lily who was dozing next to him on the round woolen rug he preferred for napping and watching television. Kipp's large amber eyes caught mine as he nodded his head. I knew him to be completely without fear and bold beyond measure. But history had recorded past "rescue" attempts between symbionts and most had been spectacular failures. If a symbiont didn't return from a time shift due to the death or incapacitation of the bonded partner, there would be no way to assist in a return. In some ways, this held a resemblance to the situation Kipp and I faced with John Gold during our Tombstone adventure. It left the returning pair with unresolved issues over not being able to actually salvage a situation. Those reasons were why no one was sent to find me after I went missing in prehistoric times when my beloved partner, Tula, was killed. To say it was one in a million that an orphaned Kipp found me would be to underestimate the odds.

"You hesitate," Claire said, as her voice dropped to almost a whisper in the small room.

Some of the candles were beginning to gutter, and I could smell the odor of the dying wicks as they surrendered to the inevitability of a finite lifespan.

I shook my head from side to side. "Maybe, Claire, just for a moment, but not for the reason you might think. I was just thinking what would happen if I were to locate Silas and the situation is not good. Do you want me to bring back the news that he is unable to time shift or that maybe something worse has happened?"

Philo leaned forward in his chair. With the toe of his shoe, he began to idly trace the pattern in the worn rug. I fell silent, waiting for him.

"Petra is right, Claire. We have no right to ask her to take on such a burden. If she were to find that Silas is dead, she would have the terrible responsibility to bring back the news." He glanced up and smiled. "It's not the thing to do to a good friend."

Kipp stared at them and then at me. I could feel the energy building in him like a volcano about to blow.

"Neither of you has the right to think you can read our minds and instruct us as to our duty in such a matter," Kipp began. His tone and stance startled our guests but not me. "Oh, I forget…you can read my mind, you just won't allow yourself to do so because of a bunch of rules you all decided to follow to suppress your natural gifts." He directed the latter at both of them, but more particularly at Philo, who began to frown. Obviously, this conversation was taking a pathway that was unexpected.

"I'm sorry, Kipp. I didn't mean to be offensive," he began, but Kipp cut him off abruptly.

"I could speak with false modesty but don't have the time or inclination," Kipp remarked. "If there are any two symbionts on earth who can find Silas, it's Petra and me. And, yes, there is a price paid by launching any such journey." Lily awoke and stretched her little cat mouth wide in a yowling yawn that exposed all her teeth in a fearsome display like a tiny tiger. Kipp paused to nuzzle her face with his nose in an affectionate box.

"I know Petra better than anyone alive because she allows me to go to the places where she holds her fear and pain as well as her love." Kipp twisted his massive head from side to side, stretching out his muscled neck. "She can handle this trip. She may not feel comfortable with the thought of it, but she can do it." Kipp glanced at me. "She doesn't need either of you to protect her."

Philo sat back in his chair and rested his head on the upholstered fabric. For a moment, he closed his dark eyes and, as I politely shut my mind to what was going on, he invited Kipp to take a journey down to where he kept his hidden self. Such a thing, for us, was unheard of, with the exception of Kipp and me. As I watched, Kipp sat back on his haunches and half closed his eyes as he gazed at Philo's face. From time to time, he would turn his head slightly, and after a few moments, his mouth dropped open into a pant.

"Thank you," Kipp said after a few minutes had passed. "I value your trust in me." He glanced at me. "I will recognize Silas from Philo's thoughts and memories of him." Kipp's eyes became vacant for a moment. "I can feel his essence lodged in your mind," he said, directing his comment to Philo.

Claire made a soft sound that could have been excitement or distress.

"You see now why this is so difficult, Petra," Philo said. "As the leader of the Twelve, I can't ask you to take this journey to personally benefit me and Claire. There is always risk involved, and I can't direct you to go."

Claire began to cry again. Without speaking, I rose, walked into the kitchen and dampened a cloth towel. Returning to the living room, I handed it to her and watched as she dabbed at her red, swollen eyes. After reclaiming my chair, I took a deep breath and glanced at Kipp. It was clear he felt we were called to go on this rescue mission. He took a couple of steps and placed his auburn head on my knees. Leaning forward, I rested my cheek upon the broad dome of his head. We stayed like that for a moment as his thoughts merged with mine.

"I've never had any interest in traveling to England during the time of Jack the Ripper," I began. "First of all, it would be difficult to just sit back and watch the events happen and not intervene to save lives of poor women who were targeted by some lunatic. But it's clear it is a great, unsolved mystery, and maybe we could come up with a reason to justify the journey."

"Why has everyone avoided it?" Kipp asked.

"Well, for one, the reason I gave," I replied. "But also, it's almost toxic for a telepath to have to be in close proximity to such twisted, dark thoughts." I scratched Kipp's chin.

"Remember what it was like to be around Sir Edward during our first time shift? His madness almost made you feel physically ill." I leaned back in my chair and gazed at the front window where my shadowy reflection stared back at me. "And, it will be a challenge to find a pair of symbionts in the midst of humans who are panicked and hysterical. The entire atmosphere will be charged."

Claire spoke up, her tone eager and hopeful. "But if you could create a plausible reason for the trip and then spend your time looking for Silas…when you return, you could give whatever reason you want to explain a failed time shift." She glanced at Philo. "No one would know but us."

Oh, yes, I could lie with ease. All symbionts could and traveling symbionts, even more so. In many ways, our job as travelers was much like an actor—assuming a role and playing it to the hilt.

Philo looked at me. "We would all be collaborating in a lie," he remarked. "I don't like the feel of it, but, at the same time, I want to find my son." Unexpectedly he smiled, and the expression seemed a little lopsided on his face. "It's one of the few times in my life I wish I'd branched off like you, Petra, and become a traveler."

I stretched my neck back. Above my head was a crystal light fixture, one I'd found in a dusty corner of a junk shop. Another cast off from a past era, I thought. A little vinegar and water, and it looked brand new to the uneducated eye.

"No, Philo, I don't think you would have wanted to travel. You're grounded with home and family." I didn't need to mention my own past when I was married, too, with a young child. But tragedy had removed all from my life, and I had no wish to return to that type of conventionality.

"We will discuss it," Kipp remarked, referring to him and me. His eyes glittered slightly across the sitting room, made darker with the escalating loss of candles. "I'm no pup anymore and will evaluate the possibilities of the trip in an analytical manner."

I put my hand to my forehead and gave him a mock salute.

"Okay, Kipp. Whatever you say," I replied.

CHAPTER 5

I was running down a dark, cluttered alley in the midst of a foggy, cold morning; the air was brisk to the point that my exhaled breath formed a visible white vapor. My boots tapped out a fast pace on the rough, cobblestone pathway, as I could feel my heart rate pulsing in my throat. I paused for a moment to gather my breath. Glancing over my shoulder, I thought I saw a shadow move several yards behind me; it began to take the shape of a faceless man.

Where was my Kipp, I wondered? He was always close by, my devoted protector and bonded partner. With desperation and fear building, I took a moment to survey my surroundings—Kipp was not in sight, nor could I feel his comforting presence in my mind. The fog began to thin, and I noticed with alarm that I'd raced down a blind alley with one way in and no exit save the path by which I had come. The dark, looming shadow stood between me and freedom.

Since there was only one choice open to me, I turned and set my feet, bracing myself for what I believed would be a violent assault. The nebulous figure drew closer until I could smell his foul breath caress my face; he was enjoying this, I thought, recognizing the savage predator for what he was. Did a gazelle feel thus when faced with the fact a lion had finally managed to grip it by the back of the neck in an unbreakable connection? Somewhere, in my mind, I thought that if I just remained motionless, the stalker would leave me in hopes of pursuing more entertaining prey. Before I could think further, the man's hand flashed in front of my face; his flesh was a sickly grayish-white. The pale hand grasped a knife, and I saw the ambient light caught on the metal blade as it descended rapidly towards me.

"Help me!" I screamed. My dream ended abruptly, and I awoke to find myself surrounded by the familiarity of my bedroom. As my heart rate began to slow, I tried to pierce the dense curtain of darkness for any evil presence, with special concern for my closet and the far, deep corner of the room. My hand drifted up automatically to find Kipp, who was resting next to me with his head propped across my breastbone, as usual.

"That was a terrifying dream," he commented, leaning forward to lick the tears that had escaped my eyes. "One of your more vivid constructions," he added, almost in an analytical manner.

"Why didn't you help me, Kipp?" I asked. He fully had the ability to enter my dreams and manipulate them as he had done in the past. I struggled to sit up amidst the tangle of damp, sweat soaked sheets.

Kipp lifted his head and stared at me. "I recall you telling me to leave your dreams alone…something along the line of them being important, and that you weren't a weakling…blah, blah, blah," he concluded.

I was irritated at myself more than I was at Kipp and finally hopped out of bed to go moisten my face with a cool wash cloth. Returning to bed, I gazed at the closed plantation shutters which were tinted with the purplish stain of color from outside that hinted at the time just before daybreak.

"And if it matters, Petra, it was almost impossible for me to not help you," Kipp said. "But if we take this trip to an emotionally complex time, you need to toughen up your responses." He leaned forward and licked my face again before nestling at my side, his head on my shoulder.

"Gee, when did you get to be so wise, Dr. Kipp?" I asked, over my fearful mood and even more past my irritation at Kipp.

"Oh, it just comes to me now and then." He laughed and turned his big head so I could scratch under his chin and behind his upright ears.

Lily had been sleeping at the foot of the bed and finally awoke in response to our activity. Since she lacked telepathy, she could not follow our dialog but her instincts told her that something was amiss. With a kittenish yowl, she began to prowl up the length of the bed until she managed to curl up on my chest.

"I'll miss the little monster," Kipp said, in reference to the oblivious feline, who refused to be ignored; her purrs resonated against my sternum.

"I won't," I replied. "Philo told me that Fitzhugh will be back at Technicorps on Monday, working a reduced schedule at first. As soon as he gets back up to speed with Peter's help, we will approach the Twelve with our plans to time shift to 1888 London."

Kipp's thoughts became quiet, and I knew he was recalling his deep descent into the mind of Philo. Odd, I'd known Philo for about three hundred years, and Kipp, a relative newcomer, knew the intimacies of his being in ways I would never understand. It had been a moment of pure trust between the two and obviously was necessary in order for us to move forward in our search for Silas. I don't know…maybe it was a guy thing. I trusted Philo without the need to push past his boundaries.

"I've never had a child," Kipp began before stopping to lick his right forepaw in a meditative fashion. "Philo let me understand his love for his son." Kipp glanced up, and his eyes were bright in the semi-dark room. "I was there when his son was born, and he held him in his arms for the first time." He took a deep breath. "Philo would give his life for Silas." Kipp paused and stared at me. "I would give my life for you but the love for a child is different, isn't it?"

I smiled and reached out to stroke the underside of his

jaw. His mind was busy trying to reconcile his thoughts with those of Philo. At times, it was hard to look into Kipp's eyes, which held a degree of inner vision that was often uncomfortable.

"Yes, your child is a part of you, and parenting involves dedicating yourself to teaching and incorporating your values to mold another being." I thought of my baby George and willed my voice not to catch. Of course, Kipp knew my thoughts and pushed his head hard upon my shoulder, his soft fur tickling my ear. With a change in tone, I added, "You'd make a terrific dad, Kipp."

Kipp mentally smiled, and I knew he was thinking how life would change for him were he to make a union with another lupine and start a family.

"Well, maybe one day. But for now, I'm a bachelor on the loose," he replied lightly, trying to ease the tense conversation. "But my understanding Philo's feelings for his son makes me want even more to go look for Silas. We must try," Kipp added, raising his head to stare at me again.

I gently moved him aside as well as Lily, who had decided to stretch her length across my body. The shutters in my room now were edged in yellow where they gapped from the sill; morning had arrived. Thankfully, it was Saturday, and I wasn't compelled to go to Technicorps and wither away my remaining years in the bowels of the library.

"Let's go for a run," I suggested.

Occasionally I strove towards fitness to ward off my slothful nature. Technicorps had an extremely well appointed gym, and I often used the treadmills for walking and running. When the weather was nice, Kipp and I walked to work, which resulted in a four mile round trip.

"Let's do and go check on baby George," Kipp added.

I wanted to whine but knew I would capitulate in the end. For some reason, Kipp urged me to go to the cemetery more often than I would have had I been left to my own devices. The trip to the grave was a good six mile round trip and would stretch my legs, as well as Kipp's. I glanced at Kipp and nodded my head.

"But when we get back," I said, "you're going to help me get this house straightened up."

Kipp sighed and rolled over on his back, his long legs sticking straight up in the air. Unexpectedly, he began to howl; the noise was deafening, and Lily did a memorable burn out, leaving scored slashes across my abdomen in her wake.

It was a couple of hours later, after I had stretched, that we took off in a light jog. I always started slowly in my neighborhood, for more than one reason, but primarily due to the rough condition of our aged sidewalks. They were due for repair; I, for one, would regret the day when the stubborn, ravaged pieces of concrete would be broken up and carted away. The jigsaw pathway reminded me of the pieces of history with which I surrounded myself at home.

Trotting politely, Kipp stayed at my side in his guise as an obedient companion dog. If only my neighbors knew the reality, I thought. After the first mile, I broke out in a mild sweat; the sun overhead was bright against a clear sky, and a pleasant breeze helped to keep down my body temperature. We passed the field where we'd found Lily, and the waving movement of the tall grasses caught my eye.

"Nothing there today," Kipp remarked.

"Thank goodness," I replied. "I don't think I could stand another Lily in the house."

With that, we resumed our journey. It must have been a quiet, stay at home type of morning, since only a few cars passed us. With relatively few exhaust fumes to inhale, the air seemed cleaner than usual, and I took a deep breath and exhaled from my mouth. Glancing down at Kipp, I caught his eye in return; his happiness and contentment radiated into the surrounding air. A few rays of light reflected off of his burnished fur as if he were made of some rare metal.

"You are way too handsome for your own good," I remarked. "It won't be long before some lupine beauty steals you away."

"No way," he huffed. He reminded me slightly of young, teenage boys who still thought girls to be icky.

My neighborhood disappeared behind us as we entered the surrounding countryside. The rolling hills of the piedmont were covered in the bright newness of spring grass, and the trees were decorated with sparse growth in its infancy; by mid-summer, the trees would be heavy with dark green foliage. Birds were busy in flocks, some migrating north from southern climes, while others were working on building nests and starting families. Everything seemed to be shaking off the effects of the rough winter we'd encountered.

We trotted beneath the iron archway that guarded the entrance to the cemetery. Only George lay there; his father, my husband, had been taken by his family to the Midwest for burial. Such things might seem strange to humans, but this was not uncommon with symbionts. Our family of origin connections were strong and persisted beyond death. My own family had been small, however; my parents were deceased, and I had no siblings. Much like Kipp, I was alone in the world. Maybe that explained part of our closeness.

"You have me," he replied in response to my thoughtful musings.

I stopped my run and began a cool down walk. We made our way up a grassy hill; George lay right below the crest.

As we walked along, I read the inscriptions on the tombstones, where survivors had attempted to capture the intensity of their feelings in a brief, memorable phrase or two. I had failed at this, and George's stone was simple, with his name and date of birth and death. For most of my kind, this information was not correct and was carefully adjusted so as to blend in with the human experience. How would mine look if I were to list my date of birth as 1604? Someone would think the stone mason's chisel had slipped!

"Yes, you look good for your age," Kipp commented. "Of course, you're twice my age, but you still look good."

I shoved at him in a playful manner. It once was

psychologically crushing for me to make this journey. But with Kipp at my side, I found that my sadness, although still present, no longer incapacitated me. This visit, once an object of dread, became less so—nor was it viewed as an obligatory sign of devotion despite grief. Kipp's strength bolstered me, and I no longer had to be alone.

The sun was approaching its zenith and shone in such a way that the plain marker cast a shadow in the thick grass, which was dry, for the most part. After making certain I would not plop my behind into a bed of fire ants, I sat, pulling my knees up to my chest as I stared off at the purple rolling hills. A breeze picked up and caressed the tendrils of dark hair that had fallen along the sides of my face. My nose was tantalized by the scent of freshly mown grass. The cooling air generated by the mild wind found its way to the back of my neck.

Kipp dropped down next to me, as his tongue lolled out of his mouth; lupines cooled their bodies in the same manner as dogs. After a few seconds, he rolled onto his side. I allowed myself to lie back and rested my head on his shoulder. Much as he had done with Philo, Kipp dug down into my memories; I felt him smile as he shared some of my happier moments with George. All of my memories were portrayed in a familiar roadmap to Kipp, and he brushed past George's death as well as the funeral.

"I'm glad Fitzhugh is coming back to work," Kipp remarked.

"Yes; no doubt he will be full of criticisms of what I've done and how I've done it," I replied, sighing deeply.

Kipp turned his head and gave me a little nudge. "You know Fitzhugh is mostly bark and no bite. He actually respects your abilities more than he does almost anyone else's."

"I don't know, Kipp. He seems to only find fault." I plucked a blade of grass and began to examine its color and texture. Putting it close to my nose, I tried to inhale the scent but found the one blade alone did not have the cachet of an entire field, freshly mown.

The warmth of the sun on my face acted as a sedative, and I almost fell asleep, not caring that my skin would betray the sun exposure as my freckles would stand out as if someone had dotted my face with a Sharpie. The sound of a car approaching roused me from my impending nap; I felt Kipp's head go up on alert. Symbionts rarely had to fear humans, because with our telepathic gifts, we could read their minds and know their intentions—both good and evil—before they made their appearance. In addition, Kipp was an impressive body guard. His size, if nothing else, was a major deterrent against unwanted advances of any sort.

It was Philo. With some difficulty, he unfolded his tall frame from the small confines of his car and walked up the hill. He was clad in blue jeans that were showing their popularity in his clothing rotation; the knee of the right leg was almost torn out, and the hem of both legs was ragged. Noticing my review of his attire, which included a sweatshirt with a large paint stain on the front, he smiled.

"Working outside today," he remarked, tilting his head back to look up at the sun.

I waved my hand out to invite him to join us. With my grand gesture, one would think I owned that lonely little hillock. He sat and leaned back on his elbows.

"So quiet here," he remarked. "I guess most graveyards are, when you think about it." He turned to look at me; his dark eyes seemed more settled than the last time I saw him. "Claire and I discussed everything again, and we withdraw our request for you to look for Silas." He looked away and shook his head. "It was a silly piece of emotional nonsense," he added as he gazed off into the distance.

The gentle hills of the piedmont brought calm to the soul unlike more breathtaking vistas to be had elsewhere. I stole a glance at him. He was solidly middle aged, with hair invaded by a premature sprinkling of gray; the silver strands caught the sunlight and caused his hair to take on more life than the dark color that was natural. Maybe getting older wasn't so bad, I thought. One hopefully grows wiser…and then there was the evolution of one's appearance to be considered.

Kipp was determined to have his say, and the peacefulness of the setting was no deterrent. "Well, Petra and I talked about it, and we're going." The gauntlet seemed to be thrown.

Kipp was one of the more determined symbionts I'd ever known, and if he set his mind, then it would be difficult to deter him. Even more, if he felt it was the correct course of action, he would not allow anyone or anything to change the direction of his intent.

Philo tensed and sat forward. He glanced at Kipp; a frown gathered on his brow, and I decided to stay out of this battle of wills.

"Kipp, it's not your call," Philo said. "It's my decision, mine and Claire's, and we have made our choice." He looked away and his shoulders, which had been straight, slumped; an air of sadness consumed him.

"You're worried we'll return with bad news," Kipp said. "But isn't not knowing just as worrisome? Don't you need closure?" he asked.

I felt like it was time for me to weigh in. "Philo, I have more concerns over this trip than does Kipp. Maybe I lack his confidence and probably always will." Smiling, I reached out and put my arm around Kipp's broad neck. "When Tula was killed, I was left behind, thousands of years from my century. I had no illusions of a rescue since I believed such things to be impossible. But it would have been good to know that I was missed and not forgotten. It might have been comforting to have news from home."

"As long as we don't change the progression of history, then why would you have any worries?" Kipp asked.

Philo shook his head. "I know that period of time is mentally poisonous to symbionts. The populace was on the verge of hysterics, and all the crazies who had dark fantasies of death and destruction were likewise whipped into a frenzy by the publicity of the murders. All of that combined with the inability to prevent the butchery inflicted upon those poor women makes it a poor choice for our kind."

A flock of crows soared overhead; their loud cawing was enough to disturb all the souls that lay resting on the somber hillside. The sun was moving, unchecked, across the sky in its predetermined trajectory, as the tombstones began to cast lengthening shadows along the grassy knoll.

"Kipp, I don't want to get into a place of authority with you that's unpleasant," Philo began.

"Then don't," Kipp replied, cutting him off.

"Okay, guys," I interrupted, my voice firm. "You are my two favorites in the world, and I'm uncomfortable with this back and forth." I reached forward and put my hand on Philo's upper arm. He placed his over mine and gave it a slight squeeze.

"Kipp and I want to make this time shift. We're strong enough as a team to do it safely and trust each other more than any other symbiont team in existence." With my free hand, I smoothed the fur on Kipp's head.

"Well, you are unique, and there's no disputing that fact," Philo answered, raising his dark eyebrows. "But no one is going anywhere until Fitzhugh is back in the saddle. He starts part time on Monday, in case you forgot."

I made a face. "No, I did not forget. He has probably been working on new ways to criticize my incompetency." A thought caused me to smile. "However, on the bright side, Lily will be leaving my home, and that is cause for celebration."

CHAPTER 6

———◆———

"Petra, where is the manuscript that references the time shift to Rome when Nero was emperor?"

Fitzhugh may have suffered a mild cardiac episode, but I couldn't discern any diminishment in either his vigor or the sharpness of his tongue and attitude. I rolled my eyes and counted to five.

"And don't roll your eyes at me," he added. Much like one's mother, Fitzhugh must have grown eyes in the back of his head.

"Peter returned it to what was supposed to be the correct place," I responded. My answer led Fitzhugh into a fit of grumbling. Peter was at the market purchasing tea and fresh local honey. Fitzhugh's rant would have to wait a few more minutes.

The symbiont pair who had made the time shift to ancient Rome returned with little evidence to suggest Nero actually provoked the great fire. The lack of definitive conclusions had been considered to be a monumental failure in our history; I hoped my upcoming trip to London would not be put in the waste bin along with some of the others. We, as a species, were just as fallible as humans and probably made the same number of errors. Symbionts could be self-serving, jealous, and take the path towards evil; the power to alter the course of history was deceptively seductive. I, for one, was glad to have the steadying influence of my partner, Kipp, who had the purest heart of any I'd ever known. Unlike other bonded pairs, Kipp chose to stay connected to me at all times. Even now, at Technicorps, I could feel him give me a comforting nudge, mentally speaking.

"I love you, too," I replied, smiling down at the table where my work was laid out.

"What are you smiling at?" Fitzhugh asked; he'd approached with the stealthy footsteps of a cat.

I put down my pen and looked up at the old symbiont. Despite our often rocky relationship, I had grown fond of him. The recognition of that fact was more than a little surprising to me.

"Why don't you find out for yourself?" I replied. At the horrified expression on his face, I laughed lightly. "We— our species—have the ability to be closer; we have to trust one another, like Kipp and I do."

I thought he would stomp away, insulted by my invitation. To my surprise, he sat down across from me at the work table; reaching up, he turned off the bright work light. I took a deep breath and relaxed; the familiar scent of old parchments filled the air. Some might find it objectionable, but I'd become accustomed to the thick, cloying scent. Fitzhugh tentatively reached out with his mind and touched the place in mine where Kipp had deposited his last message of love. Fitzhugh smiled, unbidden, and ducked his head; just as quickly, he politely left my thoughts.

"Is it always like that between you two?" he asked.

"Yes," I replied. "I wanted Kipp to remain natural and not be restricted by our modern rules," I added.

"Was it difficult?" Fitzhugh asked. "It is as if you have no boundaries between the two of you."

I leaned forward. "Our species placed those boundaries on ourselves. What Kipp and I do is natural for us."

My moment of truth with Fitzhugh was interrupted by Lily, who took that moment to tear through the library; her journey climaxed with a high, bounding leap onto the back of one of the upholstered chairs. Since she was fully armed, she began to sharpen her front claws with an excessive zeal that I found disturbing. I glanced at Fitzhugh and was even more troubled by the silly, indulgent smile plastered across his wrinkled face.

"And, no," he said, staring at me, "I will not permit you to intrude upon the part of me that feels affection for Lily."

I laughed; the notion had, indeed, occurred to me. Peter took that opportunity to interrupt us by his return from the market.

"I bought plenty of tea," the lad announced, hoping in vain to get appreciative recognition from Fitzhugh. Peter looked at me from beneath a forelock of bangs before shyly ducking his eyes away from my glance. "I'll go make a pot," he commented as he brushed past. I thought I heard a "that's about all I'm good for around here" comment but did not telepathically intrude on the youngster.

"His heart is not in this work," Fitzhugh commented. The old symbiont sighed deeply and relaxed back in his chair. It was rare I'd seen him thus; obviously, the cardiac event had depleted some of his usual energy or else he was wisely following the doctor's recommendations. "I hope, before they put me out to pasture, that I can find someone who wants to follow my lead." He looked over at me; his dark eyes were shadowed, but I knew, without intrusive telepathy, the content of his thoughts.

"It's difficult for young people," I said, "due to what they perceive to be the lure of traveling versus a tedious job here. And, no, although I am barely competent to assist you at times, this is not a good fit for me, either."

Fitzhugh's heavy gray brows drew together in a frown; a thundercloud was gathering in his thoughts with an explosion soon to follow.

"Well, Ms. Goodgame, I was not asking you. The fact that you acknowledge your minimal level of competence at least tells me you are honest." Fitzhugh placed his thin skinned hands on the arms of the chair as if to rise; the purplish veins stood out prominently, causing his hands to look more fragile than ever.

"Wait, Fitzhugh," I said, leaning forward in my chair. "I intended no disrespect to you. In fact, I have valued my time here because I've learned many things."

He puffed out his chest in agitation, and his chin dropped to his collarbone; a full gray beard shot through with strands of white pressed out like a fan against the collar of his shirt.

"I'm waiting," he finally said.

"I've learned patience from my work with you," I replied earnestly. "I have acquired a more deliberative approach to things in general and feel more calm and self-assured."

Lily managed to finally make her way onto Fitzhugh's lap. After turning a circle or two, she dropped down into a doughnut- shaped pile of fur and began to purr. Cats seemed to take on the shapes of food—now, she was a doughnut, later she would become a meatloaf kitty. Peter's arrival with a pot of tea took the edge off of the moment. The young symbiont even poured, and that was a relief to me.

"Why have no successful time shifts been made to Victorian England during the late 1880's?" I asked suddenly.

Fitzhugh didn't appear startled by my out of left field inquiry and pursed his lips as he considered my question. "Ah, the time of Jack the Ripper," he said. "We probably need to review the record and not just rely upon my memory," he began. "And I can direct you to the proper documents, if you wish." He took a sip of the tea after blowing on the brew for a moment. "I have been present in the past when such things were debated." His dark eyes met mine over the rim of the porcelain teacup. "Are you considering such a thing?"

Shrugging my shoulders, I tried to appear casual and nonchalant. I had no wish to be deceptive with the old historian but didn't have permission from Philo to make a serious inquiry. With that thought in mind, I chose a middle path.

"Kipp and I are discussing it. And Kipp, in his typically fearless manner, is pushing it," I added with a laugh.

Fitzhugh reached out and lifted the antique tea pot with care; he'd had it in his possession for at least two hundred years. The teacups had the translucent quality of fine china that was eggshell thin to the point one could see light through the sides of the cups. I always worried I would break one as result of my inherent clumsiness. The fragrance of the bergamot drifted upward to tickle my nose; a tiny drop of honey had missed its mark and slowly slid down the side of my cup. Forgetting my manners, I caught it with the tip of my forefinger and put it to my lips to taste the sweetness.

"I recognize you cannot tell me more about this proposal and respect your privacy…at least, for now," Fitzhugh said.

His neutral, exceedingly fair response provoked a pang of guilt; yes, I had a fully functioning conscience. With care, I replaced my teacup on the tray and stared at a piece of lint that was looking back at me from the fabric of my blue jeans. The fact I rarely dressed up for work was nothing new. All things considered, I was not the best representation of my kind nor was I the type of partner who could help maximize Kipp's growth. But he'd chosen me, and we were affixed to one another with a permanence that was unshakable.

"I'd like to tell you more, Fitzhugh," I finally stammered some words. "But, I don't have permission yet to reveal the focus of such a trip."

Unexpectedly, he gave a soft laugh. His bruised hand drifted down to gently stroke Lily. Oddly, she was rough with the rest of us but seemed to treat him with great care, as if she recognized his vulnerability.

"You don't need to, Petra. I trust you." His eyes glanced up to lock briefly with mine, which were no doubt rounded with a startled expression.

I broke the eye contact and tried, in vain, to locate again the little piece of errant lint. His comment was so unexpected that I lacked a coherent reply.

"And I realize that you did not expect to hear me say that to you, but my work with you over the past couple of years has helped me to understand you." He cleared his throat. "I have had to amend my hastily arrived conclusion that you are a car careening out of control with only two functioning wheels and no steering mechanism."

Keeping my head down, I laughed in response. "That is a graphic description and perhaps has been accurate in the past." The laughter left my voice. "Having the responsibility for Kipp's development has made me grow up faster than I might have wished."

Fitzhugh shrugged his thin shoulders. "I believe the reason I was so agitated with you had to do with the fact I believed you were not living up to your potential. My intuition of you was that you have profound skills as a traveler; you and Tula were remarkable, but you and Kipp are truly amazing." He took a deep breath before adding, "I probably won't be around long enough to chronicle your adventures, but I would love to have had the opportunity."

The intensity of the discussion was uncomfortable for me, so I chose a strategic shift. "I will honestly tell you that the idea of timing a visit to coincide with the serial killings of Jack the Ripper disturbs me; Kipp, of course, is not intimidated by anything. However, I lack his advanced skills, and I fear being overwhelmed by all of it."

He nodded his head, carefully steepled his fingers and stared off into the distance. From the back of the library, we could hear Peter climbing up the metal ladder, then descending, muttering as he did so. Fitzhugh darted a glance at me and smiled. "I will help you any way I can."

"So, what did Fitzhugh say?" Kipp asked.

We were free of the intrusive and busy presence of Lily now that Fitzhugh was home; I placed Kipp's bowl on the kitchen floor. He never minded sharing with the little monster, but it was definitely more relaxing for him just to bolt down his food without having to dodge her paw or head in his bowl.

It was close to dusk; coral and pink threads in the evening

sky flowed in through the rear kitchen window to coat the small room in deepening pastels. My house was old, and I rarely had time or inclination for any updates. The kitchen counter was constructed of ceramic tile, and more than a few were chipped and cracked with age. I did have a microwave and was waiting for my left over vegetarian chili to reach an atomic level of heat.

Kipp didn't know it, but I had a treat in store for him. He'd never seen *The Wizard of Oz,* which was scheduled to begin on one of the local channels in a few minutes. I'd hyped the idea of a new adventure, and he was excited; politely, he remained out of my brain so that the surprise would not be ruined. The timer on the microwave dinged, and it was in a flash that I had my bowl of chili, a packet of crackers, and a large glass of tea balanced on a tray.

"Let's go," I said.

Kipp ran ahead and was circling on his favorite wool rug by the time I entered the room. I'd closed the plantation shutters on my front windows which overlooked the street. Although my road was minimally travelled, the idea of people peeking in at me from the twilight outside was unpleasant. I clicked the remote and made myself comfortable just in time. The teaser came on; I enjoyed Kipp's wide-eyed expression.

"You look just like a kid," I said, laughing at my friend.

Kipp remained quiet for the entire movie. Since he could not use his telepathy on a televised medium, he was dependent upon his relatively new found knowledge of the English language. Except for having to ask me the meaning of a word or two, he managed quite well, I thought. When it was over, he looked at me and wagged his tail.

"I liked it, but I'm not sure I understood everything," he remarked, tilting his head slightly. By then, I was enjoying the remainder of a bag of oatmeal cookies, most of which I'd shared with Kipp.

"Well, it was marketed as a children's book, but many of the metaphors in the story cross over to adults. All the main characters are searching for something that they thought was missing, or perhaps a character flaw, only to find that when pressed, they could summon that very aspect of themselves." I stared at the last, lonely cookie longingly before surrendering it to Kipp with a short toss.

"Except for Toto," he remarked. "He wasn't complicated at all." Kipp rolled over on his back and let his legs wave in the air. "I didn't like the flying monkeys at all," he remarked, disapproval coloring his thoughts.

"They terrified me when I was a child," I said in agreement. "Believe it or not, when I was younger, I shared your struggle to learn non-telepathic language forms. One-dimensional mediums are tough for us since we rely upon our telepathy to fully understand context as well as content."

We continued to chat about the movie and the relationships within, as I took my dirty bowl and plate to the kitchen. It was late; I had no motivation to wash dishes and placed them in the sink with the sobering thought that removing dried chili would require a sand blaster the next day. I grimaced slightly at the bowl which stared back as if I should feel guilty over my slack housekeeping.

I'd showered earlier so, after stripping off my sweat pants, I climbed into bed. Kipp hopped up and managed to get comfortable, his head across my chest. His mind was still buzzing, and I finally had to shut him out so I could sleep. Perhaps I was more tired than I realized, because I drifted into a dreamless state.

Later, I became aware that Kipp was moving about on the bed, kicking his legs, almost paddling them at times. It was unusual for him to be so restless, so I joined his thoughts. He was dreaming, and the dreams were not pleasant ones. In Kipp's dream world, he was being pursued by a multitude of flying monkeys who'd launched dive bombing runs at him as he raced frantically through a dense forest. There was no obvious path, and he was laboring to keep ahead of the monkeys. It worsened as the monkeys began throwing rocks and sticks which rained down on his head.

I could have awakened him but decided to try something new…at least for me. After a couple of deep breaths to center myself, I gently and unobtrusively entered Kipp's dream. The ease with which I managed this surprised me. In the past, I'd thought that I could only monitor the dreams of another symbiont.

In the dream, I began to run while trailing Kipp. I must have been in better shape than my current status, because it took me only a few seconds to catch him as he darted past large bushes and ducked beneath low hanging tree limbs. I could hear the patter of his paws on the packed ground; overhead, I could hear the flapping of the wings of the monkeys along with their high- pitched chattering. In a moment, I drew next to Kipp—he looked at me with gratitude. His tongue was hanging with near exhaustion, and his normally burnished coat was covered in dirt and brambles.

I slowed and magically produced a large net, much like ones fishermen use. With a swirling toss that would have earned me an Olympic medal in the discus throw, I swung the net up and away. In my manipulated dream world, the monkeys could not stop and flew into the soaring net. Before my hands returned to my sides, the monkeys were safely trapped on the ground.

Kipp stared at me in fascination. "So, you can do it, too!" he exclaimed.

We awoke simultaneously, and I was rewarded for my flying monkey rescue by Kipp bathing my face with his tongue.

"I thought no humanoid symbiont could do such a thing," Kipp remarked.

"Me, too. Maybe there are a lot of things we've convinced ourselves we cannot do, and maybe we're wrong about many of them." I managed to settle Kipp down and relaxed my head on my pillow. "This will be one to share with Philo and Fitzhugh."

CHAPTER 7

"Stop pacing," Kipp suggested as he lay, comfortable and unperturbed, on the beige carpet in the anteroom outside of the large conference room where the Twelve were in session.

I stared down at him and bit back my retort. The fact that he was right and I needed to settle my body as well as my psyche went without saying. So, perhaps he should have kept his thoughts to himself.

"I heard that," he remarked. "The day I quit butting into your life will be my last," he added. Turning his ruddy head slightly, he peered up at me. The light overhead caught a living spark in the amber pools of color in his eyes.

I shook my head and took a moment to glance down at my pants. At least, for a change, I was not wearing worn jeans or stretched out sweat pants. It took a bit of searching, but I'd finally located my one pair of decent black slacks in the back of my closet where they'd fallen behind a couple of stacked shoe boxes. The white blouse I wore was wrinkled; with my aversion to ironing anything, I'd tossed the shirt into the dryer and spun it around for a few minutes to get rid of the most noticeable creases.

"You look nice, very presentable," Kipp observed.

My brows drew together in a dark scowl of uncomplimentary envy. All Kipp had to do was shake himself thoroughly, lick a paw, and he was ready for the ball. My appearance in anything less than extreme casual required an almost supernatural transformation.

The door opened, and Philo beckoned us inside. "We are ready for you two," he remarked, unnecessarily. I couldn't help but notice that his brows scooted higher up on his forehead than was usual as he tried to put my neat attire in context. Philo's attitude only reinforced my idea that I was often just shy of being thought of as a slob.

With my head up, I breezed past him to enter the inner sanctum of the Twelve. It was no secret to anyone that I detested the industrial, sterile atmosphere of the conference room. I almost didn't know what to do with my hands or body in the expansive space. Looking off to the right through a series of large windows, I sought my old friend, an ancient yellow poplar that hovered outside in its role as guardian of the garden. I'd spent many hours sitting on the bench at its base, musing esoteric notions as well as the state of my own existence. To keep my hands from fluttering and betraying anxiety, I pressed them to my sides and headed toward the chair that Philo indicated. I didn't sit, but stood, instead, with my hands resting lightly upon the back of the chair. As was tradition, the Twelve was made up of six humanoid symbionts and six lupines. While the humans rested in fairly decent chairs—although with too much chrome for my taste—the lupines were given benches. Everyone smiled, and a few hellos were murmured; both Kipp and I were well known to all. Anyone in the room could have ferreted out my purpose and recognized deceit, but we were all too polite and socialized to do such a thing. I took a deep breath and nodded at Philo.

"Petra, you asked to come here today and request permission to take a time shift…with Kipp, of course." Philo was uncomfortable with the introduction, hence his prattling on about the obvious. As the new leader of the Twelve, it was inappropriate for him to request me do the exact thing he had. The question was whether or not I could pull off the request with no one the wiser. No, it was not honest, but Philo's son was involved, and I felt the ethics of the matter could be debated at another time in the future.

Juno greeted Kipp, who enthusiastically took the bench next to her. Next to me, there was no question that his closest bond on earth was to old Juno. I had no way of knowing if she was aware of the conspiracy that was about to unfold.

"Kipp and I are fully rested following our last trip," I began. Glancing down at my feet, I recognized in horror that I was wearing different color socks; it seemed I could not even prepare for a professional event and do it well.

"I noticed out in the anteroom but didn't want you to get rattled," Kipp's whispered thoughts entered my head. His giggle resonated in the obviously empty chamber where my brain should have resided.

"I've been studying the fact that there have been no productive trips to Victorian London during the Jack the Ripper killings," I began, working up some momentum. At least I was being honest to this point; Fitzhugh and I had done a search of the available documents and only found a couple of scattered attempts that failed miserably. Continuing with my entreaty, I said, "Those past attempts were not successful due to the inability of the symbiont pairs to block the extreme emotional reactions of the day." I paused and swallowed; my throat had gone dry. "I believe that research is needed on the psychological effects on symbionts of being in close proximity to the cacophony of discordant human thoughts driven by strong emotions." I paused, somewhat pleased with my usage of impressive verbiage, while privately hoping my audience would get tangled in the underbrush of words and not question me too closely. Kipp applauded quietly in the background of my mind.

When no one spoke, I decided to plow ahead. "Kipp, due to his ability to block thoughts from me and compartmentalize his own responses, is the perfect partner. In the past, no symbiont had a Kipp who could offer his level of psychic protection to a partner."

One of the older symbionts in the room was frowning at me, his expression intensifying the longer I spoke. He was of the old guard and didn't approve of challenges to the status quo; it was enough for him that it had been attempted, and failed, and it was time to move on to fresh ventures.

"I find it difficult to understand your motives," he finally commented. His name was Mackinnon, and he had been a member of the group almost as long as had Philo. I glanced at him and smiled.

"Well, perhaps I failed to make myself clear," I replied, trying to sound helpful and neutral. "The purpose of the trip is to expand my relationship with Kipp and in doing so learn more about the capabilities of our species. We both think there are many uncovered depths and find more things on an almost daily basis that are inexplicable."

Mackinnon raised his eyebrows. "Such as?"

I was starting to become anxious and unsure; a small bead of cold sweat rolled down my back, following the gentle curve of my spine. Kipp left his bench and came over to sit by me. I knew he wanted to use the episode of my newly discovered dream manipulation skill to prod the recalcitrant members of the group to let us have some freedoms that might typically be withheld. However, the knowledge that Kipp could actually insert and manipulate thoughts was only known to me, Philo, Juno and Fitzhugh. As of that date, the only hidden skill that had been made public was Kipp's ability to learn language; that talent was being expanded to the lupines in our collective. In the secretive manner in which Kipp and I communicated, I shook him off. The insular nature of my species had truly clipped the wings that God had given us.

Kipp, clever and adaptive as usual, changed tactics on the fly. "Petra and I are convinced there are depths to the symbiotic bond that can only be discovered through rigorous challenges to the bond itself," he said. Somehow, he managed to make truthful remarks without betraying any confidences. "It makes perfect sense, when you consider the issue," he concluded, staring at Mackinnon in such a way that any sort of disagreement would only make Mackinnon look silly and petulant.

Juno, with her uncanny perceptive abilities and her connection to Kipp, probably knew more was at stake, but she managed to insert herself smoothly into the debate. She turned her head slowly due to the arthritis that had stiffened her neck and back. I caught the dulled reflection of light in her eyes made semi-opaque by the growth of bilateral cataracts.

"Kipp is correct," Juno said. "I value his honesty and willingness to explore those depths so that the rest of our species can learn from the experiences."

Slight movement at the window caught my attention; the wind was picking up slightly, and I watched the branches of the yellow poplar dance as if they were fluid arms conducting a symphony. It was rare I drove to work, and today was one of those days; it was good, since a storm was brewing.

"I think, Petra, that we can excuse you and Kipp for today. We will remain behind and discuss your proposal, which is a unique request." Philo smiled, but his expression was guarded, I thought. Knowing him as I did, I wondered if his conscience was bothering him; Philo was a very principled man who now possessed new leadership responsibilities.

After a few murmured goodbyes, Kipp and I left. It was only midday, and I was loath to leave and go home. A deep rumble of thunder from outside put a stamp upon my decision, and I decided to wait out the worse part of the storm in the basement with Fitzhugh. The old historian had grown on me lately.

"You look unusually nice," Fitzhugh said in greeting.

"Gee, thanks," I muttered, glaring at him. Kipp laughed in his easy way and trotted to the back of the library to look for Lily.

"There's a storm outside, and I thought I'd wait it out here…if you don't mind," I added, feeling oddly defensive.

The sound of the rolling thunder was muffled in the basement, and the distant sound, along with the soft lighting, caused me to feel a little sleepy. Fitzhugh obviously noticed because he announced he would make tea and disappeared for a few minutes. The fragrance of bergamot announced his return as he sat across from me, placing the tray on a small table. I noticed there was a lace doily beneath the teapot, adding a well-thought-out appearance to the display.

"I didn't mean to sound insulting, Petra," he said, glancing up at me. His dark eyes were almost lost in the droop of aged eyelids and heavy, gray brows. Without asking, he poured the tea and, knowing my preference, added some honey to my cup.

"You are a very lovely female and attract the attention of many of the males here, if only you would get your head up and notice," he said, sounding stern. "Who knows?" he added. "If I were a youngster instead of old as a glacier, I might make an attempt to court you myself."

I almost spit my tea across the room. Having never thought of Fitzhugh as possessing the typical feelings that would be considered as normal, I realized I'd not imagined him to be capable of love…except for his attachment to Lily, of course.

Kipp returned, followed by the irrepressible feline, who had managed to wrap her forepaws around his left hind leg; as he walked, she was dragged along the floor. Kipp, after giving her a mild correction that was gentle but firm, circled and lay by my chair.

"I try to encourage Petra to get out and do more things, Fitzhugh, but she's a hardhead," Kipp commented, deciding his opinions were critical to the discussion.

Ignoring them both, I took a sip of the tea. Fitzhugh possessed more talent than did Peter in that arena as well as most other things.

"I was married," I finally remarked, "lest you two forget."

Sighing deeply, I tried to roll my head on tired shoulders. The stress of the presentation to the Twelve had finally caught up, and I was fatigued. "I just never figured out how to travel and have any sort of decent relationship outside of my bonded symbiont." Leaning forward, I treated myself to a warm cup of steaming Earl Grey. "I prefer to travel with Kipp," I said. It was all really quite simple.

Fitzhugh shrugged his thin shoulders and took a sip from his cup. Lily, following her unaccustomed reprimand from Kipp, sought the pleasure of the old symbiont's lap. His thin hand, with its markings of age, drifted down to stroke her fur.

"How did your presentation go?" Fitzhugh asked, in a nice segue from my absent love life.

"Not sure," I replied. "Mackinnon was rather negative, but I think his is usually the harshest dissent in the room." I shrugged my shoulders. "The request probably seemed kind of weak, to be honest."

Fitzhugh carefully replaced the antique cup on the tray and sat back in the depths of the upholstered chair. Lily mewed softly in protest at the minimal disturbance to her comfort.

"So, why are you really going?" he asked.

I would not lie to him nor could I break Philo's trust.

"I can't tell you, Fitzhugh, because it involves someone else, and I don't have that person's permission."

Kipp was quiet, his mind oddly still as he followed the conversation. He had shut his eyes and seemed to be deep in reflection, with his thoughts closed off to me. The door to the library opened and Philo walked in, preceded gracefully by Juno.

"Where have I seen this before?" Fitzhugh asked. At Philo's raised eyebrows, Fitzhugh added, "This gathering of symbionts that spells secrecy and conspiracies…" He allowed his voice to trail off as the assembled group either chose a chair or the floor, depending upon two legs or four. "Peter has left for the day," Fitzhugh added.

Philo's eyes met mine. It struck me odd that in a room

full of telepaths, little to nothing of consequence could be said. Maybe Kipp was right about the benefits of openness. However, the large majority of us did not have Kipp's inherent goodness or honor and could not be trusted to appropriately use telepathy in an unregulated manner.

"The Twelve have asked for Fitzhugh to do the usual historical searches of other symbiont time shifts in the general area and time frame that you have requested," he said, addressing me and Kipp. "I had already made the request, since I knew it was on the horizon." He paused and looked down at the tops of his shoes; after a moment, his eyes darted to my feet. "Petra, you're wearing different colored socks," he commented, almost in an offhand fashion.

Despite the thickness of the walls and the fact we were in the basement, the booming of thunder and the occasional crack of lightening could be heard. Each time the sounds resonated in the room, Lily's ears would swivel in agitation, and I braced myself for her craziness. To my relief, Kipp reached out with his mind and, in his way, brought her a feeling of safety and comfort.

"I found some interesting facts while doing the requested research of the literature," Fitzhugh remarked, sitting back in his chair. From my viewpoint, he was looking a little pale and tired.

"You are working too hard," I observed. Fitzhugh was of the type who would fight any restrictions placed upon him. I identified with his irascibility as well as his stubborn nature.

Fitzhugh gave a soft snort of contempt at my words and literally waved me off with his thin hand. "I know my limitations. And why are you worried, Petra?" He laughed softly. "Perhaps you are thinking you'll be stuck with Lily if something happens to me?"

My feelings must have shown on my face, and the hurt I felt surprised me most of all. I'm not particularly thin skinned, and a lifetime of traveling and dealing with diverse situations and agitated humans had thickened my personal armor. But his words cut deep. I couldn't meet Kipp's anxious eyes as he reached out mentally to hold my hand.

"I'm so sorry I said that," Fitzhugh said, his typically evenly cadenced words coming in a rush. The old symbiont shook his gray head. "I learned years ago that I lack the conversational agility needed for humor." He glanced up at me, almost shyly. "I think you'd miss me if I were gone."

Philo cleared his throat. "You two are making me nervous with all this edgy back and forth. Can we move on to the findings you made, Fitzhugh?" Philo's hands grasped at his knees, his anxiety noticeable in the dim confines of the library. The storm raging outside only served to emphasize the intimacy of our secret gathering.

"Odd you should press me, Philo," Fitzhugh replied. "I think you know what I am about to say and would prefer to get it out in the open." He sighed deeply as his chest rose and fell. "Your son, Silas Marshall, was a member of a west coast group who allowed him to travel back to Victorian England to study journalism during the Ripper affair. The archives indicate he and his symbiont, Vashti, left on their time shift quite some time ago." Fitzhugh's eyes met Philo's. "He traveled under the name of Silas Hathaway. The records show no return."

Juno was clearly startled and resettled herself on the floor after shifting her stiff hindquarters from one side to the other. "So, obviously there are hidden motives behind Petra and Kipp asking to make the same journey," she remarked. There was no condemnation or accusation in her words; she was just stating facts in her calm, even way.

Philo stared at his feet again. "I asked them to go and see if they can find out what happened to Silas. Even if he can't return home, I'd like to know he is safe and well."

"And what if he is not?" Fitzhugh asked. "Such an errand is inherently risky and full of potential folly…not to mention the stress on Petra and Kipp."

"We want to go, Fitzhugh," Kipp said. "And we think that there is important research we can do if we go to an emotionally charged era." He looked at me, and I nodded my head, giving him the permission he desired. "Petra entered my dream the other night and manipulated the outcome," he added, knowing the effect it would have on the others, who were predictably startled. "My point is," Kipp continued, "we will never learn some of our potential as a species as long as we make safe trips and avoid challenges." He glanced at Fitzhugh and waited.

Fitzhugh took his time before speaking. Finally, he replied, "I agree with you Kipp, but it still is risky. If it were any pair other than you and Petra, I wouldn't assist in this piece of potential disaster, but I have faith in your abilities to, uh, do good," he said, stumbling a little as he searched for the right words.

I think by this time, nothing was really surprising to me anymore. Fitzhugh, once my harshest critic, considered me attractive, date-worthy and "good". My day really could not have gotten any better. In any case, there was a lot of preparation to be done, and it would begin with reading.

The storm passed and darkness had fallen. I walked out into the wet parking lot, my hands full of books thrust off on me by Fitzhugh, Kipp trotting by my side. Philo's words had brought him the happiness he sought with the reassurance that the Twelve had given approval for the trip, and it was our time to ready ourselves.

"You wanted it," I said, "and you got it."

Kipp laughed in reply.

CHAPTER 8

Suzanne's workshop was a tantalizing combination of old mingled with new. Samples of vintage fabrics cluttered the various tabletops, which were stacked with large books filled with pattern designs. Due to Suzanne's long held associations with mills around the world, she could request an antique weave to be remade to her exacting specifications. The cost of these endeavors was high, but it was necessary for the traveler in time to fit in as seamlessly as possible. When a symbiont team dropped into a past era, there was always plenty to worry about without having to be concerned over one's attire. We were fortunate to have Suzanne at Technicorps; she was, indeed, one of the best available in her line of work.

As Suzanne waved me to a comfortable chair, I observed her buzzing around in a typically frenzied manner. Closing my eyes, I took a deep breath; the fragrance of fabric, some musty and old, combined with the sharp odor of a hot motor posed an interesting challenge for my senses. Despite the need to do many stitches by hand so as to not bring undue attention to period garments, there was an industrial type sewing machine that was put to regular use. Suzanne's large coffee mug sat on a table, the contents no doubt having grown cold; her bright red lipstick stained the ceramic vessel. I smiled to myself—things changed slowly or not at all with us.

"So, we are working up a wardrobe for 1888 London, right?" Suzanne grabbed the mug and took a swig of the coffee; she immediately frowned and put the mug down in disgust. "Cold and horrible," she commented, glancing up at me.

Kipp chose that moment to join us and, after greeting Suzanne, circled and made a soft nest on some fabric that had cascaded onto the floor.

"I'm traveling as an American visiting London," I replied. "I will be of average means but don't want to draw attention to myself with money. So," I said, "I guess that means nice clothes—like a lady would wear—but nothing so fancy that I can't mingle with the folks who are living on the raw side of things."

Suzanne, oddly, was never interested as to the purpose of the trip. In some ways, I appreciated her lack of vulgar curiosity, since it had nothing to do with her work. She would ask sufficient questions to frame up a concept, using her sketch pad to record images. I knew enough of her skills and personality structure to simply wind her up and let her go with no interference on my end.

"Well," she began, after retrieving the pencil she kept stuck in her mass of piled up black hair, "you'll be delighted to know that crinolines were out of style by then." Her eyes gleamed as the little wheels in her brain began to spin. "I think we can recover your bustle bank that you used in Tombstone and recycle it for this journey." Her full lips turned down in a frown. "The bosses are always nagging at me to be conservative and watch costs where I can."

I realized it was difficult for a creative artist to be limited by earthly concerns. Not wanting her to think I was ungrateful, I nodded my head.

"I liked the bustle bank," I said, enthusiastically. "It really was fairly comfortable and clever, too." I knew my words would brighten her dour mood.

Kipp's thoughts twined with mine as he recalled how Suzanne had concealed money for our Tombstone trip, lest we become the victim of thieves. She created a bustle for me to wear that met 1881 fashion demands as well as conceal my bankroll. For Kipp, she fabricated a money collar, much like a money belt, but shorter.

"I'd actually like to use the carpetbag that you designed, Suzanne," I commented. "It allows me to take just enough things to get by for a couple of days until I can purchase what I need."

It was a physical fact that when we time shifted, anything in direct contact with our bodies would travel with us. Suzanne had designed a clever backpack-sling that contained clothing for me; when turned inside out, it resembled a stylish hand-held carpet bag. The story for me was always the same: my trunk or baggage was lost, and I must reassemble a wardrobe. Suzanne looked mildly relieved that she could report some cost savings from her division. Kipp caught her eye and wagged his tail, showing his support, too.

"I'm going as is," Kipp remarked.

She stared at him; humor was not an easy concept for her to manage. "What season are you aiming for?" she asked, smoothly changing the subject back to business.

"Well, I'm hoping for late spring or early summer," I replied. Our arrivals and departures were nowhere near an exact science. My thought had been to try and arrive before the Jack the Ripper hysteria struck. It seemed logical that our attempts to locate Silas would be more productive if we were less distracted by the multitude of thoughts generated by an agitated populace.

"Okay, that helps me. I'll aim for a simple blouse with a jacket or short cape and a skirt that is gathered at the back to accommodate the bustle. You will need the usual chemise and petticoats—the petticoats had waistbands with a button in the back. In winter they were made of wool but of course you will need a lighter fabric in summer, and I'm thinking of a very fine cotton flannel." She was in her element, pacing in a small figure eight pattern.

Kipp, from his vantage point on the floor, was watching her intently. Suddenly, he caught my eye and crossed his, just to be silly and absurd. This was one of those private, hidden moments between us that was lost to my fellow symbiont, Suzanne. I stifled a giggle.

"Summer hats were made of straw and could be decorated with ribbon and or flowers." She looked at me hesitantly. "Do you mind wearing the boots you brought back from Tombstone?" she asked. "They would be of the proper style and era and are much nicer than anything I can make."

Ah, I had fond memories of the boots. I'd found a boot maker while on my last time shift and replaced the uncomfortable ones supplied by Suzanne with a new pair that fit like a second, supple skin. They, along with everything else, had been archived upon my return. Travelers were never allowed to keep any bounty or articles from a time shift, and I suppose that was a good idea. If we were allowed to keep items, it might lead to time travel for the purpose of plunder.

"No problem," I replied, nodding at her. At this point, I knew she no longer needed my input, if, indeed, she had ever, and I took my leave.

Kipp and I, after walking outside to clear our heads, went in search of Fitzhugh. I pushed open the doors to the library only to find it strangely silent. My head went up, and I began to prowl through the stacks; there was no Peter to be found and no Lily to greet us. Sharing my curiosity, Kipp padded softly at my side. We reached the rear of the large room where Fitzhugh's private office was located. Since this was his inner sanctum where no mortal was allowed, I carefully poked my head past the threshold. In the dimness of the unlit room, I saw him—Fitzhugh, in his chair, his head lolled back. Lily was curled in his lap, and she stirred as we approached, blinking her eyes sleepily. Fitzhugh was so motionless that I wondered if perhaps he was dead. After all, he'd just survived a heart attack.

"I don't read thoughts, so he isn't dreaming," Kipp observed.

I tiptoed closer and reached out to gently touch Fitzhugh's

wrist to see if there was a pulse; his other hand shot up like a snake and grabbed my forearm. His sudden movement shocked me so, that I reeled backwards and struck the back of my head on the edge of a cabinet.

"Oh, Fitzhugh!" I gasped. "You almost made me have a heart attack!"

Kipp, meanwhile, fell on the floor as he literally collapsed with laughter. "That's the funniest thing I've ever seen," he said, rolling his eyes up at me.

"Why are you sneaking up on me?" Fitzhugh asked, his thick brows drawn together in a straight line.

"I thought you were dead, you old stinker," I replied. "And you don't have to be so ugly about it, either." Ruefully, I reached up with my hand and rubbed the back of my aching skull.

"Yeah, Fitzhugh. Petra was worried about your health…you should be pleased that somebody cares," Kipp remarked in my defense.

The old symbiont huffed a little, but I noted his face took on a rosy glow. My hovering embarrassed him.

"Well, I suppose thanks are in order," he finally muttered as he rose from his chair. When he looked at me again, his expression had turned sheepish. "I never used to take naps but seem to get more tired lately."

To console him, I said, "I take naps all the time." I thought that he might feel less awkward if he didn't perceive himself to be frail or vulnerable. I should have known better, however.

"That fact is no surprise—we all know you are a notorious slacker, Petra," Fitzhugh replied.

I'd had enough of extending an olive branch at that point and decided to move the conversation past the unpleasantness. "I wanted to free flow some ideas past you that I've gotten from my studies about Victorian London, Fitzhugh, if you think you can manage to wake up and help me." If he wanted it rough, I could oblige.

His head jerked up, but in the next instant he began to laugh. "I think I can do that but will need some hot tea, if you wish to join me."

While he made tea, Kipp and I went to the front of the library, and I chose what was fast becoming my favorite chair. Odd, how things changed in a relatively short period of time. I once loathed this room and felt very awkward and estranged from Fitzhugh. He'd seemed like the ultimate straight arrow who was constantly disapproving of anything I did. But I'd found him to be an invaluable helper to my endeavors and more than likely to bend rules and suggest the road less traveled when it seemed logical to do so.

Who knows what elements collide to make one suddenly sentimental, but it happened with me. Fitzhugh appeared, carrying the tray loaded with his favorite tea service. If I'd been a little more educated, I might have known the name of the pretty, delicate transfer ware, but I had reserved little time for such things.

"Fitzhugh, I, uh…" I began to stammer. Now that the time was here for me to unburden my soul, my courage flew out the window like a caged sparrow elopes from the confinement of a birdcage.

"What?" He glanced up; his brows drew together into one dark, gray-flecked line.

"Go on, Petra. Say it," Kipp mentally nudged me, since he knew what was rolling around inside the confines of my skull.

I took a deep breath. Kipp was watching. Fitzhugh was watching, and even Lily seemed to recognize that it was time to stop chasing her tail and look up at me in anticipation of an important moment.

"Fitzhugh, these things are hard for me to say, sometimes. But, I want you to know that I've grown very close to you, and that I, well, care about you."

His lips parted slightly, and the muscles in his face relaxed. After a second, he smiled. "Thank you, Petra. I find such endearments difficult to hear and even more difficult to express."

His eyes closed as he retreated somewhere to his memories. Of course, I politely averted my thoughts and allowed him his privacy, as did Kipp. Or at least, I think Kipp did. With my friend, all things seemed possible, and he was the most curious symbiont I'd ever known. He could be burrowing deep inside Fitzhugh's mind while blocking my awareness of such. But Kipp was also honorable and probably would not do such a thing.

"The last time I heard anyone say that was many years ago," Fitzhugh said, a shadow of a memory crossing his face. "My symbiont, Lydea, was attached to me in the manner of our people."

It was easy to forget that Fitzhugh had been a traveling symbiont himself when he was young and full of curiosity and vigor. Would that be my fate, if I lived to ancient years, as had he—to be thought of as old and rigid, without humor or the capacity to love anymore?

"No, Petra, I don't think so," Fitzhugh replied.

My eyes rounded as I gazed in surprise at him. "You just read my thoughts and without my permission!" I said.

Fitzhugh ducked his head and laughed. "I was just proving two points: one, I have the ability to not be rigid and to break rules, and, two, I am not without skills." His dark eyes met mine. "I know…scandalous behavior, but I am so old that I can get by with such nonsense."

He reached out to gracefully pour the tea; the steam enveloped us in a fragrant curtain, and I noticed, with gratitude, that he'd remembered to bring the honey pot for me. Kipp stuck his nose to the edge of the table.

"Do you think I could develop a taste for tea?" Kipp queried; his large black nose quivered as he examined the odor of the beverage. Our lupine brothers and sisters had the superior, evolved senses of true canines, and Kipp's olfactory sense was highly discriminating.

"Juno tried some once," Fitzhugh remarked, "but spat it out as quickly as she could. Tea is rather bitter and acidic to the untested palate."

Kipp rolled his eyes at me. It was clear he found Fitzhugh's explanation to be inadequate, since Kipp was, at heart, a bold adventurer whose courage did not pale at a new challenge.

"No, Kipp. I think you are more of a vanilla milkshake kind of guy," I said, reaching out to scratch the place between his ears that was difficult for him to locate, even with the use of extremely flexible hind legs.

"So, what did you want to run past me?" Fitzhugh asked, as he finally was settled and content in his chair.

"I'm trying to get a general feel for the place and times," I replied. Of course, I'd been alive in 1888 but had not resided in London, so research was a necessity. After another sip of tea, I leaned back in my chair. "From my studies, 1880's London was a place of great diversity. In terms of social class, there was the aristocracy and next would be the upper middle class, which would be people such as bankers or merchants. Then would be the middle class populated by doctors and maybe solicitors. Teachers, journalists, shop keepers and the like would be considered lower middle class. There were also skilled tradesmen, such as carpenters. On the lower socioeconomic rung were domestics, common laborers and soldiers." I glanced up at the ceiling as I tried to remember more facts.

"The more affluent people lived in the West End, in communities such as Bloomsbury, Marylebone, and Mayfair. Poverty was tightly clustered in the East End of London. Not all of those areas were crime infested and jam packed with poor people, but there were pockets with a disproportionately high concentration. There were estimated to be 90,000 slum dwellers in the East End."

Lily, bored with my dull recitation of facts, curled up between Kipp's paws. She looked up at me, once, and blinked her eyes slowly open and shut just to let me know she was still in the game.

"The social decay created crusaders and clergy who felt they had an obligation to try and bring improvement to the lives of the poor. The Reverend Samuel Barnett, the vicar at St. Jude's, took a strict, no-nonsense view of crime and poverty and felt the problems were due to moral decline. On the other hand, there was William Booth, who formed the Salvation Army in 1878, with a focus on the plight of endangered children. Eventually, laws were passed that provided for compulsory education and limited the ages for children who worked as well as hours worked."

As I droned on with my dissertation, it became clear to me that Fitzhugh, despite all protests to the contrary, was fatigued. Dark eyes, normally piercing to the point of being unpleasant, were dulled and sunken; his paper thin eyelids were tinted grayish-pink in a way that was not demonstrative of sound health.

Suddenly, I announced, "I'm tired, Fitzhugh. Do you mind if we pick this up later?"

The weariness left him in an instant, and he sat up, ramrod straight. "I don't know why you would be tired, Petra, since you do little work."

With that last unwanted—and undeserved—salvo fired from his battleship across the bow of mine, I stood and raised my hands in mock surrender.

"I'm going home," I announced.

Kipp carefully got to his feet and, in doing so, managed to not crush the somnolent Lily. With the lightest whisper of a touch of his nose, he grazed the top of her head in a caress and to say goodbye. As Kipp and I made our way out to the car—I'd driven that morning, thinking it would be a long day—he listened in on my vile mutterings, most of which had to do with Fitzhugh.

"You know your problem with him, don't you?" Kipp asked. His nuzzled head beneath my hand, begging a caress. A mild breeze pulled my hair off my face and away from my heated neck. On the western horizon, the sun's stubborn remnants fell from view, ushering in an early spring twilight tinged with soft, linear streaks of lilac and dove gray.

"What would that be?" I didn't really want to hear his analysis but knew he would give it anyway.

"You are too much alike!" Kipp replied.

I exhaled loudly while counting to ten internally. Kipp, on occasions, was too outspoken and perceptive for his own good.

"I'm gonna need French fries and plenty of junk food after that observation, Kipp," I finally sputtered.

"I was hoping you'd say that."

CHAPTER 9

As it was with all time shifts, there were significant preparations to be made. Not only did a wardrobe and authentic currency have to be produced, but also the traveling pair needed to have a working understanding of the culture of the day. Both Kipp and I were excused from other duties, since our studies about Victorian England eclipsed all other tasks.

We took an early morning run, enjoying the mild spring weather and the diffuse light from a hesitant sun, and returned home to continue reading. To break up the monotony, I used movies to help Kipp get a sense of the era. His command of English was a necessity to discern the subtle meanings in complex dialog presented via the television screen. Kipp and I were halfway through watching the Jeremy Brett version of *The Hound of the Baskervilles* when the phone rang. I stared at Kipp, unwilling to leave the comfort of my chair; he returned my gaze with defiance written all over his lupine face.

"Don't look at me like that," he said. "You know I can't answer the phone!"

I started to put down my popcorn bowl, but after a cautious glance at Kipp, I realized my food treasure would not be safe and took it with me to the kitchen.

"Coward!" Kipp's taunts followed me.

It was Philo, who asked if he could drop by later. After giving him an affirmative, I returned to the movie. As we watched it unfold, Kipp threw various questions my way, most having to do with the language and expressions peculiar to the times.

"There are certain slang dialects that will be difficult for us to understand," I explained. "Many of the people in the East End used a Cockney dialect, and we will depend on our telepathy for comprehension and not our command of language." I smiled at Kipp. "It's similar to translating any foreign language." He sat quietly for a moment, but I knew him well enough to realize he was hatching another question.

"What do you know about John Merrick?" Kipp asked.

"Not much," I confessed. Glancing down, I was disappointed to see that my popcorn was long gone, and only a few, lonely raw kernels were left to rattle around in the bowl. I considered another bag but didn't want to have to run a couple of miles to rid myself of the excess calories. With a sigh, I looked at Kipp. His ruddy coat was targeted by a solitary ray of light angling in through a front window to capture him—an unwilling performer—on the dusty floor of my living room. It was quiet outside, oddly so for a Saturday when the weather was splendid and should have lured people out of their homes.

"I think his real name might have been Joseph, and he was a young man who was born with no apparent problems. Then, in his youth, he began to experience physical changes; there were unusual boney growths that appeared as well as alterations to the texture of his skin. His family claimed his mother had been frightened by an elephant when she was pregnant with him, that being the cause of his maladies." I tucked my swinging free foot up under me to stop it from moving like an out of control pendulum.

"He had a severe speech impediment and was thought to be of subpar intelligence, but the opposite was true: he was bright and sensitive. A surgeon from the London Hospital took him in at the facility, and he was allowed to live there until his death."

Kipp's mind was racing with thoughts. "Is there a movie?" he asked. "I'd like to hear more about him. When we go to London, I'd like to meet him."

"Kipp, I'm not sure how our journey will go…" I began before he cut me off.

"And if I don't meet him, then, well, okay. But if we find ourselves at the hospital, I'm gonna seek him out."

It had been a while since I'd seen *The Elephant Man* but recalled that Philo had the DVD. This battle of wills with Kipp was lost, and I decided that there was no harm, after all, in the act of mere contemplation.

"I'll ask Philo to bring it," I said.

Two hours later, Kipp and I were in the small back yard of my house. The initiative that pushed gardeners to plant had hit me—a rare occurrence, to be certain. A neighbor with a truck kindly dropped off a load of flowers that I'd purchased from a local nursery a couple of days earlier. I was using a shovel to dig some holes; Kipp, eager to show he could be of use around the house, hunkered down and was busy digging, too. I stopped in amazement to watch him fling dirt backwards from between his hind legs. I'm not sure any mechanized invention could have moved earth more effectively than did Kipp.

Finally, he paused and walked to the row of azaleas. Lupines did have color discrimination in their eyesight, and he gazed at each flower in turn. In short order, he found one he liked and gingerly picked up the edge of the pot with his teeth and carefully carried it to the hole. He set it down and glanced at me—ejecting the flower out of the pot would tax the skill set of the ever resourceful Kipp. With a laugh, I dropped my shovel and walked over to him.

"Why this one?" I asked, as I gently removed the flower from its plastic cradle, careful to not disturb the roots any more than was necessary.

He turned his head and gave an analytical assessment of the plant. "I like the color," he finally answered. "It makes me feel happy."

It was, indeed, a warm but cheerful shade of coral pink, and I had to agree with him. As I patted the black soil around the plant, I felt as if I had welcomed a new member to the family. Kipp left my side and wandered towards the back of the yard, which was deep rather than wide. He stopped at a large rock that lay on the ground. Our thoughts met in midair as his eyes met mine across the distance.

Yes, he and I had buried the blanket that my sweet Tula once lay upon in that spot which was now covered with grass and unknown to all but us. I would always miss my first bonded symbiont and grieved the untimely nature of her death. But the loss of Tula had ushered in my relationship with Kipp, and there was no regret there. Maybe if there were any feelings of sadness, it would be that Tula could not be with us to experience a fresh, new loving presence in the body of Kipp.

Kipp dipped his head and sniffed carefully of the grass. I, through sharing his thoughts, caught the excitement when he realized that the scent of Tula's blanket was still discernible. He stepped back and seemed to be making a calculation; in another moment, he began digging with care at first and then with escalating energy.

"Let's place a flower here, too," he suggested.

Kipp was endlessly pushy when he set his mind to something. Recognizing his mood and attitude, I chose the flower, at his insistence, and began to pull an azalea with the promise of white blossoms from its container.

"Tula had a white coat, so this will be a nice way to remember how pretty she was," I said.

We continued to work in silence; overhead, a high flying single engine plane buzzed northward, its destination a mystery to those of us far below. Eventually, Kipp become fixated on a spot high up in a border hedge where he'd spied a pair of little Carolina wrens who were building a nest. One would think their work ethic to be motivating, but instead, I dropped to the grass to watch them toil.

"They will build a nest anywhere," I said, directing my observations to Kipp. "Once I had a clothespin container hanging from that line," I said, gesturing across the yard. "I was only gone an hour, and when I came back, the nest was built; I didn't have the heart to tear it out."

"You might learn something from them...I recall Fitzhugh called you a slacker," Kipp replied, rolling onto his back. "I'm working on my suntan, in case you wondered," he added, craning his head to stare at me.

It was getting late in the day, and I expected Philo would show up soon. With that thought in mind, I retreated inside, followed by Kipp, and changed my grass stained sweats for a pair that were clean and only had one small paint stain on the right knee. Kipp's head went up, and a moment later I recognized the thoughts of Philo and, to our delight, Juno. Kipp trotted to the living room to act as greeter, while I braided my hair to keep it off my face. Philo took a seat in the living room as Kipp and Juno exchanged moist nose greetings.

"I brought *The Elephant Man*," Philo said as he gestured towards the table where the DVD lay. He still seemed flat, his emotions tightly contained.

"I've been outside working all day," I replied brightly, thinking he'd be impressed at my rare show of initiative. "Do you want a grilled cheese sandwich?" He was obviously tense and distressed and in need of a distraction. "You remember that is one of the few things I have mastered in the kitchen."

He laughed and rose from the chair. "Let's all have grilled cheese sandwiches," he suggested. "I know Juno loves them and so does Kipp."

The crew followed me into my small kitchen; the next hour was spent with pleasant dialog and greasy food. When the last crumb was ingested, and I'd managed to return the kitchen to a semblance of order, I took my seat across from Philo.

"So, what's got you so rattled?" I asked. Even as I did so,

it seemed to be increasingly odd to me to have to ask permission to gain access to another symbiont's thoughts. Living with Kipp was having a definite effect on me that smacked of opposition toward the beliefs I'd been taught. I pushed a glass of milk across the table at Philo and began to sip on mine. Kipp and Juno relaxed on the floor, satiated after the bounty of gooey cheese and toasted bread.

Philo shook his head and tried to smile but failed. "Claire and I had a terrible argument," he began. "And you know what happens when symbionts fight…we lose that control we're supposed to have and can dig into places that hurt." He glanced at me, his dark eyes soft in the glare of the overhead light. "You remember what that's like, don't you?"

"Yes, but please don't remind me," I replied.

Immediately, Kipp became alert and focused; it was clear he wanted an explanation of what we meant.

"Kipp, when emotionally connected symbionts—like Philo and Claire or me and my husband—fight over something, it becomes almost impossible to keep the customary boundaries; you can really hurt someone you love." I remembered back, for a moment, to a spectacularly volatile argument I'd had with my spouse and opened my mind for Kipp to share the memories.

He stiffened and looked at Philo and then me. "That feels horrible!" he exclaimed. "Why does it have to be that way?" Kipp's amber eyes softened. "Petra, even when I'm upset with you, I never want to hurt you."

"Oh, Kipp, it's hard to explain. But sometimes romantic, emotional love makes symbionts—and people—vulnerable and subject to hurt and be hurt by the one loved most." I smiled at him. "Humans have an advantage in that they can't read each other's thoughts."

With effort, I cleared my mind so Kipp could release his connection with my painful memories. "Philo, do I need to make up the sofa in the study?" I asked, raising my eyebrows and smiling.

He returned the smile. "I don't think that's necessary, but

it will be a while before we are over this rough patch." There was an antique salt shaker on the table; he picked it up and gazed at it with curiosity. "You've always been comforted by your bits and pieces of the past...some stranger's past, as it were. As much time as I've spent with you, I still don't understand it." His shoulders slumped.

"So, what was the fight about, or are you gonna leave me in suspense?" I reached out and took the salt shaker from him.

He shook his head. "I'm still uncertain that this time shift you and Kipp are taking is a good course of action."

I didn't have to be a telepath to understand his concern and, at least, one of the other unspoken, fundamental issues: Philo was essentially honest, and the deception he used to manipulate the governing body bothered him and always would.

"Claire only wants answers about what happened to Silas. I don't think she is able to be worried about your and Kipp's safety and well being." He dropped his eyes to the table top, where I'd managed to miss a pile of crumbs that formed a little pathway across the scarred surface that had seen better days.

"Petra, I'm ashamed to say it, but I'm disappointed in her." He dropped his eyes again and reached out to dip his forefinger in the pile of crumbs. Philo's brow furrowed as he dragged his finger across the table, making a pattern on the surface. "And I feel bad that I'm being more than a little hypocritical in my criticism of her. After all, I want Silas to be found, too."

I reached across the table and caught his hand, putting a stop to his mindless crumb art. Kipp stood and walked over, resting his jaw on the edge of the table.

"Philo, Petra and I have made our decision. We're going, and even if you pull the permission, we're going anyway."

Philo cocked his head to the side. "You are sounding more and more like a rebel, Kipp," he remarked. The way it sounded, it could have been either a criticism or a complement—or both.

Kipp acknowledged the observation in his mind. "We have three objectives for our trip. First, we are going to look for Silas. Second, we need to work on our evolving symbiotic relationship, just as we told the Twelve. And, third, I want to meet John—I mean Joseph—Merrick."

That statement formed the perfect segue for distraction, and we moved to the living room to watch *The Elephant Man*. I hadn't seen it in years, and, of course, it was a new experience for Kipp. When it was finished, Kipp stared at me.

"Why are humans so vicious with one another?" Kipp asked. His ears drooped, and he looked rather crestfallen. He'd managed to keep up a continuous loop of information to Juno so that she could comprehend the movie. Although she was learning English, she lacked Kipp's skill to make the connection between the dialog and the feeling tones expressed.

"You're only focusing on the people who were unkind, Kipp," I replied. "There were also those who were compassionate and caring." Despite my words, he still looked a little sad—a mark of his sensitivity and abundant heart.

"Remember, Kipp," Philo said, "symbionts are capable of bad behaviors, too. If you recall Max and Andrea, both of them had evil designs that involved you. It's important, in our quest to remain humble, to understand how easily any of us—human or symbiont—can fall from grace."

Kipp rose from his worn, woolen rug and walked over to place his head on my knees. I reached out and smoothed the fur on his head, scratching the favorite place between his ears; with my mind, I also tried to soothe his worried thoughts. He was so good, noble and pure. My goal was to always try and keep him steering down the right path despite the conflicting influences of the world.

"I've got to go home," Philo announced. He seemed weary as he stood. "Claire will be worried."

I rose from my chair, walked over to put my arms around my friend, and placed my head on his chest. "Be safe," I said.

Philo rested his chin on the top of my head for a moment while Kipp hovered over Juno who struggled to stand.

"Do you have a block and tackle handy?" Juno asked, her thoughts tinged with wry humor. "It's tough getting old."

Later, Kipp and I rested in bed, his head across my breastbone as was customary.

"Petra?"

"Yes?"

"Promise me we will never fight like Philo and Claire."

"I promise," I said. "Go to sleep and dream sweet dreams tonight, Kipp."

He was quiet for a moment. "Will you love me forever?"

"I promise," I repeated. "Get some rest and don't worry, Kipp. You are mine, and I am yours."

He pressed his jaw against my chest until it hurt. Yes, we were alive, that much was a certainty. I could only hope that Silas, the missing son of Philo and Claire, would be found in a similar condition.

CHAPTER 10

A couple of weeks passed; I saw little of Philo, and when I caught a glimpse of him, he appeared harried, running from one meeting to another. I wondered if his burst of extreme vulnerability revealed to me and Kipp left him with feelings of unease. I think humans felt much the same when they unburdened their hearts to only be faced with the emotional discomfort that followed. Both humans and symbionts required parts of their souls to be hidden from sight. Kipp's constant enmeshment with me and my subsequent tolerance of such was an anomaly in my contemporary world.

Suzanne called me back for the customary fitting of my outfits, including the required undergarments. Even though I had a rough idea of her planning, it was exciting to see the finished product. She was a skilled artist, and her research into fabrics, styles and appropriate accessories was fascinating to me, as I had no aptitude for such things.

"Here, Petra. Go into the dressing room and put on the chemise, foundation garment—I fashioned it like we did the last time with laces in the front since Kipp can't help with the ties—and the petticoat."

The fabricated items were waiting for me in the cubicle. As much as it was important for me to make certain everything fit, it was equally critical I know how to don the various articles of clothing. Yes, I'd lived through those past times, but it had been a while. There were two complete outfits on padded hangers, and the rest of the pieces were neatly stacked on a bench. Kipp nosed his way past the curtain and circled before dropping down to the carpet. He watched in amusement as I struggled to master the corset.

"Inhale deeply," he instructed.

I started to make a rude comment in response but only raised an eyebrow.

"Just remember, smarty pants, that you have to wear a collar," I replied, knowing his strong dislike for any sort of confining item on his body. Kipp displayed his teeth in response.

My traveling garment consisted of a skirt that was made from a medium gray tweedy fabric with a slightly nubby texture. It fell straight with a draping of fabric in the back to accommodate my bustle. There was a simple button down blouse and a fashionable short cape to pull over my shoulders as a light wrap.

"Why did human women have to dress in such silly costumes?" Kipp asked. "Their waists were pinched in, and the bustle made their backsides look really big."

I laughed and began to fasten the dainty pearl buttons on the front of the soft cream colored blouse. "The evolution of human clothing has a history all its own." I turned and smiled at Kipp. "But I prefer sweat pants and a t-shirt, myself."

The scent of freshly brewed coffee caught the attention of my prominent nose. A second later, the curtain to the little room parted, and Suzanne thrust in her arm; a mug of steaming coffee was shoved in my direction.

"Don't spill it on the blouse, please," Suzanne ordered in her bossy way.

"Sure," I replied, raising my eyebrows at Kipp. He slowly closed one eye in a conspiratorial wink.

In a couple of minutes, I managed a promenade for Suzanne, who directed me to pirouette, march back and forth, squat a couple of times and stand on my toes. I wasn't quite sure what the squat maneuver proved, since I had no tight britches to split, but whatever, I thought to myself. Kipp giggled in my head, out of reach of Suzanne's awareness.

"I think the skirt is a little too long," she remarked. "You'll end up with the hem constantly soiled, so I think I'll take it up just a tad." She circled behind me and tugged at the back of the shirt. "I think I'll let this out across your shoulders." Putting her hands on her hips, she tilted her head to the side as she gazed at me. "Have you put on weight?"

I slowly counted to ten and turned to face her. Ignoring her comment, I gestured at my throat. The neckline of the blouse was begging for a pretty, antique brooch.

"Do we have anything in the archives that can go here?"

Suzanne nodded. "I have a tray of some that are not too expensive, and you can select your favorite…maybe a nice cameo would do." Her dark brows pulled down. "I know how tough you are on my creations."

Well, I tried to not be offended. Non-travelers really had no concept of what those of us who did encountered on a constant basis. Kipp disappeared into the next room for a moment, and then he reappeared, draped in a swaddling of cast off fabric that he'd scooped up from the floor. With his head up, he pranced around, cutting his eyes at me.

"I thought I'd dress up, too," he remarked, trying to get me to laugh.

Of course I did, but an unimpressed Suzanne left us with our mirth. Some really creative people have absolutely no sense of humor.

Somehow, Philo managed to convince the Twelve that I didn't need to undergo another interrogation. Occasionally, a second interview was required due to the nebulous nature of the trip. Since my proposal was about as fuzzy as a pair of large dice swinging from the rear view mirror of a Chevy

Bel Air, I was amazed at the lax oversight. But, in the end, it definitely worked for me.

Our departure date was set for the twenty fifth of May. That early target was purely arbitrary, but I wanted time to explore and look for Silas before the madness associated with Jack the Ripper hit the streets of London. The accuracy of our time shifts was never pinpoint, but I'd found, over the years, that my ability to hit my mark, so to speak, had grown with experience. To help us mesh as a team, Kipp and I spent countless hours reviewing maps of 1888 London, studying the topography and landmarks. I thought, after counsel with Fitzhugh, we would do best to try and land in Regent's Park. Making that initial target was always the hardest part, but Kipp's abilities had helped us to be remarkably accurate on our previous two journeys. In my guise as an American visitor, I probably would seek out a modest hotel in the West End of London. In any case, I thought Kipp and I would need distance from the congestion and chaos of the East End; symbionts' minds require rest and renewal from the intrusive thoughts of so many humans.

Two days before the proposed time shift, I found myself sitting in the basement of Technicorps, staring at Fitzhugh across a steaming tea service; the fragrance of the Earl Grey almost served as an intoxicant in the closeness of the space. Peter left at noon to do shopping for the kitchen and obviously felt no pressing need to hurry back.

"Are you nervous?" Fitzhugh asked.

"Yes," I replied. "I always am—it's a mixture of anxiety and excitement."

He nodded. After blowing on the rim of the fragile cup, he took a cautious sip. Fitzhugh peered up at me, his dark eyes sharp beneath the tangle of dark brows. His vigor, following the heart attack, had returned.

"I wish you could bring me back a packet of tea from your trip, but I imagine you'll have other things on your mind. And, besides, you're not allowed to keep souvenirs." He sighed and sipped at the tea again.

"Well, an accommodation might be arranged," I said,

laughing. "You know how I like to break the rules from time to time."

Fitzhugh relaxed in the upholstered chair, allowing his head to rest on the plush back. "I made my last time shift when I was about Philo's age," he commented. "Odd, it was to England, too, but during a different era." He glanced at me. "I liked the work but not as much as you. Kipp and you are much more curious than was I."

He broke off, and I knew he wanted to say more but hesitated for reasons known only to him. As he took a deep breath, his beard rose and fell across his chest. Kipp was upstairs, saying goodbye to his classroom of neophytes; Lily was asleep in Fitzhugh's office, and Peter was absent. It was nice to be alone with the old historian, and that was one reality I thought I would never experience.

"I met a human woman on that last trip," Fitzhugh remarked, startling me out of my lulled sense of peace. "She was remarkably bright and sensitive with an exceedingly kind nature." His eyes dropped; the room became quiet so that I could hear the soft ticking of a small desk clock with a glowing face that stared back at me from across the table. "I fell in love with her. After that happened, I really lost my zeal for time shifts."

I felt my eyes widen in response and averted my gaze so that he wouldn't see my look of incredulity. Fitzhugh capable of love? Who would have thought that could happen, I wondered? But then I considered his gentleness with Lily; he always stroked her with sensitive hands that reflected a caring heart. The long pause became longer, and I felt pressed to comment.

"I've wondered about that…if it were to happen to me how I would manage," I finally sputtered.

The falling in love part would not be impossible since symbionts and humans had so many similarities. But the human would grow old while the symbiont would stay relatively unchanged; the situation would be painfully untenable.

He didn't respond, and when the pause became

uncomfortable, I changed the subject by asking, "Will you be at my leaving party tonight?"

Fitzhugh sighed deeply and stared up at me as I stood. "Yes, with bells on."

I, in the vein of symbiont tradition, invited my closest friends over for an evening of fun and relaxation before the big event. These things were called "leaving parties" and usually ended up as more of a humorous roast with stories being told to embarrass the traveling pair. Since Kipp had no history with our collective, he would be able to sit back and enjoy my humiliation. It also fell on the travelers to prepare the feast and entertainment. I think the reasons for that peculiar tradition had been lost in history; even Fitzhugh seemed clueless.

As I worked in preparation, I looked around my kitchen in satisfaction. No one liked leaving a messy dwelling to which to return; in that way, maybe humans and symbionts had something in common. Philo had access to all of my accounts and would keep up the payment of bills and check on my house while I was gone. A huge pot of vegetarian chili was simmering on the stove. I was relatively skilled at chili, soup, and the occasional grilled cheese sandwich, but beyond that, my menu was limited.

I walked back to my bedroom; Kipp, knowing my restless mind, wandered after me. His footsteps were so soft that they could barely be heard on the aged, wooden floors. Most humans would have upgraded the flooring and fixtures by now, but I was truly a product of history and my four hundred years on earth had left me with an oddly romantic, definitely reflective sort of nature.

My traveling clothes had been delivered yesterday— Suzanne worked best with a tight deadline—and were hanging on the back of my closet door. I pulled up the hem of the skirt and looked at the tight, perfect stitches; smiling, I let the fabric drop and carefully smoothed it with the palm of my hand.

Kipp gazed at me. "What's up?" His large head tilted to one side. "You seem more unsettled than usual."

I laughed softly. "Maybe I'm getting older and thinking of our life together. At what point will all of this stop, Kipp? When will the Twelve decide it's time to uproot us and send us off to places unknown?"

He remained quiet. Sometimes one only needs to listen and not offer commentary.

"I know it's not good for our kind to get attached, but I confess I have. I love our little house—I think I know every scrape on the flooring and each tiny chipped tile on the kitchen counter." I walked to the window and gazed out at the back yard. "We just planted flowers; will we make it back to see them bloom again next year, I wonder?"

Kipp walked to my side and put head under my hand, demanding a caress. "I know how you feel, and I share those feelings." He turned his head and caught my hand between his teeth and gave me a nip. "But as long as we're together, everything else will be okay."

I knelt down and pulled him against my chest. "Yes, Kipp. I love you, too."

After sundown, my home filled with the usual suspects. Philo brought Juno; Tom, the veterinarian who occasionally had to minister to Kipp, arrived, accompanied by Fitzhugh. Suzanne also came; she was dressed in a dramatic black outfit that enhanced her bohemian, exotic nature. For the first time, I invited Peter, thinking it was appropriate he begin integrating himself into other aspects of the symbiont culture. I was old enough to be his mother, and from my point of view, she was much too controlling of his destiny. He was dressed in a casual suit and actually looked very handsome. Odd, I'd never thought of him as a looker, but he, outside of the confines of Fitzhugh's lair, was rather dashing.

"Too young for you," Kipp muttered, his thoughts active only in my brain in the peculiar way we could manage our telepathy with each other.

"Maybe I'm a cougar at heart," I replied, reaching out to lightly pinch Kipp's ear.

When Kipp and I shared our private exchanges, I understood, again, why our contemporary society avoided wholesale broadcasting of all unadulterated thoughts: it would lead to chaos, hurt feelings and the occasional fisticuffs.

While the gathering mingled, I retreated to the kitchen to check on the chili. In a minute, I felt Philo's thoughts as he approached—he was concerned, as to be expected. Time shifting was dangerous work, and although I embraced it, I was not blind to the risks taken every time Kipp and I vanished into the past. The death of Tula still resonated within my heart, and I almost lost Kipp on our first shared venture.

Philo put his arms around me and rested his chin on the top of my head. "You be careful, okay?" He took a deep breath as he squeezed my arms with his hands. "Locating Silas is the last concern I want you to have. Either that works out, or it doesn't. The most important thing is for you and Kipp to be safe and return home."

"Philo, if you start getting mushy with me, I'm gonna whack you with my big chili spoon," I replied, not needing the distraction of his sentimentality.

He laughed and released me. If things went as planned, Kipp and I would land somewhere in 1888 London in the vicinity of Regent's Park, hopefully in late May or early June. I usually tried to schedule my return journey so that it would reflect the actual time spent in another era, unless that time was extensive. So, in this case, I might be gone a few months and would return home in the fall. It was technically possible to leave one day and return the next, but it was customary to keep the time continuum linear, when practical.

I served the chili, and we all gathered in the living room with trays balanced on our laps. My kitchen—and my table—was too small to accommodate even that tiny crowd. Kipp and Juno enjoyed chopped chicken and rice from bowls I'd filled to overflowing. I think Philo worked overtime recovering old stories from my past meant to embarrass and humiliate me.

"I didn't think you'd tell that one," I remarked after one tale that left me red cheeked. Peter really had no idea about me and my capabilities until that moment; his dark eyes took on an uncomfortable glow as he stared at me. Even Kipp, who professed to have explored all the depths of my mind, looked at me with a new found respect. Yes, I had been a rambunctious cuss in my younger days.

"I may not pursue wanting to travel if I have to go through this," Peter finally remarked, spreading his hands to indicate the activity in the room.

"It's meant in good spirits and distracts the mind from worry," Juno replied.

I'd lit candles in the room, and the warm fragrance of cinnamon threaded a path through my compact dwelling. The lights were low and the gathering, though loud and raucous at times, seemed intimate. More than once, I caught Fitzhugh staring my way, causing me to wonder what was going on inside his complex brain. Our relationship had advanced greatly in a relatively short span of time. Eventually, the crowd began to thin out; Philo and Juno stayed behind, as was usual. At the door, I said my goodbyes to Fitzhugh. Unexpectedly, he turned and pulled me into his chest.

"You must be careful and come back safely," he said. Then he pushed me away from him and stared at me; his dark eyes looked stern in the dimly lit doorway. I had a fleeting thought of a barred owl with eyes so black as to appear depthless.

"I had just convinced myself that I had no need to worry about you until Philo told that last story, which somehow has escaped my notice as the one who has chronicled your reports. Perhaps you were sloppy in your record keeping?"

I averted my eyes from his; these last words at parting were always difficult at best.

"I will be safe, careful and, if you recall, in the company of the rational and supremely talented Kipp," I replied.

Kipp, upon hearing his name, darted up.

"Keep her out of mischief," Fitzhugh ordered. With that, he disappeared into the darkness and was gone. All he needed was a swirling cape and a tall peaked hat to appear like a wizard in retreat.

Kipp and I returned to Philo and Juno to spend our last moments with our closest friends. This final goodbye always provided a needed emotional boost for any traveler. As I'd already been counseled several times by Philo as to his expectations of me, there was little left to say. I tried not to cry as I watched Juno, slow and deliberate, make her way down the sidewalk. How much longer would she be with us, I wondered? The candles began to flicker as the flames on the burnt out wicks guttered; the acrid smell of smoke eclipsed the sweet, spicy fragrance of cinnamon.

"So, I thought that went pretty good, don't you?" Kipp asked.

"Yeah," I replied. My hands were in the soapy water in the sink as I managed to corral the last dirty bowl. A small bead of sweat trickled down my forehead and bobbled off the tip of my nose; I used the sleeve of my shirt to capture it. Kipp, from his viewpoint on the floor, looked up at me and yawned.

"No opposable thumbs, or I'd be glad to help," he commented.

I cut my eyes at him. "That excuse is getting worn pretty thin, Kipp," I replied.

In fairly short order, the house was neat, the dishes were put away, and I'd wiped down the counters. With Kipp trailing behind me, I walked to the small study in the rear of the house. There were a few bills that would be due, but it was too early to pay them. Philo would take care of things, as usual.

It always felt good to start a new journey with a clean body and newly washed hair, since I never knew when the next bath would come. I hopped in the shower and managed to launch my totally inadequate singing voice. Why was it, I wondered, humans and symbionts alike thought they sounded better when singing in the confines of a shower stall? I guess the echo fooled us into believing we had good voice pipes when the reverse was usually true. Kipp, lying on the tufted cotton rug on the bathroom floor, began to howl, so we had a discordant, loud duet going for a while. I hopped out and managed to share the tiny rug with Kipp, who refused to move and relocate his backside onto the cold tiles. Leaning forward, I corralled my thick hair in a towel.

"I'm glad to be a lupine," Kipp remarked, staring up at me. "You have too much to do to prepare yourself. The bath, the hair, the clothes….too much for my liking."

With Kipp padding silently after me, I went to my bedroom and began to don the various layers of clothing required for the time shift. As I tugged at the laces of the corset, which had been modified for comfort, I looked longingly at my stacked up pile of newly washed sweat clothes.

"I'm gonna miss those," I remarked, trying to not whine.

"Come on Cinderella," Kipp replied with a laugh. "Time to dress for the ball."

"Where did you hear about Cinderella?" I asked, turning to look at him.

"I've been watching some of the Disney classics," he replied. "I go down to the day care center at Technicorps…the kids love me," he added with a modest aside. "I liked all of the cartoons except *Bambi*. That one made me sad, and I couldn't figure out why they made it so tragic?"

"A lot of kids' shows have themes centered around loss," I replied as I pulled up the petticoat and struggled with the button at the waist. For a couple of seconds, I wondered if Suzanne had taken the wrong measurements of my waist. "I guess it helps children to learn from adversity, or something like that. Or perhaps the people who created the cartoons were secretly depressed."

Kipp, in an effort to distract his busy mind, began trying to recall the names of the seven dwarfs. He tried over and over and only came up with six. I finally had to throw him a life line.

"Dopey," I remarked.

"That's not very nice," Kipp replied, staring at me.

"I mean the name of the dwarf, silly," I responded. Pausing, I put my hands on my hips. "You may be relying too much on your knowledge of language and not enough on telepathy, Kipp."

He yawned and licked his paw. "I'm just restless and ready to hit the road."

I finally finished with the clothing and spent a few minutes drying my hair before pinning it up in a neat coil on top of my head. Suzanne had created a really pretty straw hat with a velvet ribbon that wound around the crown. Locating two antique hat pins in my dresser, I managed to attach the creation to my head as securely as possible. Lastly, I put on the convertible back pack that held a change of clothing and some undergarments. My money was hidden in my bustle for the most part; a small amount was in a tiny brocade reticule for easy access. Even though my travel persona was of a person of modest means, I made certain I had plenty of hidden currency to purchase an easy path if required.

"Come on," I said coaxingly to Kipp as I held out his money collar.

He lifted his lips and displayed just about every tooth in his head as he slowly approached me. I buckled the collar around his large neck, making sure to keep it loose for comfort. After turning off the lights in the room, I stretched out on my bed, taking care to prop my head so that the hat wouldn't be crushed. Kipp hopped up and took his place at my side, his jaw resting across my breastbone. After synchronizing our breathing, we began to count backwards and soon lulled ourselves into a place of deep relaxation. Then, recalling the maps and topographical graphs of 1888 London, we began to merge our thoughts and focus on the past. Pictures—as if from an album of old sepia toned photographs—flashed in our minds as we shared the grainy images back and forth.

No matter how many times I'd made a time shift, it always felt new and exciting. It was as if I was standing backwards on a high diving board before stepping off into a void, my body folding with grace as I dropped into the darkness. Kipp, with the confidence he'd developed in an astonishingly short time, led the way. I threaded my fingers into his auburn fur and let him take me to an expectant past.

CHAPTER 11

Sometimes you landed soft, and sometimes it was hard. This particular landing would not make the history books in terms of elegance, but at least Kipp and I were accurate, and in the end, that counted most. But it was jarring when I hit, and the ground, in retrospect, should have been a little more yielding. I felt something in my wrist pop and bit back an exclamation as I straightened out my left arm from beneath my body. Kipp was immediately aware of my discomfort, as I felt his anxious nose poke into the side of my face.

"Are you okay?" he asked.

I shrugged him off knowing that either way, I had to be. Modestly, I don't intend to sound overly tough, but symbionts are a pretty resilient species. Our bodies are designed to sustain bad weather, poor and inadequate food, as well as all other sorts of stressors. Many of the usual forces that conspired to attack the bodies of humans didn't seem to find us palatable. Even lowly fleas and lice were repelled by the taste of lupine flesh.

It was thankfully dark since we landed on a sparsely wooded knoll. Later, I'd learn it was, indeed, Regent's Park. Having ended up smack in the middle of a pond before, I was grateful to feel solid earth beneath me. Reaching out with my right hand, I felt grass. From the lack of adequate light, it was obvious we had arrived late in the evening or perhaps early morning. There was a moment of slight disorientation as Kipp and I struggled to reconcile our bodies and minds with the fact we had traveled over a hundred years into the past.

Turning my head, I glanced at Kipp. He, as usual, looked energetic and was on high alert, using his telepathy as well as other senses to canvass our surroundings. His tail waved slightly back and forth like a flag caught by a mild breeze.

"Somebody's coming," he announced.

With that announcement, I struggled to my feet, wincing as I put some pressure on my left wrist. Pausing, I scanned the immediate vicinity. We stood beneath the boughs of a large tree and were surrounded by a thin gathering of mature trees. There was foliage on the trees, so I knew we'd avoided winter; the temperature was on the cooler end of the spectrum but not frigid. I smelled water and knew, from my research, the source was a sizeable pond located in the midst of the park. Ignoring the discomfort in my wrist, I removed the back pack and, after laying the carefully packed garments out on the grass, turned the pack inside out so that it resembled the old fashioned carpet bag of its original design. Then I carefully replaced the items, taking care to not completely crush my other clothes. I kept the cape and, ignoring my painful wrist, managed to pull it around my shoulders and secured the clasp at the neck.

"Your hat is crooked," Kipp observed, trying to be helpful.

Reaching up, I pushed it back and forth until he nodded his head.

"Better," he said. Kipp's large jaw dropped down in a pant. "There's a man who is almost here now," he said.

Of course, I recognized the approach of a male human and picked up the flow of ideas running through the man's noggin. He appeared to be a policeman, walking a beat. The thoughts of the man were heavy, however. His daughter was at home, sick, and he was consumed with worry about her. My heart warmed to him immediately as I could read the sincerity in his thoughts.

"Hello?" A man's voice disturbed my concentration. "Are you alright, miss?" he asked.

Like an actor donning a role, it was time for me to trot out a performance. So, I turned and smiled at the man, who was shining a bull's eye lantern towards me. He was dressed in a dark uniform with the stereotypical helmet of the times. The face beneath the helmet was unlined, lean and wearing an expression of curiosity and genuine concern.

"Yes, thank you," I replied. "I am newly arrived from America and somehow became lost…me and my dog, Kipp." Kipp, on cue, began to wag his tail. This was usually helpful because his size was so intimidating that he had to overplay the role of friendly dog. Symbionts were rather shameless, so I continued, using a plaintive tone of voice. "I lost my baggage, except for this," I said, raising the carpetbag. "I need direction to a hotel, please."

"Bless you, miss. You shouldn't be out wandering around this late without an escort," the young man said. "I'm Constable Michaels, and I'll see you to a proper establishment," he added.

Of course, his mind was full of curiosity about me and my purpose since I didn't meet any of the usual criteria for suspects. Prostitutes didn't frequent isolated areas of Regent's Park because there was little chance of, uh, soliciting business. Besides, most prostitutes weren't accompanied by really large dogs who would probably scare off potential customers. I obviously was not highly placed in the social stratum since a lady would not be wandering around unaccompanied in the middle of the night. And then there was that confounding American accent which was definitely out of place.

"He seems to be a nice doggie," the constable remarked, reaching out to pat Kipp on the head. Kipp responded by dropping his jaw in a smiling pant and wagging his tail even harder.

The kind-hearted Constable Michaels decided that

despite his fascination with all the oddly shaped pieces of this puzzle, I appeared to be a harmless enough individual and was a woman in distress. All of his natural chivalry jumped to the forefront as he reached forward to take my carpet bag.

"My name is Petra Hathaway," I said. Since Silas was using the name of Hathaway, I used it, too, in the guise of his sister. This time, I was neither a widow or married or anything of the sort. I was a single gal on the town, for a change.

We walked to a nearby pathway which was graveled in fine rock; fortunately, the night was pleasant, despite some dampness. Up ahead, I saw a succession of gas lanterns illuminating a nearby street. I was curious as to the time but had no way to measure it since my digital watch, which didn't quite mesh with the current milieu, was left at home. I knew I would like to come back and explore Regent's Park but not now; it was late, dark and my wrist was throbbing. Necessity dictated we find a base of operations, and then my next chore would be to supplement my meager wardrobe before launching into a search for Silas. I already knew I would start with the offices of *The Daily Telegraph*, since that had been his professed destination, as per Fitzhugh's research.

"So, what brings you to London, miss?" Constable Michaels' voice gently prodded me out of my reverie.

"I'm looking for my brother who has gone missing," I replied. Turning my head, I caught his curious glance before he quickly averted his eyes. Clearly, he didn't want to seem impertinent or rude, but he just had not run into anyone quite like me before.

We were approaching a main road, so obviously Kipp and I had landed near the margin of the huge park. It was a massive endeavor and included private estates as well as public enclosures for walking, skating and other activities.

"I know of a smaller hotel on Nottingham Place that might be just the ticket," the constable remarked. "The proprietress is well known to me; she's kind natured and will help see to your needs, seeing as how your luggage is lost." He turned to me and grinned. "And I happen to know she loves dogs."

Kipp glanced up at me. "Well, we were lucky, no doubt. Could we have happened upon a nicer man?"

We left Regent's Park and began walking down a nicely paved road of asphalt. There were a few people in activity, mostly early morning laborers off to do the bidding of their employers. The constable seemed to know many of them as he offered greetings and tipped the edge of his stiff helmet in acknowledgment. I followed his thoughts to get a sense of the times. One man who passed us worked for a wealthy aristocrat and was on his way to be first at an open market to secure fresh produce brought in from the country. A cart pulled by a tired old pony creaked past; the driver called out a jesting remark to Michaels, who laughed good-naturedly in response. The cart was full of coal, and the driver was off to fill coal bins. All of these people toiled endlessly to meet the needs of many, but the wealth was all bundled at the top of society and little made it to the streets.

"Is it pretty much that way with all human societies?" Kipp asked.

"Yes, I think so." I managed to conduct a conversation about sociology with Kipp while maintaining a pleasant chit chat with the constable. "Even in countries that forcibly remove the wealth from their top rung and so-called distribute it to the poor, there's usually a consolidation of wealth among a few. Money is equated with power and control." I reached out to scratch Kipp's head. "There is no perfect, fair society."

"Here we are," Michaels announced. He seemed mildly anxious as he worried if I would find the hotel to be satisfactory.

In actuality, it was perfect. The brick building was narrow but deep; the fact there were only three stories lightened my heart since that meant the worse-case scenario would involve three flights of stairs versus more.

"You know, stair climbing is good for your heart," Kipp's

taunts resonated at the back of my skull.

The lobby, which was dimly lit, was small but nicely equipped with attractive furniture. Somehow, the room radiated the persona of the proprietress in that it was clean, alluring and competent. Off from the main lobby, I saw a couple of smaller sitting rooms to the left and a dining room to the right. The fragrance of baking bread floated on an air current and was starting to fill the lobby. Yes, another team of workers was up early trying to pave the way for guests to begin their morning with full stomachs and pleasant dining experiences.

A man with red, bleary eyes sat at the desk. I knew from his thoughts that he was desperately trying to stay awake while knowing he had to leave the hotel desk job for another full day of work at a tailor's shop. Despite his stress and fatigue, he was pleasant.

"Good morning, Constable," the man said, smiling with ease. It was obvious all in the immediate vicinity knew the policeman. "How may I be of assistance?" The man's red eyes nervously flicked down to peer at Kipp, who, on cue, wagged his tail, folded his hind legs and politely sat while trying to make himself as inconspicuous as possible.

"Miss Hathaway here needs a nice room, Mr. Hurley." The constable gestured at me, obviously forgetting the fact I was the only woman in the room.

"I'm certain we can take care of your needs, Miss Hathaway," the desk clerk remarked.

Constable Michaels, seeing I was in the efficient hands of the clerk, swept his helmet from his head and gave a slight bow at the waist.

"Good luck, miss, with finding your brother." He looked up and smiled at me. "I must return to my work," he said before turning and leaving.

Kipp almost caused me to lose my composure and giggle when he remarked that the constable, indeed, had helmet hair.

Mr. Hurley handed me a pen so that I could sign the register. He had courteously dipped the tip in the inkwell, saving me from that step in the process. I glanced up at him, thinking how amazed he would be to know that in a hundred years, pens, like everything else, would have evolved into a disposable convenience. The register afforded me a glimpse of the time in which I'd landed; instead of the latter part of May, it seemed Kipp and I had appeared in the first week of April, 1888. If Silas and Vashti had been anywhere near accurate in their timing, they would have been in London several months by this time.

"We have a nice corner room on the first landing that faces the front street. It has a small sitting room, too, if you have guests." The man smiled and nodded, waiting for my response.

"That sounds lovely," I replied. "In addition, in my travels here from America, I managed to be separated from my luggage. I will need someone to direct me to an establishment where I can replenish my wardrobe."

He nodded again. "There are several shops in the Marylebone district within walking distance. Some have readymade garments and, uh, the necessary accoutrements, and others have skilled seamstresses that can provide garments to your specifications."

If he thought my story to be odd or unusual, it was not betrayed in his thoughts, and I figured people showing up with next to nothing in their hands was not so uncommon after all. The man abandoned his perch behind the desk and came around to fetch my carpet bag. There was nothing left but that I follow him up the stairs. Flickering lanterns illuminated the staircase and the hallway of the first landing; lovely woolen runners extending the length of the hallway drew my admiration. The walls were painted in a deep burgundy, and the floral pattern in the runners matched the walls perfectly, demonstrating a well-thought-out artistic flair.

Mr. Hurley stopped in front of a heavy oak door and inserted a key into the lock. Pushing open the door, he asked me to wait until he could light the rooms. It only took a jiffy since the wall fixtures were gas. He then lit some oil lamps that were located on side tables. In less than a minute, the sitting room and the bedroom were bathed in a comforting yellow glow. I always had missed this while living in contemporary times—the warmth and romance of a candle or lantern lit room could not be matched by any type of modern light bulb.

The sitting room was painted dark green; a small stuffed sofa and two comfortable-looking chairs pretty much took up the space. The bedroom, to my delight, was painted a deep, sunflower yellow which was cheerful beyond words. Kipp, with his color perception, nodded his head in agreement. He liked it, too. The room was immaculate, and I smiled as I caught a faint whiff of lavender in the air. What was it about the chemistry of lavender that made the fragrance so inherently soothing, I wondered? There was another overstuffed chair in the corner covered in a pretty toile patterned fabric; it would become a friend to me in coming days, I thought.

This hotel, in the scheme of things, had many of the modern amenities of the day. After showing me the room, Mr. Hurley walked me back down the hallway I had traversed to indicate the water closet. Oh, yes, not having to use a chamber pot definitely worked for me. There was a large bathtub, too, with running water that could be heated.

"We also can bring a hip bath to your room for your personal use, if you require." Mr. Hurley spoke in a low tone while averting his gaze, as if commenting about my ablutions would violate some sort of discretion policy.

"Do you know the time?" I requested.

He pulled his watch from its hiding place in a tiny vest pocket and squinted slightly at the face. The desk clerk probably suffered from some sort of visual deficit that required glasses but lacked money to purchase what was needed.

"It is five AM," he replied. "The dining room will begin serving breakfast at seven." He paused, thinking he needed to give an explanation. "Some of our guests have early morning obligations, and we here at the Nottingham Inn pride ourselves on meeting the individual needs of our guests." He dipped his head. "We also serve a lovely luncheon as well as dinner." His eyes, which he managed to keep free of expression, met mine. "If you have guests or a dinner companion, they are, of course, welcome to enjoy mealtimes here with you." He walked me back to my room and bowed from the waist as he departed.

"Whew!" Kipp remarked. "Kind of stiff, don't you think?"

I walked into the bedroom and pulled back the heavy, brocade curtains from one of the two windows that overlooked the street. Outside on Nottingham Place, the early morning activity was beginning to pick up. A couple of horse drawn delivery carts turned and angled down the narrow alleyway next to the hotel, the sound of the horses' hooves echoing loudly in the passageway. No doubt, they were delivering food goods for the kitchen staff to prepare for the hotel guests.

"Well, he was following the rules of courtesy," I replied. "Remember that we are in Victorian times, and he was treating me in the manner in which a lady—as well as a paying guest—should be addressed." I looked over at Kipp. "I'm gonna lie down for a couple of hours and rest. My wrist hurts, and I think I just need to quit using it for a while."

With that, I removed my blouse, skirt, hat, and bank bustle, since the latter prevented any sort of comfortable reclining position. I hung up the clothing in a small recessed area that was covered with a length of exotic, woven cloth. Stretching out on the bed, I sank into a cotton-filled mattress that was softer than anything I'd experienced in a long time. Kipp struggled, once he hopped up, to not get mired down in the fabric which sucked at his feet like quicksand. Finally, after awkwardly circling a time or two, he collapsed and stretched his muzzle out across my chest.

"Sweet dreams," I murmured.

Kipp grunted in reply.

CHAPTER 12

Mrs. Sanderson was a short, round woman, even shorter than was I, with movements that were quick and purposeful. And, to my advantage, she possessed an inherently kind nature and had learned, as do all good innkeepers, to avoid displaying excessive curiosity about her guests. She fancied herself to be old enough to be my mother; in this instance, the joke was definitely on her. Consequently, she took a polite concern over my well being and made certain her staff promptly catered to my meager needs.

Kipp, though accepted in the hotel, was seen as a bit of a distraction in the dining room, mainly due to his size. Mrs. Sanderson made accommodations for all her residents, and Kipp was no exception. She made certain to seat me at a small table off to the side where Kipp could recline unobtrusively between me and the wall. As we walked into the dining hall for the first time, a small, busy terrier decided to confront the significantly larger Kipp and demonstrate that he, the terrier, was the man in charge of the room. After one sniff of Kipp, the terrier turned and ran to hide beneath the table of his master. Humans could not pick up the nuanced differences between Kipp and a dog, but any dog certainly could with ease.

It was usually a good idea to remain as unobtrusive as

possible, so with that dictum in mind, I only made a few requests of my gracious hostess. One was that the staff bring a bowl of chicken and rice to the room for Kipp, as well as supply me with a bowl I could fill with water from down the hall. Also, I made polite enquiries about where Kipp should be curbed and was told that most guests used the back alleyway as well as the small city park that was a few blocks distant. When Mrs. Sanderson brought me a pot of tea to establish a connection with her newest guest, I asked her to sit for a moment. Her eyes widened, but she dipped her head and took a seat.

Up close, I could see the lines of age that were beginning to settle on her plain, but not unattractive, face. Her blue eyes were starting to get the blurred, unfocused look of some early cataract formation. The issues of running a hotel consumed her thoughts, as would be expected. A chambermaid had just discovered she was pregnant out of wedlock and wouldn't be able to work. Mrs. Sanderson suspected the newest member of her staff was the father and would have to deal with him. She could not tolerate a seductive Lothario pursuing the female staff around and disrupting the balanced nature of her staff. All the same, she dreaded the discussion which was distasteful to the extreme.

"Why can't the girl work if she is going to have a baby?" Kipp asked, as he followed the tangled worries of Mrs. Sanderson.

"Well, Kipp, this is Victorian England. Such a thing was considered a moral failure and would hurt the reputation of Mrs. Sanderson to have an unmarried pregnant woman working here."

"So what will happen to the girl and her baby?" Kipp, with his kind heart, was a champion of the downtrodden.

"How may I be of assistance?" Mrs. Sanderson asked, her voice disrupting my private conversation with Kipp.

"I lost my baggage," I replied, smiling at her. "I need directions to a couple of establishments that can supply readymade items as well as a seamstress who can fashion some garments for me."

"Why of course," she replied. "Before you leave this morning, I will have the names you need and addresses." Her thoughts began to take on a tinge of worry again, but she shrugged them off to stay focused on me. "If there is any way I can help while you are on holiday here," she began, artfully leaving the door open for me to fill in the blanks in her curiosity over the fact a single young woman had traveled across the ocean, accompanied only by a large dog. I dipped my head, trying to look a little uncertain, hoping that would add to the mystery. Yes, symbionts are shameless actors.

"I'm actually here on business, Mrs. Sanderson. My only brother, Silas, came to London to work as a journalist. He has gone missing, and I've come here to see if I can find him and take him home."

Her thoughts refocused on me in a flash. "Oh, my! I'm sorry to hear of it and will be glad to offer any assistance that I can."

My breakfast arrived, and she left me to my solitude as I nibbled on the fare. Symbionts have odd metabolisms in comparison to those of humans. We are designed to withstand long periods of fasting in the event we're traveling in times when food is scarce. Many of us humanoids are vegetarians, but it isn't a cultural requirement. Of course, the lupines crave meat—and, in Kipp's instance, French fries, too—and are superior hunters.

I returned to my room to don my hat and cape. Kipp had already made his morning visit to the back alley, courtesy of the servants' back stair case, and I was ready to go shopping. To some, it might have seemed odd to not launch right into the search for Silas, but first I had to become grounded and comfortable in this new era. It was always like this for us travelers: the initial course of action was to establish a home base and become part of the tableau of society and activity.

On my way through the lobby, Mrs. Sanderson handed

me a piece of paper with names and addresses as well as directions. "Some of these are very close by and will afford you a pleasant walk. If you want to ride, however, there are plenty of four- wheeler cabs about. I think it might be easier for your dog to use a four wheeler than a hansom cab."

Filled with excitement, I struck out, and, I confess, my heart was beating at a faster pace. It always seemed a little miraculous to be thrust into a different age and culture just by closing one's eyes and concentrating. Of course, the physics of time shifting eluded me, and I realized I wasn't smart enough to understand the mechanics of it.

It was a very pleasant spring day with mild temperatures that were comfortable. As I inhaled, the air smelled relatively fresh, although there was some thickness of scent due to the number of horses pulling drays, carts and trams. I knew from my studies that the air would be fouler in the East End of town; the slaughter houses, furriers, and varied types of chemical manufacturers were clustered in the less affluent part of London. I drew more than one glance from gentlemen who noticed the pert angle of my straw hat as well as my purposeful walk, which definitely did not project that I was in need of assistance; Kipp's massive presence was another man-deterrent.

Following Mrs. Sanderson's little map, I cut across a couple of streets, dodging carriages and carts, until I found myself on Gloucester Place. After walking a little further, I turned into a shop that offered ready-made goods. The bell over the shop door tinkled as I entered, and I was met by a woman who glanced with concern at the overly large Kipp. I solved her worry by pointing at a corner and commanding Kipp to lie down.

"Yeah, just order me around like I don't matter," Kipp grumbled playfully. Wagging his tail, he went to the spot, circled, and lay quietly, tucking himself up into an unbelievably small reddish ball of fur.

I quickly and efficiently explained my purpose. The clerk was obviously delighted to have someone standing in her shop who was in need of a significant quantity of clothing items. With her help, I was able to select several undergarments so that my rotation of soiled pieces would be reasonably spaced out. And while they may not have met the needs of society women, I was happy with the blouses and skirts that were available. I chose three blouses and the same number of skirts; the latter needed some minor alteration in the length, but otherwise were a perfect fit. The clerk assured me the clothes could be delivered in two days to the Nottingham Inn. After paying her, I left and walked further down until I could cut through the block to Baker Street. It would have been wonderful to find a real Sherlock Holmes lurking nearby, but alas, he was a mere figment of an author's imagination. There was a dressmaker's shop as well as a milliner listed on my paper from Mrs. Sanderson. As I walked along, I took care to notice the people and attend to their thoughts as well as behaviors.

"Well, this might be the age of propriety and genteel behaviors, but there are some pretty interesting thoughts racing up and down the street," Kipp remarked. "Maybe there is a disadvantage to putting so many restraints on human nature."

I laughed out loud, drawing the curious glances of a trio of finely attired middle aged women who were out for a day of shopping and companionship.

"If there were no rules for humans, there would be chaos," I replied. "It really doesn't matter if it's here in Victorian London or in the midst of the Amazon jungle, rules must exist to keep some order." I reached down and scratched the top of Kipp's head. "The same applies to us."

We found the dressmaker's shop, and I repeated the now familiar story of having lost my luggage. The proprietress, who initially looked at me as if I were some sort of slimy creature who dragged my body from a moldy bog, decided I was somewhere approximating a lady—even if I was an American—after she heard me speak. I admit I was using my best set of manners. If I hadn't considered the fact I might require one or two nicer dresses, I really wouldn't have bothered with all the falderal. But, times being what they were and the uncertainty of Silas's whereabouts led me to consider I needed to be prepared for all eventualities.

The dressmaker—whose lack of sense of humor reminded me eerily of the temperament of Suzanne—coaxed me into agreeing to have three dresses made. Two would be less formal but appropriate for late tea or dinner, perhaps. The third would be designed for more sophisticated events, if such were to occur. Well, I thought, what the heck…I had a bustle full of money and why not do the town right? It didn't help matters that Kipp was chanting in my head, "Do it, do it, do it".

"With your coloring, I would recommend we use this lovely coral silk for the formal gown," the dressmaker suggested as she allowed the fabric to drape and cascade over her hands like a brilliant waterfall. For a moment, I had the feeling she was attempting to sell me a new car and talk me into the rust proofing that I didn't want.

"Great!" Kipp chimed in. "A good color for you."

She led me into the dressing room, stepping back so that I could precede her. A burst of mild anxiety washed over me when the dressmaker began to examine my discarded skirt while her apprentice was busy taking my measurements. Through half lowered eyelids, I watched her run her fingers carefully over the fabric.

"This is a very nice and unusual weave of cloth," she finally remarked, raising her head to glance at me over the wire-rimmed glasses perched on the end of her nose.

"Well, I don't know much about such things, but it came from an American factory in Pennsylvania, I think I was told." I gamely smiled at her. Before she could continue to query me, I brusquely moved on with the conversation by asking when she would like me to return. We set a date a few days out, and I promised her I would be back for a fitting.

As we rushed from the shop, Kipp glanced up at me. "Why would she be so suspicious of your skirt?"

I shrugged my shoulders and ducked to the side to avoid a collision with a young man pushing a cart full of produce; no doubt, he worked for some establishment and had visited one of the numerous markets. There were still stores that sold meat, fruits and vegetables, but open air markets were gaining in popularity.

"Her job is to make clothing for ladies. She sees fabric all the time and no doubt has a keen eye for something unusual." I smiled down at Kipp. "I don't think we'll need to worry that the texture of my skirt will draw attention in general."

The milliner's shop was tucked in between a quaint public house and some sort of financial business. The proprietor was a woman who looked as if she could have easily been eighty years old, perhaps even more. Her very large nose was centered in a wrinkled, round face and somehow it all came together in a pleasing whole. The vision gave me some hope for my own future, considering the size of my nose.

From a distance, she admired my hat, which I was careful to not hand to her, lest she notice the small corner of a ribbon where a frustrated Suzanne had used a hot glue gun. Really, I thought…I would need to have a talk with her when I got home. First the fabric, now the hot glue mark…ordinarily she was so particular but seemed to have slipped a little of late.

"She's in love," Kipp remarked, filling my head with his words.

"Who?" I asked stupidly.

"Suzanne…she is in love and having trouble concentrating."

"Well, aren't you Mister know-it-all," I replied somewhat irritably. "You might have mentioned the fact."

Ignoring Kipp, I focused on the milliner who was trying to speak with me. Yes, I told her I would like another couple of casual day hats, and then I would need one to match my new fancy gown that was being constructed. She was well acquainted with my dressmaker and assured me she would check the color of the fabric as well as the design and create something suitable. I told her of my return date to the dressmaker, and she indicated that she would be able to match that deadline; it seemed hat making was not a lengthy process for this seasoned professional.

One would not have thought that shopping for clothes and hats would consume the majority of the day, but indeed it had. I ended the jaunt by accompanying Kipp to the small city park that Mrs. Sanderson had indicated. It was in close proximity to the Nottingham Inn, and I knew Kipp would need to take care of his personal business; the park was preferable to the back alley of the previous evening. While he wandered off, his nose to the ground in eager pursuit of a fascinating scent, I dropped to a bench. With dismay, I realized I was weary and recognized that I needed, in the future, to approach time shifts as would an athlete view an upcoming competition. There was no question that I had become a little soft, and the amount of physical and psychic energy consumed during the shift had sapped my usual robust strength. A pair of well dressed business men passed me, deep in conversation. However, they both glanced up and tipped their top hats at me; yes, it was that frankly appraising gaze that reminded me at least a few members of the male species found me attractive. When Kipp returned, I was humming a little tune and feeling better about myself.

"So, are you that much of pushover that a couple of guys giving you the look can make you sing like a little bird?" Kipp was obviously feeling playful. He sat at my feet and rested his chin on my knees. I reached forward and scratched between his ears until he crossed his eyes in pleasure.

"Where on earth did you hear that expression, Kipp?" I asked, wondering what television shows had he been watching lately. Would he next refer to me as a moll and remark on my shapely gams? Before he could answer, I said, somewhat defensively, "Well, attention is always nice, when it's of a complimentary nature. Tell the truth—when Elani almost drooled when she was in your presence, didn't you feel like walking with your head a little higher?"

Kipp turned his head slightly so I could scratch behind his right ear. "I told you, she's just a baby, and I am no cradle robber."

I laughed out loud and a couple of women who were occupied with infants in strollers turned to glance at me in curiosity. I managed to quell my humor; as I recalled, the treatment of people deemed mentally ill was not particularly friendly during this era in history, and I had no desire to be remanded for an evaluation.

Together, we made our way back to the hotel. Mrs. Sanderson happened to be in attendance at the front desk and inquired if my shopping trip had been successful. After a moment of pleasant discourse, I confessed my fatigue. With solicitude, she offered to have my dinner meal served in my room along with a bowl of rice and chicken for Kipp. She really was most accommodating, and I accepted her offer with gratitude.

Later, after we had eaten and climbed into bed, I tried to block out the human thoughts that were drifting in and out of my mind; the intrusion of unwanted thoughts was the negative side of telepathy. Usually I was more efficient than on that particular evening, but I think my depleted energy and the constant throb from my sprained wrist had lessened my focus. Finally, Kipp managed, in his effortless way, to move in and block all thoughts until my mind was comfortably blank.

With nothing in my head except a thought of how I might look wearing my new, fancy coral colored gown, I drifted off into a dreamless sleep.

CHAPTER 13

The Nottingham Inn held a pleasant surprise within the walls of the north facing sitting room. I was wandering around, becoming better acquainted with the facility and, in doing so, ambled into one of the small sitting rooms where guests could entertain visitors for business or pleasure. On one wall was a very large dark oak bookcase with shelves loaded with leather bound books. A window that stretched from floor to ceiling allowed ample light to filter into the room to highlight an intricately patterned Persian rug spread across the floor.

"Those are for the pleasure of my guests," a voice spoke. It was Mrs. Sanderson who stood at the threshold. She had the delicate step of a cat.

"What a nice idea," I replied. "I might select a volume to keep in my room for evening reading, if you don't object." At her nod, I continued to peruse and finally found a historical volume about the Roman Empire. Well, that would be some easy, fun reading, no doubt. To find the lighter reads that would compare to contemporary mass paperback books, I would have to go elsewhere.

"Get me something, too," Kipp requested.

I kept looking until I found *The Odyssey*. "You'll like this, Kipp. It is a classic piece of literature—an epic poem—with witches, seductive sirens and a cyclops."

"Sounds good," Kipp huffed, as he closed one eye to mimic the mythological man-beast.

We spent a few days navigating the ins and outs of London. I'd learned that when entering a vast and multifaceted system, it was best to become comfortable and at least a little knowledgeable about the environment before tackling anything complicated. Finding Silas fell into the latter category. So, we hopped onto a free tram car and rode it until it stopped somewhere in Brompton. Then, we took a four wheeler cab back towards the Inn but paused at the dressmaker's shop for my final fitting. As before, Kipp lay on the floor in a compact, unobtrusive ball so as to avoid complaints from the proprietress.

As the coral gown was fit on my body, I stared at my reflection in the mirror and was pleased to see that, indeed, the tone brought out the high color in my cheeks. With my dark hair and hazel eyes, the dress was flattering, despite the fact I was not beautiful by any stretch of the imagination.

"I know you look good," Kipp's thoughts floated in to me as the seamstress stuck a pin here and there as she pulled at the fabric. "But who is gonna zip you up?" he asked. The fact it required someone to fasten a myriad of hooks and buttons up the back would confound even the cleverest symbiont.

"I'll have to get one of the maids to help pour me in and batten down the hatches," I replied, trying not to smile.

The other garments suitable for everyday wear would be delivered to the Inn the following day; the coral gown still required a tuck here and there. After departing, I wandered by the milliner's shop. She smiled upon my entrance, obviously eager to show off the hat she had made to match the coral dress gown. With a gentle hand at my elbow, she prodded me towards a mirror. With a flourish, she pulled a lovely little wisp of nothing from a pretty hatbox. Inwardly I sighed; I'd always had a fondness for antique hatboxes and would love to have taken that one home with me.

The milliner, after carefully removing my straw bonnet,

put the hat high up on the crown of my head, tilting it a little. There was some netting and delicate lace that she artfully arranged so that it looked as if the tiny, almost pillbox shaped hat, was nesting in a gossamer cloud. Gee, as I think back, it was one of the prettiest things I'd ever owned. Even though it made no sense to the milliner, I turned and walked over to Kipp.

"What do you think?" I asked, my eyes glowing. I'd spoken aloud, my voice seeming overly loud in the otherwise quiet shop.

"You are beautiful," he replied frankly, his thoughts merging with mine.

I turned back to the woman, who hovered at my elbow. "Kipp likes my hat, too."

She laughed good-naturedly; privately she thought I was perhaps a little daft. But I was, after all, a customer, and if I wanted to talk to my dog, then she didn't care as long as I paid the bill for services rendered.

The other couple of hats were ready, too, so with my hands full of hatboxes, I made my way back to the Inn. Overhead, the skies were overcast and thunder began to rumble threateningly. The first heavy drops of a rainstorm that would seem endless began to patter on my head as I entered the lobby of the hotel. Mr. Hurley, from behind the desk, snapped his fingers, and a young man who was sweeping the lobby rushed forward to take my packages. Kipp and I hurried to our rooms, followed by the boy, who I tipped for his bother.

"Let's stay here and read until the rain passes, if you don't mind." Kipp was in no mood to have to shove his way onto a crowded tram. Earlier in the day, some careless lout had stepped on his toe, and he still walked with a noticeable limp.

"We can take a cab from now on, Kipp," I said reassuringly. "There are trains and underground trains, too, if we want to brave them."

"I think I do better away from crowded areas," Kipp replied. "That man's boots had soles that were an inch thick and felt like metal."

So, to humor my friend as well as myself, we hunkered down for three days. The rain outside was nonstop and acted as a sedative on us. When we were not reading—and Kipp was plowing through *The Odyssey* as if he was an eager schoolboy preparing for an exam—we were sleeping. With our slow metabolisms, we could fall into a self hypnotic state where our bodies would conduct all the healing and regeneration necessary to help prolong an already extensive lifespan. The deep yellow of the bedroom was oddly soothing rather than being a stimulating color; from the wall sconces, the subtle hissing of the gas lanterns provided a comforting white noise that coaxed us into dreamless sleep. During that time, my new garments were delivered, so between the readymade items and the few fabricated ones, I was set for a long stay in London, if needed.

The rain was beginning to taper by the evening of the third day, and I felt we needed to hit the streets to initiate our search in the morning. Kipp, typically so active, was now over his minor snit regarding his sore toe and ready to tackle whatever lay ahead. We were in bed, his head resting across my chest as my fingers idly combed through his thick pelt of fur.

"Where do we start?" Kipp asked. He turned his head slightly so that his amber eyes met mine. We were in such close proximity, that our eyes crossed slightly in the effort to maintain a steady gaze.

"The stated intent of Silas, per the records that Fitzhugh resurrected, indicated he planned on trying to get a job, or at least an accommodation, at *The Daily Telegraph*. So, we will start there."

Simply because it was exciting for me to dress in one of my new outfits, I selected one of the readymade garments, which was plain but fit nicely. The cameo pin I'd brought with me added a little feminine touch to an otherwise uninspired appearance. I had no desire to stand out and wanted the blouse and skirt to wear doubly well if I had to walk the streets of the East End in search of Silas. I chose one of the new hats, a pleasing affair of natural colored straw, tightly woven, with a large grosgrain ribbon around the crown, the trimmed ends trailing down to almost my collar.

Pausing in the lobby, I spoke with Mrs. Sanderson and informed her that I would be gone for several hours. After that, I discretely made my way through to the back alley by way of a side hallway so that Kipp could relieve himself. Mrs. Sanderson had one of the staff to hail a four wheeler cab, and within a minute, Kipp and I were on our way to Fleet Street. As we left the northern part of the city and traveled towards the Thames, there was a definite change in the air which I associated with a major waterway as well as our growing proximity to the slums of the East End. Kipp held his head up and his nostrils were quivering with interest.

"There are a lot of animals in the city," he commented. "And I mean livestock animals, other than just horses."

"From my reading, there are areas in the East End where small herds of cattle and sheep are driven through the streets to the slaughter houses." I leaned forward to gaze out the window at the passing scenery. Our horse was clipping along at a brisk pace, and the mild breeze disturbed my neatly contained hair; I felt the long ribbons from my hat tickle the back of my neck.

"And there are other things, too, that are less pleasant and well, not organic," Kipp added.

I could smell it, too. There was a definite growing congestion in the air that was a mixture of the moisture from the Thames, inadequate sanitation, and byproducts from chemical plants as well as the smoke from countless coal burning chimneys. When there were breezy days and the humidity was lower, most likely the air would seem cleaner.

On the passing sidewalks, I saw a growing number of street vendors. There were costermongers selling meat filled pasties, girls selling bouquets of violets, and a particularly loud man trying to rid himself of some cooking pots and pans. The atmosphere was thriving and busy, and I knew, from reading the thoughts of many of the people, that there was joy as well as despair. The man selling the pots had just lost his wife to consumption and was trying to get enough money together to bury her properly. I glanced at Kipp.

"We're gonna buy some pots," I said. With that, I knocked on the seat box and drew the driver's attention. After directing him to pull over, I handed him some money and told him to approach the man and purchase all that he had to sell. The driver's eyebrows disappeared beneath the brim of his rag cap, but he nodded his head, thinking if he did as I asked, he would get a sizeable tip.

With the pots stacked on the seat next to me, the driver pulled the horse back onto the road, which was partially paved with some rough cobblestones, enough so as to make my teeth chatter. Kipp was sitting with his backside propped on the seat opposite me.

"My butt is going to be sore," he commented. Peering out the window, he glanced back at the pot vendor who was disappearing into the crowds. "He doesn't have to worry anymore," Kipp said, nodding with satisfaction.

Our driver, as did modern day taxi drivers in a congested metropolis, managed to adroitly steer the horse around slower conveyances as well as miss people who were loitering in the streets. With his skill, it did not take us long to reach Fleet Street where he gently pulled up the horse. I'd noticed, unlike some of the other men that day, our driver had a distinct tender spot for his mare, which he named Molly. Her coat gleamed, and her sides were nicely rounded, indicating sufficient feed.

Kipp hopped from the carriage, and our driver held out a courteous hand to assist me. No matter how many time shifts had involved long skirts with lots of fabric, I was inherently clumsy and lacked the skill acquired over years of consistent practice.

"Miss, you left your pots," the driver said, tipping the

edge of his worn cap with a light touch of a forefinger.

I was busy digging in my reticule for some coins. "You are married?" I asked, although I already knew the answer.

"Why, yes, bless you, miss." The man's lined face was thin. I suspected he did with less so that his family and Molly could thrive, relatively speaking. My eyes dropped down to note his waistcoat, which had been neatly patched by a loving and caring hand.

"Take the pots home to her as a gift, then," I said. I dropped several coins in his palm.

His face was priceless; his expression was one of disbelief and joy, all rolled into one. The man's voice followed me as I began to negotiate the stairs of *The Daily Telegraph*.

"My name is John Parks, miss, and if you ever need me to drive you again, you just ask for me. I drive near Nottingham Place most every day." He was honest, genuine, and not speaking up just to get more pots and pans.

I turned from the top of the staircase and looked at him. "Thank you, Mr. Parks. I'm certain I will call on you again. I'm Petra Hathaway," I added.

"Why not just engage him for the day?" Kipp asked, looking up at me. "We need a trustworthy ally, and he seems to be a decent sort," he added.

With that thought, which was a sound one, I called back to the cab driver. "Can you wait for me? I won't be long."

"Why certainly, Miss Hathaway," he replied, touching the brim of his rag hat again with a forefinger.

The lobby of the *Telegraph* was teeming with people, almost all of them male; the room filled to the ceiling with brimming testosterone. I approached the front desk where a young man sat. He looked up at me over a pair of glasses that were sitting on a nose that had obviously been broken at some point in history. His eyebrows rose as he glanced at Kipp.

"May I help you, miss?"

I nodded and put on my assertive face. "I need to see the city editor, please," I replied, making certain my tone projected a force of will, polite but firm.

"Do you have an appointment?" He uttered the standard query.

"No, but I'm comfortable waiting here until he can see me." With that, I pulled up a straight backed chair right next to the man's desk and sat, making certain to get as close to him as possible. My plan was to make him so uncomfortable that he would finally relent and let me past the castle guard.

Kipp giggled. "Nicely played." He turned his head slightly as he assessed the room and those present. "Wow, I thought things were all nice and polite in this age. But that man's thoughts are distinctly unpleasant." Kipp looked up at me, his eyes opened wide. "He just called you something vulgar."

"I heard it, too, Kipp. Let it go."

After two hours of ignoring me, the young man finally got up and retreated down a hallway. When he returned, he nodded his head. "Mr. Sidwell will see you, miss. But he's busy and only has a few minutes." His tone was cold and unemotional, his words clipped in an impolite fashion.

"Petra, I can just bite him if you want me to," Kipp suggested, looking up at me, hopefully. "This pup needs to learn some manners." Narrowing my eyes, I shook my head in a negative response.

We followed the young man down a long hallway. Kipp, behind the man's back, raised his lips so that his teeth were bared in a threatening display. I suppressed a laugh and tried to not look at Kipp, who rolled his eyes at me.

"Stop it, Kipp. You're disrupting my focus," I said, trying to sound stern.

We were finally ushered past a heavy oak door into a fairly large office; it was cluttered with stacks of papers piled on every conceivable surface. From behind a massive desk, a tall, spare man stood. He was balding, middle aged, with attractive features.

"I'm Marcus Sidwell," he said, nodding his head at me. "It took me a moment to place your name—Hathaway—which is why there was a delay in meeting you. Are you related to Silas Hathaway?" He indicated a chair, and I took a seat. Kipp circled for a minute before plopping on the floor.

"Silas had a dog, too, that followed him everywhere," Marcus commented, his eyes darting to Kipp.

I nodded. "Silas is my brother, and I've come from America to search for him. I knew he was to be working here, with your paper, in an arrangement with the *San Francisco Bee*."

Marcus nodded his head. "Yes, a very nice young man. He came with a letter of introduction asking that he be allowed to study and follow some of our methods of reporting here in London. His paper was sponsoring him." His brows drew together. "He wanted to concentrate on the East End, which can be a rough territory to cover." Marcus's shoulders drew up in a shrug. "He went out one morning, he and that dog of his, and they never came back."

"Did you search for him or report it to the police?" I asked, leaning forward.

"Why would I do that?" he responded. "Silas was not my employee and had no connections locally. For all I know, he just left here for reasons unknown."

If I'd had something to throw at him, he would have been lying on the floor in about a second. Kipp was my voice of reason.

"Don't get a head of steam up, Petra. The man is right, in a sense. Silas showed up, asked for some observation time and was not required to clock in on a regular basis." Kipp sat up and nuzzled my hand. "We'll just go and start asking around."

I stood and managed to compose myself—barely. "Thank you for your time, Mr. Sidwell. Your obvious lack of concern is touching." I could not help my last sarcastic remark. The man didn't reply as I turned and left, Kipp trotting along after me.

John Parks was waiting at the curb. He'd brought a feed

bag for Molly and was letting her enjoy a few oats while I took care of business. His right forefinger touched the brim of his cap in an automatic gesture of courtesy. It was ironic that the rough street cabbie had more inherent courtesy than the city editor I'd just left. Such things were never about appearances or class distinction, I'd learned; either you possessed such gifts or you didn't. The wearing of a silk top hat did not make a gentleman.

I walked over to Molly and ran my hand along her neck. She nickered softly before continuing to munch on the few oats remaining. She was a pretty thing, dark bay with a white blaze on her broad face and two white stockings. Her coat shone as result of the loving care given to her by John earlier that morning.

"Mr. Parks," I began before he interrupted me.

"Please, miss, call me John."

I smiled, nodding my head. "John, I have come to London to look for my brother, Silas. He's missing and probably was last seen in the East End. My Kipp," I said, glancing down at my companion, "and I need someone reliable to help. I'd like to engage you for some full days, if you can manage to do that." I hurried with my next comment. "If you can tell me what you typically make for a day's work, I will match that and more, of course, for your time."

His thoughts betrayed excitement, since his living was made day by day, but he was an honest man and had no desire to take advantage of me. So, he quoted a truly fair figure which I knew I would surpass.

"I like him, too," Kipp remarked. "Hard working, honest, humble, and he loves his family—and Molly, too."

"The East End can be a bit rough, miss. You'll need a guide that can help you steer clear of places that a lady need not go…even if she has a big dog at her side." John leaned forward and patted Kipp's large head. "I bet he'd give someone the what for if they was to try and get disrespectful of you."

"Oh, yes, John. He has before and will again," I replied.

CHAPTER 14

If John Parks thought that there was anything unusual about a young lady travelling about the streets of Whitechapel unaccompanied—except by what appeared to be a very large dog—he kept those thoughts hidden from two rather talented telepaths. He was concerned and mildly disapproving, but in his career as a driver for hire, he had seen many odd things and had learned not to burden his mind with questions. In any case, I told him I was looking for my missing brother, and that seemed to be an adequate explanation.

We were headed in an easterly direction; the air continued to gather a foulness that was fueled by a growing humidity in the indecisive skies above. I thought the rains had passed but perhaps was wrong, if the almost palpable moisture surrounding us was any measure. John, from his perch on the driver's box, was thinking the same thing. He was grateful to have my fare but had no wish to be sitting in the rain for hours on end.

"I think it will pass," Kipp offered hopefully.

We finally entered what would be considered the Whitechapel district. The people who resided there had no idea that in a few weeks a serial killer would make his mark upon them as well as history. The murders committed by Jack the Ripper would go down as one of the most sensational series of unsolved crimes in history.

"I wonder if we will solve it?" Kipp asked.

"Well, even if we do, future generations will not have access to the knowledge. We symbionts might know, but there's no way to take the information to humans without betraying our activities." I was perched forward on the seat, peering anxiously out of the cab's window. My thoughts were to have John drive us up one street and down another while both Kipp and I canvassed for any symbiont thoughts that might reveal the presence of Silas or Vashti. Yes, it was a crude method but sound. At some point, we would probably hit the streets and interview people, but not yet. Kipp, especially, worked like an efficient sonar machine and hopefully would get a ping.

Whitechapel was not completely filled with slums. There were rows of neatly kept houses—typically three stories, whitewashed, with narrow courtyards. Many times, the tiny yards were enclosed with wooden fencing or trimmed hedges to mark territorial boundaries. On other roads, we passed what would have been a large common lodging house, where people paid money to hire a filthy bed for the night; multiple people would be crammed into small rooms, sleeping on beds of straw or rags. The air reeked of sulfur, the result of coal fires used for cooking and heating. As we passed a curbside slaughterhouse, I distinctly heard the final, hopeless bellow of a cow as its throat was cut.

"Are you okay?" Kipp asked.

"Yes," I replied, not meeting his eyes. Finally, I managed to smile at him. "We become accustomed to our place in time; it's hard to visit the past and adjust to the customs of the day."

"And, remind me, what do you do for a living?" Kipp asked, turning his head slightly. A breeze entered the interior of the cab and ruffled his fur.

We spent the day in that manner, even moving our canvassing north to Spitalfields and Shoreditch. I asked John to use his discretion to stop Molly frequently, so as to not overwork her. So, we paused off and on for refreshment and relief. John, having driven over most of London for years, was well acquainted with the East End and had no difficulty steering us as he thought suitable. The day, however, was growing short. I felt as if my face was covered in soot; my hat was awry and the back of my neck felt hot and sticky where my heavy rope of hair was wrapped in a pinned coil.

"I think, John, we have done enough for one day," I said as he helped me into the carriage. "If you would take me back to the Nottingham Inn, please, I would be most grateful."

The discouragement and fatigue must have shown on my face because he immediately replied, "Why of course, miss, and we can start again tomorrow, bright and early." He peered at me anxiously from beneath the brim of his worn cap. "If you don't mind me saying so, miss, we might do better if we actually get out and talk with people. It's kind of hard looking for someone from inside a four wheeler."

I smiled. "I was hoping Kipp could pick up the scent of my brother's dog." I put my hand lightly on the back of Kipp's neck. "He has a very keen sense of smell. But, I'm sure you are right, John. Tomorrow, I may have to do something else."

It was comforting to return to my pretty yellow room at the hotel. Kipp was tired, too, after being cramped on the seat of the four wheeler for hours. Mrs. Sanderson had dinner delivered to my room, as well as food for Kipp. I also asked for a pitcher of hot water which was brought with alacrity. I managed, using the hot water while standing on a towel on the floor, to conduct enough of a bath that I felt clean and refreshed. The water closet down the hall would come in handy for washing hair as well as an all over, I thought. As I climbed into bed, Kipp hopped up; after turning a circle or two, he eased down and put his muzzle on my breastbone.

"We probably were too optimistic that we would find him quickly," Kipp remarked. "This may take some time; we don't even know if he is in London, after all."

"Kipp, we don't even know if he is alive. We could be shadowing a ghost." I sighed and ran my finger tips through the fur of Kipp's thick neck. He murmured in response. "Go to sleep," I said softly.

We spent several days, except when it was raining heavily, in John Parks' four wheeler, riding up and down the streets of Whitechapel, Shoreditch, Bethnal Green and Spitalfields. John, with his man-of-the-street appearance, obviously blended in better than did I and would ask, in his casual way, for information on Silas. I'd given him a description derived from Kipp's memories drawn from Philo, and John made an efficient detective. I would ask, too, but more often was put off or viewed with suspicion. It was clear I was not from around those parts, and people were hesitant to help me. I quickly found that a coin or two, placed in an unexpecting hand, did facilitate more dialog.

"I saw a man, what with the description you gave, being taken off to hospital," a young woman told me.

We'd stopped after re-entering the Whitechapel district, and I had offered to buy a little nosegay of violets from a street vendor. To describe her as poor would be an understatement. The girl was probably only fifteen, if that, and would end up in a life of prostitution if things did not change. She led a life of quiet desperation, with a father who was an alcoholic and a mother fallen ill with tuberculosis. The thoughts of the child were tangled in misery and anxiety.

"Stay focused," Kipp said to me, his voice a steadying one in the back of my mind. "You can't save all the tragic people here in London—or anywhere else. We need to find Silas and Vashti."

Kipp's heart was as big as any I'd known, but he was right. I did give the girl extra coin, however, and noticed the gleam in her eye. She planned on hiding the extra from her father who would spend it on ale at the local public house.

With John's steadying hand on my elbow, I pulled myself back into the four wheeler; Kipp hopped up and took his place on the seat across from me. Molly pulled us back into traffic with a gentle lurch of the vehicle. Before long, we were clip clopping along in the direction of the London Hospital. Kipp craned his large head out of the window of the carriage and was monitoring the passing streets for anything of interest. He was vastly superior to me in this, so I continued to throw out my meager telepathic net in the hopes that between both our efforts, we would hit pay dirt.

"Stop the carriage!" Kipp yelled, his thoughts ricocheting almost painfully off the back of my skull.

"John, stop, please," I called out.

"Let me out, now!" Kipp was almost frantic as he scratched at the door of the carriage with his front paws.

I opened the door, and he bolted out, racing down a small side street that was congested with narrow tenement housing. It looked rough but I, without waiting for John, hopped out, too, and began chasing after Kipp.

"Wait, Kipp! Slow down," I called after his retreating form.

John was left behind for a moment, as he tried to secure Molly. I was not concerned for my safety, since I could effortlessly read the thoughts of humans and anticipate their actions. There were a few people loitering on doorsteps; their eyes were dark, and suspicion clouded their minds at the unexpected vision of a well dressed woman chasing a big dog down the street. I passed a garbage pail full of scraps; a thin dog had his head buried in the offal as he tried to get a meal. There seemed to be nothing simple or easy in this part of the world.

I found Kipp a few seconds later; he was standing with his nose pressed against the nose of a fellow lupine. It was Vashti! But she was in bad condition, thin, her coat ragged and unkempt. She was tied by a chain tether to a railing outside of a small, dingy shop. Kipp's thoughts were almost too rapid for me to follow, as he comforted and reassured poor Vashti.

The door to the shop opened, and a large man emerged. He wore an apron, with what appeared to be the dark stains of old blood splattered on the leather bib. His forearms, massive and scarred, were bare; he was not smiling.

"Get away from me dog," he sputtered with a Cockney accent so thick that he was almost unintelligible, even with such a simple utterance. When I didn't move, he stepped towards me and raised a fist in a threatening manner. "Get away, I said," he shouted. The fact he had what looked to be an oak axe handle in the other hand did not escape my notice.

"This," I said, pointing at Vashti, "is my brother's dog." I faced the man fully, my eyes locked with his. "I am not leaving without her, and I want to know where you got her."

John raced up at that point. "Miss, we need to get out of here."

A small crowd of eager onlookers was gathering. The man who was yelling at me was well known to all; he had a vile temper, was abusive and the people assembled were preparing themselves for some entertainment at my expense. I think it was when the man referred to me with an exceptionally rude term, that it drew the chivalrous attention of John.

"Now see here, mate, there's no need to use that sort of language with a lady." John reached up to adjust his rag hat.

"I'll give you something, mate," the big man replied.

The shop keeper moved forward. Just for spite, when he reached Vashti, he delivered a kick so savage it left me breathless; she yelped and cringed, awaiting another blow. An auburn colored blur launched itself, as Kipp sunk his teeth into the man's trousers, low down at his left ankle; with savage growls, Kipp began pulling at the man's leg. Kipp was quite large and strong, and the man flailed with his arms before staggering backwards. Kipp released him for a moment, and the man took the opportunity to swing out with the club and managed to hit Kipp square on his ribs. Kipp remained silent but backed up and bared every tooth in his head. The vision caused the man to pause for just a second.

I walked forward and began trying to release Vashti by unbuckling a heavy leather collar that kept her from freedom. Of course, I could read the man's vile thoughts but didn't back down; I was just a little surprised when he slapped me across the face. The blow made my teeth snap together, and I felt a pain race up my neck and explode at the top of my head. For a moment, I saw stars.

Kipp launched into another attack, and John valiantly joined him; as Kipp pulled at the shop keeper's trouser cuff, John struggled for mastery over the club.

"What's going on here?" A deep voice interrupted the melee.

I turned my head, which felt as if it was spinning like a top, and saw two men who managed to part the crowd and approach. One had a massive build, tall and heavily muscled; he moved forward and grabbed the club from the assailant's hand.

"Jones, if you don't back off, I'll give you something to remember," the man said. His voice was heavy with what sounded to be a Scottish accent.

The other man, after pushing his way through the circle of people, reached out to cup my elbow with his hand. He was almost as tall as the giant but with a leaner build.

"Miss, are you unharmed?" His voice was soft and spoke of a cultured upbringing.

I looked up at him and felt something I'd never experienced before: this man was a stranger to me but there was a familiarity that was striking. Of course, I could read his thoughts and knew that he was equally surprised as his eyes met mine. It was one of those rare times when there is the instantaneous and uncommon spark of mutual attraction.

The man named Jones responded to the intimidating look given to him by the giant Scotsman and finally became silent.

"I'm William Harrow," the man who was holding my elbow introduced himself. "This is Michael McNish," he added, indicating the other man. Harrow's eyes were the color of blue gray that one might see when gazing at a stormy ocean. I was reminded of the waters that lapped upon the shores at Kill Devil Hills back in North Carolina. Those blue gray eyes were fixed on me; he needed explanations but was trying to proceed as would befit a gentleman. With a very gentle touch, he grazed my cheek with a forefinger as his brow wrinkled in concern.

"You were hit?" he asked. The thoughts behind his query were dark and frankly alarming as he turned to stare at Jones, who managed to look sheepish despite his brutish exterior.

I ignored the question; the hot red stain on my face where I was struck provided the answer he sought. Glancing down at Kipp, I raised my eyebrows in silent query. The blow he'd taken was well aimed, and he shifted his body with discomfort.

"I'm okay, Petra. We need to get Vashti away from here." Kipp was brave and uncomplaining, as usual.

"I'm Petra Hathaway," I said, extending my hand to William Harrow. Maybe that was not customary, but hey, I thought, I was from America and could live somewhat dangerously in terms of what was deemed appropriate. As we touched, I felt that unexpected spark again. He did, too. His fingers were strong and lean, the flesh pleasantly warm.

"I'm searching for my missing brother. This," I said, pointing at Vashti, "is his dog. I am taking her away from this," I continued, gesturing towards the filthy vestibule with my hand. I turned and stared at Jones. "I will pay whatever you want for the dog." Vashti, relieved to be on the cusp of a rescue, was sending out waves of gratitude as well as worried thoughts over the disappearance of Silas.

"Let me take care of this," Harrow said. Almost reluctantly, he released my hand.

"I can't let you…" I began, stuttering a little.

"Of course you can," he replied, smiling.

And in a moment, William Harrow had effortlessly organized all our lives without breaking a sweat. Michael McNish unbuckled Vashti; she was physically weak, and he obviously had a love of dogs, because he picked her up and began to walk towards the main street. Kipp was torn between following them and staying with me. I solved his dilemma by chasing after the giant man, John Parks trailing after me. The giant disappeared into a doorway that was centered in the front of a large building that was located on Whitechapel Road.

"John, why don't you bring the carriage up closer," I requested, pointing at the building.

Kipp and I carefully dodged an oncoming tram as well as a large dray pulled by a team of massive Shires, and darted to the doorway. Michael finally stopped, after having crossed the room. Gently, he laid Vashti down on a pile of blankets and rugs.

"There, there little girl," he crooned. "It'll be alright."

A big, gentle sweetheart with a body like a prize fighter, I thought, before turning my attention to Vashti. Her mind had almost reached a delirium; obviously, her poor treatment and malnourished body had affected her brain. Kipp moved to her side and lay down, his muzzle across the back of her neck. With the intensity only a Kipp could muster, he began to use his mind to settle her and help her reorient herself to the present.

"Your dog likes her," Michael remarked, smiling at me. He had a large, round face; the smile transformed his earlier, rather frightening visage displayed when confronting the man, Jones.

"They are from the same litter," I sputtered, trying to make the story plausible.

The front door opened and closed. Harrow rejoined us; he walked with a slight limp, favoring his right leg. Michael's thoughts were revealing as he mentally addressed Harrow as "Captain". It was clear to me that the two had seen military service together.

Harrow approached and motioned for me to take a chair.

There were a few upright, hardback chairs scattered around the large room, which was conspicuously empty. I took a quick glance; it appeared the building was in the process of some type of renovation.

Harrow's blue gray eyes met mine. He liked the color of my eyes and found the tiny specks of green gold in the hazel to be elusively fascinating. Harrow thought I was pretty and enjoyed the fact my nose was a bit too large for me to meet the criteria of a classic beauty.

I suddenly felt like a voyeur, reading this man's thoughts when they were obviously directed at me. Purposely, I shut off my telepathy and decided to fly blind, as it were. It was hard to stay focused when all the man's thoughts came back to me. Kipp raised his head and cocked it slightly to one side. He was obviously curious but decided to spend his energy on Vashti for the moment.

The door opened again and John joined us. After a couple of introductions, John, having removed his rag cap, sat in a chair, waiting for my next instructions. I liked him even more than previously, if that was possible; he was loyal and would have tried to rescue the situation with Jones, even if he had been beaten senseless in the attempt. I tried to fix my gaze on a little place on the wall just behind William Harrow's right ear; his eyes were too distracting.

"My brother, Silas Hathaway, came to London to work at *The Daily Telegraph*. He has gone missing. I engaged John—Mr. Parks—to drive me around in the hopes we could pick up a clue. A young girl told us that a man of my brother's description was taken to the London Hospital." I paused and glanced at Vashti. "We were on our way there when we discovered my brother's dog." Taking a deep breath, I met the blue gray eyes. "You know the rest of the story."

He looked away from me, finally, as his gaze fell on Vashti and Kipp. When he glanced at me again, he was smiling.

"I think I can be of assistance to you."

CHAPTER 15

---◆---

I found myself in an odd position. Symbionts typically avoided a truly personal interface with humans. Our role was as an observer...one who blended in effortlessly and completely as we examined mysteries and puzzles that existed in recorded history. It never bode well to become in any manner intimately involved with humans. To recruit and allow William Harrow's entanglement in what was a personal matter left me feeling uncertain and uncomfortable as to the ethics of the situation.

"Let him help us," Kipp urged, looking up from where he lay next to Vashti. I was gratified to see she had stopped trembling; her racing thoughts were slowing and becoming more organized and focused. Just knowing she was safe was the critical factor.

"Are you okay?" I asked Kipp. "You took quite a blow to your side," I observed.

"I'm good. But I'd like to go back and bite that man in the butt and watch him scream like a little girl," Kipp replied. He was not typically the vindictive sort, but the man's mistreatment of the gentle Vashti had almost undone the normally fair minded Kipp.

William Harrow was waiting politely for me to return my attention to him. Of course, all of what transpired between me and Kipp had taken only a second or two. We could communicate with one another with ease while simultaneously conducting business with other symbionts or humans.

"He's on the board of the hospital," McNish said, nodding at Harrow.

I opened my eyes a little wider. With caution, I let down my guard and opened my telepathy to the two men. Yes, there was a definite connection between them. They had served together, Harrow in a leadership role and McNish as a subordinate. McNish was the sort who naturally possessed a loyal nature; he would serve at Harrow's side for infinity, if needed.

Harrow glanced at McNish, raising dark eyebrows as he did so. His thoughts directed towards me were brimming with curiosity. It would be unusual, from his experience, for a young woman to travel so far unaccompanied. And following a faint trail into the heart of the worst part of London indicated a stout heart. He immediately liked me and was drawn to me; McNish possessed more of a feeling of protectiveness towards all of us. He had a daughter who might be my age…or so he thought…and he wanted to help me.

"If you are willing to assist me, then I need to tell you what little I know." I folded my hands in my lap. "My brother, Silas, came to London to work with journalists here. He was sent from his paper, the *Sacramento Bee*." Often, my job forced me to project emotion to gain a foothold with humans, but I didn't have the heart to play these two well-intentioned men. "Correspondence stopped, and I came looking for him."

"Have you involved the police?" Harrow asked.

"Not yet. I was fortunate to find a lead that suggested the London Hospital."

I could not add that Vashti was finally communicating coherently with Kipp. There had been a lorry accident that involved Silas. The last she saw, he was being taken off on a stretcher, carried by a couple of men. As she tried to follow, a man—Jones—caught her collar, ending her freedom.

"Since you have your brother's dog, which seems in need of some good food and gentle care, why don't you return to your hotel? I will make the necessary inquiries and come tell you of my findings." Harrow's face relaxed.

I glanced at Kipp who nodded imperceptibly. "We need to get Vashti somewhere safe and see to her," he said.

The big man that Harrow called "Mac" gently cradled Vashti in his arms and walked ahead of John, who led him to the four wheeler. Kipp trotted anxiously after them, sniffing Vashti's dangling legs and nuzzling them with his muzzle.

"Your dog is very attached to her," Harrow remarked. His blue gray eyes met mine; it was difficult to lie to the man.

I swallowed hard and nodded. Following the others, I could not help but notice as Harrow put his hand to my elbow to assist me into the carriage. As he shut the door, he stood close to the window.

"Where are you staying?" he asked.

"At the Nottingham Inn," I replied.

"I will be in touch soon," he said. I knew when he said it, it was a promise.

As Molly swung out into the traffic, I forced myself to not look back. Right now, my main concern needed to be Vashti. Her recovery would be vital in helping locate and assist Silas. If—which appeared to be the case—he'd been injured in some manner, there was no healing bond on earth like the one between bonded symbionts.

"Comb here, Petra," Kipp said, shoving his pointed nose at a place beneath Vashti's left ear.

John had carried her in by the back servants' entrance. I paid the young woman who saw to our needs to do two things: bring fresh food and water for both Kipp and Vashti and keep her mouth shut about Vashti's presence in the hotel—at least for the time being. I wasn't sure if it would be a problem, but Vashti wore the appearance of the worse sort of street mongrel, and Mrs. Sanderson might have raised a disapproving eyebrow at her presence.

We were fortunate in that common vermin such as fleas and lice didn't have a taste for the flesh of lupine symbionts. So, although Vashti looked rough, she carried no insect riders; she was, however, matted and dirty. As I worked to comb out the tangles in her coat, Kipp applied his tongue and vigorously bathed her.

"Thank you both," Vashti finally said. "I'd given up hope."

I was concentrating on a particularly impressive knot of fur and didn't reply. Kipp, however, reassured her that we would find Silas, too, so that they could return home.

"I want to go home," the lupine replied, her plaintive thoughts echoing in our minds. She was really quite lovely. Her eyes, unlike the bright amber of Kipp's, were deep, bottomless pits of warm, chocolate brown. Her coat, free of the tangles and filth, was a mottled gray with a pretty, feminine wave to the fur.

The maid had left me a stack of washcloths and some warm water. With apologies to Vashti, since lupines had sensitive ears, I proceeded to dig down into the cone of her ear so that I could get loose the remaining dirt that Kipp could not reach. She turned her head and sighed…that sound and sensation when something almost reaches the pain threshold but still feels good.

"Everything was going as planned," she commented. "Silas was spending most of his time on the streets, building rapport with the locals so he'd have fodder for the papers. We knew, with the Ripper murders approaching, that he would need that comfort zone with the street people in order to interview and report." She managed to stand; her right hind leg trembled a little before she steadied the limb. "The people are cautious and definitely careful around strangers. But Silas, with his friendly and open manner, managed to build bridges." Her mind started to wander to the accident that had befallen Silas. Kipp, however, warned her off.

"There's no need to fill your mind with distressing thoughts, Vashti. We will find him," he assured her. Symbionts could survive near-starvation with no real damage to their bodies. Vashti would rebound quickly due to her superior genetics and slow metabolism. While the two lupines ate their fill, I stripped off my clothes, down to the chemise. There was a dressing table with a rather nice, non-distorted mirror. I glanced at my reflection and saw, with some dismay, a bruise on the high angle of my cheekbone where Jones had slapped me. Oh, well, I thought; it was my battle scar for the day. After brushing my hair, I climbed into the soft bed, too tired to do anything else. After a moment, Kipp hopped up and took his customary position.

"May I join you?" Vashti's tentative thoughts drifted upwards.

At our enthusiastic replies, she managed to carefully climb up—leaping might take a few more days—and took her place on my other side. We became a symbiont Oreo cookie, and I was the creamy middle.

"I've missed the comfort of my kind," Vashti remarked. "Silas and I slept like this, too, and would share our reflections on the day before going to sleep."

We let her speak, since she seemed relieved to be able to communicate with us. But, before long, Vashti succumbed to exhaustion and sleep overtook her. Her breathing quickly became very deep, and as she exhaled, a soft, almost moaning sound filled the room. Kipp and I lay there, quiet after the long day we'd experienced. There was partial satisfaction in that we had met half of our main objective of the journey.

"Kipp?"

"Yes?"

"Do you believe in reincarnation?" I asked, not a devotee of the concept myself but also never having ruled it out.

"What is it?" he replied. Kipp pressed his head harder against my chest, asking for his head to be scratched. As I gently massaged the top of his noggin, I filled my brain with ideas of reincarnation and felt him busily explore my mind.

"Well, it's an interesting thought, but how would one prove it scientifically?" he finally concluded.

Yes, that was the point. There was no definitive way to rule it out or prove its existence. Theology spoke of a soul, but at what point does that soul complete a final journey? The physical body, after all, is just a finite vessel.

"You are trying to figure out why you and Harrow have a sense of familiarity and an immediate attraction, aren't you?" Kipp asked.

"Yes; it just feels odd, and I've never had this happen before," I replied. "I wondered if perhaps he has been a symbiont in some past life, and we knew one another." My ramblings were idle, since there was no answer to my query.

Vashti began to move restlessly on the other side of me; she was dreaming, and her mind filled with anxiety and fear.

"Take care of it, Kipp," I said.

And, he, with his ability to manipulate dreams in a way superior to my own fledgling skills, did just that. All worry left the mind of the gentle Vashti, like an ocean wave receding from a sandy shore.

"Miss, I'm not trying to be impertinent or nothing, but can I bring you something to put on that bruise?" Rose asked, dropping her gaze as she made the observation. She was the maid who most often met us in the morning and helped supply my lupine pack with food and water.

I reached up a tentative hand. My cheekbone was tender, indeed, but it would just take time to heal and that was that. Ruefully, I shook my head. Rose collected the food bowls from Kipp and Vashti as well as a tray for me and disappeared down the hallway.

Returning to my bedroom, I bent forward slightly and looked at my reflection in the mirror. Yes, the bruise was gathering a bit of nice color; symbionts, as a rule, healed quickly, so the bluish stain would leave my cheek in a couple of days. I was fastening the cameo brooch to my blouse at the neckline when there was a soft tap on the door. It was Rose, who arrived with a message.

"Miss, I beg your pardon, but there is a man downstairs who wants to meet with you." Her eyes were huge, and she looked a little excited. "He looks to be a gentleman, very posh and with fine manners, too." After a pause, she added, "You look very nice, Miss Hathaway. I shouldn't have said nothing about the bruise on your face."

I almost laughed in reply. Rose thought she had a soft touch but failed miserably.

"I'll be there in a moment." After she disappeared down the hallway, I turned to Kipp. "Are you coming?"

He responded, "Are you crazy? Of course!"

Vashti was resting and assured us she would be fine, so I made my way to the staircase and descended the one flight to the ground floor. Mrs. Sanderson was at the desk and nodded, smiling.

"Your visitor is in the front sitting room, Miss Hathaway."

Kipp padded at my side as we crossed the lobby and entered the larger of the public sitting rooms that were designed for guests to properly entertain visitors. A tall man was standing, with his back to me, gazing out the full length window that faced Nottingham Place. Of course, I knew who he was without having to see his face—William Harrow had kept his promise and was here with news for me. He turned and I was caught, once again, in the web of attraction that he effortlessly threw my way.

"Miss Hathaway," he greeted me, smiling. He crossed the small distance in four steps and reached out to gently take my hand, which he sandwiched, briefly, between two of his own. "What a pleasure to see you again!" The fragrance of a very subtle cologne accompanied his arrival, and I knew the scent would linger softly on my flesh after the day was over.

Many people threw out remarks just to meet the social dictates of the day; William Harrow had truthful meaning behind his words. He wore the clothes of a gentleman, to be certain, but donned them with the effortless disdain of someone comfortable in the role. I didn't actively burrow into his thoughts, but I knew Kipp was busily doing just that. William Harrow had been born into wealth and privilege which explained why he was a round peg that fit into a round hole. He wore the suit he'd been destined to wear and was finely attired in black trousers and a dove gray double breasted frock coat; the collar of his white shirt was immaculate. His black hair, which was a little long for the fashion of the day, was neatly swept back and reached past the collar of his shirt. He was undoubtedly handsome, by any measure. His face, though lean, was strong featured with a broad brow that held enough lines of worry to bring character. I wondered what issues had caused him enough distress to leave their mark on his face. The blue gray eyes met mine, and I was captivated by the extreme pull they had on me as well as the sense of recognition. I felt like a meteor caught in the gravitational pull of a planet.

"His eyes remind me of the Atlantic Ocean right after the rain has fallen, and the water is filled with light but at the same time is shadowed and dark," Kipp commented with an unexpectedly poetic flair.

"That doesn't help me any, Kipp," I replied.

Harrow, displaying a boldness considering the times, reached his hand up and lightly grazed my bruised cheek with the tip of his right forefinger. I inhaled and took in the scent of his cologne, again; that scent would remain with me a long time, evoking memories.

"I'm so distressed that you were injured," he said, meaning it. His thoughts darkened as he recalled Jones' rough treatment of me.

I backed off a step, needing some distance. "It is nothing, but I value your concern," I replied. With my hand, I indicated two chairs, and we sat. Kipp circled and took his place on the rug between us.

"Your dog seems to have recovered from the blow he took," Harrow remarked.

"He's pretty tough," I said, laughing lightly. "He goes everywhere with me and is my constant companion." I wanted Harrow to start getting the idea that where I went, so did Kipp.

"I have located your brother, Miss Hathaway," Harrow said, eager to let me know he had been successful. The excitement on my face pleased him. "He was, indeed, badly injured, but is coherent and able to receive you." He paused, uncharacteristically uncertain for such a confident man of his next move. After a moment, he finally said, "I would be glad to accompany you to London Hospital and facilitate your reunion."

"Let him help us," Kipp said again, knowing my propensity for trying to accomplish most tasks on my own. "We need allies here, for the sake of Silas and Vashti."

"I don't want to use him," I replied. "He has an attraction towards me, and I don't want to manipulate him." The whole situation felt, well, squishy.

"You aren't using him. He wants to help you find Silas. We need to find Silas. Using him would be to profess your undying love, or something like that, Petra. You need to get a grip."

Kipp usually didn't speak so harshly to me, but he was correct. I was getting my emotions all tangled up with this man, and I needed to refocus on the task at hand.

"Mr. Harrow, I accept your offer." I dipped my head, averting my eyes. "It is difficult for me, since I'm not familiar with London and some of the customs here, to navigate the streets." I rose, and he immediately stood, too. "If you will give me a few moments to check on Vashti and make certain she is comfortable, Kipp and I will be ready to go."

"You are bringing your dog, too?" he asked. His thoughts were curious, but not negative.

"I don't go anywhere without my Kipp," I replied, smiling at him. "Will it be an issue?"

"I will make certain it is not an issue," he replied. Obviously, he was accustomed to making things happen.

After telling him I would have Mrs. Sanderson have a boy go find John Parks and his four wheeler, I returned upstairs to check on Vashti. Kipp trotted behind me to see how she was faring.

"I'll be okay," she remarked. "But I don't feel strong enough to make the trip yet, and when I see Silas, I want to be whole, for his sake."

Kipp, always a gentleman, asked if she needed him to stay with her despite his burning desire to accompany me. Not only did he wish to meet Silas, the focus of our trip, but also he wanted to see if he could dig up the whereabouts of Joseph Merrick, who lived at the London Hospital.

I took a last glance in the mirror as I donned one of the new hats I'd procured since my arrival. It was navy straw, and the color helped make my eyes pop. After pulling the cape around my shoulders, Kipp and I headed back to the sitting room.

William Harrow rose, politely. "I think they found your man, Parks, and he waits out front." He put on his pocket hat, which appeared to be made of a fine, soft, black felt, and donned his silver tipped cane. "Shall we?" he asked, inclining his head.

I think we impressed Mrs. Sanderson as we waltzed through the lobby. Although courteous and very accommodating, she was basically uncertain of me. But she recognized William Harrow, for certain. I knew that any issues with Kipp or Vashti had just been swept away as I moved up a few rungs on the social ladder, without any conscious effort of my own. Yes, having one of the upper crust of society at one's side definitely made obstacles disappear.

"Do you think he could get me in to see the queen?" Kipp asked, looking up at me.

I stifled a giggle. "Don't get started, Kipp," I replied.

CHAPTER 16

Molly must have been well rested, because waves of contentment breezed back to Kipp and me, entering through the windows of the four wheeler, which moved in a gently swaying motion. Kipp, with his base connection to the beasts of the world, could read some of her more primitive thoughts.

"She had oats this morning," Kipp remarked. "Your constant work for John has afforded him with extra money to give her a higher quality feed."

"So, Miss Hathaway, where did you acquire such a handsome dog? I don't believe I've ever seen one that looks like him?" Harrow's blue gray eyes met mine across the interior of the carriage.

"Oh, he is of a type not uncommon in America," I replied, trying to say something that was not a complete lie. At least I chose to not run out my "Chinese Crested Mastiff" line with the man.

"Well, that would explain things," Harrow remarked. "I've not been to America and would be unfamiliar with native species." He continued on with polite conversation, too well bred to interrogate me openly, but curious enough to want to gain knowledge.

"I find it remarkable that you would make this trip unaccompanied...begging Kipp's pardon," he said, laughing lightly. "It is a bold move. Am I to conclude you are an intrepid and courageous adventurer?" He tilted his head slightly. It was clear he struggled with the inexplicable attraction he felt, as did I.

I averted my eyes and looked out the window at the fluid landscape of London society. We had left the West End and were headed back towards Whitechapel, where the hospital was located. Fortunately, the humidity was low today and some of the more cloying aspects of the air were lessened. It smelled fresher, and I only caught an occasional whiff of the sulfurous stench from the coal fires.

"I guess we are, at times, called upon to do things that otherwise we might find overwhelming." My eyes met his again. "We must face our fears."

His thoughts, with the complexity of the human mind, went off somewhere dark and deep within the recesses of his memories. Kipp took off after him, curious to learn what made this man tick. I didn't want to follow and managed to block off my awareness of all that transpired. It was enough that I knew he'd been in the war and had suffered some sort of damage, as might any warrior in battle.

"Where is Mr. McNish today?" I asked, struggling to keep a suitable conversation flowing. It was difficult to not speak with more familiarity, but I checked myself and my colloquialisms at the door.

"He is attempting to complete the renovations. We have a deadline, and there are commitments that must be kept." He turned his head to gaze out the window at the passing streets which unfolded into busy thoroughfares as well as tightly congested alleys.

I enjoyed the unguarded moment of being able to study his profile without being caught doing so. Yes, he was definitely handsome by any standard, and I could appreciate that, although I was never one to get overly impressed by appearances. For telepaths, the inner self was never hidden, and my kind looked for companions based upon what was in the mind as well as the heart. William

Harrow, so far, displayed a kind and gentle nature. Although he was pulled inexorably towards me, he was, in reality, helping me because he had the means and wanted to extend himself in a generous gesture.

"May I ask what you are creating?" I asked. I could have dug it out of an unresisting and unknowing brain, but I had no desire to do so.

He turned slightly and rested those wonderful eyes on me again. "There is a group of completely incorrigible boys who haunt the streets of Whitechapel." He sighed. "They are orphans and have managed to completely defy and defeat all attempts by officials to contain them and educate them." Harrow leaned forward slightly and adjusted his long legs carefully so as to not disturb me. "I have considered that any boys who possess the cleverness and adaptability as do they can learn to harness their minds and lead fulfilling lives. So, that being said, I got permission to build and open a dormitory and school for some of these boys."

Kipp was following the conversation, and I could tell he was pleased with the man.

"How will you, uh, contain them, when no one else has had success?" I asked. We hit an unexpected bump in the road; I lifted my hands to straighten my bonnet which went slightly askew.

"We will not force them. My plan is to invite them. Perhaps if it is their idea, they will be more committed to it." He smiled a bit ruefully. "It could be an unmitigated disaster, but we plan to have a go at it."

I was becoming more and more curious about what drove him since he lacked the waves of guilt that sometimes accompanied those who had been born with the proverbial silver spoon. Kipp was distracted and blocking me, so I suspected he was delving into all the inner corners of Harrow's mind.

"Are you having fun?" I finally asked Kipp.

"Nobody's asking you to make the trip," Kipp replied. Really, he was becoming sassier as the days progressed.

"I think it sounds very promising," I remarked, returning my attention to Harrow. "And once they have finished with what you can offer, what then?"

He shrugged his shoulders. "That part is still up for debate. My thoughts, and what I have presented to some of my backers in this venture, are that we will identify talents and interests and then try to place the boys in apprenticeships and other situations so that they can develop job skills." We were entering the East End. "If they stay here," he commented, "they will remain poor and desperate."

I felt my eyes tear despite my best efforts to control my emotions. Yes, it was such a small drop in an enormous ocean, but it was a wonderful thing to do. Harrow could have been living on his family's estate, fox hunting or having high tea or whatever rich people did for entertainment. But he was in the slums of Whitechapel trying to change lives.

He might have been reading my thoughts when he said, "I fear it is a small effort to tackle such a large problem."

"If you change one life in a positive manner, then it's worth it," I said, meaning it.

Harrow, again displaying a bit of a libertine attitude, reached forward and touched my hand with his forefinger. It was just a brief kiss of a touch, one to let me know that he appreciated my sincerity.

We rode in silence for a few blocks until I heard John call out to Molly, as he slowed her with the skill of a talented coachman. I heard the scuff of his boot soles as he hopped off the box and opened the door to the cab. Kipp jumped out first and vigorously shook himself after the confinement of the ride. Harrow waited while I managed to get through the aperture without getting my dress hung up on anything. I had a momentary horrifying thought of humiliation: what if I were to get snagged, fall out of the coach, land face down on the unyielding sidewalk with my dress up around my ears, my bloomers and bank bustle exposed for all to see? Kipp began to laugh, which did not help matters one little bit. John, after tipping his rag cap, took my elbow and helped me to descend, which I managed with tolerable grace. He was asked to wait as we went in search of Silas.

As we entered the front door of London Hospital, we were met by a neatly dressed man who, although polite to Harrow, was obviously alarmed that Kipp was standing at my side. Harrow started to pull the "I'm on the board" routine, but I stopped him.

"Is my brother able to be brought in a wheelchair to a patio, perhaps?" I asked. "It probably is not proper for me to visit a male ward where he is housed." In truth, of course, I was not filled with the delicate sensitivities of the day but wanted to structure the event so that Kipp could remain at my side.

The guardian man was visibly relieved at my simple solution. "Why, yes, of course. We have been getting your brother up recently so that he could enjoy the warmth of the sun." His face relaxed. "Mr. Harrow, if you would be so kind as to escort Miss Hathaway and her dog to the north solarium, I will have an orderly bring Mr. Hathaway out directly."

Harrow, having removed his hat, nodded and began to lead me down a long corridor; one side was lined with windows, the other was a solid wall. The floor was highly polished, and the odors of disinfectant and what might have been formaldehyde floated in the air. The scents were a little pungent, and Kipp drew his lips back from his teeth in dismay.

"Whew! I don't know how they stand the stink," he muttered.

In a short time, we found ourselves in a lovely, spacious solarium. There were containers with blooming flowers and hardy, dark leafed small trees that sprang from concrete planters. The sun was bright, reflecting off of the many glass surfaces, and while not quite at hothouse temperatures, the room was pleasantly warm. Harrow pulled out a chair for me from beneath the edge of a circular metal table.

Kipp was scanning the immediate area when his head went up on alert. He started to sit, but instead remained standing. I followed Kipp's line of vision and saw the form of a man, clad in dark clothing, at a distance from us. He was seated in a large chair, with his back to us, it seemed. To be honest, he was hooded, and it was difficult to tell.

"It's him!" Kipp exclaimed. "It's Joseph Merrick!" He was almost hysterical with excitement. I was surprised he didn't start jumping up and down like a child at a birthday party.

"Go on over, Kipp," I encouraged. "You might not get another chance."

He needed no other urging and trotted towards the isolated corner of the room. I was happy to indulge him, since I could handle meeting Silas on my own. As Kipp left me, I focused and could pick up the thoughts of another symbiont close by—it was Silas, of course. I could feel his curiosity directed at me, too.

"Who is it?" he asked, from a distance.

I explained my purpose and prepared him for the fact he should act as if I were his long lost sister.

"My dad sent you here?" Silas was almost unbelieving, since such a thing was rare with us.

"Good news, Silas," I responded. He was close now. "We found Vashti, and she is safe and recovering."

When they wheeled him in, he was crying, and of course only I knew the real reason: we had found his beloved symbiont, and he could consider himself whole again. I rejoiced with him, since I'd experienced the loss of Tula and understood the feelings of desperation and emptiness. To the orderly and Harrow, the tears simply looked as if my brother, Silas, was overwhelmed to see his sister again.

Harrow stood. "I'll give you a moment." Discretely, he withdrew.

"Oh, Petra, I find this almost unbelievable," Silas said, having gained some control over his emotions. His face was still wet from tears, but he'd quit sobbing.

"I'm connected to an unusual symbiont or else it might not have," I replied, reaching forward to gently pat his arm.

Silas, of course, could detect Kipp's presence but was of the modern variety of our kind who would not ruthlessly intrude into his thoughts. So he politely canvassed Kipp, giving him a mental nod of thanks.

I gave him the news from home that was relevant, basically that his parents were doing well. Silas leaned back in his wheelchair and stretched his neck so that the sun, radiating through the glass panels overhead, struck his face. He had the appearance of a nice meld of both father and mother; his face was leanly sculptured like Claire's but with the dark eyes and hair of Philo.

"What's next?" he asked.

"We need to find out when you can leave this place and proceed with reuniting you and Vashti. When you both are recovered enough to create the bond, we can all time shift back home." This seemed simple to me.

Across the room, Kipp was creating a mild distraction as he evaluated the fascinating Joseph Merrick. Glancing over, I saw Merrick reach out his unaffected hand to gently stroke Kipp's soft head. For a moment, I took my attention from Silas and focused on Merrick. He was pleased to have a live body that would not recoil from his appearance or touch. He thought Kipp was handsome, as did we all, and reflected back to early childhood before his illnesses corrupted his body; he'd had a dog and recalled throwing a stick for his dog to retrieve. These were happy memories, and I felt an emotional jolt course through his body. He was a man of contradictions: sensitive—despite the outward appearance of the flesh—perceptive, joyous and sad, all at once.

Harrow chose that moment to rejoin us, accompanied by a middle-aged man with a pleasant face, the lower half of which was covered in a dense, dark beard.

"Miss Hathaway, may I present Dr. Washburn, your brother's surgeon," he said, nodding at the physician. The two men joined us at the metal table, and I introduced Silas to Harrow. The warmth of the room was taking a toll on me due to the layers of clothing I wore. I felt a bead of sweat form and roll slowly down my back until it hit the waistband of the petticoat. I suspected Harrow was uncomfortable in his coat, too, and was pretty certain he'd like to loosen a button or two at his neck collar.

"I think your brother should be able to leave us very soon," Washburn said. "He is free of infection in the wound, and his bone has set nicely. However, he will not be able to completely put weight on his leg for a few weeks and must use crutches. So, you must consider that factor in making arrangements." He tilted his head politely. "What is your situation?"

I knew Silas could not negotiate stairs such as those at the Nottingham Inn. Silas indicated that the room he rented had been located on the fourth floor of another hotel in a different part of London.

"I have an idea," Harrow said, "if you will permit." He glanced at Silas, not wanting to sound overly familiar with a stranger but eager to state his thoughts. "I have a townhouse in Mayfair…or at least my family does. There is ample room for both of you to come, with Kipp and Vashti, of course," he added, smiling. "There is a bedroom on the first floor that is not in use that will meet your needs, Mr. Hathaway." Harrow looked at me. "And there are other rooms from which you may have your choice." The blue gray eyes were almost backlit in the bright sun of the solarium.

I could feel my shoulders creep up and forced myself to relax. There was no way that I needed more time with William Harrow. He was already much too distracting to me, and I needed all the focus I could muster to keep the wheels on the cart. Silas, however, was delighted with the offer and agreed before I could warn him off. Anything I would say at that point would only look foolish.

"Kipp, get back over here," I mentally called out to him. "We are leaving soon."

Meanwhile, Silas gave Harrow the address of the hotel

where he'd reserved a room for a month. If he was fortunate, his belongings would still be in the room, untouched, since the month's rental was still in effect. Harrow, with his manner of unobtrusively running everything, told Silas he would have his personal effects moved to the townhouse. As we prepared to leave, I leaned forward and gave Silas a gentle kiss on his cheek.

"Goodbye, little sister," he said, slowing winking one eye at me. He reached out to pet Kipp, who had reluctantly left Joseph Merrick.

With Harrow's steadying hand, I entered John Parks' carriage and managed to pull in my skirts, flouncing them around my feet. Kipp hopped up next to me, and I placed my arm around his broad neck. The carriage merged into traffic as John headed back towards the Nottingham Inn. Vashti awaited, and I didn't care to leave her for long periods.

"It was very kind and generous of you to extend your home for our use, Mr. Harrow," I said, meeting his eyes for a moment before I dropped mine. Not demure by nature, I just found it hard to maintain eye contact for long periods with him. "I fear this is a breach of courtesy on our part," I commented, "as we lack even a basic letter of introduction."

"It brings me pleasure to serve you and your brother, Miss Hathaway," he replied. "And I think I know who you are," Harrow added, smiling.

Again, I had a feeling of mild guilt; in no way did I want to use this man. Uncertain on how to proceed, uh, ethically, I pulled Kipp closer and rested my chin on the top of his head.

"It's okay, Petra," he said. "I'll speak up if I think you are going down the wrong path."

I nodded, wordlessly, as I gazed out at the passing scenery of 1888 London.

CHAPTER 17

We made daily trips to the hospital after that initial visit. When Vashti felt she could handle the emotional and physical burden, she finally accompanied us. The reunion between her and Silas was one of the sweetest moments I've experienced in my 400 plus years. Harrow sent a telegram to Silas indicating that his personal effects had been retrieved and were waiting for him in the first floor room of Harrow's Mayfair town home. I realized there was no way to retreat from that particular path. In many ways it was logical, since Silas needed the proper setting for healing that would allow Vashti to be reincorporated into his life on a continual basis. Their bond had to be re-established for an eventual time shift to occur.

Privately, Kipp and I had agreed that although we would give Silas and Vashti some history on our background together considering the unusual nature of our methods, we would not disclose the particulars of Kipp's exceptional talents, save that he could interpret and read English. After all, Silas was no Philo, and Vashti was not a younger version of the trusted Juno. On our last visit before Silas was to be released the following day, Kipp grabbed my hand in his teeth—gently, of course.

"You've got to meet him," he said. "He's remarkable."

Kipp was almost obsessed with my meeting Joseph

Merrick. Since I had no one to conduct a formal introduction, I wondered how I would manage it and not look like a totally uncouth female. But then, I recalled, I was American and could play the game a bit more loosely than might others.

"He won't care about all that silly protocol anyway," Kipp assured me.

With that reassurance, I followed my symbiont to the far corner of the solarium where the hunched, distorted figure of Joseph Merrick sat, gazing out of the glazed window into a tiny exterior garden. Outside, flowers were blooming, and the colors looked slightly distorted through the glass, much like a pretty, soft watercolor painting.

"Mr. Merrick," I said, nodding my head as he turned, adjusting his hood as he did so, "I am Petra Hathaway. I thought you might want to know the name of my friend who has become yours, too, in the past days. He is Kipp." I held out my hand in greeting; after a pause, he extended his unaffected left hand which had elegant long, tapered fingers. His fingernails were closely clipped and clean.

He was delighted to know Kipp's name, because he had formed an attachment in the brief time Kipp had visited him. Merrick's speech was so affected by the physical deformities in his mouth that it was almost unintelligible. That fact, however, served no hindrance for a telepath, and I managed to respond to him appropriately.

"Kipp, you're right. Merrick has a bright mind that is well organized as well as a gentle nature." There was a moment for sad reflection as I realized that he had a very limited time on earth; he would be found dead in less than two years.

"Your brother is leaving soon?" Merrick asked. He desperately wanted to remove his hood but was uncertain if I would be offended by his appearance.

"Mr. Merrick, I apologize if I seem forward. It is decidedly warm in here today," I remarked. "At least, I know I am a little overheated. If you wish to remove your head covering to make yourself more comfortable, it would please me for you to do so."

He almost sighed in relief; reaching up with his hand that was whole, he pulled off the hood to expose his distorted head. Since I'd seen many pictures of him, his appearance didn't startle me.

"Isn't that more pleasant?" I said, smiling.

"Will you bring Kipp back to visit?" he asked. In a secondary moment of social horror, he realized how rude he sounded. "And it would make me happy for you to visit, too, of course."

I assured him we would. "My brother will leave the hospital soon, but I would very much like to come and bring Kipp," I replied.

"He's like an oyster with the lovely pearl hidden inside," I remarked to Kipp as we left to meet John Parks, who was waiting outside for us. Kipp demanded I explain the analogy, so I filled my head with images of oysters and pearls so as to educate him.

Since we were in close proximity to the building Harrow was renovating for his school for incorrigibles, I asked John to lead Molly in that direction. Silas's physician told me he was ready for discharge, and he could be transported the next day. The streets of Whitechapel were teeming; the weather was particularly nice and accommodating for the outside vendors who were pushing their goods. Overall, the scene was busy, loud and chaotic. A couple of young boys were running down a sidewalk and managed to bump into a large woman who cursed at them in Cockney slang, using words unfamiliar to me and Kipp. The sentiments, however, were not new to us.

Within a few minutes, we arrived at the front of Harrow's proposed school and dormitory. After settling Molly and alighting from the box, John helped me down, as Kipp hopped from the four wheeler to accompany me. I entered the building; the sounds of hammers and saws and more than a little rough language filled the main room. Workmen, wearing baggy breeches and the same sort of cloth, rag hat worn by John Parks, bustled busily, carrying buckets, lumber and other items; the room smelled of sawdust and the pungent fragrance of sap from timber. From across the room, I spied a familiar figure—Michael McNish was leaning over a table; his head went up when he saw me.

"Why Miss Hathaway," he said, "how good to have you visit us again." He meant the words and experienced, again, that sense of protectiveness—the same one he felt towards his daughter. His Scottish accent was thick and distinctive amidst the many other colorful dialects floating around the large room. "Will is here somewhere," he said, winning his internal struggle to address his former officer by a given name.

In less than a minute, Harrow walked in, his head bent in conference with a workman who was showing him a sheaf of papers. Raising his eyes, he glanced at me and the look of pleasure on his face was obvious to all. Although I'm no tender flower, I felt the rush of blood beneath my skin as an involuntary blush highlighted my cheeks. He crossed the room and reached out with both his hands to take one of mine.

"Miss Hathaway, I am so delighted to see you." The blue gray eyes met mine; this time, I did not avert my gaze and returned his directly. The pleasant fragrance of his cologne made its presence known despite the competition from sweat, infrequently washed human bodies, sawdust and pine tar. He released me and reached down to greet Kipp with a friendly pat on the head.

"I really like him, Petra," Kipp said, looking up at Harrow and wagging his tail. "He's genuine and a good man."

I briefly explained my purpose and informed him that Silas was ready to leave the hospital. "It's so kind of you, Mr. Harrow, to allow him—us—into your home. Are you certain that two visitors and their big dogs won't be too much of an imposition?" Kipp had managed to convince me that Harrow would be busy most of the time with his project, thus my time with him would be limited.

"Miss Hathaway, I can think of nothing that I would enjoy more. You and your brother may stay as long as you wish." He sighed and looked around the room. "I fear I will be greatly occupied here and hope you do not find me to be an inadequate host." After a moment, he added, "Mac lives at my townhouse, too, so you will not be without a familiar face."

I wondered if he took in all the needy of London. And what fueled his desire to care for the children upon whom the rest of society had given up? There were complexities to him that probably related to his family of origin; symbionts and humans were no different in that matter.

The next day, John Parks and two orderlies struggled to get Silas comfortable in the four wheeler. Across town in Mayfair, Harrow and Mac were supposed to be waiting for our arrival. The now indispensible Parks moved my belongings from the Nottingham Inn that morning; Kipp and Vashti accompanied him and were waiting at the townhouse. This was one of my rare moments without Kipp by my side, and I experienced the sense of loss and anxiety of any symbiont who was lacking the other half of one's mind and soul.

Silas stretched his healing but badly damaged right leg across the seat. I was across from him, monitoring his thoughts from a politely reserved distance. He winced with pain, and I reacted with a sympathetic grimace. Parks eased the carriage out onto the street, and we were off. I knew, from his thoughts, that he was making a concerted effort to drive slowly and with care, avoiding potholes or sudden maneuvers.

"Petra, there's no need for you to stay here, you know. Now that I'm reunited with Vashti, we can return home when I'm ready." Silas's dark eyes met mine across the interior of the cab.

"Well, I plan on remaining until you are able to leave, Silas. I made a promise to Philo and plan on keeping it.

Besides, the other part of my reason for being here is to further explore my relationship with Kipp amidst the chaos that will hit London when the serial killings begin." I knew my face wore a determined expression. "The chances of my having found you were remote; I won't risk you not making it home."

It was starting to mist rain outside. I hated it for John, sitting up in the box, knowing he would be miserable. Of course, he took such as a consequence of his profession, and I followed his thoughts as he dug his waxed cotton cloak from beneath the box and threw it around his shoulders. He would stay dry, for the most part.

I was not well enough versed in architecture to name the style of William Harrow's house, which was made of white stone and brick and set on a deep lot on a street with many similar townhomes. All had small front gardens filled with pretty flowers and neatly kept hedges to box off boundaries. There was a curving drive that allowed a carriage or cart to approach the side of the house. A bordered cobblestone walk led to the front door, but John, after viewing the landscape, decided to stop at the side door—the one used for tradesmen—since it was a shorter walk. By now, the rain was pelting the carriage. There was an outbuilding to the rear; probably a carriage and horse would be kept there, but I didn't think Harrow had those in residence currently.

The side door opened; Harrow and Mac darted out carrying umbrellas. I sat back while they, with John's help, managed to get Silas free from the carriage and assisted him, hopping, into the house. I handed down the crutches to an older, sober faced man who appeared; I would learn shortly that he was the butler, Mr. Reeves.

Having decided to take my chances that I would not vault out of the carriage and land on my face, I started to disembark. Suddenly, Harrow reappeared with the welcomed umbrella and took my arm as he covered us both with the black canopy. His face was close to mine, and his body crowded in as he bent his head down towards me.

"What an unexpected pleasure, Miss Hathaway," he said, as a crack of lightening lit up the sky.

I laughed in reply and allowed him to steer me into the kitchen. It must have been baking day, because my knees went weak at the smell of hot, fresh bread. As John Parks darted back to see to Molly, Harrow suggested he put her in the rear building where she could avoid the worst of the storm.

"Come in, when you are done, John, so that you can dry off, get warm and have something to eat. You must wait until this lightening has passed and the rain lessens."

Parks' face relaxed. It was seldom he encountered those of Harrow's class who took such care to be concerned over his welfare. I knew there were many such people who did, indeed, have compassionate hearts, but the end result of a strongly classed society was that occasionally those hearts were not heard by the many.

Harrow shook the umbrella and placed it on the tile floor near the oven that was radiating an evenly modulated warmth into the cozy room. Turning to look at me, his thoughts once again betrayed his confused sense of familiarity with me. He didn't understand the feelings but welcomed them and was happy to have me close by. I pulled myself out of his private thoughts, again unwilling to be voyeuristic.

"Miss Hathaway, if you will permit." He stepped closer and reached out to straighten my straw bonnet that had become askew in all the hopping in and out of carriages that day. The pupils of his blue gray eyes dilated just a little as he looked at my face. Kipp, thank goodness, took that opportunity to bound into the kitchen and rushed up, almost smacking me in the knees.

"Petra, this place is great! You're gonna love it here. There are lots of books and neat little rooms for reading and just plain hiding out."

The cook, an older woman, entered the room. She frowned, unhappy that her master had brought visitors in through the tradesman entrance and not pleased at all about the big dog running across her clean floor. John entered, after carefully hanging his waterproof cape on a hook outside, and pulled his soaked, rag cap from his head. Rivulets of water ran down his plain face.

"I'm Mrs. Atherton," the cook said. "Mr. Harrow, if you will take the lady to the parlor, I will bring tea. And, you," she said, looking at John, "can have a seat there by the fire so you can dry off. I will get you some tea, too, and some bread and cheese."

Harrow looked at me and smiled. The cook had been with the family since he was a child, and this was her uncontested domain. So, with a hand to my elbow, he ushered me out, while Kipp darted ahead of us, giving a soft bark of joy. The brief separation from me had been unpleasant for Kipp, too.

Silas and Vashti waited in a comfortably sized drawing room, with large windows that faced west. There probably had been some original idea by the architect to have a well lit room for afternoon visitations by guests. Even though the temperature outside was not particularly cool, the dampness in the air had created a chill, and there was a robust fire burning in the fireplace. Mac was asking Silas about his experiences in the East End before his accident as well as sharing some of the work that had been done on the school for wayward boys that was under construction. Vashti was stretched out in front of the fire. Occasionally, she would twist her head up and look at Silas; her long, curled tail would thump, once or twice, before she would drop her head back to the floor. Kipp trotted over to join her and lie with his head upon her shoulder.

Harrow accompanied me to a comfortable chair upholstered in a pretty floral of red poppies. After seeing me to my place, he crossed over to the mantle, pausing to gaze down into the fire as if the dancing colors had placed a spell upon him. The thunder continued to roll outside, with an occasional crack of lightening that would illuminate the large window in relief. Mrs. Atherton walked in carrying a tea service which she placed on the center table. She raised an eyebrow in query at Harrow. He smiled and waved her away.

"I have no female family in residence to perform this ritual, at which I am typically clumsy, but I will attempt to provide all of you with a cup of tea." Harrow smiled and bent his head to the task.

"So, Mr. Harrow, if you don't mind my curiosity, do you have family?" Silas wore the carefully cultivated innocent expression of a busy body symbiont.

"I have a mother and a nephew who reside at the family estate in the country north of the city," he replied, looking up briefly. "It is easier, with my business being centered in London for the present, to reside here."

He favored me with the first cup, bending from the waist in a courteous bow, as he presented it to me. Silas watched all of this with amusement, since his telepathy had opened a window into Harrow's instant attraction towards me. When all were served with hot tea, Harrow took a seat and stretched out his long legs with a sigh.

"The rain was unexpected, but then that is always so in London," Harrow remarked. With practiced ease, he engaged Silas in superficial chit chat about San Francisco. Harrow was very polite but preoccupied and was feeling pressured to get back to the school since he was working to meet a deadline. Silas decided to help him along.

"Mr. Harrow, my leg is throbbing just a little. If you will pardon my ill manners, I would very much appreciate being shown to my room so that I can rest for a while."

Harrow took that moment to announce that he and Mac must return to the East End. He would leave it to Mr. Reeves and the housekeeper to help us become comfortable in our rooms.

"Mr. Hathaway, it will be much more pleasant and relaxed if you call me Will, and of course, this is Mac," he added with a sweep of his hand.

Silas smiled and nodded. "I agree. And we, too, enjoy familiarity. Please call us Silas and Petra—and Kipp and Vashti." The men all laughed.

Well, that little bit of social jousting was completed, and we were now on a first name basis. I followed Harrow's thoughts as he and Mac disappeared from the room; John Parks was happy to have another full day of work and would take them to their destination.

"Well, this is home for a while, and I don't mind a bit," Kipp remarked.

"Me neither," Vashti said in agreement. "I'm tired of life on the streets and can do with a little comfort for a while."

CHAPTER 18

The staff of William Harrow's home were as courteous and welcoming as was he. Mrs. Donnelly, the housekeeper, was a woman of middle age, with a striking appearance topped by a sweep of coal black hair untouched by gray. We tried to be unobtrusive and make few demands, but the staff simply would not let us provide for our own needs. I thought Mrs. Atherton was going to hit me with an enormous metal spatula when she caught me starting to prepare a pot of tea. After delivering a mild scolding, she allowed me to sit on a high legged stool while she made the tea. The distinctive fragrance of Earl Grey caused me to think of Fitzhugh and home; I was surprised to find myself feeling slightly homesick. When I refused to leave the kitchen and remained there, sipping my tea, she let down her guard and began to gossip.

"Mr. William is a fine master, very kind and generous. He's been that way since he was a young lad," she remarked, taking a cautious taste of her own steaming cup. "It was a shame what happened to the family."

I tilted my head in curiosity and raised my eyebrows, hoping her need to gently tell tales would override discretion and that she would volunteer the information versus my having to go digging for it. Happily, she didn't disappoint.

"Mr. William's elder brother was the heir—a fine young

man, too." She shook her head in sad recollection. "He, Nathaniel, I mean, was married to a proper lady, and they had begun a family. Mr. Nathaniel and his wife were traveling in Europe when there was an accident, and they both were killed."

"What was he like—Nathaniel, I mean?" I asked, trying to maintain an innocent expression on my face so as not to appear too curious.

She hesitated, but her desire to chit chat overrode the fact I was a guest and technically not a peer by the standards of the day. "Oh, he was very high spirited and fun loving. Mr. William was the quieter of the two, usually preferring time in the library versus entertaining guests or going to parties."

Kipp took this moment to saunter into the kitchen. Since he knew Mrs. Atherton wasn't keen on dog hair in the food, he unobtrusively sidled along the wall and hunkered down into a tight ball in the corner of the room.

"Hoping for a snack," he said to me. "There was something left from last night—kidney pie, I think—and it was really tasty." His amber eyes held that unique begging expression that lupines seemed to share with canines.

"In a minute, Kipp." I slowly closed one eye in a conspiratorial wink.

Mrs. Atherton took another swallow of tea. "Their little boy was just a wee babe when they died. Fortunately, he was too young to be traveling with them and lives at the family estate with Mr. Harrow's mother." She looked up, and her eyes were filled with tears. "Mrs. Harrow was very close to Mr. Nathaniel, especially so since Mr. William had gone off to be a soldier." She shook her head. "It was very hard on all of them."

I glanced at Kipp. We had learned more about the psyche of one William Harrow from the family cook than from all of our telepathic endeavors. There was a favored son who had been killed. William, despite his fine qualities, was not his mother's chosen child, but he was the one who survived war and lived.

"That explains the part of him that is unsettled," Kipp said, his eyes meeting mine across the kitchen.

"We all hope Mr. William will find a fine lady and settle down one day," she added. "We need to see a new generation of Harrows running around the house, breaking things and causing mischief." Mrs. Atherton glanced at me. She was hoping, despite the fact she liked me, that it would not be me. In her view, I was totally unsuitable for a gentleman of William's quality and breeding.

I peeked at Kipp and raised my eyebrows. "Well, I am certainly taken down a peg with her assessment of me."

Kipp giggled. "Well, I knew you were pretty average but didn't want to say anything to hurt your feelings."

I stood, leaving the uncomfortable high stool. "Mrs. Atherton, if it would not inconvenience you, I would like to feed Kipp. Since it's nice outside, we can go to the rear patio."

She rustled up a bowl of chopped meat and added some cubes of aged cheddar cheese for good measure. Kipp and I retreated outside, where the storms of the previous days had dissipated, and the sun was out in full force. I sat on a metal garden chair while Kipp bolted down his food which, although not kidney pie, was delicious, none the less.

"Why don't you give me cheese?" Kipp asked, delighted over this new discovery.

"I thought you might be lactose intolerant," I replied, enjoying my clever reply as I tilted my head back to let the sunlight rest on my face.

Overhead, a breeze rustled the leaves which were clad in the bright green color of early spring. Birds were busy nesting, and their songs filled the empty space above the tiled patio. A wicker trellis served as the anchor for a bunch of climbing roses that held the promise of blooms as red as heart's blood. It was pleasant there; the home was lovely, well kept, and there was plenty of food and enough coal to keep the house warm. It didn't escape my notice that five miles away people lived in squalor. Of course, there was nothing new to this aspect of the human condition.

"You're thinking about what is to come," Kipp said, raising

his head.

"Yes. By the end of August, Jack the Ripper's activities will bring chaos to the city. Just think, Kipp…one man with that much power to terrify people. And he has remained anonymous since then." I took a deep breath and stretched my neck from side to side. "It will not do for me to be idle while we wait for Silas to complete his healing as well as his task here."

"Why don't you volunteer to help Harrow at the school?" Kipp said. "You teach at a college level, so I'm sure you can handle a bunch of ruffians."

I tilted my head at him. "You know, Kipp, on occasion, you get a good thought in that big, furry head of yours. I think I might just do that."

"And before you talk yourself out of it, he thinks about you whether you are with him or not, so helping out probably won't make much of a difference in his attraction to you." Kipp nosed in the bowl and found another piece of cheese. "And I want more cheese."

I didn't see William Harrow that night to discuss my desire to help at the school. Both he and Mac were absent from dinner, and I could only suspect that the first few days of the school's opening had been not without some degree of unpredictability. Harrow, impressed with the dependability and decency of John Parks, continued the exclusive hire of his horse and four wheeler. It satisfied John, who was afforded a consistent income, and Harrow was extremely thoughtful during times of inclement weather. John would stop by in the morning to take William and Mac to the school. Then, he would circle back to check on any needs that Silas or I—or any of the staff—might have before he was free to pursue other customers before returning to pick up William and Mac.

After buttoning my white blouse, I pinned the cameo brooch to the stiff collar at my throat. If we were to stay in London until November, I would probably need to do more shopping for clothes. My wardrobe was pretty much exclusive to spring and summer climate requirements. At the very least, I would need petticoats made of wool and a warm coat. My cape sufficed for now but that would not last. And the straw hats would have to be replaced with wool ones. After brushing my hair thoroughly, I coiled and pinned it at the nape of my neck. On my own, I could not manage the hair styles of the day, but my neatly contained hair did respectably conform to societal requirements. Looking down at Kipp, I smiled.

"You look beautiful. Harrow won't be able to keep his mind on what he's doing," Kipp said.

The smile faded from my face. "I have no intention of an involvement with a nineteenth century human man," I said, my thoughts unusually stern with my best friend.

Kipp hopped up and came over to lick my hand. "I'm sorry, Petra. Don't be angry with me."

Of course, I couldn't stay mad at him, no matter what happened. Pausing, I glanced around the lovely room I'd been given. It was a spacious corner room, with windows on two fronts. The walls were painted an unusual terra cotta color; most of the furnishings were shades of green, ranging from a pale celery tone to deep forest. As were all things in the town house, it was tastefully understated in a manner that spoke of wealth and a cultured upbringing. I grabbed my tiny reticule and went downstairs. Silas and Vashti were resting in the parlor; Silas's leg was elevated on an ottoman, with a pillow beneath the calf of the injured limb.

"Hello, Petra!" Silas put down his paper and looked up, smiling at my approach.

Vashti rose from her place before the fire and walked over to touch noses with Kipp. She was much more relaxed, and the gloss and snap had returned to her coat.

I perched on the edge of a chair and told Silas of my plans. "I just can't do with this much free time," I remarked. As a species, we chafed at inactivity and were easily bored; the latter much too often led to trouble.

Silas took a deep breath. "I know what you mean. I can't

wait until I'm able to return to the *Telegraph* and get back to work."

Whitechapel was bursting with energy, almost overrun with horses pulling every imaginable form of vehicle and conveyance known to man. The sidewalks were crowded with people either trying to sell goods and wares or on their way to jobs—Whitechapel was about survival. Looking out the window of the carriage, I observed some of the rougher looking women knowing that they earned their doss money from prostitution. Most likely, everything they owned was carried in various pockets in the layers of clothing they wore. I glanced at Kipp.

"Life here is hard," I remarked.

The carriage rocked to a stop. John Parks gently helped me to descend and courteously walked me to the doorway of the school. His rag cloth hat was in his hands.

"As always, Miss Hathaway, it's a pleasure to drive you and Kipp," he said, smiling at me.

I walked into the school and was happy to see it in a finished form. The main room was now partitioned off; directly ahead was a large desk with a small reception area. Behind the large desk sat a young man, neatly attired in a black suit and white shirt. He might have been eighteen, if that. I explained I was there to see Mr. Harrow; the young man disappeared for a moment and returned, followed by William.

"Miss Hathaway! What a delight!" he said. Reaching out, he took my hand between the two of his; his flesh was warm and dry, and I experienced something akin to an electric spark at his touch. Blue gray eyes that were always lit from within with depth of feeling looked into mine. "Have I been such a neglectful host that you must come visit me here?" He asked, smiling.

"Not at all," I replied, returning the smile. I permitted myself to have a quick glimpse into his mind—his thoughts of attraction towards me had not lessened. "I'm not accustomed to idleness and have taught young learners before." I artfully left out I had taught college in the past. "I would like to volunteer my time here."

I could not have shocked him more if I had stripped down to a bikini and hopped up on a table to dance. Well, perhaps that would have been a little more unexpected. His eyes opened wide and his lips parted, but just for a second. He was too well bred to wear much on that handsome face of his.

"I don't know what to say," he finally responded.

"You say yes," I replied.

"Miss Hathaway, some of these boys are exceedingly ill mannered and completely rough around the edges. Their language is harsh and so is their outlook on life." He was torn: part of him wanted me close by so that he could have more contact with me but the other side was appalled that I would volunteer to be exposed to the vulgarity of the culture.

"Perhaps proximity to the gentler side of life might have a positive effect on them," I replied. "I will not take no for an answer, Mr. Harrow."

"I think I asked you to call me Will," he replied, with a half smile on his face.

"Only if you call me Petra." I raised my eyebrows. "While here at school, we must be more formal, of course."

He recognized the stubborn will in me and appreciated it rather than feeling the need to try and subdue it. Something about it reminded him of his own nature and his choice to go against the will of his family to join the military and forge his own path.

"Miss Hathaway, I have a small class of boys who don't really seem to fit in with the others. We have separated out the lads by interests and skills, and these few seem to defeat my careful planning. Perhaps you will spend time with them and help me to decide how best to serve them?"

Kipp followed all of this while carefully managing to keep his thoughts under control so as to not distract me. Harrow lightly touched my elbow and walked me down a short corridor, his limp noticeable. I recognized the impairment worsened when he was fatigued. Kipp trotted behind, his nose up as he canvassed the territory. Harrow opened a large oak door; as he did so, the loud talking and laughing on the other side immediately became quiet. We walked inside the room where there was a small gathering of six boys. They were all clean and neatly attired in dark blue suits; their faces had the bright appearance of skin that had been scrubbed recently—skin that normally wore a layer of filth and had not been cleaned for quite a while.

"This is Miss Hathaway. She will teach you your letters and numbers," Harrow said. "You will show her respect and courtesy." He glanced at me. "Do I need to have Mac in here with you if discipline is needed?"

"I don't think that will be necessary, Mr. Harrow."

He backed towards the door as I looked out at my tiny class. The boy's minds were undisciplined, filled with anxiety, anger, fear and rebellious notions. It was clear that the leader was actually the smallest child…a ginger-headed little tike who appeared to be perhaps eight years old. As I stared at him, he crossed his arms across his chest and glared back.

I walked towards him. "Take your seat, please." My voice was steady and firm.

"I don't like to sit; I like to stand," he replied, cocking his head to the side.

"Kipp," I said, pointing at the boy.

Kipp darted forward and grabbed the boy by the seat of the pants, taking care to not bite him in the process. Firmly, Kipp pulled him into the chair. The boy's face wore an expression of such shock that it was a struggle for me to not laugh out loud. I glanced over my shoulder at Harrow, who appeared startled.

Kipp looked at me. "Are you hearing what that child is calling you?" He cocked his head slightly. "I don't even know what that word means, but I'm sure it's rude."

"Leave it alone, Kipp," I said. I turned my attention to Harrow, who by then had managed to get his facial expression under control.

"Kipp is of a herding breed," I remarked smiling. "He knows how to keep all the sheep in the pen."

Harrow shook his head. "I'll leave you to it, then," he remarked before retreating, pulling the door quietly shut behind him.

I rubbed my hands together with delight. My inactive brain had a task and trying to corral this particular little bunch of incorrigibles would be a challenge. And, on a less self-serving level, perhaps I could change lives in a good way.

"Any worry that we are altering history?" Kipp asked, as he tried to sort out our task.

"We are not implanting thoughts or manipulating these boys. We are just identifying their strengths and pointing them in the right direction. They still have the ability, as humans, to make their own choices. Harrow already started this wheel in motion; we are just part of the machinery."

Kipp mentally shrugged. "It's okay by me…just doing a reality check, boss."

"If you recall, we did this in Tombstone, too." I felt slightly defensive.

In retrospect, perhaps my vigor to positively affect some young, desperate lives overrode the symbiont need to be cautious when interacting with humans. As Fitzhugh liked to tell me, I had a history of poorly thought out choices and could be impulsive at times.

I walked to the desk at the front of the small room. All the boys were seated, having seen what would happen if they did not voluntarily take their assigned places. The ginger-headed boy was glaring at me, his dark eyes aglow with hostility. No doubt, convincing the leader would pose a challenge. After a few moments scanning his thoughts, I was delighted to discover a complex and multifaceted mind. The boy was undoubtedly brilliant, with no formal training to help him focus his talents. He saw the world in numbers and equations, although he was not aware of it yet. He could excel as a mathematician, engineer or perhaps an architect.

"Let's get started, shall we?" I said, smiling at the covey of miscreants.

CHAPTER 19

―――◆―――

"Your sister has succeeded in getting her boys under control," Mac remarked, smiling across the breakfast table at Silas. "I wouldn't have thought it possible."

Now that the school was self-sustaining, Harrow and Mac were not on site what almost had seemed to be 24/7. They both kept a daily presence, but there were more than capable staff on hand to help with instruction as well as managing the dormitory.

I nodded my head politely and smiled at the compliment.

"She has even managed to get that trouble-making rascal Allen to sit and listen to her," Mac added.

From across the dining room, Kipp cut his eyes up to meet mine. "Hey, I'm not getting any credit for my work," he complained.

"My sister is capable and talented," Silas responded, raising his water glass in silent salute. "To the fairer sex and all that they can accomplish through a soft and gentle touch." Silas was needling me and enjoying himself in the process.

"I agree your sister is capable and talented," Harrow said, raising his glass, too. "But she does not always have a 'soft and gentle touch' as you call it. Petra has the intuition of when to be direct and focused with the boys."

Allen, the ginger-headed terror of the school, realized quickly that I would not permit his disruption of my class.

As the natural leader, I put him in charge of many things, harnessing his talent of being able to convince others of what they should do. He knew his numbers but did not know basic mathematics, so I began throwing more and more complex problems at him. Each time he successfully managed to solve the problems, he was rewarded unobtrusively with another leadership perk. Of the six, Allen was my mathematics wizard. Learning the alphabet and language was simple, too, but he excelled in math. At some point, we would have to bring in someone more knowledgeable than I to help him.

Simon was a blonde child with the face of an angel and a fragile body that hinted at past struggles with survival. His thoughts, painful for me to access, revealed significant trauma in his life. He remembered his father killing his mother as he, Simon, cowered in a corner, too small to help his mother. His father was hanged as result, leaving the boy an orphan on the streets. As I unlocked his thoughts, I also recognized his hidden gifts. As we rode in the four wheeler to the school, I sat across from Harrow and Mac, my arm across Kipp's broad back.

"Simon sees the world in color, shape and form," I remarked. "I think he could become a talented painter, if given the opportunity."

"Not to be rude, Petra, but how would you know that?" Mac, at my insistence, called me by my given name.

"Call it a woman's intuition, if you must, but I know what I'm talking about." I settled myself on the seat.

Kipp's thoughts touched mine. "Petra, it seems odd to them how you assess things and just make pronouncements. Don't hurry this so much."

"Kipp, we're only here a limited amount of time. I want to at least get a foot in the door for these boys before we leave. Maybe nothing will come of it, or perhaps it will make a difference."

Recognizing my determination, he shook his head as we pulled to a halt at the school. Harrow assisted me in my descent from the carriage by taking my elbow, before extending the moment by holding my arm longer than was necessary. The humidity had returned, and the air was thick with noxious odors that almost made my eyes water.

"Rough, eh?" Mac said, smiling down at me.

"I've had it worse," I replied, meaning it.

Harrow tilted his head and glanced at me, lifting his dark eyebrows. "And that is the lead for a completely fascinating story that I want to hear some day." Privately, he wondered who I really was but was too well bred to ask directly. Many parts of the essence of me just did not stack up in his experience of the world. But, to my disadvantage, it only made me more fascinating in his eyes. I would have been lying to deny the reality that every day we spent together, his attraction grew. As I walked down the hallway to my classroom, the sound of my steps echoed off the dark paneled walls; the floor gleamed with a new coat of wax. The school had evolved into a minor success, in that only two boys had eloped and not returned. Fortunately, Allen and Simon were neither of those two.

"You know what's bothering your focus, don't you?" Kipp asked, trotting to keep up with my brisk pace.

"No, but I'm confident you'll tell me."

"You feel a corresponding attraction towards Harrow but don't want to admit it."

Kipp was correct, but I was fighting against acknowledgment of the fact. My mind quickly went forward to the surprise we had planned today for the small class. With Simon in mind, I convinced Harrow that we needed to take a field trip to a local art gallery on the outskirts of Whitechapel that was managed by a rather bohemian Parisian fellow. It was a manageable walk if one could ignore the oppressive odors in the air which were compounded due to our proximity to the Thames. Harrow insisted he and Mac accompany us, since threading our way past some of the more congested areas of Whitechapel might be a challenge. So, with Harrow at the head of the group, we set off. I watched as Allen took up a position next to Harrow, naturally drawn to the power spot of the leader. Harrow tilted his head down, to listen to something the boy said before laughing out loud in pleasure; he rested his hand lightly on the boy's shoulder. Mac was somewhere behind us, bringing up the rear. I felt a hand tentatively grasp at mine—it was little Simon, the traumatized boy with the spirit of an artist, who needed my touch. Something about the milling crowds and shouting vendors agitated him; Kipp, reading his thoughts, pressed in on the other side, and Simon threaded his fingers through Kipp's dense pelt. Together, Kipp and I managed to support him and guide him forward.

Recently, I had visited the object of our journey during a lunch break and made arrangements for our field trip with the owner. Ramon, upon seeing me again, took my hand and kissed it in an overtly familiar greeting. The boys giggled while Harrow frowned slightly.

"Oh, boy, he's jealous," Kipp said, laughing softly.

"Put a lid on it, Kipp!" I replied. His running commentary on the obvious was disquieting to me.

While Ramon led the others around the shop to look at paintings and pottery, I kept hold of Simon's hand and took him to see an exceptionally fine painting of a three masted schooner plowing through the waves of a storm tossed ocean. His eyes widened as his pupils dilated with pleasure.

"Oh, Miss Hathaway! How do you get the green in the water to look as if light is coming through the waves like that?" Simon's mouth fell open in an "O" of astonishment as he lifted his free finger to point at a place on the canvas. His small hand tightened its grip on mine.

Ramon, although not on a pathway to become famous, was a competent artist. I had scheduled a time for him to come to our class and teach my group of boys about painting and drawing. Even though Simon was the only one with true interest, it didn't hurt the others to have a well rounded view of the world.

As we walked back to the school, Harrow dropped back and allowed Allen to take the leadership role in guiding the others. Simon skipped ahead to join his classmates.

"A successful outing," Harrow said, smiling down at me.

"I was skeptical, but you were correct."

I raised an eyebrow. "It could have just as easily gone terribly wrong," I said. "And we are not back at school yet."

Up ahead, I saw a poorly dressed man, who appeared intoxicated, stumble out in front of Allen; the man shouted something vulgar at the boy and then began yelling abuse at all the boys, who were neatly dressed and well composed. Harrow started forward as did Mac.

"Wait," I said, putting my hand lightly on Harrow's arm. "Kipp!" I directed.

Kipp, knowing his role as protector and "herding" dog, raced forward and got between Allen and the man. Without needing to growl, he showed most of his impressive teeth to the man, who recoiled and retreated, muttering obscenities. Allen reached over and hung his arm around Kipp's neck. His former nemesis was now his best buddy.

"Nicely played," Harrow remarked. "You have a good dog there." His blue gray eyes met mine. Unexpectedly he said, "Petra, I would like to take you to Regent's Park on Sunday afternoon. There is a band that plays popular songs as well as the flower walk, which I hear is exceptional this year."

"Kipp, too?" I asked.

"Why of course!" He laughed. "We might need the protection of his big teeth!"

Friday rolled around, and Ramon arrived at the school for our pre-arranged mini art lesson. Even if Simon was the only child to be excited over the lesson, it would be worth the trouble. Ramon brought some pieces of parchment, pencils, charcoal, and a box of water colors and brushes. Somewhat amused, I noticed that Harrow was present for the entire lesson. Of course, he was discrete and worked to help a couple of the boys who struggled with how to hold their pencils and brushes.

I glanced at Kipp. "Don't even think it, Kipp," I warned.

By the time Sunday arrived, I half hoped the weather

would be threatening and cause me to forfeit the date with Harrow. But the day portended to be glorious; with dismay, I glanced out the window from my room at the picture perfect blue sky. The light entered from the east to cast a lovely sheen on the warm terra cotta colored walls.

It was time to pull out one of my nicer afternoon gowns and abandon the severe blouse and skirt combinations that I used for school. As I glanced at my wardrobe, I sighed with pleasure at the coral evening gown. There might never be an opportunity for such, but it was indeed lovely. One of the afternoon gowns was a sweet little blue dress, much the color of a nugget of Sleeping Beauty turquoise. It had enough flounces and lace to appear girly without so much as to make it impossible to sit comfortably. As I dressed, Kipp rolled on the floor, squirming a little to deal with an itch on his back.

"How do you think Vashti and Silas are coming along?" I asked, struggling to tighten the laces in my foundation garment.

"Vashti is better, of course, as her health has improved. They are working on their symbiosis, but it's difficult to manage due to the pain Silas experiences in his leg. It's distracting for both of them, but overall they are gaining strength as a team." Kipp rose, shook himself hard, and trotted over to me. "Scratch between my shoulder blades, please," he requested. I complied, as he sighed in relief.

Carefully, I pulled the blue dress over my head. Except for the coral gown, I'd had all of my garments made with fastenings up the front. One never knew whether there would be a pair of hands to help with rear fastenings.

"Oh, Petra, that's a good color for you." Kipp sat and turned his head analytically. "You need the navy blue hat to finish it off."

I started to make a sarcastic comment about his looming career as a style consultant but was interrupted by a discreet tap on the door. It was Jean, the young chamber maid who Harrow, upon inviting guests, engaged as an additional helpmate to the older staff.

"Miss, I know how to dress hair, if you would like." Jean's shy eyes did not meet mine as she stared somewhere just south of my left ear.

I glanced at Kipp. "Well, there's my sign that I'm completely out of fashion in terms of hair styles." Smiling at Jean, I invited her in.

Indeed, she was quite skilled with hair. In my contemporary world, she could have made a wonderful living at an upscale, trendy salon. As her hands deftly plowed though my dark hair, I closed my eyes; it always felt good to have someone else manage one's hair.

"Oh, miss, your hair is so pretty," Jean said, sincerity ringing in her words. She parted it down the middle and then did some type of twisting roll on each side of my head that met up high in the back; the ends trailed down in a wavy mass. Artfully, she put the navy hat on my head, tilting it dramatically to the side.

After she left, Kipp gave a little bark of approval. "Harrow won't know what hit him," Kipp said. I put my hands on my hips in disgust as I glared at him from across the room.

"Kipp, you are too much."

Before we left, Kipp had one last question.

"You bought that volume of Emerson poems, Petra. When are we going to take it to Joseph Merrick?" Kipp hadn't forgotten his friend at the hospital and our promise to visit again.

"We will go tomorrow, Kipp, during the luncheon break at the school." I walked to the dresser and picked up the small, wrapped package. "It's waiting for him."

A breeze ruffled the lace curtains over the eastern windows. At least it would be a pretty day, with enough wind to keep the sulfur fumes, which too often hung in the air like storm clouds, at bay. A large oak tree hovered outside my window, casting the corner of the house in shadow; at times, the limbs would scrape the wall with an eerie, unearthly sound. I recognized Harrow's thoughts from downstairs and realized it was time to meet him.

Kipp darted ahead and raced down the stairs to hustle up Vashti. Her time with Silas was valuable, but just as important was the need for her to stretch her legs and soak up some sunshine. I heard Kipp barking at the door of the library; he was as bossy and insistent with her as with me. William Harrow waited for me at the base of the staircase; his head went up at my approach. I didn't require the gift of telepathy to recognize the expression of pleasure and anticipation on his handsome face. He took my hand and made a slight bow over it. As I thought about the matter, it seemed to me that he was taking my hand more and more often.

"Miss Hathaway—Petra—you are as lovely as this spring day promises to be."

I smiled in response and allowed him to conduct me to the front of the house where John Parks waited at the door.

"John, I thought this was your day off?" I asked, nodding my head in greeting.

"Miss Hathaway, driving you and the master on such a pretty day is a pleasure for me and Molly." John's cloth hat was clutched between his two hands.

With Kipp and Vashti secured in the four wheeler, we made the short trip to Regent's Park. Unhurried, we toured the flower walk as well as spending some time listening to the band. There were many people who had shared our notion; a couple of children propelling hoops with sticks raced by. To the left, a large field of thick green grass expanded to cover a small hillock. Kipp and Vashti decided to play dog and chased one another in circles as well as trying to engage some true canines in play. The dogs knew the lupines for what they were but appeared to decide that a game was a game, after all, and most of them entered into the robust activity. Harrow led me to a vacant bench as we sat to watch. I was laughing when I became aware that Harrow was watching me intently. Turning my head, I boldly met his eyes.

"Yes?" I asked.

"I think I just enjoy watching you when you are happy,"

he replied.

It was an intimate reply, and I turned my head away in confusion. Maybe going on an outing was not a good idea. But as Kipp had said, whether I did so or not, Harrow's attraction to me was indisputable. Purposefully, I had limited my telepathy when with him, not liking the unfair advantage it gave me over him. I was left as unguarded as any human female might be when navigating the uncertain waters of the human heart.

Harrow cleared his throat. "I must make a brief trip to my family's home," he said. I noticed he took care to not call it "my" home. "I thought it might be a pleasant trip for you and Silas—and Kipp and Vashti, too—so that you could see more of England than just London." Obviously the fact that we were peculiar Americans who were strangely attached to our dogs had settled in with the man.

"That sounds nice, if you're certain we would not be a burden," I responded. "I will leave it to you to discuss it with Silas and make the plans, if he is in agreement." There, I thought, feeling very self satisfied. If I left the decision making to Silas, then I could not question my own motives.

Unexpectedly, I became aware of some disturbed thoughts emanating from someone in close proximity to our location—sufficient in their intensity that my attention was grabbed despite the fact my telepathy was aimless and unfocused. The anger and unquenchable lust for violence almost left me breathless as I struggled to control my emotional response. Without being obvious, I turned my head and scanned the nearby crowd of people. The thoughts were decidedly male, and it only took me less than a minute to recognize the familiarity to what I'd learned about Jack the Ripper by reading his letters to the police and media. What I heard, echoing in the back of my head, were the early musings of the man who would one day be called Jack the Ripper. He was walking through the dense cluster of people, much like a wolf among sheep, thinking of how he would like to target some of them for his particular style of torture and murder. My heart rate began to accelerate as well as did my breathing.

"Petra, are you well?" Harrow asked, as he peered at my face with worry. "You are very pale and your hands are shaking." He reached out and took my hands in his as if to steady me.

I tried to smile at him. "Perhaps I am a little overheated…maybe some lemonade?"

He was off in a flash, and I took the opportunity to get Kipp's attention focused on the thoughts of the unidentified man who was circling nearby. Turning my head again, I tried to unobtrusively locate the man but was unable to connect a face to the agitation swirling in the air. Kipp darted up at that moment.

"I hear him, too, Petra," Kipp said. His fur bristled in an automatic response to a threat. Vashti followed close behind; her head went up as her nostrils flared. It was with great effort that both lupines controlled showing their teeth in an aggressive reaction.

A moment later, the thoughts began to dissipate; the man must be leaving. Stalking prey like he did in the park was just a preamble to an escalation of what was to come later. I could follow the sick, sexual perversion of his mind and recognize that as with all such budding serial killers, the mere act of walking and thinking about killing people would eventually fail to satisfy his urges. He would, and much too soon, have to act on the thoughts in order to meet the demands of his twisted mind.

Harrow rejoined us and handed me a glass of lemonade. I nodded my head in thanks and took a delicate sip. The drink was really quite refreshing, and after a couple of more swallows, I felt my mind recalibrate itself and detach the recent event from my emotional response. I'd been told that such was an adaptive response for symbionts. Too much digging in the waste dump of the human mind would result in destructive emotional turmoil if not carefully managed.

Reaching out my hands, I petted Kipp and then Vashti.

"That, my friends, was our man." I swallowed hard. "In a short period of time, he will wreak havoc on London and become infamous for the decades that follow. We will most certainly recognize him when we meet him again."

CHAPTER 20

"Miss Hathaway, what a pleasure it is to see you again," Joseph Merrick said, nodding his unbalanced head at me. "And Kipp is a welcomed visitor." If I had not been a telepath, understanding his garbled communication would have been difficult. Those who dealt with him on a daily basis had learned to comprehend, much as one did another language. He thought it somewhat odd that I understood him with ease but did not question the fact and was merely grateful. Typically, he had to repeat himself or people would merely nod, smile and feign understanding. I handed him the small package which he clumsily opened with delight, much like a little boy at a holiday gathering.

"A volume of Emerson," he exclaimed. "I have read some of his poems and essays but do not have a book of my own." Looking up, his eyes met mine. I was happy to see no shyness dwelt there. "I am very grateful."

"Well, the idea was Kipp's," I said truthfully.

Merrick laughed in response. "I am grateful to Kipp, too." Leaning forward he reached out his unaffected hand. Kipp trotted up, good naturedly, for a head and body caress, enjoying the pleasure the moment brought to Merrick.

We chatted for a while before I began to feel pressed. It was time I return to the school; Mac was with my classroom in the event I ran late. Excusing myself, I darted down the polished hallway and rushed out the front entrance. The hospital was in close proximity to the school, so I didn't bother to hail a cab. Instead, I began to thread my way through the street vendors and others who crowded the sidewalks. As I waited for a lorry to pass so that I could cross a busy street, I became aware of some unpleasantly familiar thoughts.

"Kipp, there he is again," I said, feeling unwelcomed anxiety rise in my body.

"Yes, but where is he?" Kipp lifted his head and looked around, but there were so many people that it would be impossible to single out the owner of the thoughts. "What's wrong with him, Petra? He makes me feel bad."

"Pull back, Kipp and center yourself," I suggested. Both he and I needed distance from the thoughts.

Although I knew the man posed no harm to anyone in the middle of the day and the first killings would not begin until late August, I began to rush my steps. Hesitantly, I let my mind reach out again; the man recognized me from the day at the park, mostly due to Kipp, who drew attention because of his size. The man's thoughts descended into such a depth of darkness that I was forced to take a few deep breaths in order to calm myself. A minute later, the thoughts began to dissipate, indicating the man was not following us, and I breathed a sigh of relief. I didn't want him to develop any interest at all in the school, although harming children was not something connected to Jack the Ripper. Well, I corrected myself, not that we knew of. I rushed into the school and raced down the hallway to my classroom; the fear and horror generated by the thoughts of a madman hadn't left me, and I paused outside the door to catch my breath.

"Petra, are you alright?"

I gave a visible start; William Harrow had appeared from nowhere, and the light touch on my arm shocked me from my recent brush with Jack the Ripper.

"You are disturbed," Harrow observed. His heavy, dark

brows drew together as he allowed a frown to mar his handsome face. "I should have gone with you to hospital to visit Mr. Merrick. The streets here can be mean and uncivil for a lady."

"I am unharmed," I replied, trying to give a soft laugh of reassurance but not doing a good job. "There was a lorry that almost ran us down."

His feelings of emotional connection washed over me, and I had a moment to reflect that it was nice to be cared about by another warm, living being…even if he was not a fellow symbiont. It was only a short time later that I would be forced to admit there were certain qualities in my own species that were not exactly noble.

"Will, I think Petra and I would enjoy accompanying you to your country home, if it's not too much of an inconvenience." Silas looked up from his plate and smiled across the table at Harrow. "We seem to travel with a canine entourage."

It was dinner time, and we were gathered in our usual company of Harrow, Mac, Silas and me. Kipp and Vashti hovered nearby, curled into compact balls of fur, seemingly asleep but in reality alert to all that transpired.

Silas directed his gaze at me, and, unknown to the two men, he began to tease me about Harrow's private thoughts. While I had made the decision to honor our kind and vulnerable host by not looking inside his soul, Silas shared no such compunctions and found the romantic musings of the human man towards me to be amusing. So, he and I exchanged audible chit chat with one another and the two men while simultaneously having a serious discussion with one another.

"It's something called ethics, Silas. I would think having Philo as a father you might know something about it."

"Oh, come on, Petra. Surely you can't take a superior attitude with some of the stunts you've pulled over the years." He leaned back and almost smirked at me. "Yes, I have heard the rumors."

"Maybe so, Silas, but I've also matured. It's wrong to laugh behind Harrow's back when he's being kind to you." I leaned back, too, and tried not to glare across the table.

Vashti began to mentally whine; the agitated discourse was unsettling to her. Kipp, on the other hand decided to take matters into his own hands, uh, paws. When Silas decided to defy my request and delve again into Harrow's private thoughts, Kipp threw one of his unusual mental blocks; it was as if Silas hit a lead door.

"Wow, that's pretty impressive, Kipp," Silas said, opening his eyes wider. He paused for a minute to respond to a query directed from Mac before addressing me. "Petra, I will leave Harrow alone." Before I could respond, he added, "I give you my word. I'm not interested in it anyway. All I want to do is get back to the *Telegraph* and finish my work here."

The toil at school earlier that day combined with the emotional stress of dueling with Silas left me exhausted. Kipp and I had gone to bed; I fell asleep almost immediately before awakening with a start. For a moment, I was disoriented, not sure where I was or the time. I reached my hand down to find Kipp, but he was missing. Sitting up, I looked around the dark room, not relying upon my vision since I was calling out for him in my mind.

"I'm downstairs," he replied, after a moment.

That reply left me wondering how he had exited the room. Apparently Kipp could now turn door knobs and open doors, I thought, shaking my head. What would be next?

"I'm gonna learn to play the cello," he replied, feeling mischievous.

Donning my dressing gown, I tied the sash around my waist and began to quietly descend the stairs. There was no obvious activity in the house, and the thoughts of those within were consumed with dreams or else somnolent in the dark void of sleep. Reaching the first landing, I tippy toed across the floor and made my way to the library towards the rear of the house. The door was ajar, and a soft light flickered erratically in the aperture. Cautiously, I pushed the door open. Ahead, William Harrow was sitting on the couch, his feet elevated on an ottoman. Kipp was lying on the sofa next to him, his head in Harrow's lap. Harrow's head turned at my movement, and he started to stand.

"Please, don't," I said, gesturing with my hand. "You seem comfortable and relaxed."

He smiled and nodded. "Yes; sometimes, when the day is done, it is nice just to be quiet for a time and enjoy the flames in the fireplace. After a while, it becomes hypnotic, and I get sleepy." His coat was draped across a chair and his collar was loose, so it was clear he was done for the day.

"You seem to have made a pal," I remarked, meaning Kipp.

"Oh, yes. I've always been fond of dogs, and Kipp is a fine dog. I can tell he is very intelligent...I almost get the sense he knows what I'm saying." Harrow threaded his fingers through Kipp's fur.

I tried not to laugh. "I know what you mean. I feel that way, too." Turning I started towards the door, knowing he wanted to ask me to stay—but he didn't. "Kipp can follow whenever he wishes," I commented as I pulled the door almost shut behind me.

Later, I was awoken again when Kipp climbed into bed with me. After circling a few times and crumpling with a sigh, he put his jaw on my chest. The room was too dark for me to see his eyes.

"Petra, I went into his dreams," Kipp began. "He was dreaming of you, and I think I learned more about humans tonight than I have before."

"What did you learn?" I asked, hesitant to push this discussion but knowing Kipp needed to talk.

"I learned about the capacity to experience love." He took

a deep breath. "But the concept of love is still confusing to me at times," Kipp said, with a mental frown.

I sighed—obviously, a nice relaxing chat before falling asleep was not in the cards. Kipp's brain was too busy and complex for things simple.

"Love is a word that means many things, Kipp. A parent can love a child, a man can love a woman, or a sibling can love another sibling, and so on." I took a minute to reflect on a concept that had stymied poets for centuries. "Love is a deep emotion that implies connectedness, and it can have romantic elements or not."

"So, when I look at you, and my heart feels full, that is love?" Kipp asked. I replied yes, and he pressed his jaw against my chest until I almost cringed with pain. "When I look up and don't see you, and I feel empty, is that love, too?"

"Yes, Kipp. Both of those are love."

"I think William Harrow feels love for you, then," he said. "I know you're blocking reading most of his thoughts, and I understand why. But when he looks at you, he feels deep emotions; if you've been absent and appear, he feels complete joy and happiness. When you are leaving his presence, he feels worried and sad, I think." Kipp paused before asking, "How is his love different than mine?"

I took another deep breath. "For humans—between men and women—there is love that speaks of friendship, and then there is romantic love." Combing my fingers through the fur on his head, I remarked, "There is nothing between humans like the connection symbionts share. When we bond with one another, our meshing of our thoughts almost creates a perfect whole. I think the fact you and I found one another in desperate conditions only makes our connection more intense." My eyes had adjusted to the darkness of the room. Kipp turned his head to the side and looked, for a moment, like a big dog who hoped I was hiding a squeaky toy for him to possess.

"So, how would you know if Harrow has friendship feelings or romantic love feelings for you?" He turned his head so I could scratch behind his left ear.

"Romantic feelings would be deeper and more intense than friendship. Harrow would have a physical attraction to me, in that he would want to hold me, kiss me, and things like that. When in love, it's easy to feel as if one is going crazy; you can't wait to see the other person, and it feels like a constant yearning. Friendship is more even keeled, if that makes sense."

Kipp was finally satisfied with my crude explanations. "Well, then, Harrow has romantic feelings for you. I've been listening in, so I know."

"Well, thanks a lot, Kipp. Now I won't feel uncomfortable at all when I'm with him. Why don't you turn off your brain and go to sleep?"

"Petra, if Harrow loves you, and I love you, does that mean I love Harrow?"

I rubbed his head. "Silly," I replied. "That's not a proper use of logic, but then, in love, rules of logic do not apply. Now go to sleep."

The next morning, I wished we had just kept talking, because Kipp's notions had set off a cascade of dreams that bordered on low level erotic. I had been married before and understood the dynamics of love but had pretty much avoided any entanglements for a long time; my work became my focus and then there was Kipp. It was easy to think Kipp completed me as a symbiont and that no other relationships were required. Besides him, my friendships with Philo and Juno, as well as the improbable one with Fitzhugh, seemed enough. But those dreams were disturbing, I confess. William Harrow's blue gray eyes were lovely in person, but in the context of a romantic dream, they took on new meaning.

"Well, how did you sleep?" Kipp asked, glancing up at me as I dangled my legs off the side of the bed.

"You know the answer, Mr. Busybody, since you filled my head with thoughts of kisses and passion. And I know full well you monitored my dreams last night." I almost felt some level of embarrassment. Reaching up, I tried to push my tangled hair away from my face while realizing I should have contained the mass in a braid before going to sleep.

Kipp laughed. "Wow! Petra, I take back every time I thought you were living too dull a life. I almost think I was too young to listen to your dreams...I might need counseling after that experience."

I made a face at him and lay back on the bed. It had been nice and exciting, I had to confess. Maybe it told me one thing about myself: even though I was over 400 years old, I still had a little fire somewhere deep inside my soul.

"Yes, you're not over the hill yet," Kipp commented, laughing again.

The dreams probably had something to do with my taking extra care while getting dressed that morning. Before I left the room to go downstairs for breakfast, I noticed that my cheeks had a pretty glow; I was excited, and it showed on my face.

The men were already assembled in the dining room and were partaking of coffee. Breakfast was a relaxed affair, with chafing dishes on a sideboard, so that one could pick and choose as desired. Mac, Silas and Harrow all stood, and I motioned them to be seated. Silas, I noticed, was gaining much better function of his leg, and I said as much to him.

"Yes, I'm close to the day when I can return to the *Telegraph*. My original plans were to remain in London until mid November before returning home." He glanced up at William. "I believe that Petra and I can soon look for other accommodations since we have no wish to take advantage of your hospitality for such a long period."

Harrow quietly experienced a moment of panic since he had no desire to lose me from his household. It was a testament to his self composure that he managed to keep his facial expression neutral. "Silas, it is my pleasure for you and Petra to remain here as long as you wish. As you can see, this house is much too large for me and Mac. And, in any case, it would be difficult to find suitable accommodations for the both of you as well as Kipp and Vashti. Please, as long as you are in London, consider my home to be yours."

Silas glanced at me and smiled. Although he was agreeable enough, he was no Philo and I had no history with him. I didn't care for his humor over the situation, to be quite honest, but he had promised to not interfere, and from what I could see, he had kept his word. William Harrow was a very decent man, and his feelings for me were genuine; I took all of that quite seriously and had no wish to injure his heart or soul.

"Well, thank you, Will. We accept with gratitude," Silas replied.

Kipp was probably the most relieved individual in the room, other than Harrow. The food, from Kipp's perspective, was amazing, and he figured if he just waited long enough, there would eventually be another kidney pie waiting for him.

CHAPTER 21

The whistle sounded as the train pulled away from the platform at Victoria Station. We were seated in first class; Silas and Harrow sat opposite me, while Vashti and Kipp were stretched out on the floor at our feet. Mac stayed behind in London to keep steering the various ships that were in play.

"My family's home is just southeast of Peterborough," Harrow said. He turned his head and gazed out the window as the congestion of London began to drop from view.

"Has your family been there a long time?" Silas asked politely. Both Kipp and I continued to monitor him, and he, for the present, was staying conspicuously out of Harrow's private thoughts. There was no need for him to be in there anyway.

"Oh, yes. The estate has been passed down for several generations. I don't make it home as often as I should." Harrow took a deep breath and continued to keep his eyes focused on the passing scenery. One didn't need to be a symbiont to recognize he was tense.

"It is difficult, I think, for adults to return home…especially after a long absence," I said. "Our parents will always think of us as children." I smiled, in what I hoped was a supportive gesture, as he turned to look at me.

"Yes, a very apt description of our dilemma." Harrow's blue gray eyes held the usual warmth when they were focused on me. "And I've not heard you speak of your own family," he said, tilting his head to the side.

I glanced quickly at Silas and allowed him to confabulate whatever he wished.

"Our parents are both deceased…only the two of us remain," he said, keeping it simple for me to remember the story line.

Harrow politely murmured something about his sympathies before resuming his inspection of the passing countryside. "I have only my mother and my nephew; I am his guardian." Harrow took a deep breath before adding, "It is for his welfare that I go home."

The conversation for the remainder of the journey was minimal—Harrow was too distracted by anxiety to focus. Silas had brought a stack of papers and began to read, since he was working to get back into the rhythm that had brought him to England. I had never been able to read while in a moving vehicle and instead engaged Vashti and Kipp in some private mental exercises. I would develop a mental picture and then hide it in my brain. They would, like a pack of fox terriers, try to ferret out the stray thought. Silas looked up once, aware of what I was doing; he smiled and tried to not laugh. It soon became a competition between Kipp and Vashti to see who could find the thought first. Kipp, of course, was vastly superior, and the contest was patently unfair. He, gentleman that he was, allowed Vashti to win a few times, while keeping his role in such hidden.

The trip north didn't take long, and before Kipp and Vashti could inquire "Are we there yet?", we pulled to a smoky stop at a small, rural station. Although Harrow didn't possess a personal carriage and driver in London, it was clear that his family did have both—an impeccably dressed groom driving a flashy team of matched chestnut horses was waiting. After a greeting, our minimal luggage was transferred to an area on the back of the carriage, and we were off again. Harrow's face became more drawn, the closer our proximity to his home.

The weather was pretty; a cloudless blue sky stretched from horizon to horizon, and we were surrounded by green hills and shallow valleys unexpectedly punctuated by groves of thickly leafed trees. Our carriage topped one final hill before a huge estate house came into view. I'd known Harrow must be quite wealthy, but this mansion was one of those things one saw while watching a BBC period piece on Masterpiece Theater.

Harrow caught my eye and smiled. "It's always been much too large for me. I used to get lost quite regularly when I was a child."

Kipp's head popped up as his amber eyes opened wide. "Wow! What a house!" He nuzzled my hand. "I bet they have plenty of cheese and kidney pie at that place."

The carriage swept up a curving drive as we passed stately oaks that stood like aged guardians in review. The front door of the massive house opened, and a middle-aged man dressed in funereal black stood with an unchanging face as he viewed our eclectic group.

"Good day, Mr. Murphy," Harrow said, smiling at the man, who was obviously the butler. Who else would dress in such a severe manner?

We were shown inside, and I tried not to gawk like an uncivilized heathen. After all, I had seen some pretty spectacular things in my 400 years of traveling back and forth. But that house was truly beautiful, a living museum of countless objects collected over many lifetimes. The walls were colored in the traditionally rich manner of the day, with deep, vivid reds and intense shades of green posing a pleasant series of contrasts to my appreciative eyes. The walls were covered with paintings, both oil and watercolor, and all corners were filled with statuary or delicate marble topped round tables.

A small boy clattered down a wide double staircase; he was dressed in a proper little suit and appeared as if someone had just combed his hair.

"Uncle Will!" he exclaimed, throwing himself against Harrow.

"Hello, Daniel," Harrow responded, bending forward to lift the boy in his arms. "You've grown since I last saw you." The fondness between the two was undeniable.

Daniel was a handsome child, slender built, with a head full of black hair and a serious, grave expression on his pale face. It only took me a few moments to pick up on the damage done to him by the loss of both parents. He was tense, anxious and definitely uncomfortable with what the fates had dealt. On the positive side, he seemed to have a healthy attachment to Harrow.

"Allow me to introduce you to my mother," Harrow said, directing his comment to Silas and me. The tension, which had dissipated for a moment, returned in full force. The unspoken sentiment was that the introduction was a chore he wished to be rid of.

We followed him to a drawing room off to the left; he tapped lightly on the door, which was ajar, before entering. A woman sat in the center of the well appointed room, a book in her hand; there was a regal air about her and all that was missing was a throne and crown. She laid the book aside and rested her hands in her lap. As we drew closer, I saw the blue gray eyes that reminded me of Harrow's, but sadly lacking the warmth. No, those eyes, although the same color, were cold and remote.

"Hello, Mother," Harrow said. He approached and bent over to lightly graze her cheek with his lips. I saw her tense slightly.

She murmured the requisite courteous greetings to us, but I could tell she had no interest at all in entertaining guests of her son. And even more, she laid those cold eyes on me in an appraising manner that I found unpleasant. From her perspective, I was some uncouth American lout, and she fervently hoped I did not have designs upon her son.

"Petra, what's wrong with her?" Kipp asked, looking up at me.

Indeed, she had conflicted thoughts about William

Harrow. As I eavesdropped into her thoughts, she experienced a burst of sudden shame as she realized she wished it was her son, Nathaniel, who stood in front of her and not William. Kipp looked up at me, horrified; the expression in his eyes reflected the essential goodness in his heart.

"She has no depth of feeling for him, Petra. How is it possible to feel that way about her child?" Kipp was disturbed, especially since he had developed affection for Harrow.

The moment made me sad; I reached down and lightly grazed the top of Kipp's head with my fingertips. "Kipp, the relationships and emotions of humans are complicated, just as are ours. This one is obviously full of pain and history that we don't understand."

"Thank you so much for having us as guests, Mrs. Harrow," Silas was saying, in a smooth attempt to cover an awkward pause.

I was glad he spoke up since her negative thoughts towards her son, who was a good man, had left me not wanting to engage with her unless necessary. I did, however, manage a smile and tried not to stare a hole in her. Mr. Murphy, stiff backed and silent, prepared to show us to our rooms, while Harrow remained behind to speak with his mother privately.

"Daniel, why don't you accompany our guests and show them around the house?" Harrow asked, obviously wanting to divert the child while he conferred with his mother.

Silas, after reaching his room, begged to be relieved from any more walking and plopped into a chair. Vashti promptly curled up at his feet. Although she was further in her recovery than was Silas, she hadn't quite regained the robustness typical of her fellow lupines. It would come with time. As Mr. Murphy led me to my room, Daniel followed behind us in the curious manner of a child. After intoning that my bags would be brought up directly, the butler, with all the enthusiasm of a stick of wood, bowed out.

"What kind of dog is this?" Daniel asked, looking at Kipp, who put on his happy dog routine.

"Just an American breed," I answered. "He likes little boys and is very friendly."

Daniel cut the all too familiar Harrow blue gray eyes up at me, unsure if I was being honest with him. But, after a moment's hesitation, he walked over to Kipp and tentatively reached out his hand to gently pat Kipp on the head. It was obvious that Daniel missed his mother, and for all the mysterious reasons why creatures are drawn to one another, he was drawn to me. I had two Harrow men, it seemed, who found me irresistible. In less than five minutes, he was stretched out on the floor of my room, tickling Kipp's belly and laughing when Kipp would kick his legs in response. There was a polite tap on my door, which was half open; it was Harrow, who was careful to not barge into a room occupied by a female guest.

"Daniel, it is impolite for a gentleman to, uh, be in a lady's room." Harrow tried to frown but failed. "I intended upon showing Miss Hathaway our gardens, so why don't you come with us, and you can demonstrate your knowledge of trees and flowers."

It was a nice transition, and Kipp and I completed the foursome as we went downstairs and out the front door. Kipp initiated an amusing game of chase and tag with Daniel, who looked as if he failed to get sufficient play time outdoors. Kipp, with his inherently gentle nature, felt compassion for the boy and wanted to be viewed as a friend.

"Since you have more knowledge about children than do I, I would value your opinion," Harrow began, as we slowly strolled behind the gamboling pair of Kipp and Daniel.

"Well, I don't know that I agree with that assessment but proceed," I said, smiling up at him.

"Daniel is being smothered here. My mother, who cares for him, is so consumed with the loss of my brother, that she controls Daniel. She doesn't understand the nature of being nurturing…in fact, she never did." Harrow paused to lean forward and pick up a fallen oak leaf. He began to inspect it as if all the knowledge he sought was to be found in the shape and texture of that discarded piece of nature. "There have been a succession of nurses and governesses, but the moment they try to exert any type of influence, my mother discharges them." He stopped walking and turned to look at me. "I fear an unhealthy development for Daniel." We began walking again as I politely waited for him to continue.

"I told my mother that I am taking Daniel to London with me for a while." He laughed without mirth. "She is livid, but I am his legal guardian, and she cannot stop me." Harrow stopped walking again, pausing until I made eye contact. "I fear I am not skilled at being a parent, since I've never done anything like it, but I must try."

reached out and lightly touched his arm. "You underestimate yourself, Will. I've seen you with the boys; you are very warm, and they respond to you."

High pitched laughter caught my attention, and I glanced at Daniel who was throwing a stick for Kipp to fetch and retrieve.

"Petra, what's this game he's playing with me, and why's it funny when I bring him the stick?" Kipp was clearly confused at the intricacies of fetch.

"We'll talk about it later, Kipp," I responded. "Just chase the stick."

Harrow gave me one of those intense glances that he seemed to reserve just for me. "Thank you, Petra, for being honest and supportive. It gives me strength to do the thing I must."

Of course, I felt like dirt. Yes, I was supportive, but honestly…I wasn't so sure of that. How do you tell a man, yes, I may look like you but I'm really not at all like you? And by the way, I'm a time traveling telepath, in case you wondered. Over my lifespan, there had been many times when I was not happy having to be covert about my nature, and this was one of those times. The other time had been with Perdy, but that seemed ages ago.

* * *

We only stayed three days at the country estate. Mrs. Harrow actually announced on the first morning after our arrival that she was traveling to York to visit a cousin. Harrow was horrified at her lapse in manners and worried I would be offended. Little did he know that I was constructed like a Sherman tank on two legs—symbionts were tough, and 400 years of experiences had given me the ability to toss away human disdain like a feather. Her aura was so negative that it was a relief when the door closed behind her and her tiny entourage.

Silas was not interested in a lot of physical activity, so he stayed in the library while Harrow took me, Daniel, Vashti and Kipp riding in the country in one of the spacious estate carriages. The groomsman, unlike our humble John Parks in London, was dressed in a fancy, spotless uniform decorated with more braid than anything I owned. For a change, I sat next to Harrow and watched as a happy Daniel sat between Vashti and Kipp, his arms around their massive necks. His thoughts and feelings were complex for such a young child, obviously the result of catastrophic loss. The presence of what he thought to be large dogs helped him to feel safe, and some of the ever present anxiety abated somewhat.

When we finally departed for London on the third day, the tension that had been hovering around Harrow like a storm cloud dissipated, and he almost visibly gave a sigh of relief.

"I've been gone so long, that I feel unnatural when I return," he commented as the carriage left the drive and began winding its way along a country road towards the small, rural train station. A breeze had picked up and dark clouds were gathering on the horizon. Thankfully, we would be back in London before dark.

"Well," Silas remarked, "you can't go home again." He smiled at me, pleased at his cleverness.

"A very perceptive observation," Harrow remarked, nodding his dark head.

"And a shameless theft from Thomas Wolfe," I replied, glancing at Silas.

"I am not familiar with him," Harrow said, his brow

furrowing slightly.

"An obscure American novelist," Silas commented, trying not to smile again. He enjoyed the subtle back and forth between us.

Silas and Harrow took the seat across from me in the train compartment. After a moment's hesitation, Daniel came over and sat close to me. When fatigue threatened him, he leaned against my arm and closed his eyes. I put my arm around his shoulders, and he snuggled in closer. It was hard to avoid the glance from Harrow, one of appreciation as well as tenderness.

Kipp rested his muzzle on the toe of my boot. "It's obvious, Petra, that the child misses his mother, and he will quickly become attached to you. You must, sooner than later, start planting the seed that you won't be here forever. I'd advise Harrow to find a governess quickly so that someone else can become a constant in the boy's life."

Kipp was younger than I, but often he spoke with more wisdom. He was correct of course, and I would speak to Harrow about the issue in private. But, for the moment, the child's stress was lessened. In fact, the moment we removed him from the dreary mausoleum of his grandmother's home, he began to make an effort at healing his pain. He'd learned, at much too early an age, that life was unpredictable and not safe. I was happy he viewed his uncle as a comforting and dependable refuge.

The trip back to London was quiet and uneventful; Silas remained absorbed in a book while Harrow read the paper. I closed my eyes and almost allowed myself to drift off to sleep due to the gentle rocking of the carriage. At Victoria Station, Harrow hired a carriage, and we were home within the hour. Twilight had fallen, and the western sky was crisscrossed with strands of purple and pink clouds. Harrow lifted an exhausted Daniel in his arms to carry him inside. I followed and wasn't particularly surprised to see that the thoughtful Harrow had one of the bedrooms transformed into a little boy's room in our absence. The huge, overpowering four poster bed was gone, and a much smaller,

Daniel-sized bed was in its place. The room had been painted a cheery yellow and there was a pretty mural of a pastoral scene on one wall.

"This is just lovely," I said, meeting Harrow's gaze. "It was kind of you to do this."

He shrugged his shoulders in response and pushed his hands into his pockets. As he looked around the room, I could see satisfaction on his face. "I thought he'd feel more at home." Harrow raised his eyes to mine. "Your friend, Ramon, painted the mural," he said, lifting his eyebrows with the remark.

As Kipp and I went to our room, I reflected on recent developments. In a span of three days, William Harrow had confronted his mother, which, in itself, was an amazing feat. Her remote and cold attitude had framed a lifetime of hurt between the two of them; his refuge in the city was an obvious avoidance of her. Then, he took his nephew from her control in an effort to steer the boy in a different trajectory.

"I didn't know mothers could feel that way about their children," Kipp said, as he climbed into bed next to me. For a moment, he reverted to the mind of an orphaned pup as he remembered his own cherished mother before she died.

"You and I were blessed to have mothers who loved us and cared about our welfare. But, Kipp, mothers can come to that, uh, role, with pain from past hurt. Sometimes they are just not able to nurture and feel it in their hearts. I think that applies to Mrs. Harrow more than most."

Kipp pushed closer to me. "I still miss my mother," he said. Quickly he added, "But that doesn't mean I don't love you, Petra."

I scratched the place between his ears that was a favorite tickle spot. "Kipp, I can never take the place of your mother. It's right that you should miss her."

With that last comment, I tried to purge the memory of William Harrow's unhappy mother from my mind. It would please me to have a night of dreams free from torment.

CHAPTER 22

"Silas, I'd like your opinion about something," I said, taking a seat across from him in one of the metal chairs in the small garden behind the town house. We'd gone outside with Kipp and Vashti and watched them while they ate and prowled around the garden, searching out nature in the manner of lupines.

Silas raised an eyebrow but remained silent. Our relationship was not a comfortable one for either of us. It is completely unfair to judge the son by knowledge one has of the father. Philo was my oldest, most trusted friend. And, to be quite frank, Silas was a pale shadow of someone I admired. I saw a trait in him that concerned me: his cynical disdain for humans was the overt expression of a symbiont who felt superiority to the human species. Such thoughts had led our kind astray in the past. I had made so many mistakes in my dealings with humans that they could fill one of Fitzhugh's volumes, but I never felt superior to human beings.

"How do you think we manage, when we time shift, to have the least impact possible on the natural progression of time and events?" I felt a frown pull at my face. "We are under the ethical obligation to not affect history, but I often wonder how that is possible?"

Overhead, clouds were clustering in dark gray bunches,

and it seemed we were in for another storm; the heavy air was damp with the threat of rain. Harrow and Mac were at the school for an odd Saturday meeting of the board of trustees. I'd urged Harrow to take Daniel with him; in the end, he conceded. Vashti and Kipp stopped their wandering and came over to join in the philosophical discussion that had to do with the nature of our species.

"Can one cross a dusty floor without leaving paw prints?" Vashti asked. "I think it is impossible to completely avoid altering history. Right now, for example, Daniel is having an unexpected, new experience by knowing all of us. It will change him on some developmental level."

"I think it's a fine line, Petra," Kipp remarked. "When we travelled back to the North Carolina colony, we inadvertently changed history when we became involved with a killer. Now, in the end, perhaps all of those people we encountered would have met the same fate, but we will never know."

Silas listened thoughtfully, the ability for which I'd given him scant credit. "Petra, I am involved with the *Telegraph*. People there will have a memory of me, so in that way, their lives are different. There will always be a certain element of that which is uncontrollable." He hesitated, wanting to say more, but stopped.

I put down my teacup on the small metal table; the Earl Grey was only a memory with a few, lonely tea leaves languishing in the bottom of the white porcelain vessel.

"Go on," I said.

"Your problem is that you've had the misfortune for William Harrow to fall in love with you." Silas shrugged his shoulders. "You can only think that when you leave this time and return home, he will reset his life and move on."

"So it's that obvious?" I asked, grimacing slightly.

"I removed myself from his thoughts at your insistence, but it doesn't require telepathy. It's there every time he looks at you." Silas smiled. "I'm sorry to upset you," he said lamely, not really meaning it.

Vashti nodded her pretty head. "Yes, Petra. He's

consumed with thoughts of you."

"Well, great," I replied. "I guess that goes with being wonderful," I said in a self-mocking way. "So what do I do about it?"

Kipp addressed me in the profoundly honest manner that only one's closest friend can offer. "Petra, we are committed to stay here until after the Jack the Ripper phenomenon is over. The feelings that Harrow has for you won't disappear if we leave today or at some point later this year." He walked forward and put his big noggin on my knees. "You didn't encourage his feelings. I think if you deliberately baited him, it would be wrong. When we finally leave, he will not see you again, and his life will be forced to fulfill its natural arc." He grabbed my hand in his jaws and gave me a little nip. "Settle yourself and stick to one of the reasons why we're here—you and I are exploring the boundaries of our unique bond." Kipp met my eyes, and I was reminded of how much love and trust we shared. "And in the meantime, is there anything wrong with enjoying yourself a little?"

I laughed, more than a little self conscious in the face of an audience. "You know, when I was younger, I worried much less over semantics. But then you get four hundred years under your belt and suddenly the world looks to be a much more serious place." I smoothed the auburn fur on Kipp's head. "You're right, Kipp."

A short time later, Kipp and I retired to our room, and I fell asleep without delay. Almost immediately, I became entangled in some deep level of a dream state and felt like I was fighting quicksand to pull myself free. Finally, however, I awoke. Kipp, next to me, was shaking his head to clear his mind of his dreams, too.

"Did you hear that?" Kipp asked. The room was dark with some faded, minimal illumination from a full moon that hovered outside my windows.

Yes, I'd heard it, too—the voice of someone in distress.

But since neither of us detected audible cues, it must have been telepathic and severe enough to waken us. Then, we heard it again.

"It's Daniel," Kipp said.

I rose and pulled on my dressing gown; Kipp hopped down as I lit a lamp. Quietly, so as not to disturb the others, we eased from our room and down the hall to the yellow room that Harrow had so thoughtfully decorated for his nephew. Pushing open the door, I could see the form of the child as he tossed and turned in dream-induced agitation. Kipp and I both entered into his thoughts—dreams of the deaths of his mother and father consumed him. In his child's mind, there was a large tiger that was pursuing his parents. He, Daniel, was chasing the tiger and kept trying to catch its tail in order to stop it and save his mother and father from death. He would reach out and grab the striped tail, only to have it pull free from between his fingers. In the vivid and inexplicable manner of dreams, he had the tactile sensation of feeling the fur slide tantalizing along his flesh.

Without pause, Kipp entered the dream and ran alongside Daniel; the boy leapt upon Kipp's back and, with Kipp's speed, was able to race ahead of the tiger. When they caught his fleeing parents, they likewise jumped on Kipp's back, and he saw them to safety. The child's anxiety dissipated, and his tortured face and body relaxed in the bed. Then, Kipp gently brought him to awakening. The Harrow blue gray eyes opened and blinked a few times as he stared at us in confusion.

I sat on the edge of the bed and reached out to smooth his ruffled black hair. "You were dreaming, Daniel, but all is well. You are safe." His yearning for his lost parents was working like a vise on my heart.

"Why do people have to die, and where do they go?" His face was staring up at me, pale and rigid in the yellow glow from my lamp.

"Daniel, the simplest way to explain it would be to tell you that we have a life on earth, in our bodies like we are now." I smiled and took his hand. "Like this, my hand touches yours and we feel flesh and warmth. Then, for all creatures, at some point we no longer need our bodies, and we go to another life of spirit." I didn't go to the overt religious explanation since I had no idea what he'd been taught about God and Heaven and wanted to avoid a theologically based discussion. "Your parents are in their spirit life. And while you miss them, they are still with you in their spirit life and can look down and enjoy watching you grow up."

"Will Kipp have a spirit life one day?" he asked. Kipp hopped up onto the bed and nestled next to him. Daniel threw one slender arm across Kipp's broad body, the limb almost becoming lost in the dense auburn pelt. Kipp placed his head gently across the boy's chest.

"Most certainly," I replied.

"So my parents are watching me now?" Daniel said.

I nodded. "I believe that."

Daniel sighed deeply. "I've been told that I have to be brave, but I don't want to always be brave."

I put my hand on his cheek. "Being brave doesn't mean that you cannot cry or feel sad or have bad dreams." Smiling again, I said, "You are a very brave boy. You just miss your parents."

His eyes welled up for a moment but he pulled back the tears. "Can Kipp stay in here with me tonight?"

I knew Kipp's thoughts as he enthusiastically agreed. "Why, of course," I replied.

I rose, after giving Daniel a kiss on his cheek. Taking my lamp, I crossed the room…to my surprise, Harrow was standing at the doorway as I exited.

"What happened?" he asked. He was wearing his clothes from the day, without his jacket. The normally crisp white shirt was rumpled, and the top three buttons were unfastened, exposing his throat and a little of his chest; his tie hung loose around his neck. I wondered if he ever really went to bed or just sat up, dozing, in the library.

"I heard him cry out," I replied.

"Odd, I heard nothing," he responded. The hallway was dark, save for the tiny island of light from my lamp. It felt intimate in the quiet, early morning hours.

"I have exceptionally acute hearing. Daniel seems to gain comfort from Kipp," I continued. "He might benefit from having a dog." I turned to go but stopped myself. "Have you made progress in finding a governess for him?"

He lifted his shoulders in a shrug. "I've begun inquiries," he replied simply.

I decided it was time to remind him that I would be leaving at some point. "I fear Daniel might get too attached to me because of the void left by the death of his mother. The sooner you can get a female presence connected with him that can provide some constancy in his life, the better. I don't want him to grieve over my leaving when I go home."

There, I'd said it. The expression on his face pained me as I deliberately blocked his thoughts from my mind. But in the way of a well bred, controlled man, he pulled himself together and gave a quick smile.

"Yes; you are correct, of course. I will speak with the agency and ask them to work more diligently. There needs to be someone who can commit to Daniel over the long term. He's had too much change in his life for one so young." He kept his voice purposefully low as he accompanied to my room and deposited me at the doorway after giving a slight bow. Unexpectedly, he reached out and took my hand; his lips brushed the back of it in a fleeting touch that felt both cool and hot simultaneously.

"Thank you for seeing to Daniel, Petra." Looking up, his eyes met mine. "You are benefiting his life in many ways. I liked your explanation of death, making something that can be difficult to comprehend seem natural." He released my hand. "And, I will see about a puppy, too."

The expression in his beautiful eyes almost left me breathless as I backed into my room and shut the door behind me. As I climbed into bed and pulled the light cotton covers to my chin, Kipp's mind touched mine.

"Well, that was interesting, Petra," he remarked with

humor. "Bet you're gonna have some really spicy dreams tonight."

"Oh, shut up, Kipp, and go to sleep."

"Why can't I go to school with you?" Daniel asked, looking up at Harrow as we sat at the breakfast table the next morning. The fragrance of freshly prepared breakfast fare filled the room and hung over those of us present like a heavenly cloud.

Harrow carefully set down his fork and stared across the table at the boy. "Eat your breakfast, Daniel," he responded.

"But why can't I?" Daniel asked again, persistent in the way of a child.

Harrow looked at me and then Mac. Silas and Vashti were absent; John Parks was busy taking Silas to the *Telegraph* for a meeting with the city editor. John would be back any moment to take Harrow, Mac, Kipp and me to the school as per our usual routine.

"Why not?" I asked. Since I was an American, and uncouth to boot, I could get away with ignoring society's dictates.

Harrow stared down at his plate. I knew him to be an exceptionally good man as well as recognizing the fact he was raised in a society that was highly structured with class distinctions. Even his feelings for me flew in the face of what was expected of him. I saw that reflected on the face of his mother when she first met me.

Mac caught my eyes and smiled. He knew Harrow better than anyone and loved him as a brother. But he, too, was of a different class as outlined by the current societal rules. Harrow looked up and glanced at Mac, who shrugged his shoulders before returning his attention to the cup of coffee in his hand.

When Harrow returned his gaze to me, a faint smile crossed his face. "Yes, why not," he said, and it was not a question.

So it was that Daniel began accompanying us to school

on a daily basis. He sat on my side of the carriage, his arm around Kipp's broad back. My thoughts were that the children at the school had all faced some type of trauma in their young lives. But they were tough survivors who had learned to adapt to the misfortunes in their lives. Daniel could learn much from them. In my small class of incorrigibles, it was to be the mischievous ginger-headed leader, Allen, who would connect with Daniel.

"Don't you worry, Miss Hathaway," he said to me, with a nod of confidence. "I'll show him what's what."

If I had not been a telepath, that last enigmatic comment might have left me with concern. But Allen, despite some hardening by the streets, had a basically kind nature. I was glad Harrow had rescued him before he was so enmeshed with a life of despair that he might become unsalvageable.

Our class was progressing. Some of the earlier clashes with authority had abated, and, for the most part, my leadership was respected. I kept the challenges to their brains and individual gifts ongoing. For Allen, Harrow arranged to have a friend of his who had a degree in mathematics to come to the school and challenge the boy with a series of complex word problems. I recalled those from school myself and had never fared well.

The shadows seemed to fall from Daniel's face as the days progressed. As I watched, he and the boys from my class were kicking a ball in the small courtyard behind the school; Harrow had it fenced to provide a safe play area. Daniel got tangled up with Simon, and both boys went down hard in the dirt. Daniel sat up, shocked at the impact at first; a couple of the other boys were shouting at him, in the impatient manner of children, to get up and pass the ball. He looked up at me, laughed, and hopped to his feet. Somehow, Kipp grabbed the ball in his large jaws and took off with the gang of boys in pursuit.

"I've not seen him look so in a long time." Harrow had quietly approached, and I was so focused on the boys that I didn't pick up on his proximity. He took his place at my side, and it seemed somehow natural to me that he should be there. In another place and time, I might have reached my hand down to clasp his, letting our fingers intertwine.

I turned and looked up at him. "Yes, I think being with boys who have survived their own losses has been good for him."

Harrow took a deep breath. "My mother would be completely horrified, of course, as would many of my contemporaries."

"Does it matter?" I asked. Reaching up, I smoothed back a strand of hair that had escaped the cluster of hairpins used to confine my heavy, dark hair.

His eyes followed the movement of my hand. "No, it doesn't. We happen to live in a very rigid, unforgiving society. I learned, in the military, that the background of the man next to you does not matter. What is important is his character and the trust you have placed in him." He sighed and looked at Daniel. "I hope to raise Daniel to be able to understand that." Harrow laughed as Daniel managed to wrestle the ball free from Kipp, whose tongue was lolling out. It was warm in mid-summer London.

"They are killing me, Petra," Kipp whined, glancing over at me.

"On a bright note, I've a friend who has a dog which had a litter of puppies. There is one left who has had a little basic training, in, uh, manners. We are, after school, to take Daniel over and let him have her, if he wishes."

Later that day, John Parks drove us home; I'd learned to appreciate the amount of skill it took to navigate the busy streets of London. Daniel was cradling a small terrier pup on his lap.

"Thank you, Uncle William," he said. Daniel's eyes were bright as he looked up at us.

"Just remember that she is your responsibility," Harrow said, trying to sound stern while attempting to not smile at the puppy which was licking Daniel's chin. Her pink tongue flicked out from a muzzle covered with bristles of brown fur. Harrow reached across the carriage and scratched the pup's head with his forefinger.

"What will you name her?" I asked. Before Daniel could think about it, Kipp shoved a name into his unresisting brain.

"Uh, Lily," he responded. Obviously, Kipp decided to infuse a little piece of home into the situation.

"Why Lily?" Harrow asked.

"I don't know," Daniel responded. "I just thought of it."

I stared at Kipp, narrowing my eyes; he turned his head and looked out the window of the carriage, humming a pleasant tune in the back of his mind, as he chose to ignore me.

At home, we were exiting the carriage when Harrow took me aside. "Petra, may I have a word, please?" He walked towards the small patio at the rear of the house, leaving me to follow. Daniel scampered ahead to show off Lily to the house staff; Mac followed, laughing at something he said. Kipp trailed after me, his head cocked to one side in curiosity.

"Dr. Treves has arranged to take Joseph Merrick to a play." Harrow paused, uncharacteristically uncertain how to proceed with me. "I know Treves well, since I am on the hospital board. It seems that Mr. Merrick requested that you and Kipp accompany him to the play," he said, nodding at my companion who was sitting politely.

"Let's go, Petra," Kipp said with excitement. "I've never seen a play, and we don't even have to think of a way to connive an invitation for me since I've already been included."

Before I could respond, Harrow continued, perhaps hoping he could make the invitation more enticing. "The play is quite popular—*Dr. Jekyll and Mr. Hyde.* The lead is played by the well known American actor, Richard Mansfield." His blue gray eyes met mine. We were standing in the small garden to the rear of the town house; the scents of countless flowers in full bloom comingled to make the air sweet. "As I said, it is very popular." His voice drifted off.

"Kipp, did you manufacture this?" I asked, feeling more

than a little put out with him. He was taking way too much liberty with inserting thoughts into human minds.

He stared at me with mock insult written all over his lupine face.

"You did, didn't you!" I knew then that Kipp had planted the thought in Joseph Merrick's mind. "Remind me the next time I ask you about ethics to discuss this moment with you."

"Petra?" Harrow had been left waiting.

"Why, of course," I replied, smiling at him. The relief on his face was evident. No one, human or symbiont, in this century or the next, likes to be turned down for a date. "It sounds very interesting."

"The date of the play is a week from today," he said. With a soft laugh he asked, "Will I need to send my driver?"

It was nice to see him have a little fun with our discourse. He relaxed, but not often enough for my way of thinking. It was Saturday, and we planned to take Daniel, Lily, Kipp and Vashti to St. Regent's park on the morrow, if the weather held. Through no deliberate action of my own, I was becoming a member of this little family. It was approaching mid-summer and the first murder would occur on August 31st. The passage of time would escalate rapidly as of that moment.

CHAPTER 23

The Lyceum was one of the more popular theaters in London. Treves knew the owner personally and arranged to use his private box to accommodate our eclectic party. The good-natured and dependable John Parks was to drive us.

Even if one does not possess an abundance of narcissism, it's normal to glance in a mirror and recognize one's appearance is acceptable. The coral dress was, for me, a perfect blend of color, fabric, fit and style. I was not by nature a frilly girl, and it seemed the dressmaker had discerned such from her brief contact with me. The dress was understated and beautiful. I had no suitable jewelry for adornment; my one cameo pin really didn't suit the style of the gown, which had a lovely portrait neckline. Jean, in her shy but skilled way, worked on my hair and managed to sweep it into a dramatic up do with cascades of curls trailing down my neck. She planted the tiny pillbox hat in the midst of my hairdo.

"Oh, miss!" she exclaimed. "You just look so pretty. The master won't be able to watch Dr. Jekyll for looking at you."

Of course, the remark was both ill-spoken and humorous, and I was forced to laugh in response. Kipp, on the floor, looked up at me and thumped his tail vigorously against the polished hardwood.

"Gosh, Petra. I didn't know you could look so good!"

I cut my eyes at him and darted a few severe thoughts his way.

It was quiet in the house that afternoon. Mac had taken Daniel and Lily to the park again and planned on staying out most of the day. Silas and Vashti were gone, as usual; Silas had re-engaged his position at the *Telegraph* and was busy on the street, developing the connections needed by a good reporter. When he wasn't in Whitechapel, he was at London Yard or the local police office so that he would become a trusted face for law enforcement. Silas was quickly becoming a visible figure in the area. Being a symbiont had its advantages, and since he was using his skills in pursuit of a work project, he was not violating ethics by using his telepathy to gain knowledge. I was glad we had achieved an uneasy truce in our relationship with one another.

Jean had polished my boots, which were unsuitable but all I had to wear. Great, I thought, looking down in dismay at my feet…leave it to me to wear a pair of clodhoppers with my pretty gown.

Kipp laughed but was reassuring. "Petra, your gown is long and no one will see them."

Of course, he was wrong. As I descended the staircase, Harrow waited at the base, watching me. His face lit up at my approach, and his eyes were frankly appraising. Then, they dropped to my feet and saw the boots. He tried to compose his expression but failed miserably.

"I forgot that I needed new shoes, too," I remarked, too old to be embarrassed but disappointed my grand entrance was marred by a fashion nightmare.

Harrow took my hand and leaned over it, brushing it gently with his lips. "Charming and with a tinge of eccentricity," he replied. "A very pleasant duo of characteristics." He glanced up and the blue gray eyes stared into mine. "And with such a lovely face, no one will be compelled to look at your feet."

He did not release my hand and led me to the front

drawing room. Kipp followed, tail wagging, enjoying the moment. The late afternoon sun was slanting in through the ceiling to floor length windows, bathing the room in a pinkish glow. Harrow released me and walked to the mantle, where he retrieved a small, black velvet box. He handed it to me and stepped back.

"For me?" I asked, feeling stupid for stating the obvious.

"Yes. Open it."

I lifted the lid and was delighted to see a tiny pearl necklace, perhaps 16 inches, designed to snug the neck. Of course, the piece was understated, elegant and beautiful; the perfection of nature was served best in the simplicity of the setting. And the necklace was just what I needed to finish the gown…well, some other shoes might have been nice, too.

"May I?" Harrow removed the necklace from its resting place and carefully placed it around my neck. His fingers lingered just a moment on my flesh as he managed the clasp.

There was a wall mirror in the room, and I walked forward to look at the pearls. Harrow approached; as I met his eyes in the reflection of the mirror, the moment became overtly personal, and I dropped my gaze.

"Thank you," I replied. "It's lovely, and I shall cherish it forever." When I turned, he was still looking at me with that disturbing expression of intensity. "Did you manage to pick up some shoes for me, too?" I asked.

That broke the fragile moment as he laughed. "No, I fear you are on your own, Petra."

At least I'd had presence of mind to procure a dressy cape and wouldn't be wearing the more utilitarian one I'd traveled in. So, with the cape in place and Kipp on one side and Harrow on the other, I began a trip that would be a novelty for me. John Parks removed his cloth cap, and his eyes opened a little wider. Yes, I cleaned up nicely from his perspective.

As Molly pulled us, uncomplainingly, along the busy streets, Harrow maintained a pleasant conversation while adroitly avoiding anything too personal. He did mention one thing that brought me happiness.

"I am investigating the possibility of sponsoring Allen in a private school." Harrow was gazing out the window of the carriage. "It won't be much longer before he eclipses our ability to challenge him." He turned quickly to me. "That is, of course, no slight upon you or your methods."

I laughed, not offended in the least. "You're correct, Will. Allen is much brighter than I, and don't think I don't recognize the fact." Smiling, I added, "Thank you for what you are doing for him as well as all the boys."

Kipp wagged his tail, happy over the turn of events. Harrow reached forward and patted his head.

"I think Kipp approves, too," he said.

Little did he know that was, indeed, the case.

The Lyceum was packed in a sold out showing. What might have been considered the more upper class sat on the main floor or in the boxes along the walls, while middle and lower middle class people converged in the second and third levels. The flickering of countless gas lanterns reflected an eerie glow as dancing shadows were cast upon the walls; the stage was set for a timeless drama infused with a tinge of horror and mystery.

Treves and Joseph Merrick had already taken their places but rose politely upon our arrival. Merrick, in the fashion of a gentleman, took my hand with his sound one and bowed over it as best he could. He was wearing a dress suit; his usual cape and hood were draped casually over the back of his chair.

"I'm so glad you could bring Kipp as my special guest," he said. "I don't know why, but the idea just popped into my head quite suddenly."

I stared at Kipp, narrowing my eyes. He looked away, and if he could have whistled, he might have done so. Yeah, play the innocent, my lad, I thought.

We took our seats. Harrow was to my left against the

wall of the box, while Merrick was on my right. Kipp lay on the floor between me and Merrick, and Treves was on the other side of Merrick. There was a pleasant chit chat ongoing as Treves courteously asked me about my experiences in London to date.

It was then I felt the toxic, disturbed thoughts that I'd experienced previously…the ones I associated with the man I believed to be Jack the Ripper. He was somewhere in the audience, gazing at the people, his mind filled with obsessive ruminations. He'd seen the play before and identified, to some degree, with the main character. For the most part, he thought of himself as a normal man who battled dark urges hidden within a placid exterior.

"There he is again," Kipp said, looking up at me.

"I don't want to be seen, since he might recognize us from before," I replied. Thinking quickly, I leaned towards Harrow. "I hate to admit this, but I become uneasy when sitting too close to a height," I remarked. "Would you object if I move my seat back just a little?"

Of course, he didn't; the other men were considerate and accommodating, and we shifted our positions back a foot or so. That minor adjustment pushed me so that I was concealed behind the swag of curtain that draped on the left side of the box. Although I tried to keep my focus on the play and respond appropriately at the right times, it was difficult. At certain moments in the drama, the thoughts of the budding serial killer would escalate, especially when there was a sense of a woman being threatened or placed in danger.

Harrow leaned towards me at one point. "Are you well, Petra?" he whispered. Obviously my tense body posture had caught his attention, as finely attuned to me as he was.

"Yes, thank you. I'm just enjoying the suspense," I replied. He reached out and lightly touched my shoulder in what he thought was a reassuring gesture.

He had no idea of the many brushes with death that I'd experienced as well as my having plundered through the darkest depths of many disturbed minds. No frail character was I. And there was no aspect of humanity that I had not viewed in my role of eavesdropping telepath.

Joseph Merrick reached down to stroke Kipp's back. What a gentle soul, I thought, watching his unaffected hand and fingers thread delicately through Kipp's dense, ruddy fur.

"It's amazing that he lacks bitterness for all that has been done to him because of his appearance," Kipp remarked. "I'm glad we came; I've learned more than I might have suspected."

The play was ongoing, and I partitioned off a part of my brain to keep up with the dialog and action while simultaneously querying Kipp.

"Tell me," I requested, always interested in viewing the world through Kipp's eyes versus my own, which admittedly could be somewhat jaded.

"Well, in regards to Joseph Merrick, I have seen someone who could have turned to darkness but chose otherwise. It makes me wonder if some people are just born with a good heart and soul." He paused for a moment. "The boys at the school fill me with hope in terms of the basic human spirit. They could have been crushed by circumstances but show that amazing ability of humans to adapt and push forward. Daniel, likewise, could be damaged by the loss of his parents, but he is willing to conform to a new life situation and seek happiness.

"And, in terms of Harrow, I enjoy being in the presence of a good man who has such a capacity to do things that positively affect the lives of others. He could have allowed his upbringing by a distant and cold mother to lead him to be isolative and remote, but the opposite is true. And I am learning the most by experiencing his growing love for you. It's an aspect of humanity I had not experienced to this degree."

I glanced over at Harrow and caught him, unguarded, in profile. Instinct must have warned him he was under inspection because he turned his head to catch my eyes. We stared at one another too long for casual comfort. My heart squeezed to the point my chest hurt, just a little bit. As I sat there in the box at the Lyceum, while avoiding the floating, disconnected thoughts of a serial killer that swirled in the air like a heavy fog, I realized I'd fallen in love with one William Harrow…a human man, and definitely off limits to my kind. I turned my head away in confusion and stared at the stage, but the dialog and activity was lost to me. Kipp, recognizing my state, moved a little closer and propped his head on one of my utilitarian boots.

"Petra, I'm here and will always be here for you," Kipp said. "Even if we go through some difficult times and heartbreak as a team, I'm not going anywhere."

"Thanks, Kipp," I responded. If I'd been using my voice, I think my words would have broken up through emotion. As it was, Kipp knew the content of my head as well as my heart and no explanation was necessary.

I remembered Fitzhugh's story of having fallen in love with a human woman. Odd, I'd thought him incapable of strong, emotional attachments until I saw him with Lily— the cat, Lily, not Daniel's young dog. And, unexpectedly, Fitzhugh finally expressed his growing fondness for me. Our kind was similar to humans in so many ways that I guess the progression towards love between us was not so strange after all. But it was awkward and untenable, and that was an undeniable fact.

Harrow, with characteristic thoughtfulness, did not ask John Parks to wait or come back to retrieve us, since the hour would be late. His plan was to hire a cab, but Treves offered to have his driver, after taking Merrick back to the hospital, retrieve us and take us to Mayfair. As we left the Lyceum, since the weather was very nice, Harrow told Treve's coachman that we would begin a slow walk and could be found on the Strand. After sitting for so long, I embraced the mild exercise. The gas lanterns flanking the street flickered and hissed softly; overhead, a partial moon glowed behind the fogbank that hovered around us. I don't think I could have imagined a more stereotypical stroll along a Victorian era London street.

"What did you think of the play?" Harrow asked. He looked elegant with a silk top hat resting upon his black hair; a lightweight dress overcoat extended to his knees. His limp was more noticeable, probably because he had sat too long at the theatre. The silver capped walking stick tapped out our progress.

What began as a pleasant perambulation changed in an instant as I felt a shiver crawl up my spine. Unconsciously, I pulled my cape a little closer around my shoulders. It was not cool by any means, but I was responding to the familiar thoughts of the unseen madman who lurked close by, concealed by the shadows.

"Oh, it was captivating," I replied evenly while simultaneously trying to delve into the mind of the serial killer who was obviously following us.

"He recognizes us, Petra," Kipp said. "I shouldn't have come along…my size and appearance caught his attention at the park and again tonight."

The nameless horror took pleasure in prowling the shadowed street while keeping me just in view as we would pass beneath a gaslight. He allowed his mind to drift into fantasy as he calculated the manner of my murder. Despite his dark thoughts, I didn't believe I was really at risk. Jack the Ripper arrogantly killed women of the street because he erroneously believed society would not care if women of a certain class disappeared. I was an improbable target. His thoughts, however, became so disturbing that I actually took a bad step and lurched against Harrow, who protectively caught my arm.

"Are you certain you are well?" he asked, turning his wonderful eyes on me.

"I'm wearing my clumsy boots, in case you forgot," I replied, trying to lighten the moment.

I needed to halt my telepathic inspection of the man who trailed behind us on the dimly lit avenue but could not make myself turn away. Finally, Kipp sprang to the rescue and efficiently threw one of his mental blocks between me and the madman.

Harrow neatly tucked my arm up into the crook of his elbow and gently secured my hand with his. "There...now if you fall, I'll catch you."

Kipp stopped and turned to gaze into the darkness we'd just left. Calmly, he folded his haunches under his large body and sat, eyes half closed, waiting. No one, not even a lunatic, would challenge Kipp, and the man must have melted away because Kipp released his block on my telepathy and rejoined us as Treve's carriage arrived. A young footman hopped down from the box and assisted me into the vehicle. Pulling the coral fabric inside and settling it so that I didn't look like a buoy floating in a peach ocean was an effort all of its own making.

As we returned to Mayfair, I managed to keep pace with Harrow's pleasant discourse, but it was a challenge for me. The brief journey I'd made into the hell that was Jack the Ripper's twisted mind had left me feeling disturbed and, quite frankly, unhappy. There was no way that I could resolve within myself the fact that Silas and I would stand by and not act while Jack the Ripper killed five innocent women. Maybe that was one reason why trips to certain points in time were ill advised. In my research with Fitzhugh, it was not uncommon for travelers to suffer negative psychological impact due to having landed in the midst of a traumatic point on the time continuum. Harrow escorted me into the house; in the front parlor, Silas and Mac were playing chess. Both men stood, courteously. Mac nodded his head and smiled.

"Miss Hathaway...I mean Petra....you look very lovely tonight. Did you enjoy the theatre?"

Mac had proved himself to be a consistently good-hearted man, and I liked him immensely. He possessed a character that was unshakably solid, and I appreciated the unquestionable quality of his loyalty to Harrow.

"Yes, thank you. It was a very pleasant evening," I responded.

Most games played, when pitting a symbiont against a human, were just basically unfair with the odds stacked against the human. With that thought in mind, I gazed at Silas in what was obviously a questioning manner. While assisting Fitzhugh, I ran across a story of a symbiont who went on a vacation of riverboat gambling in the 1800's along the Mississippi River. He basically stole every game and cheated his way to infamy.

"I'm not cheating, Petra, so you can wipe that look off your face." Silas's unspoken thoughts met mine. Vashti rose from her place of comfort on the rug and met Kipp with a little head bump and a soft growl.

"We need to talk, Silas," I said. "Something happened tonight that was unexpected and unpleasant."

He waited for a convenient lull in the conversation before suggesting that he and I needed to take the "dogs" outside for a breath of fresh air.

"Silas, Kipp and I have somehow managed to attract the attention of the man I believe to be Jack the Ripper." I took a deep breath. "He actually followed me and Harrow tonight, consumed with thoughts of physical mutilation and murder." Nodding at Kipp, I added, "Kipp had to throw a block to distract me because the thoughts became so intense."

Silas took a seat in one of the garden chairs on the patio to the rear of the townhouse. Overhead, a mild wind began to stir the trees causing the leaves to rustle; one lonely leaf, detached from its home, began a death spiral towards earth.

"What did you make of him, Kipp?" Silas asked.

"It was difficult to tweak out a pathway, since his thoughts are defined by overwhelming rage. Somehow, I got the impression of dead people, and this leads me to think maybe he works in a mortuary or some similar place." Kipp walked over and put his head in my lap. "I think his thoughts toward Petra are just a buildup of tension as he gets closer to actually acting on his fantasies. It could have been anyone, but it's you," he said, addressing me. "He thinks you're an unrealistic target, and his thoughts are just that and lack the impetus for action."

My fingers threaded through Kipp's ruddy colored fur.

He tilted his head back as his eyes met mine; the amber color was almost glowing beneath the half moon above.

"I understand now why trips such as this are not readily taken, Silas," I said. "How will we both feel when the first woman is dismembered, and we possessed the knowledge to stop it, but didn't? It will weigh heavy on my heart."

Silas looked away from me. For a moment, his profile reminded me of Philo but sadly lacking the depth I associated with my friend.

"Petra, I know you don't trust me and really don't care for me. But believe it when I say that I don't look forward to the events that are coming." He turned his face towards me. "This is what we do. We travel to places and times that are, by their very nature, filled with conflict and sometimes horror and despair." His gaze drifted off past me as he stared into the darkness. "If we wanted to change history and felt god-like enough to do so, we could save countless lives. Such an action would violate our very being and purpose on earth."

In days to follow, I would think back on that conversation. I'd not thought Silas to be a reflective type of man, but he proved me wrong with a few words that helped me to refocus and remember my duties as well as my obligations.

CHAPTER 24

Unless our arrival had unexpectedly altered the time continuum, the first murder would take place on August 31. It was now mid-August, and there were only a couple of weeks left. Our lives, for the most part, were continuing in about the same pattern as before. Monday through Friday, Mac, Harrow and I would go to the school and work to hopefully improve the lives of some of the young boys who had found refuge from the rawness of the streets. The success of the school was becoming well known, and Harrow was constantly approached by his peers who wished to become involved. Some of the boys—such as Allen—with remarkable aptitude would be sponsored to move on to private schools With that thought in mind, Harrow approached me one morning during a lull in my class.

"Petra, I know this sounds rather frivolous and, on the base of it, silly, but for our boys who will progress to other settings, we need to teach them some basic manners. As it is, they obviously will not fit in well and will become subject to all sorts of cruelties, I fear. I don't want that to distract them from pursuing a solid education."

Well, he was correct in that all of that society jazz was ridiculous, but it was the reality of the day, and to ignore it would be equally ridiculous.

"What are your plans?" I asked. Kipp was sitting at my side, his thoughts curiously shuttered.

"I would like for you to help me teach them some, uh, rules of engagement," Harrow replied, smiling at me. I knew I must have made a face, unconsciously, because his smile broadened.

"Oh, Will, don't you remember I'm the one who wore the horrible boots with my dress gown to the theatre?" After taking a deep breath, I added, "And you know I can't even manage to pour a decent cup of tea without spilling it everywhere."

"But you will do it," Harrow replied, knowing that I would not refuse.

Kipp almost rolled on the floor in mirth. "Ha! Petra, you're gonna teach etiquette! I can hardly believe it."

Soon after, on a daily basis, we began some small lessons on polite discourse as well as proper ways to greet people, both men and woman. In short, we were trying to help them develop some sense of what it meant to be a gentleman. Harrow pretty much discouraged the use of street slang in the school so that the boys would use proper English for the most part; that fact, at least, helped us in our endeavor. As usual, Allen, the brightest of all our lads, was watching all that transpired with his keen eyes. At the moment, Harrow was demonstrating a firm handshake.

"It should not be so strong as to crush fingers but also not so weak as to appear insincere." Harrow walked around the room demonstrating with the boys before having them practice with one another; the boys were laughing as they played mock gentlemen.

"Master," Allen asked, "what do I do when meeting a lady, such as Miss Hathaway?"

"It depends upon the setting," Harrow replied. "Let me demonstrate." He walked to me. "Let's say I am walking along the street and meet an acquaintance who introduces me to Miss Hathaway. I would make brief eye contact, tip my hat and greet her." He pantomimed the action, lacking a real hat but pretending all the same.

The boys giggled a little, enjoying watching us in the guise of actors.

"However, if we are known to one another, I might reach out, take her hand, and bow slightly over her hand, like this," Harrow demonstrated. As he did so, his eyes met mine, too long for a casual greeting.

"Are you supposed to stare at her like that?" Allen asked. Nothing, no matter how understated or subtle, got past him.

Harrow's face flushed a little, and he wore a momentary look of confusion on his face.

"Mr. Harrow was demonstrating one thing you must not do with a lady, unless she is very well known to you. Staring is not the mark of a casual greeting," I said, trying to rescue Harrow, who, for once, seemed to not be able to find the words he needed.

Harrow finally engaged a governess for Daniel. She was a middle-aged woman with a kind, nurturing nature; Daniel took to her immediately. On occasions, he would still go to the school with us since Harrow felt that his time spent with boys of a similar age was good for his development. But his governess had the main responsibility for his early education. A portion of my guilt diminished as I watched her walk down the hallway with Daniel and Lily in tow. They were going to the park, and Daniel was singing a funny song as they marched along. When I finally left later in the fall, he would have a strong female figure with whom he had some emotional bond. She, Miss Douglas, asked if I wished to accompany them, but I declined. Daniel needed to grow his attachment for her, not me.

It was Saturday, mid-morning, and I walked to the kitchen. Mrs. Atherton was baking, and the smell of bread filled the lower level of the house. There was a large table in the center of the room, so I pulled up a chair and decided to hang out. Kipp trailed after me and picked a spot where he could flop down on the cool floor. The cook no longer stared at him as if he were a criminal.

"I know what that one wants," she said, pointing at Kipp with a spoon. "He wants my kidney pie."

"Oh, gosh, yes! Petra, please, tell her yes," Kipp almost started to drool.

"Well, Mrs. Atherton, everyone knows that your kidney pie is the tastiest in London. Kipp tells all the other dogs at the park, too, so you have a true reputation." I reached forward and pulled a cookie from a warming rack. It was ginger, and I almost fell out of my chair when I bit into the warm comfort of it. With the intuition of a remarkable servant, Mrs. Atherton prepared a pot of tea and set it in front of me.

"There, lass, you just enjoy yourself," she said, closing one eye in a comical wink.

It was pleasant in the kitchen. The wind whistled in through the high transom windows—which were open— managing to efficiently displace the heat from the oven.

Mrs. Atherton was in the midst of telling me about a story from her childhood—and I'd found her to be a remarkably funny story teller—when her head went up. I knew who'd entered the room, of course—Harrow walked in, a book in hand. He was casually dressed for him, with no waistcoat, even. His white shirt was open at the neck, and his tie had been left somewhere, probably in the library.

"What's this?" he asked, a smile on his face. "Are you having a party and failed to invite me?"

"I'm sorry, Mr. William," the cook began. "We were a bit too loud, I think."

"No, not at all. I just wanted to join the fun," he replied. "Is there tea left?"

He pulled out a chair at the end of the table next to me and reached for a cookie. I was simply proud that for once in my life I managed to pour the tea without making a mess.

"You did that quite well," Harrow remarked. "Maybe our etiquette lessons are helping you, too."

It was a funny and truthful observation, and I was forced

to laugh…Mrs. Atherton, too. In a short time, Mac joined us, and the three humans began sharing recollections from their pasts. I was encouraged, several times, to share some of my own. But how was I to respond, I wondered? *"Yes, there was that time I travelled back to ancient Egypt and violated the sanctity of a sacred temple…you should have seen me skedaddle when the palace guards caught me trying to nab a little statue! What a hoot!"*

"And then Mr. William went off to war," Mrs. Atherton was saying. I snapped to attention. "He and Mr. Mac served together and probably saved each other's lives more times than they will care to admit." She leaned forward, lowering her voice. "You know how men are, Miss Hathaway."

Mac was watching me, his expression soft and unreadable to all but a telepath. "Miss Hathaway—Petra, I mean—doesn't talk about herself, I've noticed. I'd learned that if one doesn't have a good response to a potentially dangerous comment, sometimes it is best to remain silent. With that wise counsel ringing in my ears, I chose to not speak."

Harrow's blue gray eyes met mine before he began to subject another ginger cookie to intense inspection. "I am content to know Petra by her actions as well as her kind heart. Whatever else that has gone before is of no consequence." He was giving me the rare unequivocal pass.

I glanced at Kipp. "I wonder if he would still think that way if he knew who we really are?" The reoccurring flash of guilt hit me again.

"He's in love with you, Petra," Kipp replied. "I know his mind, and he really doesn't care about your past. I guess that is one aspect of love that I'm learning—unconditional love. It is a beautiful quality of humans, when they can manage it. But I don't think it happens easily or often."

I decided to shift the attention away from me. "Mac, you don't speak much of your family." It was an observation that lacked prodding, so he was not compelled to disclose if he chose.

"Well, when I left for service, I found it changed me—I

was no longer the innocent lad my family knew. I have some brothers and sisters living in Scotland, but I don't know what to say to them, it seems." Mac shook his head. "My wife died quite some time ago." He looked down at the fragile teacup resting safely between his two, large hands. "I have a daughter, but she went off and got herself married to some Yank and went to America. We had a bit of a disagreement about her leaving, and she doesn't stay in contact anymore."

It was a sad commentary from a fine man, but such things happened in the world of humans as well as my own kind.

"I think you need to go to the park today, Mr. Mac," Mrs. Atherton remarked. She pushed the platter of cookies towards him. "Miss Douglas is there with Master Daniel, and I know that they both love fresh baked cookies."

Mac's dark eyes stared at her. "So, what are you about, Mrs. Atherton?"

"I'm tryin' to get you out of that chair, Mr. Mac, where you seem much too comfortable," she replied. "Miss Douglas is a fine woman with a good heart, and she's at the park taking the air with Master Daniel. I think she would enjoy seeing you on this fine summer day."

Mac's face reddened slightly as her meaning became clear. He cleared his throat and glanced at Harrow, who raised his eyebrows in a "Why not?" response.

Mac stood and put on his cloth cap, taking care to adjust it to the correct tilt and attitude.

"Where are you going?" I asked, looking up at him.

"I'm going to the park as soon as Mrs. Atherton bundles up some cookies."

After he left, Mrs. Atherton remarked, "All he needed was a little encouragement. It was clear, every time he looked at her, that he held an interest in such a fine woman."

Harrow laughed. "I didn't realize you are a matchmaker, Mrs. Atherton," he said, winking at me. "Who will be the next to fall to your machinations?"

She glanced up from the table where she was kneading bread dough. "Oh, I think I'll keep that a secret."

Her thoughts, however, were obvious to me. She knew Harrow held more than feelings of tenderness towards me. While she might have initially had some reservations about such, she had grown some fondness for me over time. And, to her credit, she cared not that I fell short of the appropriate social standing to be considered in the, uh, running, for the eligible bachelor, Harrow.

Harrow looked at me; his blue gray eyes dropped to my throat where the pearl necklace he'd given me rested against my flesh. He smiled, and I knew he was pleased that I wore his token.

"I've heard that one should wear pearls to enhance their luster," I began lamely, before my voice drifted off.

"I've heard that, too," he said. Our eyes were locked for a moment, and I lacked the resolve to look away.

Kipp walked up and nuzzled my hand. "Petra, I need to go outside." As always, he served as my faithful friend who knew my heart and wanted to shield me from pain. "Right now," he said, emphatically.

At Kipp's urging, I stood. Harrow rose from his chair in response.

"I need to take Kipp for a walk," I said, trying to speak with a strong, assertive tone. Maybe a change in venue would disrupt the almost hypnotic effect the man had on me.

"May I accompany you?" Harrow asked. "The day is pleasant, and I've sat too long reading." He didn't mention—nor had he ever—the injury to his leg that caused pain and stiffness.

There was no way in which I could politely decline. After I retrieved my bonnet, I met Harrow and Kipp at the front door. In the brief time I'd been gone, Harrow had managed to button his shirt, apply a tie to his neck and don a coat and hat. Perhaps outside the confines of the kitchen with its homemade cookies and fragrant tea, my sense of closeness with Harrow would dissipate so that I could rediscover my focus and purpose.

"I thought I might walk to a shop and purchase a little gift for Mrs. Atherton," I said, as the door closed behind us.

"A kind thought," he replied. "Is there a special occasion I may have thoughtlessly overlooked?" He put his hand to my elbow and guided me across the street; in his other hand was his silver capped walking stick. Kipp trotted at my side.

"She baked cookies for Mr. Merrick, which I plan on delivering tomorrow," I replied, looking up at him.

He nodded his head. With a change of subject, he asked, "Do you think Mac has a fondness for Miss Douglas?" he asked.

Well, I was a telepath after all, and what was the good of having me around if I couldn't spill a few secrets?

"Yes, I'm confident of it." I started to add that I thought they had an immediate attraction for one another but stopped myself since that observation could equally apply to me and Harrow.

Harrow smiled. "Mac is the finest man I've ever known, and Miss Douglas will do well to appreciate his attentions towards her."

"I'm confident of that, too," I said, laughing.

We walked in silence for a few seconds. The sidewalk was thankfully not crowded, while the streets were only marginally congested with carriages and carts. Kipp was unusually guarded and shielding his telepathic activities from me.

"Petra, do you mind my making an observation?" Harrow asked, cautious with his query. At my positive response, he continued, "You and your brother do not seem very close."

I hated to continue the lie but there was little choice for me. "We did not grow up together," I replied, managing to not state an untruth. "In many ways, this trip is a reunion of sorts." When Harrow did not reply, I added, "Some people are just family in name only."

My remark, which was carelessly thrown like a cast off vessel, obviously hit an unintended cord, and I knew his memories drifted to his unloving mother; his face went rigid, his thoughts became distracted.

In short order, we found a small variety shop on a corner, and I was able to purchase a pretty teacup and saucer for Mrs. Atherton. Harrow tried to pay, but I forcefully told him no. It was my gift for something done for me. He was quiet and introspective for most of the return walk, only speaking enough to not qualify as rude and inattentive. Back at home, he deposited me at the base of the staircase.

"I must go to the school tomorrow to meet some workmen," Harrow remarked. "I would be delighted to escort you to the hospital, since it is close by." With that, he disappeared down the hallway to the library. His limp, once again, was prominent; his gait beat out an uneven tempo on the floor. Kipp stared after him before looking up at me.

"I guess we never completely forget some past pains, do we?" he asked.

I shook my head. "No, Kipp. They remain a part of us for a lifetime."

CHAPTER 25

"Petra, do you hear him?" Kipp's voice was urgent in the darkness of our room.

"What time is it?" I asked, trying not to groan as I struggled to sit up in the soft bed. There was no moon peeking in through my window, and the room was black as a bottomless pit.

"It's Harrow," Kipp said. "He's dreaming, and it woke me."

"Tell me about it." I yawned, my eyes too heavy with sleep to do the work on my own.

"He often dreams of the war; tonight, he dreams of trying to save someone who died. He can't reconcile within himself that the man could not be rescued, and he keeps going back, over and over again, to make an attempt." Kipp took a deep breath. "He feels panic and fear but knows he must try." Kipp ducked his head down to nuzzle my hand. "I would like to go to him, if you don't mind."

Of course I didn't object. Kipp trotted over and managed to turn the door knob with his impressive jaws. Yes, he definitely did not suffer from the lack of opposable thumbs; I would remember that tidy fact when we returned home, and he protested helplessness in terms of assisting around the house. I'd made the choice to not monitor Harrow when he was thinking about me, but there was no reason to not take a peek at his dreams about the war. I lay back and closed my eyes; Harrow's thoughts rolled into the room like a thunderstorm. The theme of helplessness against an established outcome was prominent, and I wondered if it was compounded by the death of his brother as well as the estrangement from his mother. As I monitored his thoughts, I recognized the powerful mind of Kipp as he began to gently manipulate the outcome of Harrow's unconscious, meandering thoughts.

"Kipp, what are you doing?" I hissed. He knew how I felt about that sort of thing.

"I'm just gonna tweak it a little bit," Kipp replied. "Petra, there's no need for him to have so much torment."

As Kipp worked his magic spell, I could feel Harrow relax. At some point, he awoke and was delighted to find Kipp resting on the couch, his head on Harrow's thigh. In an odd moment of connectedness, I could almost feel Harrow's fingers as he stroked Kipp's auburn fur. Deliberately, I blocked the moment; I needed sleep, even if Kipp didn't.

"Mr. Harrow said I was to wait for you, Miss Hathaway, and then bring you back to the school," John Parks said, as we pulled away from the curb and started towards the hospital. The box of ginger cookies rested on my lap, and Kipp stared at me from across the interior of the carriage. We were in Whitechapel, and the characteristically chaotic nature of the district was clear for me to observe as a traveler. The diversity of thoughts was simultaneously fascinating and elusive and provided a good mental exercise for both me and Kipp. After departing the carriage at the front steps of the London Hospital, I greeted the man at the desk, to whom I'd become a familiar face.

"Good morning, Miss Hathaway. And hello, Kipp, too," the man intoned. He laughed when Kipp barked in response. "Mr. Merrick is waiting for you in the solarium."

Having friends in high places was a definite advantage,

and I was not so humble as to not acknowledge the fact that Harrow and Treves both exerted considerable influence to pave an effortless path for me. Obviously, the staff had been instructed to greet me with enthusiasm. Kipp and I walked down the hallway, Kipp's toenails ticking on the polished floor. Gas lanterns overhead illuminated our path, creating shadows and light along the corridor. The hallway opened out into the solarium where Joseph Merrick awaited. As he stood, it was nice to see he no longer felt he needed to conceal his face or body with hoods and capes. He was nicely dressed in a fashionable suit that had to have been tailored specifically to fit his misshapen body.

Merrick's delight over the cookies reminded me of a child's pleasure with a birthday or Christmas present. We then spent a good half hour recounting the play we had attended. The symbolism was fascinating to him in that most people related to him based upon his physical appearance and never got past that to see the man inside the shell. Unlike the primitive Mr. Hyde, Merrick never reverted to the baser side of human nature.

"Don't you think that a certain degree of duality exists in all of us?" Merrick asked. "Not to the extreme of a Mr. Hyde, to be certain, but there all the less."

My mind flicked to the concept of a Jack the Ripper; yes, there was some truth in the statement.

"I think Kipp enjoys them as much as do I," Merrick commented, interrupting my private musings as he held out another ginger cookie to Kipp.

"Petra, I'm gonna get fat eating all these sweets," Kipp remarked, looking up at me. He reached his big head forward and delicately plucked the cookie from Merrick's sound hand.

"Oh, now you are worried about your waistline, Mr. Kidney Pie," I replied, trying not to laugh, watching as he polished off every crumb from the floor like a vacuum cleaner.

The levity of the moment disappeared in the next second—a man was approaching us. He was physically unfamiliar to me, but his thoughts were ones that I identified with regret since they belonged to the man we had encountered previously, the one I believed to be Jack the Ripper. Glancing at Kipp, I saw his body posture stiffen. As the man drew closer, a thick fog of horrifyingly disturbed thoughts surrounding him reached out to clutch at me. I took a deep breath and focused; it would be like a trip to hell, but this was my job. Kipp was at my side, and I knew he would help pull me out of the suffocating tar of this man's mental illness.

"Miss Hathaway," Merrick's voice drew me back to sanity for a second. "May I present a friend of mine?" he inquired politely. "I would like to introduce you to Frank Lewiston," he said.

Lewiston was a man of middle height and average build; his hair was dark and neatly combed, almost plastered to his head. In addition, he had a full beard that covered a nondescript face. His eyes, however, were memorable. As he stared at me, I took notice that they were pale, almost translucent and oddly colorless.

I'd been inside the minds of mentally ill people, the journey was not unfamiliar, but I'd never experienced anything like this. He lacked the hallmarks of classic psychosis. He was not hallucinating or feeling under the command of others. Rather, he was filled with a deep and consuming anger. For whatever reasons people become fixated, Lewiston was obsessed with violent fantasies towards women and, to a lesser degree, humanity in general. In just six days, thinking about violence would not be enough for him, and he would transition into committing murder.

Kipp, who was a braver soul than I, dove in fully and began his methodical exploration of the man's memories. The very fact of what he was attempting was stressful to him and to me, also, as his partner.

"You are the sister of the journalist who was here in hospital," Lewiston commented, his voice placid, unemotional, his glassy, depthless eyes gazing at me.

I nodded my head, not willing to speak. For some irrational reason, I didn't want him to hear my voice. It seemed that very act might give him some type of knowledge he could use to harm me.

"It was kind of you to bring cookies to Mr. Merrick," he continued. A smile flashed in the paleness of his round face, highlighted by the dark beard. When I remained silent, he made another attempt to be conversant. "Nice dog there," he said, gesturing at Kipp.

I tried to smile and ducked my eyes. Maybe if I played shy, he would go away and leave me alone. In a moment that seemed to work, because after a measured goodbye, he drifted off into the shadowed hallway; his disturbed thoughts gradually faded from our awareness as he left our proximity. I managed to regain my composure with Merrick, who effortlessly transitioned to a discussion about art. As I told him of my student, Simon, who was gifted and our trip to the gallery managed by Ramon, I privately queried Kipp.

"Lewiston's memories of his childhood are almost, well, boxed off and difficult to find," Kipp said. "I'm not even sure I got to the core of it—it's as if he buried some of his trauma in a lead vault." Kipp took a deep breath. "His early life was chaotic and unstable. His mother died when he was young, which left him at the mercy of distant family who cared not for him." Kipp looked up at me. "He definitely didn't feel loved. When he misbehaved, his caretakers would try and subdue him by making him feel responsible for the death of his mother. Overall, he felt vulnerable and unvalued when a very young boy." Kipp stood and stretched while Merrick reached his hand out to gently stroke Kipp's fur, unaware of the true beast who lurked nearby, posing as a mild mannered friend. "Lewiston is filled with rage," Kipp concluded, looking up at me.

John Parks was waiting for us, so I said goodbye to Merrick. As Kipp and I retraced our steps to the front of the hospital, I became aware that we were being watched—it was Frank Lewiston, standing in a doorway, monitoring our retreat. I disciplined myself to not turn and stare back at him. Unconsciously, our pace quickened. To say I was relieved to be in John's carriage is an understatement. Frank Lewiston didn't frighten me, but his thoughts were so profoundly disturbing that I wanted to flee.

The ride to the school was brief; John Parks pulled up Molly and indicated he would be waiting until Harrow was ready to leave. The interior of the building was oddly quiet, without the usual people found milling about during the weekdays; the boys must have been in the dormitory area. This place had become familiar and one with which I would associate pleasant memories of the people I'd met and the children I'd taught. I found Harrow in his small office; he glanced up and smiled.

"How was your visit?" he asked, standing from behind the dark oak desk.

"Mr. Merrick was in good spirits and enjoyed the cookies," I responded. To be honest, the agitating presence of Lewiston followed me, and I struggled to still a tremor in my voice. Kipp, with his innate sensitivity, nuzzled my hand.

Harrow frowned slightly and walked around the desk to me. "Are you certain you are well?"

"Pull yourself together, Petra," Kipp said. His voice in my head was enough to help me steady myself.

"Oh, yes, thank you." Somehow I managed to muster a convincing smile.

The frown left Harrow's face. "I thought we could speak with Allen together, if you don't object. He has a great deal of respect for your opinion."

Harrow left me and returned in less than a minute with Allen in tow. The boy's red hair was neatly combed; somehow the wildness in him had been subdued. Brown eyes peeked up at me, uncertain. I knew he was worried he was in trouble and on the cusp of being reamed out for some misdeed, which made me wonder what he'd been up to…I purposely avoided plundering his private thoughts. Allen perched uncomfortably on the edge of a straight back chair.

Harrow explained, patiently and kindly, how he would

like to see Allen benefit from a more advanced educational experience. The boy was bright enough to understand, but his anxiety over an impending change to his life almost filled the room.

"You mean I'd have to leave my mates?" he asked. His eyes filled with tears; although he was tough and courageous, he was still a little boy. Standing, he shoved his hands into his pockets and hunched his shoulders.

I was seated and stretched out my hand; the boy drew close. "Allen, you do not have to do anything. It's just, dear, that we can't challenge you in the ways needed to help you grow. Mr. Harrow generously will sponsor you in a private school where you will get a proper education."

The boy keenly felt the absence of a mother; he battled between wanting me to hold him, and the need to play the role of independent young man. I compromised by putting my arm around his shoulders. He smelled of soap and some sort of hair pomade that had been used to slick back his unruly hair.

"I'm certain Mr. Harrow could arrange for you to visit your friends here," I added.

Kipp pushed forward and stuck out his head expecting a caress. Allen managed to smile and gently tugged on Kipp's big, upright ears.

"Allen, I would like for you to consider yourself to be a part of my family, too," Harrow said, seating himself on the corner of the desk. "When there is a holiday, you can visit here or come to my home and visit Daniel and Mr. Mac. We will prepare you a room all of your own that will be yours."

Kipp and I glanced at one another. Was there any degree to which Harrow would not extend himself to reach out to those in need? If so, I'd not found it yet.

Allen looked down at his polished shoes before returning his gaze to Harrow. "Thank you, sir. I'd like to have a go at it." A smile split his face. "I think I can teach those posh smart alecks a thing or two."

Harrow raised his eyebrows. "No doubt."

Allen's ginger head tilted up, and he cut his dark eyes at me. "But I'll miss people here, especially Miss Hathaway and Kipp."

I gazed back at the boy. "We grow when we have the opportunity to meet new people, Allen. Just think, it was not too long ago when I first came here and met you and Mr. Harrow. See how my life has changed for the better?" I glanced over at Harrow, and the expression in his eyes made my mouth go dry.

Allen, thankfully, got my drift without any further elaboration on my part.

"Silas, can I talk with you?" I asked. We'd finished dinner; Harrow and Mac shut themselves away in the library to look at plans for an extension to the school. With Kipp and Vashti following in our wake, we went to the front drawing room. I carefully closed the door behind me since our discussion was not to be overheard. We could have managed it all telepathically, but it would appear odd to be sitting together in total silence for so long.

The parlor was dimly lit. A tall candle was burning; the fragrance of vanilla and cinnamon filled the room. I was sitting in a low arm overstuffed chair while Silas faced me from the opposing couch. Kipp and Vashti lay close together on the woven rug that stretched the length of the room.

"Kipp and I have determined the actual identity of Jack the Ripper," I began. "He works at the London Hospital and has befriended Joseph Merrick," I began. Between Kipp and me, we filled in the facts we had determined from our trip to the hospital.

"But why did Vashti or I not hear any of this?" Silas asked, frowning. "Kipp, even you during earlier trips didn't pick up on his thoughts."

Kipp sighed and stretched his neck. "This Frank Lewiston has managed to somehow box off his thoughts that are toxic." If Kipp could've managed it, he would have physically shrugged. "I'm not an expert on the human mind, but it feels like it's some type of adaptive response so that he can manage to work and focus like a normal man. Despite that, it breaks loose at times—like at the park—when he loses a grip on it."

"Well, that makes sense," Silas replied. "And what better place to hide himself than among the dead." He looked at Vashti and grinned. "I think we'll be spending some time at the hospital," he said.

I was startled and bit back a loud exclamation. "Are you crazy, Silas? Why on earth would you tempt the devil? You know that you cannot take any chance of changing the future arc of events."

"Petra, don't be naïve," he replied. "We will have a unique opportunity to study the mind of an infamous killer."

And there it was, again: that arrogance and lack of humility which led Silas to believe he was untouchable and infallible. His dismissive comment addressed to me was infuriating—even more so when I realized there was no way for me to stop his foolhardy behavior.

Agitated, I stood. "If you are set on this poor choice that is inherently dangerous, then there's nothing I can do to stop you." However, to Kipp, I maintained a secondary, private dialog that I blocked from both Vashti and Silas. "Your job, Kipp, is to monitor Silas and keep an eye on what he's up to. I don't trust him due to his questionable judgment." From past experience, I knew Kipp could be actively present in Silas's mind without leaving a whisper of a trace.

Vashti rose from her place on the rug. "Please, let's not fight with one another. Silas and I can carefully monitor the man from a distance with an eye on preserving the future." She looked up at me. "Petra, I assure you, we take the dictates of caution as seriously as do you and Kipp."

I knew she was sincere, but I was uncertain if she could exert sufficient influence on Silas to keep him in check. The evening had come to an abrupt and unpleasant end as far as I was concerned. I left the room, Kipp on my heels. In the hallway, we met Daniel who was taking Lily for her constitutional. Kipp and I trailed along hoping, perhaps, that the fresh air would make me feel somewhat renewed. It was approaching darkness outside; I turned to look at the house where the yellow light from the interior lamps highlighted the windows at the rear of the dwelling. A safe refuge for us, perhaps, but many others had no such place.

"You are thinking about Frank Lewiston, even if you aren't aware of it," Kipp remarked, ducking his soft head beneath my hand. Ahead of us, Daniel was playing hide and seek in the small garden as Lily chased him, barking in her high pitched voice.

"How's that, Kipp?" I asked.

"Here in the dark you are reminded of the vulnerability of humans whose senses are limited." He paused before adding, "Frank Lewiston will be another unseen danger as he follows women whose only crime is to be alive. He wants to destroy and horrify; he will feel powerful if he can take life." Kipp collected his thoughts to summarize. "The little boy who was helpless can make others feel that same way."

For one with no formal training in psychology, Kipp had managed to decipher the trail that led to the disturbed psyche of one tragic human being.

It was Miss Douglas' evening off, and I assumed the responsibility for helping Daniel prepare for bed. He'd bathed and changed into his pajamas; as I tucked him into bed, I caught a whiff of lavender from the pillowcase while leaning forward to give him a gentle kiss on his dark hair.

"Miss Hathaway?" he began, unsure of himself.

"Yes?"

"I like Miss Douglas very much," he said. His blue gray Harrow eyes met mine. "She's a good teacher," he added before lowering his voice to whisper, "but I like your class better."

I laughed. "Well, it's not a fair comparison since my class has other boys your age and you can find playmates." I pulled the light cotton blanket up until it was neatly folded beneath his chin. There was something wonderful and indefinable about being tucked into bed by a loving hand. "You get to learn different things at both places, and that is a good thing."

"Uncle William tells me it's important to understand how to get along with all sorts of people," Daniel said, his face thrown into partial shadow.

I reached over to turn down the lantern; the mural on the far wall—the one so carefully painted by Ramon—was lost in the darkness of the room like a far away landmark at twilight.

"You should listen to your uncle," I replied. "He is a wise man and one of the best I've ever known." I reached forward to stroke Daniel's ruffled hair. "Your uncle has a good heart, and you can learn much about kindness from him."

Kipp climbed up on the foot of the bed and was trying to soothe a restless Lily by licking her face and head. I tried not to laugh as he back combed her fur into a rather alarming spiked style of brown and brindle hair. I was so busy watching them and listening to Daniel that I did not hear Harrow's light step as he entered the room. Without speaking, he crossed to the other side of the bed and sat, so that he was opposite me with Daniel between us. I knew without bothering to delve into his mind that he had heard my complimentary comments about him. I raised my face and met his eyes across the brief expanse.

"It is time for you to go to sleep, Daniel," Harrow said, his voice soft. He stretched his hand out to smooth the blanket over Daniel, and his hand almost met mine.

Inadvertently, I let down my guard and the intensity of his thoughts almost made me gasp. In wonder, I listened in as he fantasized what it would be like if he and I were married and were sitting, thus, tucking in our own child at bedtime. The doorway to Harrow's mind suddenly shut, and I glanced at Kipp, who'd stopped grooming Lily.

"Don't do that to yourself," he cautioned me, his amber eyes bright despite the softly lit room.

"I knew better but just had to allow myself, once," I replied. "He's thinking of children—which we can't have—and he wants me to be the mother of his." I closed my eyes for a moment. "This is very difficult, Kipp."

"Petra?" Harrow's voice disturbed my descent into what was very likely to become a profound state of self pity.

"Yes?" I replied, turning back to him. Somehow I managed a smile and stood. "We need to let Daniel get his rest."

I left first, followed by Kipp and then Harrow. "Good night," I said firmly, knowing I did not want any lingering discussions in the hallway. I felt too raw, too vulnerable, and my emotions were threatening to spill over at any second. Harrow's instinct served him well because he let me go without pause.

Back in my room, I undressed in the darkness. Kipp hopped up in the bed and waited for me. With a sigh, I slid between the sheets which felt cool against my overheated skin. Kipp tried to amuse me for a while by pushing funny images and thoughts into my weary mind. Finally, he took a deep breath and rested his head across my chest. I prayed for a deep sleep, free of dreams—good, bad or otherwise. My mind needed an interval of blank numbness for a change.

CHAPTER 26

I lacked an alarm clock, since I'd relied upon the one I could set on my watch; that timepiece definitely would have been an attention getter in my current circumstances. Kipp, however, was an acceptable alternative as he nuzzled my chin and gave it a quick sweep with his tongue. The sun was breaking through the clouds after a night of rain, and a few feeble rays found their way into my corner room.

"It's happened," Kipp said.

Of course, he didn't need to explain himself, since I, too, picked up on the thoughts that drifted up through the wooden floor like smoke rising into the air. The murder of Mary Ann Nichols had taken place—Jack the Ripper had begun his assault on the sensibilities of Victorian London. There had always been violence in the world, but Jack the Ripper applied a horrific element to the taking of a life that made him a sensation.

I was not in a particular hurry to dress. It was a school day, and I selected one of my plain, utilitarian outfits that almost had become a uniform. Slowly, I walked down the stairs, allowing the humans an opportunity to settle themselves. The news had come by word of mouth—first the coal man and then the delivery boy from the fresh market. Both shared the story that was circulating on the streets with the rapidity of wildfire. Many of the facts were incorrect and understandably distorted, but that was a common occurrence in the passing of any tale. I entered the dining room to find Harrow, Mac and Silas conversing; they stood, as a group, despite my hand gesture indicating they should not. Kipp trotted ahead and bumped noggins with Vashti before lying down on the floor next to her. My eyes wide with pretended innocence, I glanced around the table.

"Is something wrong?" I asked, knowing I'd have to prod it out of them, with the exception of Silas.

Harrow met my gaze, his expression impassive. "It is not a suitable topic for a lady, I fear," he replied.

He was obviously disturbed, despite the control he managed to exert over his handsome face, and it was clear that a violent crime in such close proximity to the school was worrisome to him. Mac looked away and didn't comment, but Silas couldn't wait since he wanted an open discussion and my being there had put a damper on the dialog.

"Petra isn't fragile," Silas remarked, looking at Harrow. He then went on to "surprise" me with the news of the murder. "I think she should know, Will, since she is often in Whitechapel and will need to take care."

Harrow carefully folded his napkin and placed it slowly on the table. He did not look at me but stared at Silas.

"Petra does not need to go back to Whitechapel, since there is obviously a lunatic running around with no compunction to not murder women." Harrow's voice barely contained a subtle tremor.

His reply set off a dueling banjoes moment in which he and Silas discussed, at length, what I would and would not be doing. I glanced at Mac once and caught his amused expression; he seemed poised for the moment for me to step in and clarify things for the men in my life.

After pouring myself a cup of coffee, I cleared my throat and held up my hands. "Gentlemen, I need to say something, please." There was a lull and I continued. "I will decide what's best for me, and I will decide if I go to Whitechapel or not. I do not require anyone in this room telling me what I may or may not do." I was feeling pretty cocky at that moment, a modern day American "woman" declaring her freedom from male intrusion. "As it were, I have business in Whitechapel, both at the school and the hospital." I glanced at Harrow, who wore a look of total consternation on his face. There was no malice in my reply since I knew he loved me and was trying to do what he thought was in my best interests. Silas, deliberately provoked the moment, but in a good way, since I needed this opportunity to make myself known.

"Will," I began, looking at Harrow, "I'm a very deliberate, cautious person and will not take any unusual chances. And, you forget, I have my Kipp."

Harrow was struggling with his innate need to be protective and his conditioning, as a man of the times, to be dominant and advise a woman living under his roof as to the wise course of action. Bless him…he didn't realize that I needed neither of those things from him. I was probably the safest being on all the streets of London, since I knew the face and name of the killer and could predict his movements.

My face and my tone softened. "I promise I will be careful. And anyway, most of my time traveling is with you or Mac, so I think my safety is assured."

That last comment was what he needed to hear; I wasn't rejecting his need to help me, just redefining it a little. Harrow tried to smile at me from across the table as he took another sip of coffee.

The ride to Whitechapel was made in almost complete silence. Harrow and Mac procured the first run of the daily papers and were pouring over the facts, most of which were erroneous. I was not offered a paper, since the information was considered coarse and indelicate. Kipp winked at me.

"If they only knew, Petra, how rough and rowdy you can be."

Smiling, I reached over to put my arm around his thick neck and rested my chin on the soft fur on top of his head, while staring out the window at the passing tableau. We were entering Whitechapel district, and the anxiety from the street notched up significantly. People living there already dealt with crime and poverty; now, Jack the Ripper gave them something else with which to contend. I could feel Harrow's eyes on my profile.

"Yes?" I said, turning to him.

"I was thinking about Kipp," he replied. His blue gray eyes were bright in the confines of the carriage. "There is no doubt in my mind that he would deal a significant blow to anyone who dared to cause insult or injury to you."

"Oh, you don't know the half of it," I replied, momentarily forgetting my place and situation.

"Why don't you tell me about it?" he replied, his voice serious.

Feeling foolish, I realized I needed to regain my discipline. This was a job, and I was working. Playing word games with a human man who was in love with me was ill advised and could only lead to a mishap unless I was very careful. Mac folded his paper carefully and was waiting, too, for my response.

Kipp, as was often the case, sprang to my rescue and began barking at a small dog walking along the edge of the sidewalk. Of course, I knew that Kipp had absolutely no designs upon that poor little dog but instead was putting on a grand show to divert the attention of the men inside the carriage.

"Don't say that I've never done you a favor," Kipp huffed, in between barks. The small dog, to its credit, lobbed a few rather aggressive barks back towards our departing carriage. The moment was sufficient so that we arrived at the school without any further interrogations of me. However, as I departed from the carriage, Harrow took my hand as an assist and held it longer than necessary.

"I've not forgotten our conversation—despite Kipp's interruption—and will resume it at a convenient time and at your pleasure," he remarked, bowing slightly over my hand.

* * *

I spent a pleasant morning with my small class, which still included Allen, who was privately a favorite of mine. There was something about his brash, independent attitude that probably reminded me more than a little of myself. As soon as Harrow could work out all the details, Allen would leave us for a more sophisticated setting, and he, no doubt, would leave his unique footprint wherever he would go.

Harrow arranged an afternoon field trip to the London Zoo for my covey of boys. Although they had spent their short lives in London, they had never experienced the zoo. Harrow asked John Parks to engage a second four wheeler, and all of us crowded into the two vehicles for the journey, including Kipp, of course. As the boys excitedly darted ahead, Harrow kept an anxious eye on their activities to make certain no one climbed over a wall and ended up in a cage with a tiger.

"See here, Simon!" he called out before trotting ahead of me and Kipp to approach the boy who was in the midst of taking some silly dare from Allen. I noticed, tenderly, the slight impairment to his gait; he was a man who had suffered with no complaints uttered. At one point, Harrow turned and looked back at me, smiling. The moment felt as if it were frozen in time, and I felt my heart thud heavily against my chest wall as my mouth went dry. Poets might write about unrequited love, but the reality of it was that there was too much pain to equate with beauty and grace.

"Pay attention to the animals," Kipp suggested, attempting to distract me from the desperate thoughts of the lovelorn.

Dutifully, I gazed at the exhibits as we continued to walk. "This is a little sad to me, Kipp," I remarked. We'd stopped in front of a cage that displayed a Barbary Lion. A few steps back, there had been a Portuguese Ibex, which looked bored and unanimated in the confines of captivity. "These animals become extinct in the next century."

I stopped to examine the lion, which returned my gaze with his unblinking, yellow eyes. "What a wonderful and rare treat to see them here today," I murmured. Kipp nuzzled my hand.

"Nothing lasts forever, Petra," Kipp said. "Some things disappear because of the interference of man; some are due to nature itself. Do you think the primitive tribe with whom you resided actually survived the ecological disaster that would have killed us, too, had not we bonded and left that time?" He folded his haunches and sat while he and the lion engaged in a staring contest. "All living creatures have a finite span on earth."

"Yes, that's true. But it is sad when the last one of a species is gone. Something irreversible has happened." I sighed and turned away.

Harrow returned, slightly short of breath. "I think we've been much too permissive with Allen," he said. "The boy is in need of some type of corporal punishment, no question about it."

I laughed as I looked up at him. He was frowning slightly. Staying my hand, I resisted the impulse to straighten his slightly askew tie.

"You couldn't spank him if your life depended upon it," I replied. It was warm, and I felt a bead of sweat slowly roll down my back between my shoulder blades. Why people had to wear multiple layers of clothing in the middle of a heat wave, I knew not.

Harrow smiled in response. "Well, perhaps not, but he needs a good talking to from time to time."

"That's what comes with being intelligent, I fear. He will be a challenge to all adults since he can outthink us." I turned back to the lion. "Will, do you ever consider what will happen when animals, such as him," I said, pointing at the cat, "are no longer on earth?"

Harrow was never one for a frivolous reply. "I recognize the reality of extinction and can only hope that I do nothing to hasten the end of any species—including my own."

I looked up at him. "Me, too."

"Petra, you can't believe what I've learned today," Silas

began. His voice was almost shrill in my head.

We were sitting in the outside chairs to the rear of the house. There were a few late summer flowers still in bloom, including one variety unfamiliar to me but extremely fragrant. I tilted my head back to peruse the twilight sky. A little brown bat darted to and fro in search of insects; his haphazard zigzagging was oddly fascinating. Kipp and Vashti could actually pick up on his echo location soundings that were undetected by my inferior ears.

I let Silas rattle on endlessly. He'd spent the first day after the murder canvassing the Whitechapel district looking for subjects to interview. As was often the case following a notable crime, there were as many opinions and assumptions as there were individuals to give them. I'd not seen Silas wear such an expression of excitement, and although I understood why, it was still disconcerting. After all, a woman had been murdered.

"Oh, don't be so holier than thou, Miss Perfect," Silas said, frowning at me. "You've made plenty of trips to conflicted times and had to be just as thrilled when you were on the cusp of an important discovery."

I shrugged my shoulders. It was what we did, and perhaps the transparent inelegance of it was suddenly more apparent to me.

"Silas is right," Kipp commented.

"Okay, guys, I get it," I finally replied, feeling irritated. "I don't need a tutorial in job responsibilities today, please."

Vashti typically waited until everyone weighed in with an opinion before expressing her own. Maybe, one day, she could be an important figure in terms of imparting wisdom…sort of a Juno—type contributor…but not yet. She was still a little uncertain and too tentative to take a leadership role. But I valued her kind, compassionate input, nonetheless.

"Petra, the loss of human life is tragic. I've been bonded to Silas for a very long time and know his heart; despite how it may seem, he does not take it lightly. But you must agree that we have a unique opportunity to explore not only the effect that these events have on society, but also to delve into the mind of Jack the Ripper himself." She paused as her dark eyes stared off into the shrubs; something tiny and furtive was rustling in the undergrowth. "We might learn something of value from examining the killer further."

"I'm not arguing with any of you," I finally said. My shoulders drooped a little; I was tired but didn't care to admit to the fact. The time we'd spent here was the most difficult I'd ever spent on any time shift, with the exception of when Tula was killed. The constant attention paid towards me by one William Harrow caused me to have to constantly guard my thoughts and deny my natural gift of telepathy. The analogy for a human would be to suddenly be without one of the five senses.

"I'm going to visit Merrick," Silas said. "My hope is to draw out Frank Lewiston and do a more in depth examination of his mind."

I laughed. "Good luck with that, Silas. You recall that Kipp tried and didn't get too far." Suddenly, things didn't seem quite right to me, although I couldn't really pinpoint the issues. "So, Silas, how do you plan on getting Frank Lewiston to talk with you?"

He almost smirked but caught himself at the last moment and controlled his facial expression. "I plan on asking him to join me and Merrick, since he seems to be friendly to Merrick. Then, I will appeal to his vanity and discuss the murder—since it is a current hot topic—and ask him his thoughts since he works in a morgue and has seen all manner of deaths."

Silas's judgment was questionable from my way of thinking, but I was neither his supervisor nor his mother. I started to tell him to be careful but bit back the words and shuttered my thoughts.

"Don't worry, little sister, it will be fine," he said, rising from his chair. "He'll never know what hit him."

Vashti darted one look over her shoulder at me and Kipp as she trailed after Silas. I knew she was trying to talk with me, but I continued to block her. I'd had enough of Silas, Jack the Ripper, bank bustles, time travel and everything else…except for Kipp and, perhaps, a man named William Harrow.

"Stupid hard head," I finally muttered. Looking up, I saw the little bat had returned in search of a second course of dinner. "What do you make of him, Kipp?" I asked, nodding up at the circling brown ball of fur with wings.

"Hungry, hungry, hungry, is all I can hear in his mind," Kipp replied. "He is not without some level of intelligence, but right now all he wants to do is eat." Kipp stretched his head back and gazed past the bat to a far tree. "There's an owl in that tree, and the bat knows the owl is hungry, too; he's being careful right now and will dart in and out of the shadows to conceal his movements."

I finally rose and began walking towards the house. Kipp reluctantly followed me.

"It'll be okay, Petra," he said. "Vashti has more influence on Silas than you believe; she can and will get him to modify his actions if needed."

Reaching down, I scratched the top of his head. "I hope you're right, Kipp. I really do."

CHAPTER 27

The next murder took the life of Annie Chapman on September 8, 1888. Frank Lewiston obviously escalated his need to defile others because he didn't stop with a mere slashed throat—this time he progressed to mutilation of her corpse. The papers hinted at the horror; I knew the details from Silas, as well as from my own study of history before taking his journey. The ugly side of humanity was that the masses were hungering for someone to accuse, and there had been a near lynching of one unfortunate man. Based on a scribble on a wall, the following drum beat of craziness would be to blame the Jewish population. Hysteria is not a pretty thing.

The tension over the entirety of London was significant, but it intensified every time I journeyed to Whitechapel. Eventually, the killings would focus so much attention on the impoverished districts that the government would finally intervene and try to improve the plight of the residents. The premature death rate was atrocious, as was rampant illness, crime and hopelessness. Harrow's school was an island in the midst of an ocean of pain; there were other people also trying to do good, but it was too little an effort to make a sizeable impact.

By the end of September, there were two other murders, and Jack the Ripper had doubled his activities. The police believed he was interrupted while committing the assault on Elizabeth Stride on September 30th. Her throat was cut but her body was otherwise not damaged. In an apparent rage of frustration, the murderer went out in search of another victim, which he found in the body of Catherine Eddowes. This time, he was able to fully indulge his terrifying compulsion to mutilate her body.

It would have been difficult to find any house in which the topic of the day failed to include the turmoil brought to the city by the actions of a serial killer. Harrow, to some degree, kept the discussions in his house to a minimum. I knew that his main concern was Daniel; the boy had enough anxiety from having lost his parents and certainly didn't need to worry about Jack the Ripper. Harrow and Mac, however, both took to carrying their service revolvers whenever venturing to Whitechapel. Although I didn't require the protection of either man, I humored Harrow, lest he worry himself to death over my safety, and allowed one or the other of them to accompany me if I left the confines of the school.

Silas made frequent visits to the London Hospital under the ruse of seeing Joseph Merrick. Often, to his delight, he would encounter Frank Lewiston and even engaged him, as planned, in conversations about Jack the Ripper. Silas and Vashti used their combined telepathic skills but simply could not recover much of use from the man. Only Kipp had the ability to push past barriers of repression and ferret out deep and important memories. As much as I did not wish to get involved, I understood the value of understanding the mind of this uniquely disturbed and destructive man.

With that thought in mind, Kipp and I finally agreed to make a trip to the hospital to coincide with Silas's visit with Merrick. The opportunity arose when my class was busy playing outdoors in the fenced area behind the school; one of the other teachers was watching my boys as well as some others from another class. At Harrow's insistence, since he was occupied, Mac accompanied me on the short journey to the London Hospital.

"You seem to enjoy visiting Mr. Merrick," Mac commented. His hat was set at a jaunty angle, his dark eyes peering at me from beneath the brim. He tried to stretch out his legs but was simply too large a human to comfortably fit into the four wheeler he'd hailed.

"He has a gentle soul and is one of the few people who has remained calm and unaffected by all that is happening now," I replied. Mac would be one of those humans who I would remember for the remainder of my days...sort of like Perdy.

Mac nodded. "I think Mr. Merrick has seen the underbelly of the beast and understands the heart of evil. In any case, I think I'll keep my revolver close by," he said, patting his pocket.

Mac chose to remain with the carriage, so I, accompanied by Kipp, made the now familiar trip up the stairs to the front entrance. In less than two minutes, I was greeting Merrick, who was sitting in his favorite corner of the warm solarium. Silas expressed mock surprise to see me and Kipp and even jumped up to give me a light kiss on my cheek.

"I asked Mr. Lewiston, Joseph's friend, to sit with us, Petra," Silas said, nodding his head as if he was coordinating high tea at the estate of some lord. "I happen to know he enjoys the ginger cookies that we bring."

Kipp was standing before Merrick, allowing the man to caress his head. I didn't need to turn to recognize Frank Lewiston as he approached from the rear; his thoughts preceded him like the stench off of a rotting carcass.

"Ah, Mr. Lewiston," Silas said, acting again as a social arbiter.

I was forced to turn and did so reluctantly. Lewiston's colorless, depthless eyes stared at me, but not long enough to qualify as ill-mannered behavior. Lewiston murmured a soft greeting and took his seat across from me. Kipp kept playing with Merrick, but his mind was busy as it began to penetrate the layers of Lewiston's mind.

"Terrible stuff that is happening in Whitechapel now," Silas began, sipping delicately at the cup of tea.

Merrick nodded his assent and murmured something soft; I knew he was uncomfortable speaking of it in my presence. Lewiston stared at Silas, his eyes flat and cold. As he reached out to take a cookie, I observed a very fine tremor to his right hand.

"Here, boy," he said, holding out the cookie to Kipp.

Kipp rose, appearing as would a marionette's puppet pulled up by strings. It was with effort he kept his hackles from rising. His pursuit of the repressed memories of Lewiston was inherently agitating and struck some primal cord of fear in my friend. He took a few slow steps and stretched out his neck to take the cookie.

"Good boy," Lewiston said, a smile flashing from behind the heavy, black beard he wore. "I've always wished to have a dog, a companion of my own."

I knew that was a true statement. He was, at heart, a lonely man. With a horrible soul hidden within the shell of his body, he could not truly befriend anyone. What sat across from me on the sun lit solarium at the London Hospital was an actor, playing a civilized part in the little daily drama of life.

Kipp returned to my side, thoughtfully munching the cookie, as he continued to plunder Lewiston's memories. Silas made a few more references to the murders, but not so much as to appear insensitive to the fact a lady was present and obviously much too delicate for such discussions. Lewiston mentally enjoyed reliving the events to the degree I had to block him and restrict my telepathy. I saw Vashti blink and cringe once and knew she was struggling with the same issue as was I.

"Well, I must go," I remarked, standing. The men all stood, politely, Merrick struggling a little to get his balance.

"Oh, yes, you must get back to the school," Merrick said, innocently.

Privately, I fumed at my stupidity and Silas's. Lewiston's curiosity immediately peaked, and I knew he would ask questions about the school and my activities after I left. Although historically Jack the Ripper didn't appear to prey upon children, our appearance here could have changed the trajectory of time. He could do something different that would terrify London even more, if that were possible.

Feeling a degree of urgency to return to the school, I almost ran down the stairs, my skirts secured in one hand, my hat anchored by the other. Mac was waiting for me in the carriage, and it was only a short time later that I was knocking on the door to Harrow's small office. He taught classes, too, but also possessed the administrative responsibilities that often kept him bound to his desk.

"Come in," a voice called out.

As I entered, he stood and began to don his coat which was hanging nearby.

"Please, don't," I said. "It's much too warm for that."

He nodded with gratitude. "Yes, I agree." Frowning, he tilted his head slightly. "You appear distressed, Petra."

"Will, I need to ask you to do something that may sound irrational, but I just need you to trust me." I sat forward on my chair.

"Anything at all, with no questions asked," he replied. There was a fine sheen of perspiration on his face. Most likely, he'd been with the boys during their midday break, chasing a ball or somehow exerting himself. Most of his peers were at restaurants having luncheon as he sat in that office, sweating, while working out the budget to hire another teacher and expand services. I knew he preferred the latter choice.

"I want you to hire an armed guard to stay here after hours when you and Mac are not on the property." I took a deep breath and tried to settle myself. "With the recent killings so close by, I fear the school could become a target. I also think you need to make certain that access points are secure after we leave each day."

"Wait here," he said. With that, he rose and went to the door to summon Mac. There was a brief conversation before he returned. "Mac will take care of it, and there will be someone here tonight."

I exhaled carefully. "You must have someone here nightly until at least mid November."

He smiled and tilted his head slightly to the left. "Why until then?"

"Call it woman's intuition, I suppose. Just promise me." I tried to smile in return but it came with difficulty.

"I promise." He hesitated before speaking again. "Petra, there is a society gathering for charity this Saturday—there will be dinner and dancing. It's important for the school, since I have become a charity, I believe." He grimaced slightly. "I would consider it an honor for you to attend with me."

I glanced down at Kipp. How on earth would I manage to get Kipp into something such as that? Kipp blinked his amber eyes at me and began to pant softly; the heat in the small office was affecting him, too.

"I think I can finagle some way to bring Kipp along," Harrow said, reading my mind from my actions. "I know he's important to you." He hesitating, hoping to not offend me. "I understand you feel safe when he is around, and I don't question the need to feel safe. We all do the same thing in different ways, I suppose."

I couldn't look at him and longed to tell him the truth about me and Kipp and my entire existence. But as good a man as he was, the truth would be unbelievable and unacceptable.

"Yes," I answered simply. "It will give me a good reason to dust off the coral gown," I said, managing a soft laugh.

"You might want to rethink the shoes this time," he said, raising his dark eyebrows.

"So, Kipp, what did you find out?" Silas could barely restrain himself.

Kipp was slightly annoyed with Silas's schoolboy-like enthusiasm and voyeuristic attitude. But he tried to control his reaction and remained focused on the task at hand.

"Frank Lewiston's mother committed suicide," he began.

We were in the front parlor; it was early evening, and Mac and Harrow were still at the school meeting with the subcontractors. Miss Griffin was upstairs with Daniel and most of the servants had gone to a street festival for entertainment, with the exception of Mrs. Donnelly, who had stopped in early on to see to our comfort. Her kindness extended to bringing us a pot of tea. Silas was more of a coffee person, but I had always enjoyed tea, my fervor stoked, perhaps, by many hours spent with Fitzhugh.

"Lewiston never met his father and apparently his mother only made negative remarks about him being a bad, worthless man. They were desperately poor, and he never knew when they would eat; often he was hungry. His adult speculation is that his mother made money as a prostitute. Anyway, when he was six, she killed herself. He found her hanging by a bed sheet from the door in the room they shared, on and off, with another family."

Vashti whined softly; the thrill of tragic discovery was not a part of her nature. She naturally possessed the compassion that Silas seemed to lack. I recognized her constant struggle to bring balance to their bond.

"Amazing, Kipp!" Silas remarked. "How on earth do you find this stuff that I can't even get close to?"

"I'm very good," Kipp replied, his tone cool and controlled. "Obviously, that sort of event is very damaging to a child. He was sent off to distant relatives who didn't want him....or at least, he felt unwanted. He was made to work hard and often punished excessively. Over time, he became angry at everything and everyone. Initially Lewiston hated God before he decided there is no God. He hates the church, too, because his mother was refused burial in consecrated ground due to the manner of her death. And he has learned to wear that passive, inoffensive mask to conceal his inner rage. In truth, he hates everyone, not just women. Lewiston walled himself off from any meaningful relationships, and as he saw other men forming bonds with women, he began to feel frustration that he did not have a woman of his own. Somehow, he twisted his frustration to make it the fault of all women that they don't like him. He almost builds this up into a frenzy of rage until he can kill; the power he experiences at having the say- so over the life and death of another being is intoxicating." Kipp glanced over at me. "I feel dirty, soiled almost."

"I'm sorry, Kipp," I replied, feeling the pain that resonated in him. "I don't want you to go there again."

"What are you talking about, Petra?" Silas asked. Standing abruptly, he began to pace back and forth in front of the mantle. "This is a unique opportunity to learn about the mind and patterns of a serial killer. We need Kipp to meet with Lewiston again, shortly before the November 9th murder, to track the build up before he kills Mary Kelly."

It wouldn't have taken much on a good day, but Silas finally managed to enrage me. I stood, too. "Silas, Kipp is my partner, not yours. He is not going to be exposed to Frank Lewiston again. He has given you what you wanted, which is a collection of memories you were not skilled enough to obtain on your own." I felt the blood rush to my face. "Any concurrent thoughts you should be able to get from your own skills, unless you are incapable of acting independently." I glanced at Vashti. "I don't even think Vashti wants to make that journey with you."

Previously, when I had spoken up for Kipp in this manner, he would usually warn me off and assure me he was a big boy, able to take care of himself. This time, he remained silent. The trip into Frank Lewiston's memory vaults had disturbed him, leaving him depressed and weak. Silas's face flushed bright red as he barely managed to contain his hostile response.

"I don't need you, Miss Goodgame, to lecture me on my job, ethics, and, most of all, on my relationship with Vashti. I know you think you're hot stuff, you and Kipp, and my father probably thinks you're wonderful. But I'm not excessively impressed."

Vashti rose from her place of comfort on the Persian rug and crossed over to stand before Silas. "Please, both of you,

say no more before things are said that cannot be forgiven."
She looked at me, her dark chocolate eyes looking as if
they would melt. "I don't think we need to stress Kipp
anymore. Certainly, we have a good idea of Frank
Lewiston and I, for one, applaud your efforts, Kipp." The
light in the room was caught in the waves of her gray fur
bringing a deceptive softness to her appearance. Kipp
walked to her and they touched noses. I decided to follow
his example and approached Silas, who was still breathing
heavily as he audibly huffed his agitation with me.

"Let's try and work through this Silas," I said, feeling
very adult and pleased with myself at my attempt to broker
a peace agreement. "I think this is why past teams have
avoided this place and time. The stress on society is
affecting us, even when we are not really aware of it. We
cannot allow ourselves to dissolve into bickering that will
destroy this time shift."

Kipp nodded his head. "Remember, one of the reasons
given for our journey was the exploration of what happens
to the symbiotic bond under extreme duress." His auburn
head tilted back as he stretched to relieve the tension in his
neck and shoulders. "Maybe we are seeing one of the
effects, now."

Silas's anger was so intense, that he experienced the
tunnel vision that affects human and destroys their sense of
reason. I politely monitored his thoughts, not too
intrusively, and admired the manner in which he gained
self control. He might be quick to anger, but he was equally
quick to calm himself.

"Everyone is right, I think, with the exception of me," he
finally said. "I think I've worked so long with journalism,
that the pursuit of a story—this story—became critical and
all other matters were no longer important." He looked up
at me, and I caught an unexpected flash of Philo written
across his face. "Maybe I need to consider another line of
work," he added with a rueful smile. "I'm sorry, Vashti.
Instead of achieving a balance with you, I've been selfish
and dominant for far too long."

I knew he'd experienced some sort of corrective emotional epiphany, which obviously had to do with his relationship with Vashti. At least, I wasn't quite arrogant enough to think that I had cracked open that thick skull of his to impart wisdom. The relationships between us and our symbiotic partners was the closest imaginable, one that transcended marriage, parenthood or friendship.

Kipp and I decided to leave them at that point, sensing they had some repair work to do. That activity was also an important part of our bonds—the clearing out of interpersonal junk that impeded the connection between life partners. As we climbed the stairs to our room, Kipp glanced up at me.

"I'm glad we finally got that over with," he remarked.

"What?"

"The fight between you and Silas. You know you are an opinionated hot head, Petra, so it was only a matter of time…" He allowed his thoughts to drift off as he purposely did not complete the sentence.

"I am not a hot head," I replied defensively, feeling stung.

"I love you anyway, despite all your flaws," he said. Reaching over, he grabbed my hand and caught it between his jaws. "There—I gave you a love bite." He raced ahead and was waiting for me on the landing, his tail wagging like a flag. "Tomorrow, we need to go shopping for some pretty, new shoes for you to wear to the dance." Twisting his head, he asked, "How do you think Harrow is going to get me into the party?"

I shook my head. "That's a mystery yet to unfold, Kipp," I replied.

CHAPTER 28

"Miss, your hair is a lovely color, so dark and rich," Jean commented as she ran a brush through the heavy mass. I'd not had it trimmed since coming to London, and it now stretched past the lower margins of my shoulder blades.

"I happened to be in a shop picking up something for Mrs. Donnelly, when a posh lady came in to find a gift." Jean's eyes were huge in her slender face, reminding me of a fragile doe, poised for flight. "Her hair was done in the latest style…I'm gonna try and copy it for you, miss," she said, peeking over my shoulder to obtain my nod of approval.

At some point in the exercise, Daniel wandered in, having knocked politely on my door. It appeared that his uncle's admonishments about a gentleman entering the bedroom of a lady had stuck. After asking my permission, he climbed up on my bed and turned, on his stomach, his face propped up by his hands. Lily, after some hopping, managed to scramble up next to him.

"Why do ladies have to go through such silly stuff in order to go out in public?" he asked. The Harrow blue gray eyes met mine in the mirror.

"That is a question that has been asked for thousands of years, I suppose," I replied. He didn't know that I shared exactly the same sentiments and was, at heart, a simple creature, who would prefer sweat pants and a good book to having my hair styled.

"Master Daniel is gonna teach me how to play chess this evening while you and Mr. Harrow are gone," Jean said, looking at him over her shoulder and smiling. "Mister Mac has taken Miss Douglas out to the park for the evening," she added.

"I wasn't asked to go along," Daniel remarked, allowing his bottom lip to pucker out in a childish pout.

"The day will come when you will understand why," I replied. Across the room, my coral gown hung on a padded hanger, impatient to head out for the evening. Beneath it on the floor sat a pair of delicate slippers; they were a bronze color with beading on the top. The shoes seemed fairly comfortable, and I hoped I could dance in them, but a significant part of me longed for my running shoes which rested in my closet back home.

"Do you know how to dance?" Kipp asked.

Jean continued to prattle on in her soft voice, talking about fashions and hair dressing, while I attended simultaneously to both her and Kipp.

"Well, yes, I do, Kipp. Although I admit I'm not the most skilled, I can manage to keep up with my partner." I felt mildly disappointed that he would have so little faith in me.

"I just wondered," he replied. "You lack natural grace and usually stumble when we are out running." He sniffed at his right paw before applying his tongue to some spot needing attention.

I recognized he was needling me to dispel any anxiety I might have. And it was at that exact moment I realized I was, indeed, nervous.

"Thanks, Kipp."

Sometimes a good friend gives us the reminders we need. Yes, although I'd managed to subdue my anxiety, it was there as a part of the upcoming event with William Harrow. His feelings for me were obvious, despite my having shuttered my telepathic window into his mind. And then there were my feelings for him that existed despite the impossibility of an intimate relationship between the two of us.

"I wish I'd not agreed to go, Kipp," I said. Turning my head was difficult, since Jean was looping a coil of hair and needed to secure it with a mouthful of hairpins. But I could see him from the corner of my eye.

"So, why did you?"

"I'm not sure," I replied, forgetting for a moment that lying to Kipp was impossible.

"Now you're not being honest with yourself, Petra," Kipp said. "You're going because you love Harrow, and the opportunity to dress up, be beautiful, and have him hold you in his arms is just too overpowering to refuse."

Well, if your life partner can't lay things out in that brutally honest fashion, then you just don't need to have one.

"Now, don't cry, or you will mess up your face," Kipp admonished me. "Jean put rouge on your cheeks and some stuff—I don't know what that is—around your eyes, and it'll get all runny, and you'll look like a demented clown or something."

The demented clown comment caused me to laugh. Jean looked a little puzzled.

"Did I say something funny, miss, about hair styles?"

I shook my head, afraid to speak.

It was the first of October, and thankfully the heat of the summer had passed. I had no desire to be square dancing—or whatever we would be doing—with William Harrow as rivulets of sweat poured down my face. When I purchased the pretty shoes, I also bought a heavier weight petticoat made of wool flannel; the school, despite Harrow's efforts, was drafty and would probably become unpleasantly cool in the coming months. Since all of my garments were light weight, I procured an inexpensive coat to wear, as well as one wool hat in a neutral gray color. Our time here was drawing to a close, and I only could justify the one hat. In any case, I would leave my clothes behind for someone to inherent and enjoy. Symbionts, by our nature, were meant to leave a small footprint—arriving with little and departing with the same.

I descended the now familiar stair case, Kipp at my side. I'd brushed him until he gleamed; there was not a stray hair out of place on his body. We were both ready for the ball, in case anyone wondered. Harrow stood at the base of the stairs, his top hat in hand. Having been born into wealth, he wore his finery with an attitude of indifference. I, on the other hand, felt like a little girl playing dress up in my mom's nicest clothes. Playfully, I pulled up the front edge of my gown to display my new shoes while endeavoring to not flash him with an excessive amount of petticoat.

"Ah, the boots are gone," Harrow said, smiling. "Your new choice is perfect with the gown. In fact, everything is perfect."

The expression in his blue gray eyes was intense and intimate. I ducked my head with the awkwardness of a schoolgirl out on a first date, perhaps on my way to the senior prom with the boy named most likely to succeed. How silly, I chided myself. I was over four hundred years old, had been married with a child; I was no novice, and this was not my first rodeo, by any means. But there it was, regardless, that sense of mystery and rush of excitement. I knew, despite my attempts to relax, that a flush—other than the rouge applied by Jean—stained my cheeks, bringing high color to my face. Unconsciously, my fingers drifted up to lightly touch the pearls Harrow had given me which were secured about my neck; the white beads were cool against my flesh, which suddenly felt heated. Harrow leaned over and gently kissed my hand. I was glad I'd taken time to try and tidy up my fingernails, which were often overlooked. Looking up, his eyes met mine.

"Mac has taken Miss Douglas out for dinner," he said, raising his eyebrows. "Perhaps there is romance in the air tonight?"

The double entendre could not be overlooked, but at least

I was wise enough to not make a jesting remark in response. Instead, I chose a neutral, cautious reply.

"Mac and Miss Douglas make a fine couple," I said, taking the coward's way out with my passive response. Ignoring my comment, Harrow took my wrap and carefully placed it across my shoulders. I'd left the tiny pillbox hat upstairs since we'd be dining and dancing, and I didn't want to sling the hat across the dance floor as we spun around the room.

Harrow engaged John Parks for the evening, and we went through the now familiar routine of entering and subsequently departing a carriage. Kipp was correct in that I was inherently clumsy, but I thought that all the maneuvering in and out of conveyances while wearing long skirts was sort of like charm school—instead of walking with a book on my head to correct poor posture, I vaulted in and out of carriages while wearing Victorian clothing. Maybe there was an Olympic event? The air held an undercurrent of coolness, a promise of winter to come. Kipp sat close to me, his warmth radiating like a kerosene heater to help keep me comfortable, my arm resting lightly along his back.

"Your brother is occupied tonight?" Harrow asked. Occasionally, he would glance out the window at the homes we passed. London stayed busy and active, no matter the time of day. Many tradesmen worked all hours, despite the inclement weather or any other factors. Patrons of the theatre and other entertainment were likewise hurrying to their destinations.

"Yes, in pursuit of a story, as usual," I replied, trying to smile. Lingering in the back of my mind was a nagging worry that Frank Lewiston might escalate his activities to include the vulnerable children at our school. The connections between me and Silas were obvious, and the leap to other things important to us was simply made. In addition, what better way to terrify and escalate the emotions of London than to kill a child? Lewiston, no doubt, achieved some type of perverse sexual gratification when he killed women, so he might not target a youngster. But at the same time, his need to have power over life and death had no age limits.

"You're just worrying about something with no basis," Kipp said, trying to bring me back to ground.

I pulled him closer and rested my chin on his head. Harrow watched; there was no longer curiosity about my need to have Kipp at my side. Harrow, since he loved me, just accepted that I might have an inexplicable oddity and viewed it as a part of the charming whole.

"He brings you great comfort," Harrow remarked. His features were momentarily lost in a passing shadow.

I nodded. "How did you explain his presence to our hostess?"

Harrow dipped his head and laughed softly. "A gentleman hesitates to fabricate stories, so I tried to keep the margins of the truth intact. I told Mrs. Cummings that you had suffered a traumatic event at some point in the past and feel secure when your dog is present." He smiled. "She is a great lady who would never incommode a guest and was very gracious. Besides, she loves dogs and has several in her house as companions."

"Oh, great," Kipp moaned. "Now I'm gonna have to fend off a bunch of yapping ankle biters all night."

The carriage pulled to a gentle stop as we heard Parks call out to Molly. He hopped down from the box before Harrow could stir; the usual cloth cap was in John's hand as he assisted me from the carriage. He nodded to Harrow and smiled at Kipp.

"I'll be back by eleven, if that's what you wish, Mr. Harrow," John said, nodding at my companion.

"If it's not too late, John," Harrow replied, meaning it. He could just as easily find another cab and not disturb John's evening. Of course, he would give John a sizable tip for the inconvenience.

With my hand in the crook of Harrow's arm, we were met at the door by a black clad butler—I'd decided the ability to maintain a poker face must be part and parcel of the job of butler—who took my wrap and Harrow's top hat and overcoat. Mrs. Cummings, our hostess, was a delightful woman who must have possessed some degree of eccentricity in her soul, since she saw nothing unusual in my bringing along my 'dog' to a charity ball. With just a little eavesdropping into her thoughts, I was happy to find a truly kind soul who sincerely enjoyed helping the less fortunate. She was, as were most of the other people present, very interested in me. Harrow was considered one of the most eligible bachelors in town, who had somehow managed to evade the efforts of the marriageable young ladies of London. As far as Mrs. Cummings was concerned, he was one of her favorite people, and if he found this strange American woman—whose large nose kept her from being called beautiful—to be a compelling draw, then that was just fine. The need to have a dog in constant attendance was not so peculiar from her way of thinking. She toted her Pekinese dog, Millie, literally everywhere, including the theater and opera, and she had raised a few carefully groomed eyebrows by bringing Millie to church.

A man, who was unfamiliar to me, excused himself before dragging Harrow out of sight, leaving me in the kind arms, figuratively speaking, of Mrs. Cummings. Meanwhile, a curious Millie was busy inspecting my Kipp. Unlike most dogs, she was not avoidant of him and seemed excited and rather star struck.

"I think Millie likes your dog," Mrs. Cummings said, laughing softly.

Kipp looked up at me, horrified. "Petra, do something. She won't get away from me," he said, referring to the low lying bundle of fur with legs. Millie's pink tongue flashed out from the dark mask of her flat face.

"Face it, Kipp; the ladies love you," I replied, amused at his discomfiture.

"Speaking of liking, Miss Hathaway, how on earth did you manage to capture William Harrow's attention? He is notoriously circumspect and has not been forthcoming with

many of our eligible ladies." Mrs. Cummings was being
overtly nosey, but not in an unpleasant sense. She liked
Harrow and found herself liking me, too. After all, anyone
who loved dogs, as did I, must have some good qualities.

"Well, I don't think I've captured him, to use your
words," I replied. "Mr. Harrow has been very kind to me
and my brother following my brother's accident. He is a
generous man," I added.

Mrs. Cummings raised her pencil-enhanced eyebrows.
"A very true statement, but I still think he is more than just
a little fond of you."

Fortunately, it was time for dinner, and I was spared any
further interrogation. Harrow courteously escorted me to
my chair and managed, somehow, to include me in the
flow of conversation at a table of strangers. After dinner
and some mild mingling, the majority of the guests
gathered in a spacious room for dancing. The walls were
covered with various large paintings; gas lights hissed from
ornate sconces carefully placed in a row down the length of
the room. The floor gleamed with polish; if there had been
many dances in that room, I couldn't tell it from the pristine
condition of the flooring. A string quartet had set up and
began to entice a few couples to take to the floor. I enjoyed
the spectacle as the women swept by, their gowns forming
swirling splashes of color in the room; the men were
uniformly clad in dark formal wear in contrast to their
partners who reminded me of gaily feathered birds.

"May I?" Harrow approached me, bowing slightly, as he
held out his hand.

Suddenly, I felt self-conscious and uncertain; my dancing
was less than adequate, and I realized these people would
watch for the slightest misstep.

"Will, I've not danced with anyone in a long time," I
began, looking up at him. "I'm appallingly awkward and
am known for stepping on toes."

"And I walk with a prominent limp, in case you didn't
notice. Neither of those things is of any consequence, and I
will not allow you to leave here tonight without our having

danced together." He leaned forward. "Dance poorly and perhaps some of these people will feel sorry for me and pledge more money for the school."

I surprised myself in that I danced with more skill and grace than I'd done so before. Were my feelings for him transformative, or had I just finally developed rhythm? His hand that clasped my waist felt as if it burned my skin through the thin barrier of coral silk. As we made another circuit of the room and swept past Mrs. Cummings, she nodded and smiled at me. Yes, I knew what she was thinking. Some of the people present wondered why William Harrow would choose a woman who was not a member of society. Mrs. Cummings seemed unbothered by such social mores and issued her tacit approval. After all, I loved dogs.

"May I tell you something?" Harrow asked, his voice deliberately soft so that others would not listen in on our conversation.

"Hmm?" I replied, my eyes focused on his throat. Taking a deep breath, I inhaled the fragrance of his cologne.

"I was dishonest with you," he continued.

Startled, I looked up at him.

"Whether you danced poorly or not, I have already maximized all the pledges and more. Tonight has been a grand success, and you were not compelled to dance with me." He waited a moment before breaking into a broad smile.

"Will, you lack the ability to be dishonest," I replied. "It's not in your nature."

His eyes drifted down to gaze at the pearl necklace. I knew he wanted to touch it with his fingertips, but such a thing would draw attention, and not in a good way. Vulgar displays of emotion were not typical of the day. As we moved past Kipp, who watched from the margin of the dance floor, I saw him thump his tail in support as he relayed more than a little sense of surprise that I'd managed to not get my feet tangled and go down in a heap.

"Well, thank you all the same," Harrow said. The music

stopped, and he escorted me back to the margin of the room. "I think we will be taking our leave soon, if you've had your fill of society for one evening." He deposited me at a chair, where I could wait for him to say his goodbyes. Harrow's eyes met mine before he bowed and lifted my hand to his lips for a brief kiss.

Despite his birthright, he didn't crave that type of setting and preferred the solitude of his library or chasing the children down the corridors at the school. But he needed the support of his peers to make his dream a reality. Already, young lives were being changed—hopefully in a long lasting way. While he made a last circuit of the room, I patted my knees so that Kipp would place his chin across my lap. Leaning forward, I rested the side of my face on top of his big head.

"I know, Petra," Kipp said. "This night was difficult for you, considering your feelings for Harrow. But wasn't it also exciting?" he asked. After a tiny pause, he added, "I hope one day to feel the way you do right now."

Yes, love was intoxicating and being in love was exciting, to use Kipp's word. But it was also stressful. Looking across the room, I caught the eyes of Mrs. Cummings, who held Millie in her lap. No doubt her maidservant spent countless hours removing dog hair from her mistress's fine gowns. Smiling, she nodded at me. Yes, Mrs. Cummings was a fan.

CHAPTER 29

"Good morning, Miss Hathaway," Mrs. Atherton greeted me as I walked into the kitchen. The smell of fresh bread almost caused my knees to buckle; a couple of loaves were cooling on racks on the large table in the center of the room. A porter must have delivered fresh food because several baskets of vegetables were sitting against the far wall. I spied one that contained perfect deep burgundy apples that made my mouth water.

Kipp remarked, "Those look tasty, but I'd rather have kidney pie."

I had slept poorly following the dance, but my slumbers were oddly dreamless. Kipp must have wiped the slate clean despite my disapproval of his interferences in my subconscious thoughts. Mrs. Atherton looked harried; it was baking day, and she had multiple projects going simultaneously.

"Your brother and his doggie left an hour ago," she said. "And I need to get this pot of tea to the master in his library," she added.

"I can take the tea," I offered.

"Bless you, miss," the cook replied with gratitude. She raised a flour coated hand to push back a lock of hair that had fallen over her eyebrows; in a flash, a smear of white dust coated the right side of her forehead.

With Kipp following anxiously, I managed to carefully balance the tray, hoping one of the fragile cups would not go flying off. At the entrance to the library, I tapped softly, while using my right knee to help keep the tea service from tumbling to the floor.

"Come in," Harrow called out.

Of course, the minute he saw me, he leapt to his feet and came around his desk to take the tray from my hands.

"So, we've put you to work?" he asked, smiling. I noticed dark circles beneath his eyes; he appeared weary and fatigued. It seemed his sleep also had been disturbed.

"Just helping a little since Mrs. Atherton is baking." I laughed. "I didn't want anything to interfere with a snack of some wonderful bread later on today." I turned to leave, thinking my job was done, but he reached out and lightly touched my shoulder.

"Please stay and have a cup of tea with me," he requested.

It was warm and invitingly cozy in the library. Since November had arrived, the fireplaces were all in use, and I allowed Harrow to lead me to the couch that faced the mantle. A row of pictures stretched across the top of the wood, and I realized I'd never looked closely at them. Stepping forward, I saw a face that stood out…the face of a man who greatly resembled Harrow. Turning, I raised my eyebrows in query.

"My brother," he remarked, controlling his facial expression. "A terrible tragedy with long lasting consequences for the family," he said, shaking his head as he sat at the opposite end of the long couch. Harrow began to pour the tea, not waiting for me to offer. I suppose he knew by then that there were many such tasks at which I did not excel, nor did I wish to. The delicate fragrance of English breakfast tea unexpectedly filled the room.

Harrow was dressed for the day. It was Sunday, and Mac and Miss Douglas had taken Daniel to church. Harrow never attended, and I didn't ask him why. From the limited glimpses inside his mind, I knew him to be a spiritual man but obviously there was no lure from organized religion. As with most human nature, there was probably a story lurking there, but it was one I didn't need to know.

Somehow my brain, mimicking the processing of the human mind, made the rapid association between religion and spirituality...and something demonic: London thought that Jack the Ripper was done with his evil mischief, but the last recorded murder would take place on November 9th , a few days hence. Poor Mary Jane Kelly would meet her fate in a squalid little room off of Miller's Court. Involuntarily, I shuddered; Harrow mistook my tremors and thought I was cold.

"No, thank you, it's very pleasant in here," I replied in response to his query.

We began to share impressions from the previous night. More than a few were humorous, and we laughed out loud, enjoying the moment. Kipp stretched out on his side in front of the fireplace; occasionally, he would share in our humor by thumping his tail on the floor.

"And you are a very good dancer," Harrow said, raising his teacup in a silent salute.

"Well, not really, but thank you, kind sir, for your compliments."

"Between my gimpy leg and your new slippers, I thought we managed a respectable outing," he replied nodding his head. The smile left his face as he suddenly became serious. "I told you last night that I was a coward, and you tried to convince me otherwise. But, I am a terrible coward who lacks the, uh, confidence, to say the things I must."

I felt my mouth go dry. Perhaps my bringing the tea to him was not such a good idea after all.

"Silas told me that you will be departing before the end of November." His blue gray eyes searched my face. "I don't want you to leave." Harrow looked down at his hand which was clasping the teacup so tightly that the fragile vessel appeared it might shatter from the pressure. He set the cup on the tray as carefully as if it was made of the paper thin shell of a robin's tiny egg.

"The first time I saw you standing in the midst of that miserable courtyard, I had the most inexplicable feeling that we had met before." Harrow shook his head slightly. "But I suppose that is just hopeful fancy on my part." He took a deep breath and slowly exhaled. "The fact is, my dear Petra, that I love you." His face softened as he hurried on in a rush to finish. "I've not said anything before because it felt improper for me to declare my feelings while you resided under my roof. I felt more urgency to do so since your leaving has become a certainty." His breath became a little ragged as he struggled to express all that he'd contained for so long. "I want us to marry and have a family together."

Well, there it was; I'd known it was coming but didn't know when or where. Kipp did know, of course, but had kept his knowledge private. He stretched his neck back so that I was in his line of sight. Kipp thumped his tail again in support but curtailed telepathic dialog with me since I had my hands full with this wonderful human man.

I began speaking slowly and deliberately. "Will, my trip to London has changed me in many ways. Knowing you has been and is one of the greatest experiences of my life." Pausing, I searched for the right words. "But I don't think I would be the best partner for you for many reasons." He started to speak, but I held up my hand. "I'm not a member of society, and you most certainly are. A marriage with me would only hurt you with your peers. And, there is another matter that is difficult for me." I took a deep breath and felt my shoulder rise and fall with tension. "I cannot have a family with you…what I mean is that I'm incapable of having your children."

The tension on his face lifted immediately. "Oh, Petra, that's not important. There are so many children who need a family…we can adopt and give a child—in fact several—a stable, loving home." He rose quickly and moved over to sit close to me on the couch. Harrow reached out and took both of my hands in his, leaning forward to softly kiss the back of my hands. "Can you look me in the eyes and tell me that you don't love me?"

My moment had arrived. Did I lie to him and let him think I didn't care, hoping he'd eventually find someone who reciprocated his feelings? Or was I honest, for once, in telling him that I did care but that a future was impossible. I glanced at Kipp, hoping he would help me, but he remained silent.

"I do have feelings for you, Will," I began but didn't get to finish that sentence because he unexpectedly leaned forward and pulled me into a kiss.

It was not as if I'd never been kissed before, since I'd been married and was no untouched innocent…although that seemed to have been ages ago. But this experience was different for me. My husband and I married after many years of friendship, and in many ways our union was just the cementing of the bond between two people with great fondness for one another. And, yes, we had a good marriage, were happy, and were blessed with a wonderful baby boy. But that kiss from William Harrow scorched me from the top of my head to the tips of my toes and shook me to my core. I suppose we often don't realize what we've missed but that lesson was quickly shown to me in a brief instant. He released me and pulled back; his pupils were dilated so that the unique blue gray of his irises was lost, as he struggled to regain his composure. With an unsteady hand, he pushed tremulous fingers through his thick black hair which was still surprisingly neat. Yes, damn it, we were caught up in the intense emotional field that was as wonderful as it could be destructive. I dared a glance at Kipp, whose eyes opened wide.

"Wow," Kipp remarked. "That was something! I may have to rethink my bachelorhood."

I tried very hard to ignore Kipp, since there was nothing vaguely humorous about the moment.

Harrow finally managed a smile. "I know, despite your cautious nature, that you care for me as I do you." Reaching up, he gently tucked a curl of my dark hair behind my ear, having managed to get the tremor in his hand under control.

With a light caress, he cupped the side of my face in the heated palm of his hand. "I am asking you to marry me."

I felt tears brimming at the back of my eyes and knew they would spill at any moment.

"Will, there are so many things about me that you don't know," I began. The moisture finally escaped and began to trickle down my cheeks. Harrow gallantly retrieved his handkerchief and dabbed lightly at my face; the scent of lavender wafted in the air as I realized Mrs. Donnelly had probably tucked some dried lavender into the wardrobe with his clothing.

"Petra, I am not without history…none of us are if we are honest. I have done things during the war which still cause me distress." He took a deep breath and sighed. "Whatever haunts you, I care not. I know all I need to know or want to know, and I trust you. That should be enough, don't you think?"

Reaching forward, he captured my hand and laced his fingers between mine; I could feel his raw strength, something he normally concealed beneath the polished exterior of a gentleman.

"I'll not press you further, since you must reconcile within yourself these past issues that you're hesitant to drop." His eyes met mine. "It is enough for me, now, to know that you love me as I love you."

It was said as a question, and he awaited my validation of what he'd said. I could lie and tell him that I did not fully reciprocate his feelings…perhaps that was the merciful route to take. But it felt instinctively wrong to deceive him since he had exposed his feelings in such a blunt and forthright manner. The fact was that I did love him, but I couldn't have a relationship with him. I peeked over at Kipp who continued to stare at me. There was no help to be found, but I couldn't blame Kipp.

"Will, I do love you. I love you enough that I'm unwilling to make promises to you that I can't keep." I shook my head. "I wouldn't bring injury to you in any manner."

He sat back, his spine resting along the rear cushion of

the couch. With his hand still grasping mine, he turned his head to gaze at the fireplace.

"Petra, I've had a lifetime of achieving that which I was told was impossible. Perhaps, I no longer believe in the impossible." Harrow turned back to me. "This, between us, is not impossible. I know it in my heart and soul," he said, touching his chest with the palm of his hand. Leaning forward again, he allowed his lips to gently touch mine. "And at some point, perhaps you will trust yourself enough to say what bothers you."

I was glad he instinctively understood my issue was not one of trust with him. Kipp, recognizing the moment was right for his planned interruption, rose and walked over to thrust his big noggin in between us. Harrow laughed, and reached out to ruffle Kipp's dense, auburn fur, which was toasty warm from his close proximity to the fireplace.

"Kipp," he said, staring into Kipp's amber eyes, "your timing is appalling, but despite that fact, you're welcome to stay, too."

Kipp barked in response, his auburn tail wagging like a flag.

Harrow stood, holding out both of his hands to me. I extended mine in return and allowed him to pull me to my feet. Standing, the top of my head came to just beneath his chin. He put his fingers gently at the margin of my jaw and tipped my head up for another gentle kiss Harrow's eyes dropped to where the pearls he'd given me encircled my throat. A shadow of a smile crossed his handsome face.

"Let's go to the kitchen and see if we can steal some fresh bread from Mrs. Atherton," he said.

As we entered the kitchen, the outside door opened, and Daniel bounded in on a current of cool air, closely followed by Miss Douglas and Mac. Somehow, instead of retreating to another common room, we all ended up gathered around the large table, enjoying the warmth of the room along with one of the fresh loaves of bread Mrs. Atherton had cooked. She placed several plates on the table along with a crock of fresh butter and apricot preserves from the larder.

"So, Daniel, how were services today?" Harrow asked, as he carefully buttered a slice of the still warm wheat bread.

Daniel didn't make eye contact and instead mumbled some reply. From the corner of his eyes, he looked over at Mac who returned a stern glance.

"I beg your pardon?" Harrow said, not willing to let the boy get by with a rude non answer.

"Tell him, Daniel," Miss Douglas said. Her plain face appeared animated with a flush of pink color along her cheeks. Yes, love was transformative, and she looked pretty on that day.

Daniel's slender shoulders slumped a little. "I misbehaved," he said softly. "During one of the prayers, when it was really quiet, I tried to pass a top to Jonathan, and it fell to the floor." His eyes became huge in his child's face. "You can't imagine the clatter it made." Daniel glanced at me. "The prayer stopped as everyone turned to look at me." He grimaced. "That top rolled all the way to the back of the church before it hit the rear wall and stopped."

Harrow was frowning at him, but I saw his lips were compressed too tightly for anger; indeed, he was trying to not laugh. I, too, having been caught in countless embarrassing situations knew the danger of the falling top, to borrow a metaphor.

Mac cleared his throat. "Not to take away any of the drama from today's adventure, I have something to announce." He glanced at Miss Douglas and smiled. "I've asked Margaret to marry me, and she has kindly agreed to be my wife."

Daniel was immediately relieved, since the spotlight was off of him. Harrow stood and went over to Mac to shake his hand and clap him on the shoulder. I, too, stood and embraced the governess, happy for her upcoming transition in life. Mrs. Atherton, after giving an exclamation of joy, began to prepare a fresh pot of celebratory tea.

"Fabulous news, Mac!" Harrow exclaimed. He glanced at me, and I knew he wanted to be able to make a similar announcement but lacked my go ahead.

"In many ways, little will change," Mac said. "There is a townhouse nearby with a cottage out back. You know Samuel Heatherton, Will," he added. "He will rent it to us for a very reasonable amount, and we will be within a pleasant walking distance of here. Margaret will continue to be Daniel's governess, and I will keep on working with you and the school."

"And where will you be going on your honeymoon?" I inquired, trying to engage Margaret, who was soft spoken and reserved.

"Mac would like to take me to the Highlands, since he grew up in Inverness," she said. "I've never been outside of England and know there are many wonderful places to see to the north."

I actually had been to the Highlands during one of my past time shifts, a story too long and involved to recount. Feeling happy over their announcement as well as discombobulated by Harrow's passionate declaration of love, I forgot myself for a moment.

"Oh, yes, the Highlands are wonderful. I've been to Inverness myself," I started before catching the curious stare from both Harrow and Mac.

"Uh, oh," Kipp murmured in my head. "You better watch yourself, Petra."

"Begging your pardon, miss, but I thought this was your first trip overseas," Mac said. His warm, dark eyes were on my face; I could feel the blood rush beneath my skin in a tell tale stain of color.

I glanced at Harrow as my mind went completely blank. He simply smiled in response, and I knew he didn't care. Short of me declaring myself to be Jack the Ripper, he really just didn't want to be bothered with the other potentially sordid details of my past. Love, for him, was indeed blind.

"Petra is, and will always be, a delightful combination of contradictions," Harrow finally said, winking at Mac. The remark was a release, of sorts, telling Mac that the topic was off bounds and of no consequence.

"As are all ladies," Mac replied, raising his teacup at Miss Douglas, who smiled in response.

Kipp, to rescue me, made a big production of going to the door and whining. I knew he could probably open it himself, but I excused myself and let him out, following behind him outside into the rear garden. All the pretty and fragrant flowers from spring and summer were long dormant; the trees thrust their bare limbs up into the flawless, blue sky. The air was cool with a brisk cleansing wind from the northwest; only the mildest scent of sulfur hung in the breeze.

I heard steps behind me on the cobblestone pathway—it was Harrow. Courteously, he removed his jacket and placed it about my shoulders. The garment contained the warmth from his body, which felt like velvet against me, as well as the subtle scent of his cologne. I turned to look at him.

"I told you I didn't care," he said, his face neutral. "I meant it."

He was referring to the Highlands slip I'd made. I knew he was curious…he had to be…but his love was greater than his busy, inquiring mind.

"I'm so happy for Mac and Margaret," I said, choosing to not reply to his comment. "He's had many tragedies, and it's time he finds lasting joy."

"I agree," Harrow said, as he raised his face up to gaze at the sky arching overhead. "Maybe some of the recent horrors are truly behind all of us, and we can move forward and plan for the future."

He was thinking of Jack the Ripper, his and Mac's past in the war, as well as the loss of his brother and sister-in-law. Kipp crossed over to him, and Harrow's hand moved down to caress his large, upright ears. Kipp's eyes closed in pleasure at the gentleness of Harrow's touch.

"Right now, the priority will be to help Mac and Margaret plan their wedding," I replied, smiling a little too brightly. My future was set and unchanging, as best I could see.

CHAPTER 30

"You know, Petra, you can make the choice to stay here and marry Harrow, if that's what you want to do." Kipp was still reclining on the bed. He'd rolled on his back, and his feet were sticking up in the air towards the ceiling. "I'm content and happy to be anywhere you call home," he added. He stretched his head back and looked at me from an upside down position; his jowls sagged, exposing his teeth in a gruesome display.

I was struggling with the strings on my modified foundation garment, thankful it was not a full-fledged corset designed to crush my rib cage. It was another school day, and I was running late to meet John Parks and begin the daily routine. The past few days had been a little sad and perhaps unconsciously led me to lag that morning. Harrow had finished the applications and dear little Allen would transition to his new school in a couple of weeks. Although Silas had made clear to Harrow that he and I would be leaving towards the end of November, Harrow pretended to ignore that fact in the hope that I would change my mind and stay behind with him. Consequently, he was making no preparations to replace me at the school. After his initial declaration of love, he thankfully did not hound me on a constant basis, nagging me to stay. I appreciated his character in that he made his feelings known and then stepped back to allow me time to consider. But his feelings were present, written all over his face every time he looked at me. There's a certain softening of features when someone is deeply in love, and I saw it played daily against the harsh masculine angles of his face.

"It's happened again, as scheduled," Kipp said, changing the subject abruptly, as he rolled over off of his back and onto his belly. Jumping to the floor, he shook his coat hard; I saw hair fly off into the air to be caught with dust particles floating erratically in the light. "Mary Kelly has been found, mutilated."

He was picking up on the news floating up through the wooden floor boards from downstairs. Since the last killings had been in September, London had relaxed her vigilance, thinking the killer was done and had either moved on, been killed or maybe incarcerated. But, no, after disappearing for a while, he was back at his grisly task as the time continuum predicted. Silas continued to make trips to the London Hospital, hoping for the occasional encounter with Frank Lewiston. So, I knew that some of the historical speculation that perhaps the man responsible had been jailed for some petty crime, thus accounting for the lapse in killings, was incorrect. Lewiston just chose to not seek out another victim for reasons of his own. Silas and Vashti came to the conclusion that he was playing with the police and the press by his haphazard patterns of what he did and when.

I finished dressing in one of my utilitarian outfits and was wearing the recently purchased wool flannel petticoat, which helped a little with warmth and comfort. In addition to the coat I'd bought, I purchased a wool short jacket that I could wear over my blouse at school to combat the ever present draftiness inherent inside a large building with tall ceilings. With a last glance in the mirror, I fastened the pearl necklace around my throat and dashed downstairs, followed by a galloping Kipp. It was obvious the men had finished breakfast as the dining room was empty, so I raced through to the kitchen. Harrow and Mac were donning their coats and hats as I arrived.

"I'm so sorry," I gasped. "I overslept."

Harrow smiled. "We haven't left, so it's not a problem, Petra," he remarked. "We will wait while you have some breakfast."

I insisted I not hold up our departure; Mrs. Atherton, ignoring my protests, thrust a small package in my hands. Like a schoolgirl, I had my bagged lunch ready to take onto the school bus.

"Your doggie there snuck down earlier, and I gave him something to eat," she commented, pointing at Kipp.

"And you didn't bother to wake me," I said to Kipp, narrowing my eyes. He chose to ignore me and ran out the door that Mac opened.

A blast of cool air hit us as we crossed the yard to the carriage. John Parks was bundled up for the day he'd spend outside, with a wool muffler concealing most of his face. Despite the temperature, he removed his hat as I approached; the northern wind caught his hair and dislodged strands that had been slicked down by pomade. John would always have a certain degree of protective fondness for me.

As the carriage began the trip to Whitechapel, I peeked inside the cloth bag from the cook. It contained a biscuit, some cheese and one of the pretty apples from the fresh market. Kipp was on the seat next to me, so I crumbled off some biscuit to give to him. Mrs. Atherton didn't know that my symbiont constitution would protect me from hunger and deprivation. I could actually go days with little to no food, as long as I had access to water. Across from me, Harrow and Mac wore looks of amusement on their faces.

"Losing your sharpness with your time, aren't you?" Harrow remarked, wanting to tease me.

"I didn't sleep well," I replied, looking out the window. Despite the cool weather, the activity in London was unchecked. Vendors selling fresh meat pies, as well as other men and women hawking their wares, were shouting out in competitive voices made shrill from fatigue as we passed. Numerous wagons delivering coal to homes and businesses crowded the streets. An enormous dray full of lumber rumbled by as its weight seemed to make the street surface tremble. London's growth was marching onwards regardless of Jack the Ripper.

"Sometimes people don't sleep well because their minds are full of worry," Harrow remarked, trying not to smile. "They go to sleep thinking of things they've not taken care of…unfinished business, so to speak."

"Or," Mac chimed in, "they have decisions to make, and it just weighs heavy on them until they do so."

I stared at each of them in turn. "Okay, thank you both very much for your analysis of my sleeping patterns." Raising an eyebrow, I remarked, sarcastically, "I'll take the information under advisement."

Harrow laughed lightly. "However, Petra, on a more serious note, there has been another murder attributed to Jack the Ripper. It occurred at Miller's Court, which is not too far distant from the school." He turned to peer out the window, his beloved face lost to me for the moment. "I need to ask you to continue to be careful and allow one of us to accompany you if you leave during the day."

I started to protest but stopped when he glanced at me, and I saw the expression on his face. I don't know how to describe it except that he already suffered enough over the uncertainty of my response to him without my compounding the issue by causing him worry over my safety.

"Yes, I promise," I replied meekly, although passivity was not typically part of my nature. Kipp pushed closer, and I draped my arm around his neck. His warmth was welcomed as were his thoughts.

"We'll make it through this together, Petra, no matter the outcome." Kipp nuzzled my cheek before sticking his nose into the cloth bag, begging for the piece of breakfast cheese.

* * *

At recess time, I accompanied my class outside to the courtyard to let them get some exercise and burn off any mischievous scheming attributed to built-up excess energy. As I stood watching their antics, I felt a duo of familiar thought patterns: Silas and Vashti quietly approached from the rear.

"I need to talk with you," Silas said, nodding his head.

Another teacher was in the courtyard, so I begged to be excused, and we walked to my classroom, which was empty. After closing the door, I sat down at my desk, Kipp close by. Silas began to pace back and forth across the worn floor; Vashti seemed distressed, but her thoughts were carefully guarded, and I didn't intrude on her privacy.

"As you know, there have been many letters sent by people purporting to be Jack the Ripper," Silas began. "Some are forgeries, some are from nut cases and probably some are journalists trying to stoke a frenzy in order to sell more papers." He stopped walking and came over to sit on the edge of my desk. "We received one at the *Telegraph* today, and I think it is the real deal. It was addressed to the city editor and me, by name, and the reference that concerned me was one about 'suffer the little children.'"

Silas's eyes met mine across the short distance. From outside, we could hear the high pitched shouts of the boys as someone obviously kicked the ball harder than expected. I thought I could hear Allen's distinctive voice above the others.

"Are you happy now?" I tried to keep my voice low but was so furious that if I had been a more physical person, I probably would have slapped Silas until he begged for mercy. "I told you to leave it alone, but, no, you just had to keep going back. You've attracted the interest of a lunatic, and now he wants to strike something close to you that will be even more horrible, if that is possible."

He immediately began defensive backtracking. "But Petra, that behavior would be atypical for a serial killer driven by sexual urges to suddenly change his target." Silas shrugged his shoulders. "Maybe it's another crank message."

"You know it's not, Silas," I replied, trying to keep my voice low. "You tried to analyze and outthink a killer. Did it occur to you there may be a part of him that does this stuff just to get a reaction to the horror…so that he feels powerful? What would be more terrible than preying upon children? Maybe Frank Lewiston is changing his game plan as a part of being clever and unpredictable."

I was definitely not an expert on psychology, nor was I interested in becoming one. But common sense dictated that when you poke at a cobra, he might just strike back. It was then I violated some of our rules, and I didn't even bother to ask Kipp to do it covertly. Brazenly, I merged my thoughts with Silas's and dug deeper than is conventionally acceptable. His face reddened as I found what I wanted.

"That intrusion was totally uncalled for," he protested. "I will tell you what I know without that sort of assault."

"I don't trust you, Silas, in case I've not made that fact clear. At this point, I don't even have words for you. From your last meeting with Lewiston you knew what he was thinking but covered it up and hoped he'd change his mind. Then you managed to talk Kipp and me into a deeper exposure and involvement. The letter to you just validated what you already knew. You are despicable." I glanced at Vashti. "I'd hoped you could keep Silas in line, but I see that my worries were well founded." Her ears folded back as she ducked her head. I knew she despised conflict, but she had a responsibility as a member of the partnership she formed with Silas. I stood, no longer able to sit still and feel as upset as I did.

"But I didn't know, Petra," Vashti began before I waved her off.

Silas must have blocked the information from her, and she wouldn't have intruded into his closely guarded thoughts. At that point, I didn't care.

Kipp stood up and came over to nuzzle my hand. "Petra, take a deep breath and calm down. We need to problem solve, and you can't help if you stay this agitated."

There was a soft tap on the door, and it opened before I

could call out. It was Harrow.

"Is there something wrong?" he asked, frowning. From the agitation he could sense in me to Silas's red, avoidant face, I knew that it would be stupid to say "no" and hope he'd leave.

"Yes, Will, there's something wrong." I managed to make myself sit at my desk. Harrow walked in, followed by Mac, who closed the door to the classroom so we'd not be overheard.

"Silas received a letter at the *Telegraph*. It was from someone who claims to be Jack the Ripper, and he made a not-so-veiled threat at children. We both think he means the children here." I looked up at Silas, who finally managed to get his breathing under control. He looked at Harrow and nodded his head.

"This is all very confusing to me, Petra," Harrow said, crossing his arms at his chest as if the action would help him think more clearly.

"I've been asking a lot of questions of people since the killings began," Silas said, pulling Harrow's attention from me. "I think I made someone angry."

"But who would associate you with the school?" Mac asked.

"I have a suspicion as to the identity of Jack the Ripper, but it's nothing that can be proved. I've made a point of spending a lot of time in his vicinity, and since Petra is my sister, she has been with me often. He became aware of her involvement in the school." Silas shrugged his shoulders. "Our best guess is that he's being vindictive and thinks he's clever by shifting his targets."

"So, who is this man?" Harrow asked. He'd taken a seat on the corner of one of the student's desks.

"He works at the London Hospital, but, as I said, there is not one iota of proof against him." Silas looked over at me; the flush was gone from his flesh, leaving his face pale and drawn. At Harrow's prodding, Silas mentioned Frank Lewiston's name, but the man was unfamiliar to Harrow.

Mac sighed. "Maybe the proof is in what happened. But

if we have no evidence for the police, I don't know where to go except to protect the school, as we've been doing."

Harrow's eyes met mine. "What do you think, Petra?" He asked because he trusted me; he'd never been sure of Silas.

"I think you need to guard the school well," I answered. Kipp put his jaw on the edge of the desk as I scratched between his upright ears.

Silas began walking towards the door. Vashti, after a moment's hesitation, rose and followed. "I think I'll stay at the *Telegraph* for a few nights," Silas said, nodding at Harrow, who did not argue. "The city editor has a cot in his office for anyone who's in the doghouse at home."

"In the doghouse?" Mac repeated. "That's an odd turn of phrase."

Silas shrugged. "In any case, I think I'll make myself scarce until Petra can cool off a little." He avoided my stare.

"From the look of things, that might be a while," Harrow replied.

CHAPTER 31

"Where is Mr. Harrow?" I asked, as Mrs. Donnelly passed me in the hallway to the library. I'd already looked, and he was missing from his usual corner chair, the one closest to the fireplace.

Two days had passed since my altercation with Silas. So far, nothing unusual had occurred, and Harrow continued to employ an armed guard at the school. There was a male teacher who boarded there and oversaw the second level dormitory for the boys, but he was not armed. I thought I'd probably be more useful in a fight than would he.

"Mr. Harrow said something about the guard being ill, and he took off in this cold, wet weather to go stay at the school overnight." Mrs. Donnelly nodded courteously and disappeared towards the kitchen. I could hear the sound of metal on metal and recognized Mrs. Atherton was putting away cooking pots.

Kipp looked up at me. "What do you want to do?"

"Well, what do you think we should do, Kipp?" I asked. Obviously my judgment was clouded by my feelings for Harrow, so I had to trust my partner.

Kipp looked at the front door. "I don't like the idea of him being there alone; maybe it's intuition, but I want to go down there and check on him."

Well, it would be truly intuition, since even with Kipp's

exceptional abilities, he couldn't read the mind of Frank Lewiston and determine his intentions from halfway across London. I needed no further encouragement, and, after grabbing my coat and hat, we quietly exited by the front entrance. Rushing along the mist dampened street, we had to cross a couple more before we found a vacant four wheeler for hire. Before I could second guess the rashness of my actions, the driver slapped the reins along the back of the horse and off we went into the darkness.

I'd told the driver to hurry, and he drove as fast as possible, considering the elements; that particular night was moonless, and the gas lights were doing little to ward off the impenetrable blackness that enveloped the streets. I almost felt like we were hurtling down a tunnel to some terrifying destination. Kipp pushed in close to me as I placed my arm over his back. At one point he turned and licked my chin.

"It'll be okay," he said, in the way a friend makes a meaningless promise just to console one's heart and spirit.

As we pulled to a halt, I almost leapt out of the carriage and, after giving the driver some coins, raced up the front steps to the now familiar school. Pausing, I took a moment to catch my breath; corsets did little to facilitate efficient sprint running.

"Kipp, look!" I said. The front door was ajar, just a sliver, but it was unlocked all the same.

Kipp began to pivot his head back and forth, throwing out his telepathic net as well as using his superior senses. I saw his body stiffen, and a strip of hair rose from his head down along his back to his tail.

"He's close by," Kipp said. "I can't tell if he's inside or somewhere else on the grounds."

It made sense to check inside first, since that's where the children were clustered. My hand trembled slightly as I reached out to push the heavy door inwards. I followed instantly, Kipp pressed against my right leg for support. Once inside, I took a moment to allow my eyes to adjust to the dimness; there were a few lanterns flickering along the corridors. Ahead, I saw a body crumpled on the floor. I knew immediately who it was and ran forward without consideration for danger. Kipp raced along by me, while continuing to try and telepathically pinpoint Lewiston's location.

"Will!" I cried out softly, dropping to my knees next to him. At first I thought the worst, since he didn't respond. Placing my forefinger and middle finger on his neck, I felt for a pulse. Thankfully, the beat was strong and regular. Gently, I ran my fingers along the back of his head until I found it—a large lump where someone had struck him with some blunt object. When I withdrew my hand, I felt dampness, and the metallic smell of blood confirmed the injury.

"I think the skin was broken when he was hit," I said to Kipp. My partner, however, had other, more pressing concerns.

"He's in here, somewhere," Kipp remarked, his thoughts focused and intense.

I could hear Lewiston's thoughts, too, when I took a moment to listen. They were the thoughts of a demented predator who was, at that moment, enjoying himself as his excitement spiraled, since he knew we were in the building with him.

"I want you to go upstairs and check the dormitory," I said. "I'll wait here with Harrow until you return."

"I'm not leaving you alone down here," Kipp replied defiantly.

Without speaking, I turned to Harrow's body and reached inside his coat to an inner pocket. Carefully, I withdrew his service revolver. Kipp's eyes opened wide as he saw the heavy object in my hand.

"You know how to shoot that thing?" he asked.

"Oh, yes," I replied confidently. A friend of mine on the Durham police force had taught me the basics. I was no professional, but I could handle myself.

Although neither of us wanted to be parted from the other, it was the only thing we could do in a bad situation. Reassured as to my safety, Kipp turned and began to race towards the back staircase that led upstairs. "Be careful," his voice trailed off in my head.

"You, too, Kipp."

Adjusting my position slightly, I managed to pull off my wool coat and spread it over Harrow. There was obviously some risk of him going into shock, and lying on the cold floor wouldn't help things a bit. Picking up the gun again, I took a moment to test the heft of it in my right hand. The soft squeak of a door close by broke my concentration. Looking up, I saw one of the classroom doors slowly open into the corridor; a pale white hand was grasping the edge of the wood. A second later, a man appeared, dressed in dark clothing with a type of oilcloth mackintosh around his shoulders. He wore a hat pulled down low, but I knew who he was and nothing would hide his identity from me.

"Hello, Mr. Lewiston," I said. Maybe if I could keep him busy, it would give Kipp time to return; it would take both of us to deal with this man.

"Aren't you the clever one?" he replied. Almost as an instinctive act of courtesy, he pulled off his hat.

He took a step towards me, then another one. His hand reached into one of the deep pockets of his greatcoat; as he pulled it free, the glint of metal in his hand was caught by the low lighting of the gas lantern overhead. Harrow moaned and moved slightly on the floor.

"In fact, all of you think you're cleverer than me, but I'm the one with the knife, and I'm the one the police can't catch." He took another step closer. "Mr. Merrick will be sorry to hear of your death, miss."

I stood and raised the gun towards him. Recalling my lessons, I assumed a classic stance, using both my hands to steady the weapon. I'd always been told that one needed to be willing to pull the trigger or else you didn't need to have a gun in your hands. There was no doubt in my mind that I could pull the trigger.

Lewiston didn't seem fazed and laughed softly. "I took the liberty of removing the bullets," he said. Reaching into his left pocket, he pulled out a handful of metal objects and dropped them to the floor. The bullets cascaded down, hitting the wood surface with an echoing sound. "I hope you don't mind," he added.

Stupid, stupid, stupid, I thought to myself, almost wanting to tap my forehead in frustration. The instructions from my friend echoed inside my empty brain—always check to see if the gun is loaded. With few other options springing nimbly to the forefront, I decided to try and delay the man as long as possible. "Your days of killing women are at an end, Lewiston," I began. "All that history will record is a pathologically sick man who preyed on helpless people. But the death of Mary Kelly is your last."

"And how would you know such things?" he asked, smiling at me again; his teeth looked sharp and gleamed in the manner of a hungry animal. "You'll be a step up from the others, what with your fine self."

"Maybe I'm a time traveler from the future and know your destiny," I replied, trying to shake his confidence by what would seem to be a nonsensical comment.

It was then I heard the quick pace of Kipp's paws as he raced back down the steps. He pulled up short next to me and took a position at my side as we stared at Jack the Ripper.

"I'll cut the heart out of your dog just to have fun and get my knife warmed up for you," Lewiston said. The smile left his face, which became terrifyingly expressionless.

Kipp took a step towards Lewiston and lowered himself into a crouch; his growls echoed in the dark hallway. From Lewiston's thoughts, I knew he was blustering in his boasts about Kipp. Being faced by a very large dog which was showing almost every tooth in his head in an aggressive snarl would disconcert even the boldest person. Kipp knew Lewiston's thoughts, too, and began to press his advantage by moving a step forward to try and intimidate the man.

"Well, Kipp, we have a standoff," I said. "What do we do now?"

Kipp started to reply but was interrupted when the front door to the school swung back. The tall, familiar figure of

Mac, who'd come once Mrs. Donnelly told him I'd disappeared in a hurry, stood in the aperture. Mac, with his military service, summed up the potential danger in a flash. Lewiston, seeing his plans had suddenly disintegrated, turned and ran down the hallway, angling sharply into the last classroom. Without hesitation, Kipp charged after him, his claws scrabbling for a purchase on the polished floor. Of course, I took off after Kipp. Symbionts are just like that, I suppose. Mac began to follow but paused, for a second, to check on Harrow, who began moving and was trying to get to his knees.

From the room ahead, we heard a terrible crash and the shattering of glass. Kipp darted in, with me a step or two behind. One of the large windows had been broken out and all that was left was a jagged hole where the cold night air began to blow into the room. Kipp ran up to the sill and, after gauging the jump, leapt out and into the darkness.

I've never claimed to be the most courageous symbiont, but there was no way I'd let Kipp chase that man alone into the blackness of Whitechapel. So, after kicking free any obvious glass with my boot, I stepped up on the sill and jumped to the ground below, which was on the same level of the window. I stumbled upon landing and fell on my right side. A sharp pain in my lower leg made me catch my breath, but I didn't pause to examine the injured limb. Clumsily, I lurched to my feet and began to run down the alleyway after Kipp.

As I fought the constriction of my corset and the cold air that was trying to force my respiratory passages to shut in protest, I raced along after Kipp, gauging his path by the startled reactions of onlookers as well as his retreating thoughts. Unexpectedly, from ahead, I heard the high pitched scream of a man. Continuing my flight, I saw a crowd beginning to gather at the edge of the street. A ragtag cluster of people surrounded a large dray pulled by a team of four draft horses; beneath the front wheels of the dray, was the body of a man.

"Poor sod, he never had a chance," one man muttered,

removing his hat. "He just ran out in front of that team like a daft fool." Other people began to utter similar comments while the shrill sound of a police whistle tore the night air.

Kipp unobtrusively ducked his way back through the crowd and returned to my side. As he looked up at me, the light from a gas lamp post caught the spark of amber in his eyes.

"Frank Lewiston won't hurt anyone again," Kipp said. Tilting his head, he added, "Wasn't this the way it should have happened, only the five deaths and no more?"

Reaching down, I dug my fingers into his dense fur. "Yes, Kipp, the timeline has been unchanged."

Turning our backs on the spectacle, we began to retrace our steps to the school. My adrenaline surge had expended itself, and unwillingly I surrendered to the pain in my leg and began to limp. I needed to stop and examine the injury but didn't want to hike up my skirts out in the middle of Whitechapel. Kipp poked his nose down towards my boot and gave an exclamation.

"You're bleeding!" he said. "I can smell it."

I reassured him I wouldn't die before we could get back to the school. Despite my confident thoughts, there was no one happier than I to see the familiar building take shape in the darkness. As I pushed open the main door, I was mildly surprised to see several people present, including Harrow—who was finally on his feet, with Mac's support—along with a uniformed policeman. Harrow's head went up, and he walked to me, although his gait was none too steady. Forgoing the usual Victorian sensibilities, he pulled me hard against his chest.

"Oh, Petra!" he exclaimed, tightening his arms around me. I knew he wanted to say more but couldn't find the words.

I allowed myself to melt against him and be held, despite what anyone else might think. After a long moment, he pushed me away, his hands on my upper arms, so that he could inspect me.

"Are you unharmed?" he asked.

"Yes, I think so, except my leg hurts," I replied. "Are the

boys safe?" I asked, raising my head to look around the lobby.

He gazed down at the floor where blood was pooling around my right boot. I followed his glance with surprise and looked back to see a bloody trail that tracked from the front door to where I was standing.

"Oh, my!" I cried in dismay.

Harrow was still unsteady and had not regained his balance, so without any words exchanged between the two, Mac walked over and picked me up as if I was a feather. He carried me into Harrow's office and sat me down, Kipp following, his nose touching my feet with worry.

"Not to be impertinent, Petra," Mac said, "but I need to check your leg."

Harrow followed us, wobbling slightly, and pulled up another chair so he could help. "Put your foot on my knee," he instructed. I propped my heel on his knee and tried not to wince at the pain.

Mac, as delicately as possible, pulled up my skirt hem. My right stocking was soaked in blood, from the area below my knee to my foot. Obviously, I'd been cut on the outside of my right lower leg from the glass when I stumbled as I vaulted from the window sill. Since I thought it would embarrass the men to have to pull off my stocking, I leaned forward and did it myself. Yes, there was a sizeable gaping wound roughly three to four inches long; blood was flowing freely but at least it was not arterial spurting, so I knew I'd live.

The sight of my injury must have cleared the residual fog in Harrow's brain because he began barking commands. Fortunately, we were near the London Hospital, so he directed one of the police to go and fetch back a surgeon. Another man was sent upstairs to get some linen and the third was made to go to the kitchen and begin heating water. It must have been his military background that gave him the ability to quickly prioritize needs and give orders.

So there I sat, my bare leg resting on the knee of the man who loved me. The moment could have had interesting possibilities but the timing was wrong. Kipp glanced at me, and his tongue lolled out in a lupine smile—he only wished he had an eyebrow to lift in whimsical humor. The moment was not lost on him.

Harrow used one of the clean towels to apply pressure to the cut. While we waited on a surgeon, the police inspector joined us to get a statement. I took it on myself, in consideration of the fact that symbionts must try to not change the arc of history, to plant a suggestion with the police…one, I hoped, which would lead them to not consider Lewiston as a viable Jack the Ripper candidate. If it worked, history would continue to consider the Whitechapel murders to be unsolved.

"I think my brother Silas, in all of his interviewing, drew the attention of a copy cat killer, someone desperate for attention. It was clear his target was children, not the women from the streets of Whitechapel." I looked up at the inspector and gave him my very best innocent face.

"Good one," Kipp chimed in. "You're faster at lying than I am."

"A skill honed by years of practice, my son," I replied.

I relayed all the important points of what had occurred, tactfully omitting the part where I told Lewiston that I was a time traveler and the fact that Kipp and I were telepaths. Somehow, that probably would have confused the issue—and not in a good way.

Harrow stared at me as I talked, occasionally shaking his head in amazement. Mac tried not to smile as I described my leap from the shattered window sill. His mind wondered if there was something inherently cheeky about these Americans that their women felt emboldened to chase armed killers through unfamiliar streets.

"Remind me, later, to tell you how angry I am that you put yourself in danger," Harrow said. His blue gray eyes wore an unusually stern expression.

I looked down at my leg; the blood was starting to seep through the thin towel. When I glanced up at him, his face had relaxed. I knew his statement was made out of fear for my safety.

"Will," Mac said, "it was the boldest thing I've seen in a long time. She and Kipp were standing in between Lewiston and you. I got the feeling if he'd made a move towards you, she and that old dog of hers would have torn him to pieces." He laughed and shook his head. "An amazing sight for this soldier to see." Mac nodded at me. "Will tried to get up and follow after you and toppled over again; I managed to catch him before he hit the floor."

"Who is an old dog, might I ask?" Kipp said, coming up to put his head in my lap. "I'm a young lad, still."

I leaned forward and pressed my cheek against his fur. "Oh, Kipp, you are just too wonderful for words," I said, my mind conveying all the love I felt for him. Turning my head, I caught Harrow's eyes on me in an unblinking stare.

"Yes?" I asked, raising my eyebrows.

"You are an amazing woman, Petra Hathaway," he replied simply.

The surgeon arrived and tended to both me and Harrow, who had a cut to the back of his head but no permanent damage from what seemed to be a mild concussion. Having lived through the next century into modern times, I can categorically state that contemporary syringes and needles are vastly superior to the old, reusable kinds. The needle tip, after multiple uses, tends to get dull, and I think I got a needle that had been used at the zoo on the tough fanny of a rhinoceros. Kipp, who kept his head on my lap during the entire procedure, whined a few times in the sympathetic reaction of a bonded partner. The surgeon was none too happy at having a very large canine staring at his every move, but there was no way for me to convince Kipp he could leave—Harrow either, for that matter. Yes, the two guys who loved me most of all were in close attendance.

While the surgeon was finishing up with me, I was slightly surprised to see Silas, who'd been fetched by a thoughtful Mac. Not past my last agitated encounter, I greeted him with all the frigid coolness I could summon.

"Is she going to be okay?" he asked the surgeon. At the affirmative reply, Silas's shoulders, which were bunched up almost to his ears, suddenly relaxed.

"I'm so sorry, Petra," he said, his words audible for the others to hear. "This is my fault for involving you."

"It's over now," I replied. Telepathically, I added, "No one else will suffer and the timeline of history should be intact." Looking up at Silas, I added, "And that's all that really matters."

"Miss Hathaway will need care to make certain that her leg heals properly," the surgeon muttered in a monotone voice, as he began to replace the tools of his trade into a leather bag.

"I will have my personal physician follow up on your much appreciated work," Harrow said.

"And you," the surgeon said, pointing at Harrow, "need to go home and rest. A knock on the head can have consequences too, and the best thing is to let your body recover."

Mac and I almost simultaneously replied that we would make certain Harrow rested as ordered. The ride to Mayfair was made in relative silence. The surgeon gave me a pain killing powder to take as soon as I arrived home, and although I was not usually apt to take medications, I changed my mind and drank the powder mixed in a little water. My leg throbbed, and I would never sleep unless the pain lessened.

Climbing into bed, I pulled up my gown and stared at the neat row of stitches. The surgeon had done an efficient job of patching the wound, which needed both internal and external sutures. Kipp examined the wound, his perceptive nose a millimeter from my flesh.

"I'll have a scar," I replied. "It's a good thing I'm not overly vain or it could be a problem."

Settling back into the dense mattress, I felt the opiate powder begin to take effect. Reaching out, I pulled Kipp close, and he rested his head against my breast bone.

"Kipp, don't let me dream tonight, please," I requested.

"I promise," he replied.

CHAPTER 32

The close encounter Kipp and I had with Jack the Ripper left Silas profoundly shaken, and, after another impolite invasive sifting of his thoughts, I believe he found humility at last—or at the very least was on such a journey towards introspection. Learning that our actions have consequences that can harm others is the first step to thinking with more deliberation and care. However, he hadn't returned to Harrow's house, and our date for leaving for home now loomed. There was no need to remain in London, and every day I did so only mired me more deeply, emotionally, in the time. I tried to think of Kipp, too, despite his declarations that he would be happy anywhere—as long as he was with me.

"But it's true, Petra," he said, as we strolled down a neatly kept Mayfair sidewalk. It was mid-November and one of those blustery, gray days with threatening dark clouds looming overhead. As much as I enjoy a cheery blue sky, I equally find pleasure and solace in a stormy day. Maybe my inner angst is unexpectedly soothed in the midst of a storm, when the wind-tossed rain lashes the window panes, and the air is raw with uncertainty.

"I am happy with you. As fate would have it, I live with you in modern day North Carolina. You could have just easily visited my time from any place else in the world for the past three hundred years or so." He twisted his large head and looked towards the heavens, smelling rain with his keen nose. "We need to start home," he observed. "And I mean home here," he added, nuzzling my hand.

We began a slow circle and doubled back. At one point, I had to grab the brim of my gray wool hat when the wind got under the lid and almost popped it off my head.

"I'd miss Lily, Fitzhugh, Philo and Juno, but other than that, life goes on," Kipp remarked. "And you know, there are symbionts here in London; we've just not made attempts to find them. I feel the remote pinging of at least two pairs somewhere."

"I didn't," I replied, widening my eyes as I looked at him.

"Well, you aren't as good as am I," he answered smugly but honestly.

I'd begged off from any "family" events for the past couple of days, by claiming that my leg bothered me. In truth, it only was the least bit sore; I was making my separation from the others. To help Daniel with the upcoming transition, occasionally I reminded him I had to return to America. He expressed some dismay, but he had, in a healthy way, developed attachments for his dog, Lily, as well as his governess. So our leaving would not leave a gaping hole to be filled. Mac's heart was complete with his love of Miss Douglas, so he was sad but happy at the same time. Harrow, I avoided completely.

We ducked in the doorway just as the storm began. Both Kipp and I laughed as we shook off the few raindrops that assaulted us before we got inside. Mrs. Donnelly met me, taking my coat and hat, and gently explained that dinner was almost served. Again, I managed to lie competently by claiming pain in my leg. She offered to send up some clear broth and toast, but I declined and told her I might raid the kitchen later after resting. The housekeeper raised her dark eyebrows, since it was not in her nature to allow a guest to function so independently in the confines of her domain, but there was little she could do to launch an argument. In the comfort of my terra cotta colored room, I lost track of the time. I was reading one of the volumes from Harrow's extensive library, when there was a tap on my door—it was Jean.

"Miss, if you beg pardon, please, the master asks if you can join him in the library for a moment." She gave a neat little curtsey and disappeared down the hallway. A sweet natured child, I thought, as I watched her retreat. She was fortunate to serve in a household that was led by an ethical, kind man; many were not so fortunate.

Kipp and I traded glances. His tongue lolled out but not in his usual smiling fashion. I recognized he was mildly stressed, too, with all the hidden agendas and uncertainties. Leaning forward, I scratched between his ears as he began to pant.

"Let's go."

As I tapped on the door to the library, I looked down and smoothed the front of my blouse. My fingers went up to touch the cool strand of pearls around my neck. This, I thought to myself, will not go to the company vault at Technicorps. The necklace was a gift to me, and I planned on keeping it.

The door swung back; Harrow stood in the aperture, neatly dressed as was typical for him. I'd caught him rumpled or untidy a few times, but usually after he'd fallen asleep on the couch in the library. His black hair, still a little long for the day, touched the crisp white collar of his shirt; he wore a vest but no coat. I thought he'd not shaven, since his face looked shadowed from a couple of day's growth of potential beard.

"Come in," he said, standing back and waving me inside with a gesture. He was pleasant but seemed politely cautious and reserved.

Heat radiated from the fireplace into the room. Oil lamps were in use instead of the more modern gas fixtures; the result was changing levels of light, flickering and with mysterious reserve. Outside, the storm was beginning to escalate; I jumped involuntarily when a flash of lightening outlined the two large windows. The burst of static in the air caused Kipp's hair to rise momentarily so that he looked like a big, red puffball.

"Since you didn't come to dinner, I asked Mrs. Atherton to prepare a small tray of sandwiches so that we could share a meal," he remarked. The tray was sitting on the low table in front of the couch. He didn't wait for me but moved to the couch and sat at one end, facing the yellow light glowing from the fireplace. Kipp walked ahead of me and curled up in the prime spot in front of the fire, his face pointed at the couch. I joined Harrow, sitting at least a couple of feet from him. In truth, I was not hungry, but reached out and took the cup of tea he poured.

"And how is your wound?" he inquired, sitting back and crossing his long legs. It was obvious he had no interest in food, either.

"Oh, better," I replied. "Still sore at times, but thankfully without inflammation." Blowing on the rim of the teacup, I took a cautious sip. The steam rising off the beverage tickled my nose.

"Silas visited me at the school today and informed me that you will be leaving in two days," Harrow remarked.

I nodded my head and reached out for a quarter of a watercress sandwich, placing the morsel on a small, delicate plate. Maybe if I kept eating and drinking, he would leave all of this pointless dialog and go on to other topics. But I knew he wouldn't.

"A year ago, I made a trip to visit an old university friend of mine who now is a master at the Normal School of Science." Harrow paused to sip at the fragrant tea. It was still too hot for pleasant consumption, and he replaced the cup on the tray. "I met an interesting young man admitted under a scholarship. His name was Herbert G. Wells, and I was struck by his fanciful thoughts and creative turn of mind." Harrow glanced at me across the softly lit room. "He had begun work on a story about time travel and was very convincing in some of the ideas he proposed."

I felt my heart push up into the back of my throat. My choice to not monitor his thoughts was again leading me into unnavigated waters. I looked at Kipp who yawned, showing every tooth in his head. Deliberately, he blocked his thoughts; I was on my own, obviously. Harrow dug into one of his narrow vest pockets and pulled out something small and shiny.

"You gave this to John Parks," he said, reaching out to hand the object to me. "I'd like to know what it is and how it came into your possession."

Holding out my hand, I waited while he dropped the object into my palm. It was a coin; I held it closer to my face for viewing. It happened so quickly that I could not control my expression of dismay, as I realized I was holding a 1982 American nickel, complete with Jefferson's profile on one side and Monticello on the other. Raising my eyes, I stared at Harrow, unable to think of anything plausible to say. In the next second, I thought of ten thousand lies I could have told, with the adaptive skill of my kind, but I lacked the heart to do so.

"How long have you had this?" I asked, willing myself to speak.

Harrow uncrossed his legs and scooted down the couch until he was close to me. With care, he reached out and took the coin from my fingers which were numbed with anxiety.

"John gave it to me several weeks ago," he answered simply. "When I was on the floor of the school and beginning to regain consciousness, I recall hearing you say something to Lewiston." He looked up as he attempted to recall the memory. "You told him that perhaps you were a time traveler and knew his destiny."

"Surely you misheard me," I began, but stopped speaking when I saw the expression on his face.

"Can you explain this coin?" he asked.

"No, I can't. Please don't ask me to, Will."

He took a deep breath as he gazed intently at the coin, which rested in the palm of his hand. "Admittedly, I was the most inadequate student at university in applied physics. And I have always lacked the poetic nuance to craft a meaningful story of any sort. But, I learned one thing from my time as a soldier, and that is the world is filled with the inexplicable. I saw men on the battlefield who should have, by all the laws of human physiology, died, but managed to live. Was it a miracle, I wondered? Or was it something that defied nature itself and just happened because it was meant to?" He smiled and replaced the coin into his vest pocket, patting the wool tweed fabric gently as if he was carrying a gem of incalculable value next to his body.

"I understand the need to embrace the inexplicable and not always search for answers and meanings in all things." Harrow seemed weary as he stretched his neck back, tilting his face towards the ceiling. His chest rose and fell as he sighed deeply. "Perhaps that is the mark of a shallow mind...or at least my mother would think so. But in any case, I'm content to not demand an explanation from you, since it might imply things that I cannot intellectually accept. Are you married?" he asked, unexpectedly.

"No."

"Do you have family?"

"Only Kipp," I replied.

"Not even Silas," he asked.

"No, not even Silas," I responded.

"Must you leave?" he finally asked, his eyes searching my face.

"Yes, Will."

"Will you come back?" His face was open, raw and vulnerable.

I looked away from him and into the fire. Kipp raised his head and looked at me, waiting.

"I don't know the answer to that," I finally said, my voice soft.

Harrow smiled, but the animation didn't quite make it to his unforgettable eyes. "Ah, you did not say no, and on that indefinite I can maintain hope." His face became serious again. "You have been remarkably circumspect as to your feelings toward me, and I believe I'm owed an honest answer, since I have not demanded a full explanation of all these other, uh, inconsistencies in your stories." He rested his palm on the side of my jaw and gently turned my face towards his. "As I've bared my soul, I believe it's not uncouth for me to require at least one heartfelt response from you." There was a slight pause before he asked, "I asked you once, and I am asking you again, do you love me?"

I smiled and put my hand up to touch his. "Yes, Will, I do love you. I thought that was obvious."

He shook his head. "Nothing in this world of confusion is obvious, Petra," he replied. "Our time on earth is shockingly brief, and we owe it to one another to not waste time with games that tug at the heart and soul of us."

Of course, my time on earth was not as brief as was his, but nonetheless his words rang true with me. Kipp finally stretched out on his side. As I glanced at him, he thumped his tail in support. His thoughts remained blocked from me, but I recognized his physical thumbs up from the tail wag.

Harrow leaned forward and kissed my lips. It was not the same kiss as before, the one filled with passion that left me feeling as if I'd been ignited like a bonfire. This one was gentle and wonderfully sweet.

"I'll wait for you, Petra Hathaway, and will expect you to return to me." He drew back, a slight frown on his face. "That is your name, isn't it?"

"Petra Goodgame," I replied, with a little shrug of my shoulders. A dark strand of hair had fallen across his brow, and I reached up with my hand to smooth it back from his face. It was the first time I'd touched his hair, and it was like touching silk. Suddenly, his chest looked inviting, and I leaned into him, not caring a whit about Victorian rules of the road. He caught the back of my neck, his hand warm against my flesh. Gently, he tucked my head beneath his chin. It was quiet in the library, with the exception of the slowly swinging pendulum of a grandfather's clock that stood like a sentinel in a far corner of the room. Outside, the storm was beginning to abate; a fine, drenching rain continued to patter upon the soaked ground. With my ear pressed to his chest, I could hear the beat of Harrow's heart, strong and steady. The cologne he wore acted like a soothing dash of aroma therapy, because I fell asleep with the ease of a child whose mind is unburdened by the demons of worry.

My last day in London was to be on Tuesday, and Silas and I planned to leave very early the following morning. Several days earlier, I began to gather together small gifts and tokens for my friends. There was no way for me to deny that I'd developed an unhealthy attachment to this place and the people…at least, the attachment was not advisable for my species. We were so conditioned to leaving not so much as a footprint, and here I had left lasting impressions that would have more impact than I might have desired. But, as Kipp reminded me, we did the same with Perdy, and I believed, without a doubt, that she remembered both of us until her dying day. As I walked into the school lobby for the last time, I took in all the familiar scents and sounds as my eyes lovingly caressed the dark wood balustrades and polished floors.

My boys—most of whom had developed sufficient couth to move on to other classes—huddled around me as they expressed their sorrow over my leaving. For Allen, I had a burnished leather satchel for him to take to his new private school; he would look just as nicely put together as the rest of the boys. Simon received a paint set with some basic watercolors, brushes and rolls of parchment. I tried to keep each gift personal and targeted towards the interests of each child.

With those thoughts in mind, I also selected objects for the people in Harrow's household. All of them had welcomed me and treated me as if I were precious cargo. I knew that Harrow set the tone, and he surrounded himself with fine people. With no desire for sad goodbyes, I asked everyone to gather in the wonderful kitchen on that last evening, where the fragrant dried herbs hung from hooks and woven baskets with fresh fruits and vegetables were pushed against the far wall. It was a far cry from my own little kitchen back in North Carolina, where the chipped tiles on my countertop begged for attention.

Daniel climbed onto my lap and was quietly pleased with the leather collar and leash I'd given him for Lily the dog. I also found a very nice tea set for Mac and Miss Douglas, one they could use in their cottage after they were married. It was quite possible I embarrassed John Parks when I presented him with a new oil cloth duster length coat that would keep him dry in times of inclement weather.

Harrow sat at the end of the table, his face shadowed; he laughed, however, and seemed to join in with the others as they gave exclamations of delight or joy at another little surprise. When all those present had been gifted, I excused myself to dash to the parlor, returning with a rectangular package wrapped in brown butcher's paper and tied with string. Feeling uncharacteristically shy, I presented it to Harrow and quickly returned to my chair. Carefully, he untied the string and pulled the paper free. I could tell, from his expression, that he was happy over my choice. Without speaking, he raised it for the others to see. I had found a small watercolor painting at Ramon's gallery that depicted a woman and a dog standing at the shore of the ocean, looking off to the horizon. The setting was sunset and the early twilight colors bathed the woman in a soft, ethereal glow. I felt it perfectly captured the sense of longing of the human soul, and the dewy symbolisms could not be overlooked.

"It's lovely, Petra. I will cherish it all my days," Harrow said, his eyes meeting mine across the room.

I said my goodbyes to him earlier in the day at the school when things were structured, and I could not surrender myself to an emotional moment. My instructions were that he was not to see me off in the morning. Not only would it make me sad, but also it would disrupt the concentration I needed to make the time shift with Kipp. It was time for me to do my job and focus. With apologies to all, since I had an early departure, Kipp and I retired to our pretty room for the last time. Yes, this place had felt like home for us.

I spent a few minutes packing my belongings in a valise that Silas had delivered. Of course, I'd leave the bag on the train for some lucky person to inherit a few nice clothes. The only things I planned to take, other than the clothes I'd brought, were the pearl necklace given to me by Harrow and a packet of Earl Grey tea for Fitzhugh. Symbionts were supposed to give a full inventory upon return but I really didn't care and planned on lying, a skill I'd mastered over a lifetime of practice.

Thankfully, we actually got a solid night of sleep. Kipp helped me soothe my thoughts, much like one pulls at a rug to make it lie flat on the floor. It had been a long and difficult day, and I think I fell asleep within five minutes of my head hitting the pillow.

It was still dark, in that interval between late night and early dawn. The air was damp; cold, dense fog crowded in against the houses and streets. With the valise in hand, I carefully made my way down the staircase. As per my request, the landing was empty of people, and there were no tearful goodbyes at the door. I quietly exited, Kipp at my side, out the front door and walked towards the waiting four wheeler; Silas and Vashti greeted us as we climbed inside. Harrow's thoughts penetrated the thick atmosphere, and I looked back at the house; he stood in one of the windows, gazing out at me. After a moment, he extended his hand and placed his palm on the inside of the glass as a silent salute. I raised mine in reply and tried to smile. The driver called up his horse, and we pulled away from the curb.

"Don't look back," Kipp advised, pushing close to me on the seat.

I was not easily given to tears but began to cry, silently, as I stared straight ahead at a place on the opposite carriage seat just to the right of Silas' shoulder. Vashti hopped over and crawled up next to me, placing her head in my lap. Kipp leaned over and began to gently lick the tears from my face, his tongue like fine sandpaper on my cheeks. The carriage gave a slight lurch as we navigated a sharp turn, and I clutched at Kipp. Silas, wisely, remained silent and avoided staring at me. I appreciated the fact everyone was trying to be supportive of me.

"Tough trip, this one," Silas finally said. "For a lot of reasons," he added.

Closing my eyes, I nodded my head in agreement. "I think I want to stay home for a while."

Silas had purchased tickets for a train leaving from Victoria Station that was traveling north, since its destination did not really matter. Our first class compartment was private, and as we felt movement out of the station, all four of us began preparations for a time shift. The basic mechanics were the same for all symbionts, but each bonded pair handled it just a little differently.

I had the few things I would take back in my convertible carpet bag; this I pulled across my back and put my arms through the backpack type straps. Kipp moved over and laid his head across my lap. My concentration still suffered, and I was not surprised when Silas and Vashti disappeared from view; yes, it was logical they could literally get their act together faster than could I. But, of course, I had Kipp who used his talents to help me block off distracting thoughts, and it was not long after that we felt the familiar sense of rushing down a funnel only to dive off of a precipice into the darkness of time.

CHAPTER 33

"Get out of bed and get your clothes on," Philo barked through the phone. "I'm on my way over…we're going out to Duke Forest," he said.

I started to fabricate a reason why not, but he abruptly hung up on me. Kipp was next to me in the bed; it was seductively warm in my little house, and I was reluctant to stir, knowing it was unpleasantly cold outside. Kipp stretched his head over to my chest and managed to squirm around so that his nose was almost touching mine.

"He's right," Kipp said. "You can't avoid getting back to life, Petra." His raspy tongue flicked out to lick my chin.

It was the first week of December. Silas and Vashti actually made it home four days earlier than our team, so the overall accuracy was pretty good. Kipp and I had completed our debriefing, which was uncharacteristically short and uninformative. I felt compelled to omit Silas's misbehaviors and then there was the small episode of my having fallen in love with a human man. Somehow, I believed the Twelve would not appreciate the latter, with the exception of the soft hearted Juno who was my champion in all things. For once in my life, I wasn't sure of Philo's possible response. Since my return, I'd only seen Fitzhugh once to schedule time for me to resume work with him. Without any formalities, it appeared I was Fitzhugh's reluctant helper, doing the job no one else wanted. I hadn't even given him the smuggled packet of tea; my heart just wasn't ready for the gesture.

Making myself leave the comfort of my bed, I finally managed to pull on some sweats that weren't worn too thin. Rambling in a drawer, I found a wool cap and retrieved an insulated jacket from my closet. When I'd left for my time shift to England, it was spring, and some of my winter clothes were still packed away. Kipp followed me, staring at me with concern.

"I'm worried about you, Petra," he said, his eyes resembling large pools of liquid copper.

I walked over to my vanity—one of those from the thirties with a large round mirror set low—and sat there, staring at my reflection. The wood surface needed refinishing, but I never managed to make the time for it. My face was pale with an unhealthy grayish tint to the flesh. On the table top was a small, velvet covered box; I opened it to find the pearl necklace Harrow had given me. With hesitant fingers, I pulled it free of its container and let it puddle in the palm of my hand.

"You have to move on," Kipp continued, moving close to me.

I turned to stare at him, fighting back the tears gathering behind my eyes. "Oh, Kipp," was all I could manage before I started to cry again.

A knock on the front door interrupted me, and, after quickly drying my eyes with the cuff of my sweatshirt, I went through to the living room to greet Philo. He walked in, without any greetings, and stared at me.

"Have you been crying?" he asked.

I was irritated at him, myself, and our entire species. He could easily determine the content of my heart, if he would allow himself. But, no, we'd put so many arbitrary controls on ourselves that we didn't function as God intended. And then there was the issue of us masquerading as human beings when we were not. Just little children dressing up for Halloween, I thought dismissively.

"I don't want to talk about it," I replied, my voice cool and controlled. A moment later, I impulsively added, "If you want to know, you can just go looking for it, Philo."

His face reddened. "I'll be out in the car." Turning, he stomped outside and slammed the door to his little car so hard that I was surprised the window didn't break.

We dashed through the countryside on our way to Duke Forest, Philo driving in his usual careless and slightly terrifying manner. Kipp managed to convince Philo to stop at Hardees and get a bag of egg and cheese biscuits as well as coffee for Philo and me.

"These are good," Kipp said, staring at Philo in the rearview mirror. "I found, while in London, I developed an appreciation for cheese as well as something called kidney pie."

Philo laughed before abruptly changing the light-hearted subject to one that was more painful. "You might help me, Kipp, understand what's wrong with Petra. I used to think I was her best friend and that she trusted me, but now I'm not so sure."

Kipp didn't answer him and instead began to wolf down another biscuit. I turned to stare at Philo; he did the same with me and only returned his eyes to the road when Kipp gave a yelp as we crossed the center yellow line.

"Silas's debriefing was rather brief to his governing body, as was yours. However, he called me later to privately tell me that he'd had some ethical lapses that caused stress between you two and him and Vashti."

"Really?" I replied, somewhat shocked Silas did such a thing.

"Yes. Silas said you were instrumental in trying to keep him focused on the right course of action as well as assisting him in his journey. I think he's grateful, although he might not let down his guard enough to ever say that to you."

He parked and, after a few sips of coffee, we set out.

Within a few steps from the parking area, we disappeared into Duke Forest, which was empty and barren since plant life had gone dormant for the season. I was grateful for the scattering of conifers which brought some variety to the bare, skeletal landscape that otherwise matched my somber mood. Layers of decaying vegetation were crisp underfoot; it seemed our footsteps echoed much too loudly for three insignificant adventurers.

Kipp didn't run ahead in his usual manner and, instead, walked with his left shoulder pressed against my leg. The warmth of his body almost burned me through the pants I wore. At one point, he ducked his head beneath my hand so that I would scratch the favored place between his ears.

"You can trust me," Philo finally said.

"I know that," I replied. "I just can't talk about it yet. Something happened—and I don't mean with Silas—and I'm just not ready."

Oddly, I found just that tiny admission helped me; perhaps the loose stone in the dam of my emotions was dislodged. The walk became more pleasant as we reminisced about past times and amusing episodes. With shock, I heard my laugh reverberate throughout the trees, which stood as silent watchtowers, looming overhead. Later that afternoon when Philo dropped me off at home, I didn't invite him in nor did he ask. He placed his hand on my forearm before I departed the car.

"You need to be at work Monday," he said, frowning. "Fitzhugh has a new project and needs help." Philo thrust his face closer to mine. "Promise me."

"Okay, I'll be there," I grudgingly replied, raising my eyebrows in what I hoped would appear to be an expression of innocence.

Monday arrived too soon for my liking. After the exchange with Philo, I couldn't beg off with headaches or an upset stomach. So, with my usual disdain for dressing, I looked in my dryer for the sweats I'd washed the night before. As I pushed my legs into the pants, I had a sudden and unexpected recall of the coral gown I'd worn to the play as well as the dance.

"Remember the boots you wore the first time?" Kipp asked, laughing, his tongue lolling out.

"Oh, yes, a definite fashion faux pas." I managed a slight smile in response.

The cold was unceasing and combined with it was the threat of snow, so I decided to drive. Fortunately for me, Philo had cranked my ancient hulk of a car weekly while I was gone, and it started after a few rough coughs. With a belch of exhaust smoke, Kipp and I wobbled down the street towards Technicorps.

"You need one of those," Kipp said, pointing his nose at a vehicle we passed; it looked to be a new Jaguar sport sedan. "Something like that, and we can ride in style," Kipp remarked, his eyes rounding at the sight, as he day dreamed over how he'd look hanging his head out of the window of a more trendy car than our current, dilapidated coach.

"You pay for it, and I'll drive it."

Inside Technicorps, Kipp and I separated; he had resumed his work teaching English to the lupines. Not able to stop myself, I threw a teaser at his departing backside.

"Elani is waiting," I called out.

He gave me the mental equivalent of the middle finger as he disappeared down a hallway.

I entered the library and was surprised at the comfort that the dark, rich colors brought to my soul. Since Fitzhugh had chosen a decorative palate popular during Victorian times to decorate his space, I had the odd sensation that I was home again—with Harrow, Mac, Mrs. Atherton and all the other dear people I'd met.

"Petra, good morning," Fitzhugh's voice greeted me. "Peter will not be here today, so it is just us two. And Lily, of course, but she's asleep in my office."

I narrowed my eyes at the old librarian. The unexpected absence of Peter, who served as a dilution in our brew, was unexpected. Shrugging my shoulders, I hung my coat on the brass coat rack and went to my usual table.

"Oh, Fitzhugh, I've been meaning to give you this," I said. Reaching into my hoodie pocket, I withdrew the packet of tea. I placed it in his outstretched hand and enjoyed watching the delight spread over his aged features as he realized the treasure he held.

"Thank you so much," he replied. His gray flecked thick eyebrows rose to almost disappear into his hair line. "You broke all the rules, as usual, but this time I benefit so I'm glad." Fitzhugh's dark eyes wandered down to my throat. "And I see you are wearing something new, too," he observed.

Since coming home, I maintained my practice of wearing the pearls given to me by Harrow, but usually they were kept tucked beneath my clothing. Apparently, they had been dislodged when I removed my coat. My fingers went up to touch the cool strand, and I guess that familiar action brought back the associated memories and sadness. With effort, I controlled my facial expression as well as my thoughts, although I knew Fitzhugh was not probing my mind.

"I'm going to brew this tea, and we will enjoy it together," he said.

I followed him to the back of the library, as I was in no mood to start work and would rather drink tea and let my mind be numb from worry and pain. He saw me hovering and told me to wait in his office. Lily was asleep on the top of his desk, so I tippy toed in and sat in a worn work chair in the corner. The fragrance of bergamot threaded its way into the small room and a moment later, Fitzhugh appeared with the tray. I noticed the thoughtful inclusion of honey and nodded my head in appreciation.

Fitzhugh began to pour and handed me a cup. "I missed you, Petra," he began. "That fact surprised me more than I might have imagined."

I raised my cup in silent salute and took another sip.

"You seem different, changed somehow," he went on, his brows drawing together over his eyes. "I think you need to tell me about your trip," Fitzhugh said, his voice gentle.

Unconsciously, my fingers went to the necklace again as I stared at Fitzhugh across the small space.

"May I?" he asked, and I knew his intent.

I nodded, wordlessly, and he began a gentle, polite intrusion into my mind. His expression changed as he probed the love I felt for Harrow and the dilemma of conscious and duty that the mere fact implied. Fitzhugh's dark eyes met mine as I began to cry. He concluded his telepathic inspection and paused to refresh both our cups with the vintage tea.

"Love changes humans as well as symbionts. Our physiology is different, but the way our emotions are built is almost identical," he said. "Your trip has changed you forever, Petra." As I dabbed at my eyes, he cocked his head to the side and asked, "Would you rather have never known Harrow?"

Well, that was the all important question, and I knew the answer. "No, I'm thankful I knew him and wouldn't do any of it differently if I had the opportunity," I replied.

"Well, then, it's worth the pain you feel," he said, a smile flashing over his face. "Would you consider going back?"

I shrugged my shoulders. "Kipp has asked the same thing and assures me he would be happy in any other time, as long as he's with me."

"And I suspect Kipp means that wholeheartedly," Fitzhugh replied.

"Yes, but there are other issues to be considered. The biggest one is how would I explain my nature to Harrow and what would be his response?" I laughed mirthlessly. "He knows I have secrets, but he would never guess the main reason I was less than forthcoming with him."

Fitzhugh allowed a nod of his head. "True, it would be a significant issue, but perhaps you don't give the man the credit he deserves. From your thoughts, he appears to be a sober minded man who is able to think outside of the proverbial box." Fitzhugh turned from me and hit a key on his computer keyboard. "Let's Google him," he said. After typing in a few letters, he leaned forward and began to read passages as he scanned the page.

"William Harrow was a noted philanthropist of the Victorian age. His greatest achievement was the establishment of a school for orphaned boys who lived in the destitute Whitechapel district of London." Fitzhugh used the roller ball to move down the page. "It goes on to recount his upbringing in wealth, his time in the army serving as a captain during the war in Afghanistan—he was highly decorated, did you know that?—and then his later life."

I leaned forward; a picture of Harrow in monochromatic gray hovered on the margin of the screen, along with words to small for me to read. In the flat, one dimensional depiction of him, the depth and passion of his remarkable eyes, the ones that reminded me of the stormy Atlantic Ocean, was lost. Surrendering myself to a fragile moment of self indulgence, I recalled the scent of his cologne and almost willed myself to be back in the library, sitting quietly as he read a book, his dark head bent in rapt concentration. With the realization I was holding my breath, I finally slowly exhaled.

"It says he never married and died at the age of eighty-three. His nephew, Daniel, continued his work and the school evolved into a highly regarded specialty program for disabled children."

My mouth went dry. So, he didn't marry; he told me he would wait, and he apparently did just that.

Fitzhugh sat back in his chair. "If you ever make the decision to return to him, you would not change the timeline of history, since he didn't have offspring."

I raised my eyebrows. "Are you encouraging me to give up my life here, with my kind, and just float off to the past to live with a human?" Smiling, I said, "That seems like an extremely romantic notion coming from someone as serious and dedicated to our species as are you."

His face lightened as he laughed in response. "Perhaps, but do you remember my story of having fallen in love with a human woman?" At my nod, he said, "Don't think that the idea never crossed my mind to return to her." Fitzhugh sighed. "At some point, they will rotate you away from this place and, in the way we control one another's lives, will set you down in the midst of a colony of strangers to start over." He looked at me. "Is that what you want?"

"No, Fitzhugh; I don't want that," I replied, my voice gaining strength. "I'd miss Philo and Juno..." my voice drifted off before I added, "And you."

He nodded. "Thank you for that inclusion. I didn't expect myself to become attached to you, but I have, Petra. And I want you to do what is best for you and not our collective or necessarily our species."

"Fitzhugh, you have the soul of a libertine," I exclaimed, with delight. "What else lurks inside your heart?"

He smiled. "There are some secrets that an old symbiont must keep private." Frowning, he added, "But at least I never defaced an ancient picture or piece of statuary."

Ah, the old Fitzhugh was back with a vengeance. In the next moment, he was barking orders and marching me to the front of the library to my usual desk. A stack of parchments were laid out for me, and, after stretching my neck and popping one stiff knuckle, I began to work. Without Peter there, I was left with his usual chore of cataloging my discoveries. At one point, I felt Fitzhugh staring at the back of my head. Turning, I gazed at him.

"Yes?"

"Glad you're home, Petra."

I smiled. "Me, too."

THE SYMBIONT
TIME TRAVEL ADVENTURES
SERIES

*Turn the page for a
teaser from*

THE GENERAL,
1862

The Symbiont Time Travel
Adventures Series

Book Four

———◆———

T.L.B. Wood

Petra and Kipp face a new challenge when they become mentors to a pair of apprentice symbionts: Peter, the assistant librarian, and Elani, a beautiful lupine harboring a secret crush on Kipp.

Neither Petra nor Kipp suspect Peter's primary goal is to become engaged with the Great Locomotive Chase, when the mighty General is stolen by an audacious team of Union raiders deep in the heart of Georgia.

Soon, Petra and Kipp find themselves in the middle of the American Civil War, caught between the North and the South.

THE GENERAL, 1862
available in print and ebook

T.L.B. Wood began her appreciation of literature at an early age, encouraged by her mother who was an English teacher. T.L. is a certified adult behavioral health clinical nurse specialist and works as a case manager as well as a clinical instructor at a school of nursing. She and her husband share a love of nature, and more than one rescued dog or cat in need of a caring family has found a forever home with the Wood Family. When not feeding and caring for her menagerie, T.L. can be found at her desk, writing, or taking long walks as she envisioned new stories to be told.

You can contact T.L. through her publisher at
TLBWood@epublishingworks.com

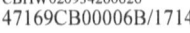